# Novels by Kelly Cheek

All We Hold Dear

Trial by Fire

The Lost Colony

JackSimile and the Phantom Fury

Spirit Breather


## The SpiritSense Trilogy

In Restless Dreams

First Light

When We Were Gone Astray


## The Facebook Trilogy

Profile

Private Messages

Poked

# In Restless Dreams

Kelly Cheek

Cover and book design by Kelly Cheek

ISBN: 978-1-7335022-4-5

Printed in the United States of America

For Linda,
my greatest and favorite fan

# Prologue

The moon looked down on the nefarious activities below like an unblinking eye. It made neither judgment nor comment but, like a willing accomplice, it cast deep shadows for the two men to take advantage of. Struggling with their burden, they slipped quietly along Cowgate, staying in the shadows of the once grand houses which were now dirty, drafty slums, crowded with poor tenants.

At the Fishmarket Close, they went a block north to the High Street. Their trek eastward from Greyfriars Kirkyard had been uneventful, and they looked forward to being compensated for their trouble, hopefully in the morning. A wheelbarrow, or something of that sort, would have made the transport easier, but it would also have been noisier, and they wanted nothing drawing attention to their activities.

As they approached Burklaw's Close where they were to turn, they heard two sets of footsteps on the cobblestones behind them, one set heavy, the other lighter and a little faster. A couple out for a late-night stroll, perhaps. Glancing at each other, the men hurried into the close and flattened themselves against the shadows of the wall as much as they could, allowing their blanket-wrapped charge to slip to the ground between them. As it did, a corner of the shroud fell open and an arm dropped to the side, a hand lying just outside the blackness of the shadow.

The two men looked down and saw the hand illuminated by the moon. To their eyes, it was a blazing white beacon. The taller man started to stoop down to move the hand when the footsteps suddenly became louder as the couple came alongside the entrance to the close. Now unobstructed by the walls of the buildings enclosing the close, the sound echoed around the two men as they froze in place.

The man facing the entrance of the close, holding his breath, saw the couple, well-dressed, perhaps walking home from the theater. However, as they walked past, they didn't turn their heads to look into the close.

9

*Moments later, the footsteps faded away. The two men exhaled, the clouds of their breath heavy in the cold air. The tall man wiped beads of sweat from his forehead, despite the cold temperature, and wiped it on his coat.*

*He nodded at his partner as he stooped to replace the errant arm back inside the blanket. Hoisting the body, they continued on their way, deeper into the darkness of the close.*

uzy Quinn liked candles. Whenever she was relaxing at home, she often had at least one burning nearby. There was something about the warm glow that she found calming.

Suzy especially needed that now.

She pulled her feet up onto her sofa as she sipped her Earl Grey tea and looked out across the harbor. The scattered lights of mainland Marblehead sparkled amidst the reflections of the candle flames in the window. Though she purposely avoided looking to her right, through the corner window, she could still peripherally see the green glow from Marblehead Light. The glow registered in her consciousness, causing her to turn her head a bit, to look more southward, away from it, toward mainland Marblehead.

The light, while not a traditional photogenic lighthouse as most think of them, was the only one of its kind in New England. The original light, built in 1835, along with the accompanying house for the keeper, had been a more traditional white tower, lit by ten whale oil burning lamps.

Sixty years later, the current light replaced it. Standing on the extreme northern tip of Marblehead Neck, an island connected to the mainland by a narrow two-lane isthmus, it was a simple reddish-brown metal framework instead of an actual enclosed tower. The lamp was now a constant green.

Some people felt a certain chagrin at the romantic charm that the current light lacked. Suzy was ambivalent. For her, the light was burned into her memory, and it had nothing to do with its construction.

It was a year ago today. As her eyes wandered, she looked down toward the pier and boathouse. The boathouse was empty now.

She shook her head and took another sip, forcing herself to look beyond the harbor and the light, out toward the open ocean. She could just make out the rocky protuberance that held Fort Sewall, the remains of a British fortification originally built in 1644. But the waves crashing against the rocks just beyond it were a reminder, too.

Heaving a heavy sigh, she pushed herself up from the sofa and pulled her sweater tighter around her. She knew she should have made plans. This was not a good day to be alone.

Her phone started vibrating in the pocket of her sweater, and simultaneously, she heard the warm opening piano notes of John Lennon's *Imagine*. It had been Mark's favorite song, and it had been Suzy's ringtone for years.

She pulled the phone out of her pocket and looked at the screen. Against her will, she smiled. *I should have known*, she thought.

"Hi, Rachel," she said.

"Hey, Suzy, how are you doing?" Rachel's voice carried that thick sympathetic tone often used by people who don't know what else to do or say.

"I'm fine," Suzy replied. Even she had to admit she didn't sound very convincing.

"Why don't we go out?" Rachel asked enthusiastically, choosing not to comment on Suzy's tone. "Let's go down to Boston for the evening. It'll be fun. We'll get you out of the house and have a nice dinner together."

"Thanks, Rachel, but I don't feel like going out. And I sure don't feel like being in the city."

"Honey – okay, I'm not going to lecture you. I know you're a grownup. But I also know this is a difficult time for you. Experts agree that this is not a time to spend all by yourself."

"Thank you for not lecturing me."

"Smartass. But you know I'm right. You shouldn't be alone."

"You're right. So, why don't you come over?"

§

Suzy lived in her family's home, which they had always referred to as, simply, "The Estate." Though Suzy's grandparents had sold a couple of parcels of land over the years, her family still owned more property than most of their neighbors on Marblehead Neck, Massachusetts, an old fishing village on the North Shore, just a few miles up the coast from Boston, and right next door to Salem.

The Estate had been in her family for generations, since the turn of the nineteenth century when Phillip Drummond, a Boston ship builder, settled there. Drummond had made a fortune and decided that this was where he wanted to raise his family.

The house itself was, Suzy thought, a bit ridiculous. A sprawling structure with aspirations of being a castle, it was made of stone and heavy timbers, with later additions being added, in an apparently haphazard fashion, in similar stone, brick, and even painted clapboard. When Suzy was young, her parents had done a massive remodeling project, modernizing and opening up parts of the interior, though Suzy's décor now celebrated its earlier maritime history.

She couldn't help but feel that The Estate must be somewhat less impressive now than it had been when it was new. The house itself was larger now, and the interior was quite nice and comfortable, but the surrounding property had settled into a bit of disrepair. Some parts were overgrown, and numerous small outbuildings had been long neglected.

When Suzy's parents died in an accident several years ago, she was living in Boston. She had stayed there after college, though she hadn't started pursuing a career, or even deciding on one yet. She was in the process of discovering the limited options available to a history major. The property became hers, as the sole heir, and she moved back. She thought it was a good place to raise a family, as well.

When she married Mark, he was only too happy to live here, too. As her parents' remodeling efforts from her childhood were now dated, she and Mark had embarked on an ambitious endeavor to clean up the place, and they had made a nice home for themselves. When Emma was born, the work slowed, and eventually stopped. But they had been a happy family, living in a beautiful home.

Until last year.

Thanks to Suzy.

§

"I'm glad we did this," Rachel said, taking a swallow of her wine. She slid another slice of pizza onto her plate as a Telemann trumpet concerto played in the background and candle flames danced around them.

"Yeah, I am, too," Suzy agreed. "The comfort food and the upbeat music should stave off suicide for at least another day."

Rachel just shook her head.

"You know, some people may appreciate your smartass attitude," she said around a bite of pizza, "but I think you should be a little nicer to your best friend."

"You think you're my best friend?" Suzy asked with a smile.

"I don't see anybody else here with you on this particular evening."

"Yeah, well . . . you're right," Suzy conceded and smiled at Rachel. She was pensive for a few moments. "Mark liked it." Rachel looked at her with a quizzical expression. "My smartass attitude. In fact, I think I got it from him."

Suddenly, she was with Mark on that last day, a year ago, remembering the last smartass exchange she had with him.

They had a boat then. It wasn't a big one, just a small pleasure cruiser. But Suzy loved to take it out and open up the throttle. Though most of the boats had been brought in for the winter, a few were still tied to their moorings in the harbor. Suzy wanted to go out that day, but Mark was not as enthusiastic about it.

"It's Oc-freakin-tober," he said. "It's freezing out there."

"It's only the *first* of October. It's not that late."

"But, it's cold. I'm talking about the weather, not the calendar."

"Well, you know, they have these newfangled contraptions now called coats," she shot back. "They're meant to keep you warm in cold weather."

"Suzy Q, it's too frigid out there." He looked her up and down, allowing his eyes to linger in certain places. "Why don't we stay inside and make some heat to ward off the cold." He raised his eyebrows meaningfully.

Feeling herself being undressed with his eyes was warming her up as well, and causing a bit of a tingling sensation, but she didn't want to admit that. Maybe when they got back.

"It's not *that* cold out there, you big weenie."

"Weenie! See? You've got sex on your mind too!"

"Mark, Emma's right up there in her room." She lowered her voice to a whisper to make it more significant.

"I can be quiet. What about you?" He gave her a look that almost melted her resolve. "You *really* look great!"

"I wish you'd reconsider."

"Okay, you look like shit, but I still want to have sex with you."

She struggled to not smile at his remark. She didn't want to be distracted from her own argument. She knew she was being stubborn and a nag, but he finally gave in, and of course, Emma was up for it.

She remembered climbing aboard their boat, tossing the rope up onto the pier. She remembered the thrill of revving the engine and working the boat out of the harbor. It was pretty easy when the harbor wasn't so crowded with other boats. She remembered gliding past the green light on the right, and opening it up as they neared open water.

She remembered turning toward the north and being pleasantly distracted by Emma's excited laughter behind her. And she remembered seeing the overturned rowboat submerged just below the surface, and jerking the wheel to the left at the last possible moment. But it wasn't soon enough. Their boat was listing hard to port when it glanced off the rowboat.

She was still holding her breath when she spotted the rock ahead of her, and she jerked the wheel back to starboard. This, also, was a glancing blow, but the rock was less forgiving.

Once the immediate danger was passed, Suzy turned to check on Mark and Emma. She didn't know which of the turns or impacts had been to blame, but they were gone. They hadn't been wearing life jackets over their heavy coats.

They went down fast. Once Suzy got the boat under control again, she went back to get them. But she couldn't find them. The boat was damaged from the impact with the rock and difficult to control, and by the time the Coast Guard responded to her distress call, she was soaked and freezing herself. The boat went down seconds after they pulled her aboard.

When the divers recovered the bodies the next day, Mark had his arms wrapped around Emma, as if he had been trying to comfort her in their last moments.

"Well," Rachel said, breaking Suzy's link to the past, "Mark was a pretty special person."

Suzy was quiet for several seconds. She could feel tears coming, but she willed them away, surreptitiously wiping her eye.

"Yes, he sure was."

Noticing her distraction, Rachel had an idea.

"Weren't you tracing your family tree, or something like that?"

"I've been doing that off and on since I was a teenager," Suzy said, dragging her attention back to Rachel. "Why?"

"I think you need something to occupy your mind. I know you enjoyed that. Why don't you get back into it?"

"You think immersing myself in dead people is what I need to get my mind off my dead husband and daughter?"

It hurt to say it, but her smartass attitude helped to dull the pain.

"It's something to focus your mind on."

Suzy sighed.

"I don't know," she finally said. "I'll think about it."

It was 11:00 when Rachel left, and it was only after making Suzy promise that she was going right to bed, that she was not going to pine over photos or videos.

It was an easy promise to make. Suzy didn't need photos or videos. The memories were as vivid in her mind as if they had happened yesterday.

## 2

Leaning against the door as he pushed it closed with his butt, Finley MacKinley dropped his keys in the bowl on the table that stood beside the door. That feeling in his chest was back again. He struggled to dismiss it, but it had happened too many times to just ignore it.

The feeling wasn't one of illness, or of any kind of physical infirmity, but it was chronic. It was something that he had lived with for most of his life.

He stood with his back against the door for a few moments, trying to decide what he wanted to do. Finally, he pushed himself forward and went into his library where he had a wet bar, taking an Old Fashioned glass from the cabinet. He splashed some 21-year-old Ben Nevis into a glass, followed by a few drops of filtered water. He swirled the glass a couple of times while he inhaled the aroma.

*Taking a sip,* he thought, *our hero appreciated the incongruity of the cool liquid warming his throat.*

After a few moments, he realized that he was staring out the window. It wasn't quite dark yet, which made the whole evening that much more pitiful. The cluster of aspen trees outside the window had lost some of their leaves, but those that hung on were a rich golden color.

Fin bought his home southwest of Denver after he had made his first million dollars. He had said that to a friend once, thinking it was kind of funny and definitely pretentious, but it was also true.

Fin was a writer. He had been writing for as long as he could remember, most of the stories immediately forgettable. A few of them, though, he thought were pretty good, and he tried getting publishers interested in them. There were a couple of nibbles, but nothing ever panned out. After innumerable rejections, he finally decided to self-publish, figuring it would always just be a hobby which brought in a few dollars a year, as a meager supplement to his monotonous day job.

One of his books, though, caught the eye of a big publisher in New York, and they signed him on to put his creation out on the mass market. The publisher also had contacts in Hollywood, and the rest was history.

He knew that his success story was a one in a million thing, like E.L. James or Andy Weir. He was still Facebook friends with several indie writers who were still plugging away for a Kindle sale here and there, like he used to be. He made it a point to not brag too much on his personal account.

But his novel, *TimePlex*, a time travel themed love story, became the literary success he had always hoped for. Having Ryan Reynolds' and Jennifer Lawrence's names connected to the movie, due out next year, didn't hurt, either.

*TimePlex* opened the door, and suddenly there was interest in several of his earlier novels, as well.

Still, Finley MacKinley wasn't a household name. Fin had never been one to draw attention to himself, so he had written under a pseudonym. Even now, he had mixed feelings about the fact that Michael Jones got the credit for the books that Fin wrote.

The rather generic pseudonym was related to other issues that, in his mind, wove the fabric of his undoing. Fin just wasn't a typical guy. He was, in his words, a high-level geek. He could explain the physics behind what powered the warp drive of the Starship Enterprise but didn't know the first thing about fixing a car engine. He enjoyed role-playing games but shunned sports. He attended Comic-Cons and Renaissance festivals, in costume, but couldn't understand the point of wearing a Broncos jersey on game day.

He had known from an early age that he was different from his contemporaries, and had learned to be self-conscious about it. He tended to fade into the background, and that's where he usually preferred to be, instead of having the attention on him. Growing up, he had managed to develop a sharp wit, but few were aware of it. When it came out, people were often surprised to hear it from him.

Being an introvert, now that he was a famous author, there were numerous times he was glad for the anonymity of the pseudonym. But there were other times when he wished he could point to his novels and the movie, and even his lifestyle, and throw it all in the faces of those who had teased and bullied and made fun of him growing up. He knew it was silly and superficial, but in a sense, he felt a certain validation from his success.

It didn't help that he was a naïve, hyper-romantic. Due in large part to that, relationships he was able to start often accelerated quickly, but turned into a disappointment for one or both of them.

Case in point, Cindy. He had met Cindy on a dating site he had used, MySoulmate.com. The bits of his personality that came through in their correspondence prompted Cindy to agree to meet him in person.

They met at a Starbucks that was somewhat halfway between them. Lingering over their coffee, Fin was happy that sports never came up once in the conversation, and Cindy didn't seem to have a problem with his geekiness. They talked for nearly three hours before Cindy asked if he wanted to go somewhere. Fin agreed so they went out to the parking lot, where they started kissing.

The heat built up quickly between them, and Cindy suggested they go to one of their houses. They determined that Fin's was closer, so he led her there. Fin had never been the kind of guy who would jump into bed with a woman after just meeting her. He had never hooked up with a woman with just sex on his mind. That evening, three hours became his record.

After that first night, they embarked on a relationship that involved a lot more sex. Being perpetually aroused by Cindy, Fin's naïve heart latched on to her as his next and last love. He didn't realize that love had absolutely nothing to do with it.

Not until she told him two weeks later.

"Love has absolutely nothing to do with it, Fin." She looked at him with an expression of amazement on her face. "We've known each other for a couple of weeks. How can you be in love with me? You hardly know me. We don't even really have any kind of relationship. All we do is fuck and go out to eat."

At the time, she was sitting across from him in her little dining room after breakfast, almost wearing a robe. The parts of her that were *not* wearing the robe were a little distracting, but he tried to stay on topic.

"Oh, come on," he said a little indignantly, even hurt, "I didn't say that I was in love with you, just that I thought I *could* fall in love with you. And besides, that's not all we do. Last night, I thought we did some pretty tender lovemaking."

"'Making love' is just a gooey phrase people use to try to give deeper meaning to their fucking."

"Wow, I never realized what a romantic you were," he replied with a dry tone.

"I'm not sure why. I thought that my jumping into bed with you three hours after I met you would have told you where I was coming from."

"I thought you were really attracted to me."

"I *was* attracted to you. I still am. You're a good-looking guy, and a great lay! But Fin, come on, attraction is just an evolutionary device for perpetuating the species. It doesn't have anything to do with that syrupy, archaic notion of love. I'm kind of surprised you've fallen for that!"

He suddenly felt like a silly, wide-eyed elementary school student.

"But you're on a site called MySoulmate.com. Doesn't that kind of indicate that you're looking for something more than just a shag?"

"It might if I actually believed in such stupid shit as a soulmate. Sometimes I just need to feel a man next to me, and inside me. I'm not looking for a great love, Fin. I just want a little human contact from time to time. But unfortunately, I've found the caliber of most of the guys at Copulation Corner a little lacking."

Despite the depression that was beginning to settle over him, Fin had to give her high marks for her clever wordsmithing.

But Fin was a little in shock. Admittedly they hadn't really had any deep discussions, so the idea of a purely sexual, no-strings-attached kind of arrangement had never occurred to him. He just assumed Cindy was looking for what he was looking for: someone to grow old with.

It was seeping into his brain that assumptions without discussions were not really the basis for a lasting love. So he sat there dumbly looking at her, not knowing what to say. Finally, she saved him by interrupting his blank stare with an imploring statement.

"Come on, Fin, you're a good lay. Don't spoil what we have by calling it love."

A good lay. He had to admit that *kind of* felt good. Over the last couple of weeks, he had learned how much of a sexual goddess Cindy was, with nearly boundless energy and many years of experience.

She had taught him many things – new positions, exotic techniques, and an openness to try new things. They had copulated in more places than his house had rooms. The bed and the bathtub were, to him, obvious places to start. But from there, they spread out to the sofa and the easy chair in the living room, the dining room table, a dining room chair, the kitchen counter, and the floor in various places as well, depending on where they happened to be standing when the urge struck. One time, they even did it in his closet, between his clothes, with Cindy holding on to the bar. They also did it in various places at her house as well.

So for someone of her experience to call Fin a good lay felt like a compliment, but it was one of the backhanded variety. He wanted more than just a fuck-buddy. He wanted to find the woman he was meant to be with. Their hearts would connect and they would know that they would end up living happily ever after.

He was gradually realizing how naïve he really was.

That was a couple of days ago. This evening, Cindy broke up with him.

*Another one bites the dust, as the late, great Freddy Mercury once said.*

He sighed and turned away from the window, sitting down at his computer. He woke it up, pondering whether to go back on MySoulmate.com, but decided it was too soon. He just didn't feel up to it.

It was too exhausting and discouraging. Trying to sound like something he wasn't, he knew, wasn't the way to go, but being completely honest about himself didn't seem to have satisfying results, either. Online, Fin was able to converse fairly easily. The distance and the time delay allowed him to compose his messages with a ring of authority, even doing a little quick research when necessary. He usually tried to steer conversations away from topics he had no interest in, like sports. That was often a difficult thing to do in Denver, a city with a major league team in practically every sport imaginable.

Fin remembered when "sports" was generally considered the domain of men, in which women had little or no interest. While he didn't begrudge women their interest in formerly male-dominated areas of life, it just added another category of people he now had a hard time relating to.

The women he met through the dating site often seemed disappointed by real-life Fin. Like those who use twenty-year-old photos as their profile picture, he was just too different from his online persona. If his boredom with sports or his geeky interests came up in conversation, which they inevitably did, he often saw "the look." The look could consist of a number of things, in a variety of combinations. Glazed over eyes, puckered eyebrows, the "I don't get it" expression, the clumsily looking around for something to say, or just dead silence. And those to whom he revealed his alternate identity, that he was Michael Jones, author of *TimePlex*, could scarcely believe it.

He didn't feel like he was up for any more.

*The story of my life.*

He had managed a marriage once. Kay had been a friend before she became his wife, so she was aware of his "affliction." But after a while, she started making comments, suggesting things that might make him a little less embarrassing to her. At least that was Fin's take on it.

He agreed to watch the Super Bowl one year when the Denver Broncos were playing. He lasted about a half hour. Over the course of a couple of years, Kay's comments went from suggestions to criticisms to outright insults. Fin's lack of ability or interest in so-called manly things, and his preference for geeky enterprises, apparently had sealed their doom.

In time, their relationship became little more than thinly-veiled hatred and resentment. They finally divorced a few years ago, weeks before *TimePlex* was discovered. That ended up being a pretty nice consolation prize. He missed being in a relationship, but the money and fame helped to spackle over the fresh hole in his life. It had taken a while for him to sign on to a dating site.

He sighed and took a sip of his Scotch. As he did, one of the bookmarks on his browser caught his eye. For several years, he had engaged, off and on, in tracing his genealogy through a website called FamilyLine.com. When he was afflicted with writer's block, he often went there to continue his search for his roots. The genealogy was interesting enough that he sometimes stayed there longer than the writer's block lasted.

He opened up the page and logged in, perusing the family tree that he had built so far. The tree was fairly robust. He had traced back through both of his parents into the past, to varying distances. His parents had started him off on his search, giving him a little insight on what they remembered about their relatives, and this tree was what he had grown from it.

The deepest root he had dug up was in the MacKinley line, or Mac an Léigh in its original Gaelic form. Apparently the spelling had been Americanized when Lachlan Mac an Léigh arrived from Scotland.

Something about Lachlan had puzzled Fin for as long as he had been digging, a family legend of sorts. Lachlan, a wealthy nineteenth-century ancestor, had been known in Scotland for his kind, philanthropic nature. He spent much of his time trying to help the poor, labored tirelessly to improve working conditions, and especially seemed driven to help the poor souls forced to live in the vaults, the underground caverns beneath the streets of old Edinburgh.

When he came to America, though, he was very different. Sullen and miserly, he seemed to keep to himself. While Fin identified with the 'keeping to himself' part, he always wondered what the turning point was. What must have happened to Lachlan to cause that change in him.

Sometime after that, Lachlan seemed to have just disappeared altogether, leaving behind a pregnant widow.

The time Fin spent perusing the page was all it took to reignite the flame. With Cindy all but forgotten, he began anxiously investigating the notices of possible leads that had been sent to him since the last time he had been on the site.

## 3

Cold and impotent, the sunlight dissipated weakly through the drab overcast, as the Coast Guard boat bobbed on the iron-grey waves. Divers surfaced, struggling with the burden between them. Their companions on the boat reached down and helped them, lifting the stiff bodies of Mark and Emma over the gunwale. The heavy coats were saturated with seawater and added greatly to the weight.

Their skin was a waxy ashen color, but still, it looked like they were only sleeping. In a protective spooning position, Mark's arms were wrapped around Emma, their legs bent as if she were sitting on his lap.

Suddenly, Mark opened his eyes and turned his head which, as usual, had the effect of jerking Suzy instantly awake.

Sitting up in bed, she folded her arms across her knees and rested her head on them. The dream was usually pretty much the same. There were slight variations, though. Sometimes Emma was the one to look at her, sometimes both of them. Sometimes one or both of them reached out imploringly toward her.

Thankfully, she hadn't actually seen the recovery of their bodies nearly twenty-four hours later. Somebody had said that their bodies had lodged against a large rock, or else the tide would probably have dragged them out to sea. But her imagination had taken what she had heard and constructed this dream which she was subjected to every now and then.

She turned her head and looked at the numbers glowing beside her. It was nearing six o'clock. Almost an hour before sunrise, but she knew she wouldn't get back to sleep.

She pushed the covers off and got up, pulling a soft, fluffy robe around herself. The windows that descended the stairs around the corner turret allowed the green light to the northeast to catch the corner of her eye, but Suzy made a point to ignore it.

She picked up the kettle on the stove and found that there was still water in it. She turned the burner on and set about spooning tea into the infuser basket in her tea pot.

Rachel had once commented on how much faster and easier it was to stick a cup in the microwave. But to Suzy, tea wasn't just about drinking the end product faster. It was the experience, the process of making it. The journey was the destination. The ritual in itself was comforting to her.

Besides, what did she have to hurry for? She didn't need to be anywhere. She thought about the fact that she hadn't worked a "real job" in several years. She had partnered with Mark in a number of his entrepreneurial enterprises, some more successful than others. While that, obviously, had come to an end, she frequently volunteered her time at numerous local charities. But overall, she had very few demands on her time.

Pouring hot water into the tea pot, she set the timer on the microwave and left the tea to steep while she went into her breakfast nook. Leaving the light off, a little light spilling in from the kitchen, she sat in the built-in booth and looked out the window. The eastern horizon was just beginning to become visible as the sky turned a lighter shade of darkness than the sea.

Suzy put her hands out on the table, palms up, and closed her eyes. Breathing slowly, she concentrated on each breath flowing in through her nostrils, then out her mouth. It was harder than usual this morning, but she focused all her attention on the circular flow of air, blocking everything else from her mind. She visualized the cadence of the air being pulled in through her nose, traveling down her trachea, expanding her chest as it filled her lungs, then reversing to be expelled from her mouth. The rhythm was relaxing.

She could feel the calm, though it wasn't settling. It tickled her senses, teasing her, but it was as if it was just out of her reach. And it was shattered altogether when the timer started beeping.

Suzy sighed and got up, punching the "Stop" button on the microwave. She poured tea in her cup, along with a little agave and half-and-half, and stirred, closing her eyes and inhaling the steam. Maybe the tea would help her regain her calm.

§

After attempting her informal meditation again, and failing, she tried a more formal approach. She sat cross-legged on her yoga mat, repeating the process she had tried in her breakfast nook while her tea steeped, but this time with no time limit.

Fifteen minutes passed and she still hadn't been able to cross that threshold.

"Dammit!" she exclaimed. She pushed herself up and looked out the window. The sun was shining and, though it was probably cooler than it looked, it appeared to be a beautiful Indian summer day. Wondering, vaguely, whether that was a politically correct term, Suzy turned and wandered through the house, hoping to seize on something that might help her throw off the shroud she was under.

A year ago today had been the most difficult day of her life. She was 99.9% sure that Mark and Emma were dead, but the lack of concrete confirmation kept that tiny spark of hope alive. Then, in the afternoon, that spark was stubbed out when Officer Vincent told her quietly, sympathetically, that the bodies had been recovered.

She shook her head and sighed, trying to push the memory from her mind. Having wandered through the house, and finding nothing to take her mind off the past, she remembered Rachel's suggestion last night. She thought about the genealogy, and while she did find it interesting, it just wasn't grabbing her attention now. Drawn to the window again, she realized that she didn't want to stay shut up in the house.

She could see the grey-blue water of the harbor, and one boat caught her eye, working its way out for, possibly, the last outing of the season.

*Please be careful!*

She dropped her eyes down toward the backyard. The improvements that she and Mark had made were only on the house itself. The grounds and outbuildings were looking pretty shabby. Looking out the back window of her bedroom, the little carriage house caught her eye. It had been converted to living quarters nearly two hundred years ago, but nobody had lived in it for at least as long as she had been alive. It had been locked up her entire life, and who knows how long before that.

She vaguely remembered when she was little that it was rumored to be haunted, and while that kept her away when she was young, she hadn't really thought about it in years. There had just never been a need to go in there. Now, it seemed like the perfect project.

It crossed her mind that cleaning up the carriage house was just busywork, a distraction to procrastinate from what Rachel had suggested.

"She's not the boss of me," Suzy said under her breath with a grin, realizing the grin was wasted with nobody to see it. Still, the project was something to get her mind off the horrible anniversary.

She was sure Rachel would approve.

§

The carriage house was a traditional looking little structure. There was a large rectangular area to the right of the door that had been filled in, but the stones didn't quite match those around them. Part of that area had been left open and a window had been installed. Suzy figured that area was where the large door had once been which allowed the carriage to enter.

There was a large, ancient, rusty padlock on the door, and she had no idea where the key might be. But she did have a hacksaw. A couple of minutes later, the carriage house was unlocked.

Opening the door, she went inside, looking around with a childlike sense of wonder. This was a place that had been forbidden to her since she was a little girl. Seeing it for the first time was fascinating.

It was still filled with eighteenth- or nineteenth-century furniture, but it all looked grey as everything was covered with a thick layer of dust. Opening the door for the first time in well over a century allowed the cool breeze of the October morning to stir up the dust a little, further casting a haze over everything.

She closed the door, but could barely see in the murky interior, so she went to the two windows on the side wall and pushed the heavy curtains aside, stirring up another cloud of dust. She did the same with the window beside the door.

Suzy turned around. Despite the open curtains, and the bright sunshine outside, it still appeared dark and hazy. Maybe one of the first things she needed to do was wash the windows.

She looked around the little apartment. There was what she would call a living room and a very old-fashioned kitchen, with a little iron stove. Near the kitchen, there was an area with a small, but beautifully carved, wood table and three chairs with delicate turned spindles. In the back, there was an enclosed bedroom, but there was no bathroom. She assumed there had been an outhouse once, but it had been removed long before her time.

There was a small bookshelf standing in the "living room," and since Suzy loved to read, she curiously went to peruse the titles that were there. The shelves weren't full, but of the few books that still resided there, she didn't rec-ognize a single title or author, except one. The title, *The Fair Maid of Perth,* meant nothing to her, but the name Sir Walter Scott was familiar enough. She carefully opened the cover, hearing the old, dry binding crackle. Gingerly turning to the title page, she was surprised to see that the book was a signed copy.

*To the fairest maid of Edinburgh.*
*With affection, Wattie.*

Drawing the conclusion that 'Wattie' was a nickname for 'Walter,' Suzy was a little chagrined that the inscription didn't name the person it addressed. Who could this 'fairest maid of Edinburgh' be? And how did she, or at least this book, come to reside in this carriage house in Marblehead, Massachusetts?

Intrigued by the mystery, Suzy turned her attention back to the apartment. The floor was covered with a large braided rug, which sent a cloud of dust into the air with each step she took. There was so much dust on everything that it was difficult to tell the color of virtually anything in the apartment.

Looking up, Suzy realized that the walls were bare. The only art she saw was a small simply-framed portrait in a corner near a chair and side table arrangement, beside a fireplace. There was a candle in a holder on the table, and a well-worn pillow on the chair. She went closer to get a better look at the painting. The background was dark, but the man was well-lit. Seated in a dark red chair, his pose was casual, his elbow resting on the arm of the chair, his chin resting on his hand. He had dark eyes, dark hair, and a close-trimmed beard, and a slight smile played about his lips.

The portrait was hung low, near the candle, and Suzy imagined the occupant of the apartment, the fairest maid in Edinburgh, sitting in the chair, perhaps sipping a cup of tea, and gazing at the man in the painting. She wondered who the man, and the occupant, for that matter, had been.

She straightened up and turned to continue looking around when she felt something loose under her foot. She rocked back and forth on her foot, and she could see the rug raise up a bit in front of her shoe.

*Maybe there's a treasure buried under the floorboards,* she mused to herself as she bent down and pulled the rug aside, stirring up more dust. Being that close to it, she felt a tickle and she put a hand over her mouth and nose to try to filter the worst of the dust.

The loose floorboard lifted up easily, and she laid it aside. She could see some kind of bundle in the space below, and her half-serious remark a few seconds earlier suddenly seemed plausible.

It was so dark in the space in the floor, though, that she didn't want to just reach in blindly. She moved around so that some of the meager light coming in the windows could reach it. She could see now that it wasn't crawling with spiders, her main fear, so she gingerly picked it up.

She took it to the table near the kitchen area, where the light was a little better, and looked at it. It was fourteen to sixteen inches long and nearly a foot wide. The outer wrapping appeared to be some kind of blanket, thin and fragile now in its current condition, but she could just make out the plaid design of it.

As she stood there looking at the little bundle, Suzy felt a prickly feeling on the back of her neck. She was alone, she knew, but she felt as if someone was looking at her, watching her closely. The air around her seemed to be pulsing, as if the carriage house was breathing, and its respirations were intensifying with emotion. She knew the thought was ridiculous, but the feeling was too strong to ignore. She couldn't help it. She turned to prove to herself that she was being silly.

That's when she saw the woman's face looking at her.

She stepped back in terror and bumped against the table, and her heart jumping into her throat pushed a scream past her lips. The face was only there for a moment, though, and Suzy laughed derisively when she realized it was just the slowly swirling motes of dust making patterns in the meager light filtering through the windows. Even as she watched, the "face" slowly changed into a more generic cloud shape.

"Damn, Suzy," she muttered to herself, pressing her hand to her chest as she tried to catch her breath, "you're losing it!"

She blew out a long breath and pushed her hair out of her face, turning back to the table. She looked back down at the bundle and started carefully unwrapping the blanket. It turned out to be long and narrow, more like a shawl or a sash, and it took several turns to unwrap it. Inside the sash, she saw what appeared to be old and brittle newsprint. Again, exercising extreme care, she started peeling away the layers of paper. The paper practically flaked away in her hands, and it was now such a dark brown that she could scarcely make out any words printed on it.

As Suzy kept peeling paper away, she saw a front page with the masthead, announcing that it was the Marblehead Gazette, dated January 13, 1827. Surrounded, now, by bits and pieces of dusty flakes of newsprint, this was the final layer. Inside the newspapers, the bundle was wrapped in what Suzy guessed had once been white linen, but was now brown and grimy.

Suzy felt that feeling again. Goose bumps rose on her arms, and she felt chilled to the bone. Once again, the air seemed electric, waves of pressure pulsating against her. Amidst the emotion she felt in the air, she had the distinct impression that someone was watching her, but when she turned, again, nobody was there.

*Of course there's nobody there, you big wuss!*

She took a deep breath and turned back to the little bundle on the table. She found an edge of the soiled fabric and pulled it aside, unwrapping it carefully as she had the sash. Peeling off the final layer, she screamed as she revealed the head of a mummified baby.

Suzy took a deep breath to calm herself. She looked with horrified fascination at the little head, the skin stretched tight, its toothless mouth slightly open. The rest of the body was wrinkled and brown, the skin hardened. The skeletal arms and hands were pressed tightly against the chest in permanent indentations. The legs were drawn up against its belly, the feet and lower legs crossed over themselves. Suzy couldn't see the genitals, to determine if it was a boy or a girl.

*Not exactly the buried treasure I was hoping for.*

§

Jay Gilbert leaned in close, examining the baby on the table, sometimes with a large magnifying glass, and snapping a few pictures with a flash. He often moved around to different angles to get better light in the dimly-lit carriage house. He looked up at the windows, apparently flooded with light from outside.

"It's kind of dark in here, isn't it?"

"I know," Suzy said. "I need to wash the windows. And I think the air is still kind of hazy in here from all the dust I stirred up."

Jay bent back over and spent some time looking at and photographing the bits of newspaper scattered about on the table as well. Finally, he straightened up and looked at Suzy, his eyebrows raised.

"So, what do you think?" Suzy asked. Jay looked at her seriously and left a dramatic pause hanging in the air for a few seconds.

"I think it's a baby," he finally replied. "Or at least it used to be."

"You know, I have to say I'm really glad I called you," Suzy snarked back at him. "I had a feeling your expertise would be invaluable."

Jay was a curator at a local museum, the Marblehead Historical Consortium. Suzy had known him for years, having met him in college in Boston, and they even dated a couple of times years ago, before she ever met Mark. They had both been history majors, and they had stayed friends ever since, despite Suzy feeling a little jealous that he had been able to actually use his degree. Jay was very familiar with the Drummond house, and he had even been consulted on a couple of other issues dealing with the property during some renovations a few years back.

"I'm glad you called me, too," he smiled.

"Honestly, though, I didn't expect *you* to come when I called," Suzy replied.

"What, you thought I'd just blow you off?"

"No, now that you're a curator, I figured you'd be too busy and would just send an intern or something."

"That would have been nice, but we're a little short-handed. We're actually looking for an intern or two, just to do some of the mundane stuff that we don't have time for, filing, even research and provenance depending on their experience and skill sets."

"My first thought on finding a dead body under the floorboards," Suzy continued, getting back to the original reason for her call, "was to call the police. But whatever happened to it, I figured it might be a little beyond the statute of limitations."

"Well, the police would have just bagged it, catalogued it and filed it away. Eventually, it would probably have just been disposed of. I doubt they would have devoted any manpower to investigating it. Cold cases don't get any colder than this."

Suzy looked at the dried up little body and, despite the grotesque look of it, she felt sympathy for it, and sadness. She thought of Emma wrapped in her father's arms on the floor of the bay, but she pushed the image away.

"So, no clues?" Suzy asked quietly.

"I'm afraid not." Jay turned and looked at the baby, as well. "My first impression, though, is that it was loved. You know, it wasn't just discarded in the woods, or tossed into the ocean. Somebody took the time to wrap it up, like swaddling clothes. But as far as the identity is concerned, I'm afraid I don't have any idea."

Suzy nodded, disappointed. She felt her heart going out to this child, and its mother who, for whatever reason, chose to bury her baby in this way.

"If you don't mind, though," Jay continued, "I'd like to take it with me. Maybe if I get a chance, I could do a little more investigating."

"Please!" Suzy said enthusiastically. "I hate the idea of the poor little thing just lying in a cardboard box in some evidence locker."

As Jay carefully placed the baby in a padded plastic bin he had brought with him, along with the larger bits of newspaper, Suzy felt that prickly feeling again on the back of her neck, and the sensation of being watched. But this time, it didn't feel frightening.

## 4

I found a record," the notice said, "of your g5 grandfather, Lachlan Mac an Léigh contracting with my g5 grandfather, Robert Drummond, to bring some of his personal property to America from Edinburgh, but he never paid for the transport. Drummond sued him for the money. Do you have any records of that suit, or of the outcome? By the way, are you from Scotland?"

Fin looked at the time stamp on the notice. It had been sent over a year ago from someone in Massachusetts, a Suzy Quinn. So it had been at least that long since he had been on the site. He found the genealogy folder on his computer and refamiliarized himself with the documents he had gathered in the years since he had started his quest. He saw nothing resembling what this person was inquiring about.

"Sorry it's taken me so long to respond," he replied. "I haven't been on in a while. I'm afraid I don't have anything relating to that suit. (You're not going to make me settle up, are you?) And no, I'm from Colorado."

Being a writer, he took his time to edit his response. It had been over a year since the original message had been sent – what difference would a couple of extra minutes make? Being a stickler for proper grammar and punctuation, a so-called grammar Nazi, he took a minute to review his response, then clicked "Send."

Another of his quirks as a writer involved phrases forming in his head in various situations as if he were writing about them. Sometimes they were hokey and exaggerated, "dark and stormy night phrases," he liked to call them. Sometimes he would utter them out loud, as if he was narrating the event, which sometimes caused interesting reactions if somebody was nearby. Other times, he would just think them to himself. Sometimes, if he thought the phrase was a good one, he'd make a note of it, to possibly use later.

*Deal with it, babe,* he thought as he considered his growing reputation as a grammar Nazi. *You're never gonna change me. Don't even try.*

Deciding that was one of the dark and stormy night variety, he shook his head and turned his attention back to his family tree, and at other notices he had received. But it wasn't holding his attention as it had at other times. His mood was probably still affected a little by his breakup with Cindy.

He closed the browser and opened up his latest work in progress. *TimePlex*, he found, was a tough act to follow. He had published two novels after it, but they hadn't sold nearly as well. It had been enough to keep him in the lifestyle to which he had quickly become accustomed, but so far, there had been no movie deals.

His current novel, tentatively titled *A Place Made of Time*, was an unexpected sequel to *TimePlex*. This one, actually inspired by his genealogical research, was another time travel story, this time set against the backdrop of old Edinburgh. But it had been giving him some trouble.

After staring at the screen for a few minutes, though, he decided it just wasn't going to happen tonight. He closed the Word document. Something was still tickling his brain, though. The brief visit to FamilyLine.com and the notice about his Scottish ancestor, as well as perusing his current work in progress, had been enough to start it up.

"Alexa," he said, "play the Tannahill Weavers." As far back as he could remember, Celtic music had exerted a pull on him that he could only describe as homesickness. Even though he had never been anywhere in the British Isles, traditional Celtic music always stirred up feelings deep inside that he had never felt for his actual hometown of Littleton, Colorado.

One acquaintance was certain that this was evidence that Fin had lived in Scotland in a previous life. Fin thought that was a pretty cool theory. It had certainly fueled plenty of best-selling fiction. After that, he had spent a little time day-dreaming about what his life might have been like in his Celtic past.

But he figured it could just as likely be genetic memory, the idea that the thoughts and memories of ancestors were stored, to some extent, in the cellular material and passed on genetically to descendants in their DNA.

Whatever it was that caused it, he leaned back in his chair now and allowed *Wild Mountain Thyme* by the Tannahill Weavers to raise goose bumps on his arms.

§

Sometime during the night, Fin woke up with a thought banging around in his head. A result of the genealogy communication and the Scottish music, combined with trying to work on his novel, he realized that what his current story was missing was authenticity. He had been trying to give it a Scottish flavor, but never having been to the land of the Scots, he decided that the story had the quality of mere hearsay. He was developing the style based on other books or movies based in Scotland, but it lacked actual knowledge of the setting.

Perhaps a trip was in order. If he could go there, he could see what the location was actually like. Surely, there must be places where the past still exists in some form. He had seen photographs of Scottish castles that seemed steeped in the centuries, places made of time.

He would go there, he would see those castles, he would allow the past to wash over him. Maybe then, he could give his story a feeling of authenticity.

*Pleased with his decision, our hero fell asleep with the sound of bagpipes playing in his head.*

## 5

**D**on't go in there, Suzy told herself, but she didn't know why. The door to the carriage house stood open, but it was still dark inside. Even so, she walked through the door, looking around, seeing the interior as she had that morning.

She didn't understand why there was still so much dust. It was everywhere. After Jay had left that morning, Suzy had spent hours cleaning the place. She had washed the windows and dusted. Since there was no electricity in the carriage house, she had strung extension cords out there and vacuumed. Still, there was only the dimmest light illuminating the little apartment.

A breeze swirled around her, through the open doorway, and the layers of dust rose up and formed shapes more substantial than she knew they were. One cloud directly in front of her, though, took a shape that was immediately recognizable. A flame became visible, followed by the candle upon which it was burning, floating in midair. Finally, the cloud of dust took the form of a woman, dressed in nineteenth-century clothing, a few feet away from her, holding the candle. Her face glowed in the spectral candle light. It was pretty but careworn, her hair dark, her features delicate. Suzy recognized the face that she thought she had seen watching her in the carriage house that morning.

The woman's lips moved, and Suzy heard her voice, sweet and quiet, and fairly heavily accented.

"Thank ye," she said, "for looking after me wee one."

"Of course," Suzy replied sympathetically. "I'm so sorry I couldn't have done more."

The woman tilted her head and gave a sad smile and a shake of her head.

"There was nothing ye could have done. He was doomed from the start."

"So he was a boy. What was his name?"

"Aye. His name was Caden, like his father. But he was stillborn, and there was nothing to be done for him."

Suzy looked at the woman for a few moments, and the woman tilted her head self-consciously, it seemed, but she kept her eyes on Suzy.

"What's your name?" Suzy finally asked.

"Me Christian name is Fiona. At the end of me days, I was buried in the family plot of Drummond, though in me heart, I shall forever be Fiona Loganach."

"Fiona Loganach," Suzy repeated. "I'm Suzy Quinn."

"Aye, I know your name, lassie," Fiona said, "and now I know your heart."

Suzy opened her eyes and found herself looking up at the shadows of the ceiling of her bedroom, nestled in a deep feeling of contentment.

§

Suzy sat in the booth in her breakfast nook, looking unfocused across the harbor. Her index finger rested distractedly in the handle of her cup as the steam coiled languorously toward the ceiling. The early morning sun was glancing off the Marblehead Light to her right, but Suzy didn't notice. The contentment she had felt during the night had given way to a different feeling.

She had long been open-minded about paranormal and supernatural phenomena. She was even pretty sure that she had been visited on more than one occasion by dead friends and relatives, though there was still some skepticism.

Since Mark and Emma's death, especially, she had hoped for some kind of visitation from them. She loved them both so much, and she worried about them. She had never grieved so deeply for anyone before. But she was sorely disappointed that there had been no contact from them. While she, admittedly, didn't know for certain what awaited them after death, she suspected that there might be something more.

After her experience in the carriage house yesterday morning, followed by the dream in the night, she was now quite certain of it. But that just made her disappointment about Mark and Emma that much more intense. If she could be visited by a total stranger, separated by almost two hundred years, why couldn't she have seen her husband and daughter again? When their death was so recent, her feeling of loss so great, so profound, why didn't they visit her to let her know they were alright?

There were several theories marching through Suzy's mind now. Some have suggested that people who die, but whose spirits stick around afterwards, do so because they have unfinished business to care for. With Fiona's baby buried, all but forgotten, under the floor of the carriage house, that theory, Suzy thought, certainly could apply to her. But really, wouldn't practically anybody who died unexpectedly have unfinished business? Words left unsaid, deeds left undone?

Some feel that if death comes suddenly and unexpectedly, the victim might not even know they're dead, and they continue going about their business as if they were still alive, but unseen to those around them. Suzy remembered the ending of *The Sixth Sense* and the pain and sadness that resulted for Bruce Willis' character with this scenario, and she ached for Mark and Emma if that was the case.

Of the people who have had "near-death experiences," the majority invariably speak about seeing a bright light. It's believed that going into the light takes the person to the next place, wherever or whatever that may be. Perhaps that light goes out after a while. The portal closes, so it's imperative that spirits go through it in a timely fashion lest they be left behind.

Maybe Mark and Emma had to do that or risk missing passage into the next realm. Perhaps Suzy, so deeply ensconced in her grief, just hadn't been ready or receptive enough back then to see them, so they had to move on.

One theory she didn't like to consider, but which invariably haunted her mind, was that maybe Mark and Emma blamed her for their death, as she herself did. God, how she wished she had stopped nagging about taking the boat out that afternoon and just stayed home and made love to Mark like he had wanted!

On the other hand, maybe death really was the end. Maybe Fiona was just a dream.

*One way to find out,* she thought as her eyes focused on her cup. She picked it up and took a sip of tea.

§

Settling in front of her computer, she opened her browser and pulled up the FamilyLine.com web site. After logging in, she saw that she had a few notices, but she ignored them to begin with. She had more important work to do. She went directly to her family tree and traced back the Drummond branch.

There was Phillip Drummond, the ship builder, the one whose name was now forever attached to The Estate. But his wife's name was Helen. Hmm. It was too soon to feel disappointment, though, so Suzy pressed on.

They had two sons, Robert and Michael. Suzy and her family came from Robert, who was born in 1796. He would have been thirty-one years old in 1827, when Fiona's baby died. His wife's name was Judith. Hmm, again.

Something clicked in Suzy's brain at the name. There were a few paintings in the house that were signed simply, "Judith." Suzy knew they had been done by someone in her family's past, but she never knew the connection. Some were fairly ordinary, but a couple of them Suzy liked enough to keep on the walls. Now she put it together. Judith Drummond, Robert's wife, had apparently been an amateur artist.

Suzy hadn't gathered as much information on Michael Drummond, but his wife's name was either Mary or Marie, depending on the documents consulted.

Suzy sat back in her chair, pondering the apparent setback. Thinking back on her dream, she realized that Fiona hadn't said that she *was* a Drummond, just that she had been buried in their family plot. While that would imply marriage, it certainly wasn't irrefutable evidence.

Suddenly, she got up and grabbed a jacket and her keys. She realized that it would be easy enough to find out how Fiona was buried, assuming she actually existed. Suzy knew that the Drummond family plot was in an old cemetery on the north side of mainland Marblehead. It took less than ten minutes to drive there.

Getting out of her car, she walked toward the big white marble mausoleum that marked Phillip Drummond's final resting place. His wife, Helen, was buried there with him, while other family members occupied graves in front of the structure.

There was Michael's grave, marked by a stone of the same white marble. Mary – with a 'y' Suzy noticed – was next to him. A few feet farther on, she found Robert's stone, and next to him was Judith. Their only child, Martha, was buried nearby.

Suzy figured that, even though she hadn't found physical records, Robert must have remarried. Otherwise her family's branch of the Drummond line would have ended with him. But she knew that Robert was her ancestor so, unless Robert had an affair and Suzy's family was descended from some illegitimate offspring, there must be a second wife. Besides, other relatives would likely have raised a stink about a bastard inheriting the family estate.

She continued moving past Robert's grave. At that point, the border of the Drummond family plot seemed to blur, as others with different names became interspersed with Drummonds. Suzy figured they were probably in-laws. She knew her own parents, her uncle and a few other family members, while actually Drummonds, were buried some distance away from here.

Finally, several plots away from Robert, she saw a simple little worn, grey stone. Its markings were plain and austere but poignant:

Fiona Drummond
Loyal wife and mother
April 4 1807 – January 12 1858
Her body lies here,
but her heart remains in Scotland

Suzy's heart was pounding. Fiona was real! She really existed! Suzy's eyes actually filled with tears as she looked at the stone.

She thought that "loyal wife" was an interesting choice of words, instead of "*loving* wife." But that, along with the inscription below, was in accord with what Fiona told her in her dream. *"I shall forever be Fiona Loganach."*

§

Suzy double-clicked her Genealogy folder, which still resided on her computer desktop. She had a few folders inside that, with the names of different entries on her family tree. She opened Robert Drummond's folder and looked at some of the documents inside. One of them was a copy of a death certificate for Judith, his wife, dated June 14, 1825. She was only twenty-four when she died.

Since she had given Robert only one child, and a daughter at that, he likely felt some pressure to remarry, to produce an heir to the Drummond name. Suzy wondered how Fiona came into the picture.

## 6

Brooding in front of his computer, Fin frowned, staring at the page. *A Place Made of Time* was a pain in the ass, he thought. Occasionally, he considered dumping it and starting on something else. But he had told his publisher about it and they were eagerly anticipating it. Somehow, he had to finish it.

He remembered his revelation during the night, about visiting Scotland, to get a feel for the place. The more he thought about it, the more he wanted to do it. What a great Renaissance festival that would be!

But he couldn't do it for a few months. He had the New York Comic Con in a couple of days, and his agent had arranged several stops in a book tour over the next few months to promote his last novel, to try to drive up sales. Scotland would have to wait.

After spending what seemed like hours sitting and pondering, he did what he usually did. He indulged in procrastinations. He logged in to Facebook and followed up on a few notifications. Then, out of curiosity, he logged in to MySoulmate.com, and found that Cindy was already back on. *Maybe she never left*, he thought bitterly.

Finally, he logged in to FamilyLine.com. Since the previous night, he had received a new notice. It was a reply to the response he had sent last night.

"Ha! No, I won't make you settle your ancestor's debt. I was just curious. It's okay, I haven't been on in a long time, either." Then, down below, in a line that seemed tacked on as an afterthought, "You don't happen to have any other information about the Drummonds, do you?"

After spending a few minutes scouring his genealogy folder, he responded.

"No, I'm afraid I don't have any information on any Drummonds. I've reached kind of a dead end myself. My ancestor Lachlan Mac an Léigh has vanished, and frankly I'm distraught. (True, it happened almost 200 years ago, but who says there's a time limit on grieving?!) I'd love to see the information you have about him and the lawsuit, meager as it might be.

"By the way," he added, "my name is Finley MacKinley."

§

When Fin couldn't procrastinate any longer in front of his computer, he decided to procrastinate outside. It was a beautiful early October day, sunny, but with just a bit of a nip in the air. He pulled on a jacket and went out his back door.

His neighborhood was sparse, the houses spaced far apart, and his was the last one before the road ended at a trailhead up into the foothills. The back of his house faced west, so the back door of his walkout basement was the one he went out of when he wanted to take a walk in nature.

The walk cleared his head, helping him to purge the unsuccessful search for romance from his mind, at least a little. And he was able to work through a few issues he had with *A Place Made of Time*.

He sat down at his computer, ready to get to work, but the window for FamilyLine.com was still open in the front of his browser, and he saw a new notice. He clicked on it and saw a response to his earlier reply.

"Finley MacKinley?! Really? That's quite a moniker. With a name like that, you ought to be living in Scotland! (I'll bet you never got teased!) My name is Suzy Quinn.

"I've attached JPEGs of a couple of documents, one an old newspaper notice about the lawsuit, the other a page of a letter that Robert Drummond wrote to a friend in which he mentioned being bamboozled by that ignoble, dastardly ancestor of yours. I expect you to be suitably penitent after you read it."

With a grin, Fin clicked on the paper clip icon and looked at the documents that were attached. To the genealogist in him, they were mildly interesting, but neither contained much useful information.

"Thank you, Suzy," he replied. "Not exactly the bounteous fount of information I was hoping for, but I appreciate it nonetheless.

"By the way, my friends call me Fin."

*Those who don't know me at all call me Michael Jones,* he thought. *But why spoil a fun exchange if it isn't necessary?*

## 7

Rotating her head to stretch her neck, Suzy closed *The Fair Maid of Perth*. Being unaccustomed to nineteenth-century prose, reading it was a bit of a chore to start with. But after a few pages, she felt a little more familiar with it, and she could feel herself gradually being immersed in the culture of the earlier time. She knew nothing about the events that the historical novel was based on, but she was determined to keep at it.

Not now, though. She decided that she wasn't in the mood to read.

She got up from her chair and went to the window. A misty twilight was draping itself shamelessly over the harbor, and she could see the fuzzy glow of lights across the water on the mainland.

Suzy wondered what Fiona had thought about the book. Did it mean something special to her? Or was it just another book, simply one among many books contemporary to her time?

Judging by the inscription, she figured that it was more than just another book.

Suzy felt restless. She had gotten out of the house to go to lunch with a couple of friends, and that helped to get her mind off of Mark and Emma, as well as the melancholy story of Fiona. Now that she was back, now that she had spent hours immersing herself in the language and culture of the past, regardless of how difficult it had been, she didn't know what to do with herself.

She found herself wandering aimlessly around the house, as she had yesterday morning. This time, she ended up in front of her computer.

Fiona's story, and particularly how she came to end up married to Robert Drummond, and becoming Suzy's great-great-great-great-great-grandmother, had been poking

Suzy's mind for hours. She sat down at the computer and pulled up the FamilyLine.com site.

She read Fin's response, and she smiled.

"Hi Fin," she replied. "Yeah, I know those documents weren't exactly noteworthy. So you might imagine how they've tickled my curiosity for the past few years. And especially now."

Stopping there, leaving that thought hanging there incomplete, Suzy knew she was vagueposting, but she also knew how crazy her recent experiences would sound. How would this stranger react to her seeing and talking with a ghost? She just wanted to test the waters, ease in slowly.

As it turned out, Fin was online. He responded right away.

"Why 'especially now'?" he asked.

*Here goes.*

"Because I spoke last night with my g5 grandmother, and it's only made me curiouser and curiouser!"

This time, there was a long pause. A couple of minutes passed. Suzy tried to imagine what Fin must be thinking. Finally, there was a response.

"Really?"

"You must type really, really slow," Suzy replied, hoping to lighten the revelation.

"She must be at least 200 years old!"

"210, but she doesn't look a day over 40."

"Okay, forgive my skepticism, but it's not every day someone tells me they spoke to their 210-year-old ancestor."

"Yeah," Suzy replied, "this is a first for me, too."

"So, I guess there must be a story there."

"You could say that."

## 8

Not sure what to make of Suzy's disclosure, Fin stared at the computer. Being a fantasy writer, he certainly had a lot of experience with ghosts and more, as far as research and story-telling goes. But he had never experienced any first-hand contact. To be honest, he felt a little envious of people who had such experiences, short of a full-on haunting, of course.

But he was also aware of how many people who claim such knowledge and experience turn out to be victims of what he liked to call CranioRectal Inversion Syndrome.

Having just met Suzy, he didn't know her from Eve. So, operating on the assumption that he may have come in contact with a nut case, he read the account that she was sending him a few paragraphs at a time. Her description of the carriage house was certainly creepy, and his interest was definitely piqued with the finding of the mummified baby. Her sighting of the woman's face in the dust cloud was possibly coincidence, but he didn't respond.

Dreams were a difficult subject for him as well. He didn't know if there was any special significance or prophetic meaning in them, or if they were just a way for the brain to flush out the weirdness of the day.

But he had to admit that finding Fiona's grave after hearing her name for the first time in the dream was somewhat persuasive. Though it's possible that Suzy might have seen the name somewhere else at another time and, while her conscious mind forgot it, her brain stored it away to use in the dream. Brains can be sneaky like that.

Still, it certainly made for an interesting story, and the author in him made notes of ideas he might want to use at a later date.

"Well, that was certainly an interesting tale," Fin replied noncommittally after she had finished.

"You don't believe me, do you?" Suzy asked. "It's okay, I don't blame you. But it has definitely given me a kick in the butt to get back into tracing my genealogy, if only just to find out more about Fiona and her baby." After a few seconds, she added, "Unfortunately, you've been absolutely no help at all!"

"Sorry," he typed with a smile. He liked her sense of humor. It would be just his luck that she's married, or weighs three hundred pounds, or is eighty years old. Not that it made a bit of difference, since she lived two thousand miles away. "I've been a little busy myself lately."

"Oh yeah? What do you do?"

*Moment of truth.*

"I'm a writer."

"Cool! I'm a reader. What do you write?"

"Novels. Usually fantasy or sci-fi."

"Hmm. I don't think I've read your work. I think I'd remember 'Finley MacKinley.'"

"Well, no, you definitely wouldn't have read anything by Finley MacKinley. I write under the pseudonym Michael Jones."

Several seconds passed before Suzy's response came across.

"Michael Jones? Michael 'Time-Freakin-Plex' Jones? I don't believe it."

"I don't blame you. Sometimes I don't either."

A full three minutes passed before she finally responded.

"I have that book in my library. I just went to get it. Hmm. You're kinda cute."

Okay, she didn't sound like a married woman. At least not a *happily* married woman. Unless he was reading more into her remark than was really there. Still, that didn't rule out three hundred pounds or eighty years old.

"Thanks," he typed. Seeing an opportunity to, hopefully, find out more about Suzy, he seized on it. "I'm afraid you have me at a disadvantage, though."

"How's that?"

"You know what I look like."

He waited for a couple of minutes before her next message arrived. It was a photo she had shot with the web cam on her computer. Her eyes were crossed and her tongue was sticking out.

Well, she's not three hundred pounds, and definitely not eighty years old. And if he could undo the silly face, sort of reverse-engineer the expression, he thought she might actually look pretty.

Of course, she was still two thousand miles away. But he knew he was being silly. He didn't even know her.

"Gorgeous!" he replied.

"I can't believe I just made a face at a famous author," Suzy responded. "Of course, people can say they're anybody online. You could just as easily be my creepy next door neighbor."

"Fine," he typed a couple of minutes later, attaching a photo of himself with some fake buck teeth that he remembered that he had in a drawer.

"Alright, I guess you're really you," Suzy replied. "By the way, I think this should be your next author photo."

"If I can ever finish the damn thing, I just might consider it."

"Having trouble?"

"Not so much with the story, but the atmosphere. I can't get the feel of it right."

"Hmm. Wish I could help you, but I'm definitely not a writer."

"At the moment, I'm not much of one, either."

"Says the man who wrote the New York Times best seller, and the basis for an upcoming blockbuster movie. By the way, I never told my husband, but I've kind of had a crush on Ryan Reynolds. I think he's a good choice to play Spencer."

There it was.

"Ah, you're married?"

Several seconds passed.

"I was," she finally replied. "I'm a widow."

"I'm so sorry!" he typed, feeling an indescribable, and completely illogical, mix of sympathy and relief.

"Thanks," she replied quickly. "Listen, I should go. It's getting late."

"It's only 7:30."

"It's two hours later here. Good night, Fin."

*Shit.*

## 9

Amazed at the online conversation she just had, Suzy looked back at the messages she had exchanged with Fin, aka Michael Jones. The smartass remarks came naturally to her, although that was usually the case with people she knew well. She was surprised at how easily they came with this guy she had only met online yesterday.

Then, she had to mention being a widow. Dammit! She had typed and sent it before she even realized it. Feeling awkward, she suddenly had the ridiculous sensation of being unfaithful to Mark.

Still, she had just exchanged witty banter with the dynamic Michael Jones!

What must he be like in person!

Wiping away a tear, and trying to overcome that nagging feeling of unfaithfulness, she put her computer to sleep and went to her bedroom to do the same herself.

§

"You're real!" Suzy exclaimed.

"Begging your pardon?" Fiona said with a confused expression.

"I wasn't sure if you were real or just a dream, a figment of my imagination."

"Ah, and now ye know?"

"I found your grave." Suzy's voice changed to a more reverent tone. Never having been put in the position before, she wasn't sure if "I'm sorry" was an expected remark to make to someone who was dead. It just seemed so inadequate.

Fiona smiled, but only with her mouth. Her eyes still looked sad.

"What's wrong?" Suzy asked. "Are you missing your baby?"

"Suzy Quinn, ye're a dear girl," Fiona replied. "I've been without me wee laddie for a long time, but I knew where he was. It's not him I'm missing, but me husband, me love."

"Robert Drummond?"

"Robert Drummond was me savior, but he wasn't me love."

"'Your heart remains in Scotland,'" Suzy recited quietly. "That was on your grave stone. You said your baby, Caden, was named after your husband. He died in Scotland, didn't he?"

"Aye, at least that's what I was told. I ne'er knew for sure what happened to him."

"Caden Loganach?" Suzy asked? Fiona nodded, looking momentarily hopeful. "I'm sorry, I haven't seen anything about him." Fiona's hopefulness was replaced with disappointment. "In fact, in tracing my genealogy, I haven't found anything about you, either, except for your grave stone which, curiously, wasn't in the rest of the family plot. My family name is Drummond, and I know we came through Robert's line, but he and his first wife only had a daughter."

"Judith died years before. She was already buried in the plot next to Robert's."

"You had children, though?"

"Aye, I had three bairns, a son and two daughters."

"What were their names?"

"Me daughters were Finella and Roberta," she said with the first sincere smile Suzy had seen. "Me son was named Patrick."

"So, Patrick Drummond is my great-great-great-great-grandfather." Suzy smiled. Fiona returned the smile, but again, the sadness remained in her eyes. Suzy noticed, and her heart went out to her. "I sure wish there was something I could do to make you happy."

"Ye're a sweet lassie, but I only want to know what happened to me dear husband."

56

"I'll find out," Suzy said resolutely.

§

The next morning, Suzy pondered again her receptivity to communication with a woman who had been dead for over a century and a half. And again, she wished, with a feeling of deep regret, that she had been able to do the same with Mark and Emma.

Suzy went downstairs and began her tea-making ritual. As the tea steeped in the pot, she thought about her conversation with Fiona.

She didn't know if she could be held accountable for promises made in dreams, but she wondered how she could make good on her promise to a ghost. How was she going to find out what happened to an obscure person in Scotland almost two hundred years ago, one who, apparently, didn't father any progeny that lived?

She did have his name, thanks to a ghost, no less. But what kind of records would have been kept back then about a poor nobody?

Pouring tea into her cup, she added some agave and half-and-half, stirring it to a warm, creamy tan.

This morning, she sat on the other side of the breakfast nook booth. Instead of the lights switching off across the harbor, the wrap-around windows gave her a view of part of her back yard, including a portion of the carriage house, dimly illuminated in the early sunrise.

She felt a little agitated and, as was her common reaction, she lit a candle. Staring into the flame, she reflected on the fascinating occurrences of the last twenty-four hours, marveling again at her ability to commune with the past through the spirit of a dead person.

Even as she thought this, the flame blurred before her, and she felt a tingling sensation throughout her body. She blinked her eyes, but it didn't help. She looked out the window and saw that her view of the back yard and the carriage house began to change as well, blurring, dissolving, melting into an unrecognizable mosaic of colors. Watching the view of her back yard altering before her eyes, she experienced a moment of panic, and she wondered if she was experiencing some kind of medical emergency, like a stroke.

She tried to focus on the neglected trees and shrubberies, some wearing their October colors, some having shed their raiment, leaving them scattered at their feet. But she couldn't hold on to it. The view wavered like heat on a distant highway, fading into a very different scene.

## 10

Being eighteen, pretty and the last unmarried daughter of Taran MacGregor, Fiona was aware of several sets of young – and not so young – eyes on her as she crossed the room. She knew some of them judged her as independent and head-strong. Others who didn't know, or who did know but didn't care, looked more favorably on her. Regardless of their judgment, she ignored them as she continued toward her goal, the fifty-four-year-old, greying man leaning on a cane standing near the fireplace. As 1st Baronet, he was known to most people as Sir Walter Scott, but as a long-time friend of the family, Fiona addressed him much less formally.

"Wattie!" she said, her face beaming. "I'm so glad ye could come!"

"'Tis lovely to see you, me dear," he replied, taking her hand in his, and blushing a little as she kissed his cheek.

"Is Charlotte here?" Fiona asked, looking around.

"Nay, I'm afraid she's not feeling very well this evening."

"I'm so sorry. Please give her me love."

"Indeed, I shall," he smiled at her. Glancing around at the crowd, he looked back at Fiona. "'Twas most kind of your father to invite me tonight."

"How could we not invite ye?" she asked with a tone of mock indignation. "Ye're family!"

"You're very kind, lass," he said warmly. At that time, a young, attractive man approached carrying two glasses of champagne. He held one out to Scott.

"Here you are, father," he said.

"I didn't ask for me," Scott replied with a sly smile, "but for the young lassie." Scott turned toward Fiona. "Fiona, me dear, may I present me youngest son, Charles. Charles, this is Fiona MacGregor, daughter of our host tonight."

"How do you do, miss?" Charles said quite seriously, with a slight bow. He presented the glass of champagne, which Fiona took a little hesitantly.

"Pleased to meet ye, sir," she replied. "Although I think we may have met when we were younger."

"Aye," Scott replied, "ye did play together a few times when ye were bairns. When ye weren't running off."

"That sounds like me. Me father still scolds me for not being aware of time and wandering off on long walks at the least opportune times."

"It's a wonder your parents allowed you to keep coming. Especially since we weren't exactly of your class."

"What are ye saying?" Fiona protested. "You're a baronet. I suppose I should be calling you Sir Wattie."

"But I only gained that title four years ago. Before that I was primarily a scribbler."

"Psh," Fiona said with a shake of her head. "Anyway, the division of classes is such a ridiculous thing."

"Well, ridiculous or not, if your father wasn't such a patron of the arts, we likely would ne're have met."

"Then I thank God for me father's love of the arts," Fiona replied with an affectionate pat on his arm.

"As do I," Charles added, with a purposeful look at Fiona and another slight bow.

Fiona felt a little flushed under his gaze. She was relieved when somebody nearby vacated a chair, and she saw an opportunity to shift the attention off of her. She asked that Scott, still leaning a bit unsteadily on his cane, sit down. He limped toward the chair and eased into it. Taking a sip of the champagne, Fiona decided to change the topic of conversation.

"Do I detect a hint of an English dialect in your speech, Mr. Scott?" she asked Charles.

"Aye, perhaps you do," Charles replied. "I've been studying law at Brasenose College in Oxford. I suppose I may have picked up a bit of the accent. As classes have just let out, I decided to come back to Edinburgh for the summer."

"And not a moment too soon," Fiona replied.

"How do you mean?"

"Ye need to be immersed in your native tongue before too much damage is done."

"Indeed," Charles chuckled. "So, does your father do this often?" He motioned toward the people conversing in various small groups about the hall, a few of which included some recognizable faces.

"At least once a year, me father likes to promote the arts among the populace. Although I suspect a part of it is a desire to be seen among artists." She grinned as she looked across the room to where her father, his white hair bouncing as he gestured enthusiastically, was engaged in fervent conversation with William Turner about one of Turner's paintings hanging on the wall.

"He's not as superficial as she makes him sound," Scott said with only a slightly scolding tone.

"Nay, indeed he's not," Fiona agreed with an affectionate smile. "I think it has to do with me brothers and sisters having their own lives. Since it's just me father and me here now, he likes to see the house filled up from time to time. And he needs to justify the cost of the staff."

Scott shook his head and rolled his eyes at Fiona's joke, but he couldn't help smiling at her. Fiona laughed and touched his shoulder affectionately.

"Sir Wattie's right. Me father is a true lover of the arts of various disciplines. And he really does enjoy introducing artists and their works to others."

"Very commendable," Charles said. "And what of you, Miss MacGregor? Are you an artist yourself?"

"I'm afraid not."

"Nonsense," Scott spoke up. "Fiona is quite an accomplished painter."

"Wattie," Fiona objected, "ye're much too generous." She turned back toward Charles. "I dabble. But putting blobs of color on a canvas does not put me anywhere near the level of those in attendance tonight. However, I must admit a particular fondness for the literary arts."

"Well, of course. After all, my father's sitting right here," Charles said slyly.

"Wattie is one of me favorites!" Fiona said enthusiastically, happy to have turned the conversation away from her. Turning to

Scott, she continued, her eyes glowing. "I loved The Bride of Lammermoor. And The Pirate. Oh, and Ivanhoe!"

"Father, it seems you have a devoted admirer."

"Oh, I am indeed. But not only of your father's. I'm a ravenous reader. I've recently finished a fascinating historical novel, Valperga, by Mary Shelley. Have ye read it?"

"I have," Charles replied, and Fiona noticed the slight look of disdain on his face.

"Ye did not care for it?" she asked.

"No, not much. If I wanted to read a romance novel, I think I may as well read Jane Austen."

"Oh, well I like Jane Austen, too. But Valperga was so much more than simply a romance novel. There was political intrigue, there was –"

"Yes, I've heard the arguments about the undercurrent of good versus evil."

"Nay, not so much good versus evil," Fiona said, pondering. "More right versus wrong. It was wrong of Castruccio to make Euthanasia choose between him and freedom. What a horrible position to be placed into."

"Yes, well," Charles responded, "of her works, I much preferred Frankenstein. Have you read it?"

Fiona shuddered a bit.

"I'm afraid I've not been able to bring meself to read it yet. It reminds me too much of the resurrectionists."

"Oh, yes, the body snatchers. Well, a comparison may certainly be drawn there."

"When her mother died," Scott said quietly to Charles, "her body was taken from her grave." Charles leaned closer as Scott continued in a whisper. "It was later found in the university where it had been dissected."

"Oh, Miss MacGregor, I am so terribly sorry," Charles said, truly horrified.

"Thank you," she replied quietly.

"Do ye mind if I interrupt?" Fiona heard her father say behind her. She turned toward him, thankful for the interruption.

"Of course not, father."

"Fiona, I'd like to introduce Mr. Lachlan Mac an Léigh." Fiona looked at the man she had been hearing of lately, his face the absolute personification of kindness. "He's been agitating some of our guests with talk about those unfortunate souls living in the vaults, and I thought that ye might be the one person in attendance here tonight who may be able to converse sympathetically with him."

Fiona smiled at Mr. Mac an Léigh.

As her heart pounded, Suzy sat there watching the vision fade, and she sighed with relief as her breakfast nook appeared around her again. Hesitant to move too much, she glanced cautiously out the window. The back yard was still there, including the portion of the carriage house.

Judging by the light, it appeared that only a few minutes had passed. Taking a fortifying sip of her tea, the heat of it confirmed that conclusion.

"Cool trick, Fiona," she muttered. "Please don't do that when I'm driving."

Suzy pushed herself unsteadily to her feet, keeping her hands on the table top. Breathing a little more regularly now after her immersion in the past, she blew out the candle, picked up her cup and went into her office, waking up her computer.

She decided she needed some backup information.

§

Edinburgh, Scotland was a city built on hills. The Scots were a hardy people, well-suited to life in the rugged terrain. Edinburgh had already existed as a settlement and a town for eight hundred years when they came up against the English at the Battle of Sark in 1450. After defeating the English army, they built a wall around the city, effectively setting a limit to the point to which the city could expand.

The Battle of Flodden in 1513 had a very different outcome. The English, better-armed and with cannons that could inflict great damage on the wall, were the victors this time. Despite the different outcome, the Scots' defeat had a similar result. They built another wall. Taller and thicker, the newer, more robust wall was outside the first one, thereby expanding their limits. But it was still a limit nonetheless.

The hills on which the city was built were separated by deep valleys, which early on were used as pasture ground. But as time passed, and with the city limit literally set in stone, the only way to build was up.

Bridges were built to traverse the valleys, the stone arches supporting them still allowing passage of cattle below. In time, though, the pasture ground was turned into human tenements, some buildings reaching as high as twelve stories. As more and more building took place, and life was conducted at bridge level, many of the lower stories subsequently became cellars.

There was scarcely room for streets, so many of the buildings had only narrow passages between them, called closes. Little more than tight alleyways, they allowed almost no light to filter in between the towering tenements.

Eventually, structures were built right up against the bridges, enclosing the arches, or vaults, below ground. Those vaults were divided up into different levels, and were saved as storage and workspace for merchants who occupied space above them.

However, as Edinburgh's sewage system was comprised of buckets, windows and city streets, with seepage through the cracks and porous stones, the vaults below ultimately became a dank and smelly system of caverns that the aboveground owners finally abandoned. They were all but forgotten when the poorest of the poor found them and took up residence.

*So, those were the vaults that Lachlan Mac an Léigh was concerned about.* Suzy thought about Fin and what he might think about her having a vision of his ancestor. Hell, he probably thought she was crazy the moment she told him she talked to the ghost of her own ancestor. She noted, though, that she could see a resemblance between Lachlan and Fin's author photo.

Having read a bit of Sir Walter Scott's book, and now having seen him, she was curious about him. It turns out he had been born in rather poor circumstances. Six of his siblings died when they were babies, and as an involuntary sob escaped her throat, Suzy wondered how mothers back then could possibly survive that kind of grief.

Walter himself contracted polio when he was two years old, which left him lame. After a series of spa treatments in Bath, England, and summers spent plodding around the Scottish Borders with his aunt Jenny, he became somewhat rehabilitated, though he walked with a limp for the rest of his life.

And the body snatchers! Back then in Scotland, the only legal source of bodies for use in medical schools was from criminal executions or those who had died in prison. In the nineteenth century, due to a lessening in the severity of sentencing in the courts, fewer people were being executed or sentenced to long terms in prison.

As a result, there was a serious shortage of cadavers for dissecting. This led to a morbid black market, the practice of digging up newly-buried bodies and selling them to the universities. This was a problem in several countries, including the United States, but it was most prevalent in Scotland and elsewhere in the United Kingdom.

It became so common that various deterrents came into being. Among them, iron cages called mortsafes being erected over and around graves, to prevent would-be body snatchers from gaining access to a newly-buried body. Stone watchtowers were erected in some cemeteries, so guards could watch over the graves.

When the deterrents became too much of an impediment, some found other methods. William Burke and William Hare found that they could avoid all the digging and sneaking around cemeteries by simply killing people and selling the bodies. By the time the dismal duo were apprehended, they had killed sixteen people.

It didn't sound as if Fiona's mother had been one of their victims. But still, to have her body stolen and later found partially dissected in a university must have been horrifying to Fiona.

Now that the shock of the vision had worn off, Suzy decided that it had been really cool actually seeing a scene from history. Obviously, a famous literary figure like Sir Walter Scott was a big deal. But the others, too. Common people living their everyday lives.

Although these people weren't so common. Fiona, obviously, came from a fairly well-to-do family, and the people at the party were, for the most part, not your average citizens. But still, being able to actually see them, how they related to each other, to hear how they spoke, see how they dressed, it was fascinating!

The only thing that would make it better would be if she could have interacted with them.

She idly wondered what Fin, aka Michael Jones, would think about her time travel.

*I'll bet his research wasn't as cool as mine!*

§

Today was a little cooler than yesterday, bright and sunny, but a little more seasonal. Suzy pulled her jacket tighter around her as she opened the door to the carriage house.

Walking in, she was again baffled by how murky the carriage house was. On the outside, the windows were flooded with sunlight, but little of it seemed to be making its way into the apartment. She had washed the windows inside and out, but it was as if the glass was filtering out the light. It was also freezing, much colder than outside.

"Fiona?" she said, struggling to keep her teeth from chattering, and feeling a little silly calling a name in an empty apartment. "Fiona, can we talk face to face?"

She walked around the apartment, waiting for a response. As she approached the upholstered chair and table, she bent over to look again at the little painting on the wall. She knew now that the face in the portrait must be Caden, and she looked at him with renewed interest. She didn't know how good the likeness was, but the face seemed kind.

She felt that prickly feeling on the back of her neck, and it was accompanied by a deep feeling of apprehension. She stood up and turned. She half expected to see the pretty apparition made of dust clouds that she had seen in her first dream.

But she saw nothing.

"Fiona?"

The apprehension increased as the temperature dropped even more, and Suzy felt the sensation of fluctuating pressure. It was almost as if the carriage house was breathing, and with each inhalation, she could feel the pressure against her own body, expelling the breath from her lungs in a cloud of vapor. As the breathing became more rapid, her apprehension changed to dread.

Her heart speeded up, as did her breathing, but with the ebb and flow of the external pressure against her body, it was difficult to suck the necessary air into her lungs.

As the dread turned to panic, she became aware of a building vibration. The vibration shook her whole body from the inside out, and she felt as if she might vomit.

She couldn't pinpoint the source of the vibration, but as it reached a peak, it seemed to coalesce into something recognizable. The vibrations consolidated into a series of sounds. It was not quite a voice, but there were words in a frequency that she felt deep in her chest, and that she understood in her head. A simple sentence, loud and drawn out.

"Leave me alone!"

## 12

*I hope they grow back*, Fin thought, as he looked at the clumps of eyelashes and eyebrows stuck in the plaster. He looked at his young reflection in the mirror and was glad to see that they didn't *all* come out.

He looked back down at the plaster object in his hands. Now that the pain and the panic were subsiding, he was pleased with the outcome. In the plaster, he could see the inverted image of his face, and he realized belatedly that he should have put some Vaseline on his eyes and eyebrows.

Fin was fourteen when he went on a California vacation with his family, and of the attractions they visited, Fin was most intrigued with the movie studios. The demonstrations of movie makeup and special effects had made an impression on him, and one of the first things he did when he got back home was start on an ape mask, like he saw demonstrated in connection with the original *Planet of the Apes* series of movies.

The first iteration bore little resemblance to the makeup used in the movies. He started with a particle mask, the kind often used by painters, made of white fiber, molded into a semi-circular shape, and with an elastic band to hold it on. He cut it horizontally for the mouth, then coated it with a papier-mâché concoction. The final product was a full-face mask, complete with a faux fur material to cover his head.

When he pulled it on, it was tight enough that it moved when his face moved, and it sort of reflected his expressions. But not really. Not well enough for Fin.

People he showed it to were impressed. Fin knew he could do better.

Studying books he checked out from the library on the subject, he knew that he needed to get plaster and liquid latex. The mold of his face, painful as it had been to get off, was what he made a positive impression from. Once he had that, he could use modeling clay to create the shape of an ape's face that would fit perfectly onto his own. Another plaster cast of that, and he had the negative mold for the latex prosthetics.

While his friends were outside playing baseball or football, or learning death-defying acrobatics on their bicycles or skateboards, while his sister was out with her friends, doing things extroverts do, Fin was applying latex prosthetics to his face with spirit gum and shopping fabric stores for the most realistic looking faux fur.

After several years and several moves, Fin didn't have those early ape masks anymore. His recreations of super hero costumes had also been discarded. Over the years, his interests gradually changed. But he always favored the cerebral and geeky pursuits over the physical.

Thus, as the author of a New York Times bestseller, and the basis of a Hollywood blockbuster, Fin was hiding away his secret identity and Michael Jones was on his way to New York Comic Con. But he wasn't taking a costume. He was going, this time, as a celebrity guest.

§

*Gazing about the complex, our hero was a little star-struck.*

Sharing the program with him was Jennifer Lawrence, the female lead of *TimePlex*, and he had to admit he was enamored with her honest, enthusiastic, girl-next-door persona. Ryan Reynolds was there, as well, whom Fin had liked since he first saw him on the sitcom *Two Guys, a Girl and a Pizza Place*. The young director of the movie was also there, whose name Fin couldn't remember just now. But Jennifer Lawrence was the one who had his full attention.

Walking around the floor of the main hall of the Javits Center earlier had been a thrill. He had attended the Denver Comic Con a couple of times, before they changed their name to the Denver Pop Culture Con in an attempt to be more inclusive in their description. But the size and scope of the New York convention amazed him.

Even more amazing was being on stage in one of the auditoriums in front of cheering fans. He knew they were there mainly for Jennifer Lawrence and Ryan Reynolds, but still, the concept of being there, 'on their level,' was almost unthinkable to Fin.

The setting was casual, the four guests being seated on a long sofa, a coffee table with drinks in front of them. Bob, the emcee, sat to the side in a chair of his own. Fin was seated on the end of the sofa.

Next to Jennifer Lawrence.

He had mixed feelings about the discussion itself. The emcee was fielding questions from the audience, as well as asking some of his own, but they were mainly directed to those connected to the movie.

He knew his story had been changed quite a bit for the movie, as is usually the case in writing a screenplay. While he knew it was necessary to fit the story within roughly two hours, and he was excited that his book was even chosen for such an honor, still he felt a smidgen of resentment that such liberties were taken. And he was glad it wasn't up to him to do it.

His mind came back to the panel discussion again when Jennifer started responding to a question from the audience. She was so animated in answering questions, and in telling funny stories about the movie production, that she sometimes bumped Fin or Ryan, often following it up with a "sorry" and her husky laugh. Fin didn't mind.

But he found his mind wandering again when the director began talking about other projects he was working on. One was a ghost story, and it made Fin start thinking about Suzy again.

He wondered if there was anything to that story she told him. The whole idea of visiting with a dead ancestor from nearly two hundred years ago was just so creepy. Of course, what Suzy said about their meeting wasn't creepy at all. It was cordial, almost sweet. But still . . .

"Michael?" Fin jerked his attention back to the discussion when he realized that one of the questions had been directed to him.

"I'm sorry," he said, fiddling with the earpiece of the microphone headset. "I'm afraid I didn't hear the question."

"The young lady asked about your motivation concerning the love story in *TimePlex*."

"Oh, of course." He thought for a moment. "Well, I guess my main motivation was Jennifer," and he grinned at her. "I just wrote what I wanted her to do or say."

The audience loved that and applauded, and playing to the crowd, Jennifer leaned against him and put her arm through his.

"Unfortunately, not everything in the book will make it to the screen," Ryan Reynolds said, his voice soft and apologetic. There were a few groans from the audience. "I know," he said earnestly. "I'm as sorry about that as you are!" Jennifer elbowed him.

"That's right," the director chimed in with a slight accent, and a contrite look on his face. "I'm afraid we're going for a PG-13 rating." There was more applause, and a few more disappointed laments from the crowd.

"What about a sequel?" somebody shouted.

All eyes turned back to Fin again.

"As it turns out, I am currently working on a sequel, but I'm afraid I don't have a release date yet."

There was a smattering of applause, and Bob asked a follow-up question.

"Can you tell us anything, yet, about the story in the sequel?"

"Well," Fin said, pondering briefly, "unlike *TimePlex*, which went into the future, in the sequel, *A Place Made of Time*, I have Spencer and Gisele going into the past, to old Edinburgh, Scotland. I'm building on the relationship they started in *TimePlex*, but the look and atmosphere will be completely different."

"What inspired you to go in that direction?"

"Partly my own situation. I'm Scottish on my father's side, and I've spent a lot of time tracing my family tree back to Edinburgh, learning about my ancestors, and I just find it fascinating. So it's pretty much self-indulgent. I thought it would be a great setting for a story since I'm so inexplicably drawn to Celtic culture."

"Wow, that's cool," Jennifer said, placing her hand on his arm. "Maybe you lived there, like, in a past life." Fin didn't know if she was being serious or not.

"I've actually heard that theory before," he replied. "And I admit that I'm open to the possibility. I just haven't really given a lot of thought to that whole afterlife thing. Not until recently, anyway."

"Recently?" Ryan prodded. "Why? What happened recently?" Fin hadn't meant to take the discussion in that direction.

"Well, I was talking with a friend a couple of days ago about a supernatural experience she had. She thinks her house is haunted by a ghost, from Scotland, coincidentally. One of her ancestors. So yeah, it's recently been on my mind."

"Maybe a joint ghost story is in our future," the movie director replied.

Fin knew his response to Ryan's question had been vague, but it was enough to keep his mind on Suzy, while the questions turned now to the movie production. He didn't like the way his last conversation with Suzy had ended, and his subsequent messages to her had gone, so far, unanswered.

He made a mental note to try to contact her again once he got back to the hotel.

## 13

The little Church of Spiritual Science was just a few minutes away from Suzy's house. Surrounded by homes at least a century and a half old, the shingle-sided building sat next to a small parking lot. On a Friday, the parking lot was empty except for Suzy's MINI Cooper and the Chevrolet Malibu owned by the pastor.

Suzy had visited this church a few times after Mark and Emma died, and though she had decided not to continue attending, she had pleasant memories of her time here. She liked their inclusivity, not only in their acceptance of people of all walks of life, but also in their beliefs. She went to the back of the church where the pastor's apartment was located, and she knocked on the door.

The door was opened by a sixtyish woman wearing old bell-bottom jeans, a thick, nubby sweater and round John Lennon-style eye glasses.

"Suzy!" she smiled.

"Hi, Leanne," Suzy replied, smiling in spite of the tension still clinging to her.

"It's good to see you. What brings you here?"

"I was wondering if you might have a few minutes to talk."

"Certainly. Come on in." She stepped back, opening the door wider so Suzy could step past her. "I just made a pot of tea. Would you like some?"

"Oh, that sounds good!" Suzy knew it would be herbal tea, probably chamomile, instead of her favorite Earl Grey, but as chilled as she still was, she couldn't refuse.

She sat on one of the stools at the counter in the cozy little kitchen while Leanne got a second cup from the cabinet and poured the tea. It was chamomile. She set one of them in front of Suzy and scooted a little Lazy Susan with condiments and sweeteners closer to her.

Leanne watched silently as Suzy selected the honey and squirted a little into her tea and stirred it. As she put the spoon down and picked up the cup with both hands pressed tightly against it, she still hadn't noticed Leanne watching her as she took a sip.

"You seem uneasy," Leanne finally said.

Suzy exhaled. She meant it as a disdainful laugh, but it sounded more like an inverted gasp.

"Yeah, I'm uneasy," Suzy replied with a bit of a chuckle, staring into her cup.

"It was just about a year ago, wasn't it?"

Suzy looked up at her, surprised. Not that Leanne had remembered, but because Suzy realized that the anniversary hadn't encroached on her mind for several hours.

"Yes, it was. But that's not why I'm here."

Leanne sat on the stool next to her and waited. Suzy took a deep breath and another sip of tea before speaking again.

"What are your beliefs about ghosts?"

Leanne's right eyebrow raised a little as she gathered her thoughts.

"Well, I think there are a number of viable concepts." She peered closely at Suzy. "Is it Mark or Emma?"

"I wish," Suzy said regretfully. "No, I've recently discovered that a rumored ghost on the property is, in fact, real. I'm just not sure how to deal with her."

"Hmm." Leanne took a sip of tea. "Is this ghost being disruptive? Do you feel like you're in danger?"

"No, nothing like that. At least she wasn't. It hasn't really been your typical textbook haunting."

"There's no such thing as 'textbook' where hauntings are concerned. Ghosts are as different as people."

"Of course," Suzy nodded. "I mean it hasn't been rattling chains and levitating dishes." Leanne smiled and nodded. "Fiona has been a very sweet person, very forthcoming with information when I spoke with her."

"You've actually conversed with this ghost?"

"Yes, well, sort of. We had a couple of conversations in dreams, and I had one waking vision."

"Interesting. What kind of vision?"

"It was as if I was watching a scene from a historical movie. But it was an episode from early in Fiona's life."

Leanne sipped her tea, her eyes wide.

"But the conversations in my dreams were fascinating, too. What started the whole thing," Suzy hesitated, "well, on the morning that I first went into the carriage house, I found a mummified baby under the floorboards."

"Oh my God!" Leanne gasped.

"It turns out it was Fiona's baby, and in my dream, she thanked me for taking care of him."

Leanne, her eyes growing wider, looked at Suzy open-mouthed. When she spoke, it was barely above a whisper.

"Why did she put her baby under the floorboards?"

"I don't know. We haven't talked about that, yet."

Leanne watched Suzy, flabbergasted, for a few moments after she stopped talking, before she was able to compose herself.

"Okay, so what are you wanting to do about this ghost?"

Suzy looked at her and sighed.

"I don't know. It's not like she's changed my life drastically. She hasn't run me out of my house or anything like that. I never even knew about her until I opened up the carriage house a couple of days ago. But she doesn't come in my house, except in my dreams and visions."

"Of course, but dreams and visions can be disruptive, too."

"But they haven't been. They've actually been pretty cool. Fiona's a very sweet person. And I saw Sir Walter Scott!"

Leanne's eyebrows puckered in confusion, but she pondered quietly.

"You probably think I'm crazy," Suzy said, "talking to someone who's been dead for over a century and a half."

"No, not at all," Leanne replied, setting her cup down. "There have been numerous documented cases of spirits of the dead communicating with the living." Suzy looked at her skeptically. "I know," Leanne continued, "for the most part, it's not scientific documentation. Frankly, the scientific community doesn't take that sort of thing seriously.

"But think about how many beliefs in the past were considered 'occult' before science discovered an 'acceptable' explanation. Back in Fiona's day, if you pulled out your cell phone and talked to someone on the other side of the world, you probably would have been hanged as a witch."

"So, you think science is just opposing it because they don't have a scientific explanation?"

"I think it's possible. I think *a number* of things are possible." Leanne leaned forward a little toward Suzy. "I'm curious, why did you come to me with this? Why didn't you go to a priest, or a medium?"

"Well, I'm not Catholic. I wouldn't know what to say to a priest. And mediums just seem shady, like con artists."

"Some are," Leanne agreed with a nod, "just like in any other business."

"But I know you. I know you're open-minded, level-headed, and very wise."

"Oh, baloney," Leanne replied with a smile, but her face reddened a bit.

"Besides," Suzy continued, "wouldn't a priest just perform an exorcism?"

"Possibly, if you wanted him to. Is that what you want?"

"No." Suzy pondered a moment. "I don't know. I don't think so."

"Then what? If the conversations and the visions have been 'cool' as you called them, then why have you bothered coming here to talk to me?"

"Well, because this morning, something else happened." Suzy took a few moments to steel herself, then related the scene in the carriage house earlier.

"Hmm." Leanne sat quietly for several seconds, looking absently into her cup. "Keep in mind that ghosts were human. Obviously, they're not flesh and blood anymore, but their feelings and emotions are similar to what we experience every day. They're just not tied to our physical world any longer, or bound by our physical laws. That's why they're able to do things that we consider supernatural.

"But they react to things they experience. They respond to things they think about. And it sounds like this Fiona has had a couple of emotional days, having her dead baby disinterred. Even having her private abode for the last century and a half invaded can be traumatic."

"You're saying I just have a ghost who's subject to mood swings?"

"It's very possible," Leanne said with a chuckle.

"Can she hurt me? I mean can she do me physical harm?"

"No, I don't think so. The physical realm is ours. Just because a ghost is still hanging around doesn't mean it has any influence over us in the physical world."

"Seemed like she had a fair amount of influence this morning."

"Just try leaving her alone for a while. Don't go looking for her. See if she gets in touch with you again."

§

Suzy didn't hear from Fiona for a couple of days. When she did, Suzy was sitting on her yoga mat, meditating, as several candles burned around her.

"he problem is a complicated one," Lachlan said. "The industrialization of our country in recent years has produced a higher standard of living, but the mechanization that facilitated the industrialization means that, while more work gets done, fewer people are needed tae do the work."

Fiona and her father sat in their parlor at tea time, with their guest, Lachlan Mac an Léigh. Fiona sipped her tea and set the cup down in the saucer in her left hand, thinking about what Lachlan had said.

"So," she replied, "while our country becomes richer, a much greater percentage of the population become poor because there are not enough jobs."

"Exactly. And the problem is aggravated by thousands of migrants from Ireland, or those put out of their homes in the Highland Clearances. They come tae the cities looking for work because they have nowhere else tae go. The Irish are routinely thrown back oot, but Scottish people from the countryside are simply left to flounder."

"I can't say I'm sorry about the Irish," Taran MacGregor said.

"Father!" Fiona replied with a scolding tone. "They're just people looking for a better life."

"There is just nae adequate housing for everyone," Lachlan continued quickly. The Scottish prejudice against the Irish was common, and he didn't want to get in the middle of an argument with his friends about the issue. "The tenements are packed tight, with as many as ten people in a single room."

"Which likely makes them a hotbed of disease," Fiona added.

"Exactly. But 'tis difficult tae cultivate specialized aid for individuals because so many of them are transient. I've met certain individuals and taken note of their needs, then returned one or two days later in hopes of offering some relief, only tae find them gone.

"And those making their home in the vaults under the bridges, well, ye can't even imagine the mean conditions that exist there. The lodgings are as crowded as those above ground, but the stench and the crime, and the pitiable condition of the residents," he paused to utter a heavy sigh, "'tis almost more than I can bear tae go doon there."

"It's so commendable that ye even try," Fiona said warmly.

"I admit I have personal motives. Me brother is one who, I fear, will be finding his way there soon."

"Your brother?" Fiona replied, shocked.

"Aye, I'm afraid Duncan is a bit of a scoundrel." He paused, looking down at his hands, as if the subject pained him. "He's known in certain parts for his carousing. He's become a little too familiar with the drink, and with fallen women." His face reddened with the last revelation.

"Oh, Mr. Mac an Léigh, that must be so distressing to you."

"And tae me family. Me father has recently cut him off from the family fortune, which is why I fear for him. Me brother has ne'er known want, and he has no skills to speak of. Without me father's money, I don't know how he'll survive."

"I suspect you'll keep trying to help him, though."

"I do try, but Duncan's nae very accepting. He'll take money, if I offer it, but real help tae improve his situation, which requires effort on his part, I'm afraid he spurns."

"I'm so sorry." Fiona's heart went out to Lachlan, and he began to feel a little embarrassed with the kind of attention he was receiving.

"Well, I thank ye," he replied. "That's why I tend tae focus on some of the others. Many of them are doon there through no fault of their own, and they appreciate the help and might be willing tae put forth the effort to improve their situation, if only they knew what tae do."

"I applaud your undertaking!"

"Och," Lachlan said with a dismissive wave, "'tis naught but what any others might do."

"Your humility does you fully as much justice as your charity, Mr. Mac an Léigh. But it's clear that others do not attempt what ye are doing."

"Perhaps because it is so complicated," he replied, steering the conversation back to the more general. "'Tis clear tae me that a more comprehensive solution must be introduced, from a state level, for 'tis more than can be accomplished by any individual."

"But I have the feeling that you'll still keep trying," Fiona smiled.

Realizing that she hadn't heard a response from her father since his remark about the Irish, she glanced over at him. His head was down, his chin on his chest. A tuft of white hair had fallen forward and was fluttering with each exhalation as he snored softly through his mouth.

"Perhaps I should take me leave," Lachlan said quietly as he smiled and placed his cup and saucer on the table beside his chair. Fiona did the same and walked him out of the parlor, pulling the door closed silently behind her.

"Miss MacGregor," he said as they paused outside the door, "I don't know if me intentions have become clear tae ye, but I like ye very much. I should like tae see ye again, if ye were agreeable tae it."

Fiona looked up at him, a little startled by his admission, and amused to observe the bashful boy he had become. And she was pleasantly surprised to find that she felt similarly.

"Thank you, Mr. Mac an Léigh," Fiona replied with a smile. "I must admit I've grown fond of you, too. I should like that very much."

Lachlan smiled and exhaled as if he had been holding his breath awaiting her answer. They looked at each other a little nervously before turning toward the foyer.

There was a knock at the front door, and almost immediately, Murdoch, the MacGregors' steward, appeared to answer it. He opened the door as Fiona and Lachlan approached.

"Good afternoon," Fiona heard Charles Scott say, "I've come to see Miss MacGregor."

Murdoch turned toward her as she and Lachlan arrived at the door.

"Thank you, Murdoch," she said, and Murdoch gave a courteous bow. Fiona noticed the awkward expressions that appeared on both Lachlan's and Charles' faces when they saw each other.

## 14

T he dizziness and disorientation were not as bad when this episode ended as they were after the first one. Whether that was because this one involved fewer people and less activity, or just because Suzy was becoming more accustomed to it, she didn't know. Still, she sat there on her yoga mat for a few minutes, exhausted and pondering what she had witnessed.

Finally, she took a deep breath, exhaled it, and stood up. Her next stop, like the first time, was her computer. Though this vision was of people she had already 'met' in her previous episode, she was curious about some of the information that had been shared with her.

There was still the slightest element of doubt or skepticism in Suzy's mind about the reality of what she was experiencing, and she wanted proof of the claims that Lachlan had made concerning the industrialization of Scotland, the crowded conditions of the tenements, even the prejudice against the Irish. Being a historian, she wanted evidence of the minutest details.

After just a few minutes, she had proven to herself that everything presented to her in the vision had been accurate. The next thing that occurred to her was that she was acquiring information about, not just her own ancestor, but Fin's as well. Remembering how she had abruptly ended their correspondence a couple of days before, she felt guilty.

The moment the FamilyLine.com site came up, she saw that she had a message. It was from Fin.

"Hey Suzy, how's it going? I'm sorry if I said anything that offended you. I didn't mean to make you feel bad in any way.

"I'm in New York for the next couple of days. I was a guest at the Comic Con here to promote TimePlex (the movie). Killing two birds with one stone, my agent arranged a reading and book signing engagement at a couple of book stores.

"No pressure whatsoever, but if you'd like to meet face-to-face and talk about dead people, let me know. I'd be happy to hop up to Boston."

At the end of the message, he included his phone number so she could contact him directly instead of going through the genealogy site. She looked at the message for a few moments, trying to decide how she felt about it. She knew her feelings of unfaithfulness a couple of days before had been silly and unfounded.

First of all, on a purely logical level, Mark was dead. He had been gone for a year. Suzy was no longer married. Of course that thought was never just purely logical, but still, she knew there was no marriage to be unfaithful to.

Secondly, there was no romance involved in her contact with Fin. They had simply exchanged information about a shared interest.

If she were to look at it purely functionally, the phone number made sense. Communicating through Fami-lyLine.com was clunky. It was a nice feature of the web site, but it wasn't meant for extended, detailed conversations.

She looked at the date stamp of his message. He had sent it yesterday. He was still in New York. She pulled her phone out of her sweater pocket and opened her text app.

"Okay, buster, I'll meet you in Boston, but considering the financial hardship your ancestor caused my family, I think it's only right that you pay for the coffee."

Thinking it best to save him from having to rent a car, she picked a Dunkin' Donuts that was across the street from the airport car rentals. He could ride the shuttle to it and back to the airport.

She clicked "Send" and heaved a sigh.

## 15

Dunkin' Donuts?!" Fin replied. He was happy to see her response, but he had actually hoped for a nicer venue, maybe an Italian dinner in the North End, or a lobster dinner at virtually any seafood restaurant in or around Boston.

After he checked about changing his flight, though, he saw that her suggestion made sense. He could schedule a six hour layover in Boston during the day, which would not require him to book a hotel.

"Hey, Dunkin' Donuts is a staple around here," Suzy responded. "It was founded in Quincy, a suburb of Boston, and you'll find one on every other corner."

"Sounds like Starbucks in my neck of the woods," he replied after booking the change to his flight. "Alright, I'll buy you coffee, and maybe even a donut if it will finally settle the tab that my scurrilous ancestor started."

He sent her the time he would be available, and it was a date.

§

The morning was grey as Fin sat in the Dunkin' Donuts. After exchanging a couple of text messages with Suzy, he purchased a coffee for himself, a toasted almond latte for her, and a couple of Boston Kremes. He placed the order on a table in front of a window and sat down, taking a sip of the steaming coffee. Less than a minute later, he saw a little red and white MINI Cooper pull up.

*Seeing the pretty brunette get out of her car, our hero wondered if she was the one.*

He watched her, trying to determine if she could have been the woman who made the silly face in the photo she sent to him. He didn't have to wait long. He received his answer when she saw his face through the window and waved.

In the seconds it took her to walk to the door and come in, Fin wondered about the best greeting. Would a hug be appropriate, considering the fact that they had already engaged in several conversations? A kiss on the cheek? Both, he had discovered, were completely appropriate in the show business world. He and Jennifer Lawrence had actually exchanged a quick show-biz kiss as a greeting at the Comic Con, but he knew that wasn't the case in the real world.

He got his answer as she approached with her hand outstretched.

"Hello, Fin," she said. "It's nice to meet you."

"You too, Suzy," he replied nervously as he shook her hand. "Have a seat."

"Have you been waiting long?"

"No, I just sat down when you drove up."

"Good." She took her latte and one of the Boston Kremes. Biting hungrily into it, some of the cream filling squirted out over her fingers. She reached for a napkin and wiped her fingers.

"I can't believe our first date is in a Dunkin' Donuts," Fin joked.

"Stop the presses, book boy," Suzy barked, wiping chocolate roughly from her mouth. She glanced around, realizing that she had said it louder than intended. She lowered her voice. "This isn't a date."

Having grown familiar with her sarcastic sense of humor in their written correspondence, Fin wasn't entirely sure if the severity of her statement was serious or not. Her face did look pretty stern, he decided.

"Sorry," he said meekly. "I didn't mean anything by it. I was just joking around."

Suzy looked at him for a moment and then shook her head.

"I know," she sighed. "You'll have to forgive me." She looked down at the napkin she was wringing in her hands.

"This is kind of a tough time for me. A few days ago, I just passed the first anniversary of my husband and daughter's death."

"Oh my god," Fin said, "Suzy, I'm so sorry!"

"Thanks. I just haven't been able to think about where I want to go from here."

"I completely understand."

"I didn't mean to bite your head off, though."

"It's okay. It's been bitten off before. It just keeps growing back." Suzy smiled.

"You're like Jack Jeebs," she said, "on – "

"*Men In Black*!" Fin finished excitedly. "I love that scene!"

They both laughed, and Fin felt the atmosphere lighten a bit. His inner geek suddenly felt a little closer to Suzy, but he thought it might be best to keep that to himself.

"So," Suzy said, "New York Comic Con, huh?"

"Yeah. Ryan says hi."

"Shut up."

Fin smiled again, beginning to feel a little more comfortable.

"Well," Suzy said, "I've always thought that would be fun to go to, but I never got around to it."

Fin looked at her, wondering if she was being serious. He had never met a woman who thought that would be fun. Of course, he was aware they existed. He had seen enough green Orion slave girls and Wonder Woman clones that he knew female sci-fi geeks were out there. He just never had the good fortune to meet one.

Rather than expend too much time or effort puzzling it out, he decided to move on to a different topic.

"Have you dug up any more information about your ancestor?"

"I've done a little more than dig it up," Suzy said, leaning forward excitedly. "I've witnessed it. And not just about *my* ancestor, but yours, too!"

"Huh?"

86

Suzy took a sip of her latte and wiped her mouth with a napkin. She spent the next few minutes describing the two visions she had experienced, and for Fin's benefit, focused especially on details about Lachlan Mac an Léigh.

By the time she had finished, Fin was just staring across the table at her, his mouth hanging open a little.

"I – I don't even know what to say," he finally managed.

"I know, it's crazy!" Suzy agreed.

"You're pretty lucky to have such a friendly, cooperative ghost."

"Well," Suzy said a little hesitantly, "don't get ahead of yourself. It hasn't *all* been friendly. A couple of days ago, she was a little less than welcoming." She related the "confrontation" in the carriage house. Seeing Fin's concerned expression, she tried to put his mind at ease. "Don't worry, I have it on good authority that ghosts can't physically harm us."

"Can't harm us? Didn't you see *Poltergeist*? Their whole house got sucked into the ground!"

"Yeah, you do understand the difference between real life and movies, right?"

"Well, yeah," Fin said sheepishly. "But, okay, what about *The Exorcist*? That was based on a true story."

"*Based on!* Besides, wasn't she supposedly possessed by the devil?"

"Alright," he replied in a conceding tone. "Just be careful, okay?"

"Of course," Suzy smiled, feeling warmed by the worry on his face.

§

After a couple of hours, they had exchanged extensive information about their respective genealogical searches. They also shared a fair amount of personal information as they both relaxed in each other's company.

Fin glanced at his watch.

"I guess I should get back to the airport."

"Already?" Suzy replied, surprised at the disappointment she felt.

"Afraid so. But it sure has been nice getting to know you, Suzy."

"Yeah, you too." Suzy thought briefly about offering to drive him to the terminal, but decided she wasn't ready for that. Spending two hours with him here was about as crazy as she was willing to get. She was relieved when Fin craned his neck to look out the window and down toward the car rental complex.

"A shuttle just drove up. If I hurry, I can sneak in with the actual customers."

D riving north along the coast from Boston, Suzy spent a good deal of the drive thinking about her meeting with Fin. That nagging feeling of guilt was returning, primarily because she had actually enjoyed the time she had spent with him. He was handsome, intelligent and sensitive, and she couldn't deny a feeling of attraction to him.

*Dammit!*

As she drove, she looked around for something to take her mind off the time she had spent with him, and his annoying appeal. As she was passing through Lynn, she remembered its checkered past.

Despite its colonial-era beginnings, during the early part of Suzy's life, Lynn, Massachusetts had been a hell-hole. It languished between the preserved colonial history and exciting nightlife of modern Boston, and the picturesque seaside charm of Marblehead and Salem without contributing anything of note to either, an industrial pothole on the road connecting two destinations that people actually wanted to go to.

An unfortunate but well-deserved reputation for high crime a few years back led to a taunting rhyme about Lynn that had become known throughout eastern Massachusetts – "Lynn, Lynn, the city of sin, you'll never come out the way you went in, what looks like gold is really tin, the girls say 'no' but they'll give in."

Suzy smiled grimly as she recalled the lines. She remembered that, with the goal of putting an end to the insulting rhyme and reputation, there was some city official back in the late 1990s who tried to have the town renamed to Ocean Park, apparently figuring that Ocean Park would be more difficult to rhyme with. His efforts, however, were without success.

Various other attempts to clean up Lynn's reputation had also been met with grave disappointment. Travelers tended to either actively ignore Lynn, or just didn't notice it as they passed through it to get to their real destination.

Fortunately, more recent efforts to actually renovate and revitalize Lynn, rather than just alter public perception, met with greater success. Empty vacant buildings were turned into stylish lofts, and large murals, sponsored by the city itself, were painted on some of the buildings to add to its artsy charm. It was now a pretty town with a lovely seaside drive, and was considered a trendy and desirable place to live.

Suzy was happy that pondering Lynn's recent history killed a couple of minutes for her. Until she found herself wondering what kind of history Fin's home town had.

*Dammit!*

§

Suzy stood in front of the fireplace in the family room. The fireplace was cold and dark, but she was looking above it, at the pair of urns standing on the mantel. There was the larger brass urn with the brushed nickel finish which held Mark's ashes, and the smaller ceramic one with the multicolored glaze design that reminded Suzy of a boisterous flower garden.

She looked at the photo of Emma which stood beside that urn, remembering her daughter's happy personality, her easy laughter. Before her eyes clouded too much with tears, she shifted her gaze to Mark's photo, smiling at his sarcastic sense of humor. He had been the perfect complement to her own smartassery.

Suzy recalled a couple of friends who had recommended "getting back out there." She was young and pretty, there was bound to be someone else out there for her. As if Mark had been a dog that died and it was time to replace him.

She knew that they had meant well, but their insensitive remarks irritated her. Thinking about it now, she realized that she hadn't seen them in a while, and she realized that it had been her own choice.

Suzy flipped the switch next to the fireplace and heard the soft pop as the gas flame started. She turned and sat down on the loveseat that she and Mark had spent many hours on. She picked up one of the big pillows that she kept on it and hugged it in front of her, as she slipped down to lean her head back. She had done this numerous times a year ago, slouching down in a comfortable position that allowed her to keep her eyes trained on the photos.

She remembered the attraction that she had felt for Fin that morning, and she felt that twinge of unfaithfulness again. She wasn't ready for another relationship. She knew that. That attraction was simply a physical reaction hard-wired into the body, genetic programming that drove them to perpetuate the species.

She still loved Mark, and she missed him more than ever. She wasn't ready to replace him.

She stared absently into the dancing flames and felt herself relaxing.

My time here is nearly over," Charles said as he looked intently at Fiona in the MacGregors' garden. His voice was firm, but he was trying not to sound as if he was reprimanding her. "Next week, I shall return to Oxford, and I should like to go knowing that you and I have an understanding."

"Mr. Scott, we've scarcely known each other for two months," Fiona replied, her voice expressing amused disbelief. "Do ye not think ye might be rushing me a bit?"

"No, I don't, Miss MacGregor. My parents were engaged after three weeks."

"Well, I don't make such decisions that quickly. I need time to ponder me choices. I admit I am flattered by your attention, but I'm afraid I'm not ready to make a commitment after this short a time."

Charles pinched his lips together as he regarded Fiona from beneath his furrowed brows.

"Ponder your choices? You mean Lachlan Mac an Léigh?"

"Mr. Mac an Léigh and I have become friends, as have you and I, but that is all. I have known him only as long as I have known you. I assure ye I am no more able to accept his proposal after only two months, had he offered one, than I am yours."

Feeling simultaneously appeased and scolded, Charles relaxed a bit and leaned back against the stone wall.

"Of course, Miss MacGregor. Please forgive me. It is only that I find your company so agreeable. I do not mean to make you feel put upon."

"Thank you, Mr. Scott," Fiona replied sincerely. "But I must admit I wonder at my company being so agreeable to you, when you are of such a serious nature, while I am quite contrary and intractable."

"Oh, not intractable. Steadfast, perhaps."

"Aye, a gentlemanly way of saying that I'm stubborn," Fiona smiled.

"Only where my wishes are concerned," Charles joked. "But I shall not compel you further."

"Thank ye again."

"Well," Charles said, "I should take my leave. My parents are expecting me for dinner, so I should begin making my way home."

"Very well, Mr. Scott. I wish ye well. Meanwhile I shall spend me time contemplating me proposals." Charles raised an eyebrow at her, but he smiled as he opened the garden gate.

After he left, Charles remained on her mind. His serious, traditional personality appealed to her in a way. She knew that, upon graduating, he would likely obtain a stable job as a lawyer, in which his sobriety would serve him well.

He was joined in her mind by Lachlan, and Fiona was surprised that two men of such different backgrounds and personalities could be vying for her attention. Lachlan, who had all the money he would ever need, seemed to care little about it, aside from what he could do with it to help others less fortunate.

As it was a lovely late afternoon, and she knew that dinner would not be for a couple more hours, Fiona decided to stay outside and go for a walk, to reflect on her situation. A nice walk always cleared her head and helped her to think clearly about anything that might be on her mind.

She went in the back door and poked her head in the library where she knew her father was.

"I'm going for a walk," she said brightly. "I'll be back soon."

"Sure ye will, lass," her father chuckled, knowing her propensity for wandering.

She went out the front door, onto sunny Saint Andrew Square. Crossing the street, she followed the path that went through the square and around the Melville Monument which had just been erected the year before. Styled after Trajan's Column in Rome, it consisted simply of a prodigious stone base surmounted by a tall fluted pillar. Fiona heard that a statue of Henry Dundas, Viscount Melville, was ultimately going to be installed on top of the column.

Continuing southward, Fiona was enjoying the sunshine until, when she was nearing the South Bridge arch over Cowgate, she realized that the sun was low and casting long shadows. With the sun going down, the narrower streets of Old Town allowed less of the sunlight to reach her, and she started feeling chilled.

She turned to head back north, toward home, and as she did, she almost ran into the man who was close behind her. His face was dirty, his hair and beard unruly and matted. His breath reeked of whisky and he smelled as if he hadn't bathed in weeks. That Fiona could detect the smells was noteworthy considering the stench that permeated much of Old Town.

"Oh," she exclaimed, "excuse me."

She stepped to the left to go around him, but he mirrored her move. When she stepped back to the right, he did too, and he pushed her against the stone wall of a tool maker's shop.

Fiona cast a quick glance around, but the narrow street was deserted at the moment.

"Sir," she said shakily, attempting to reason with him, "please don't do something you'll regret."

The man leered at her and, looking down toward her body, shook his head.

"You're a fine lookin' lassie. I don't think I'm apt to regret this."

Seeing that reason was not going to work, Fiona tried to pull away from him, but his grip tightened on her arm, and he pushed her harder against the wall. Looking around, he pulled her back a few steps into a gap between the tool maker's shop and the next building, a space not even wide enough to call a close.

The narrow alleyway was filthy and littered with refuse of every kind imaginable, and Fiona struggled to get free. Keeping his right hand gripped tightly around her arm, he grabbed the neck of her dress with his left hand and was able to pull her in.

Rearing back, Fiona kicked him in the shin as hard as she could. With a pained grunt, the man let go of her arm, but the fabric of her dress was easier to hold on to. As she fell back, her dress ripped open and Fiona screamed. She ended up lying on her back, with the man still holding on to the ripped fabric of her bodice.

The man pulled himself on top of her and let go of her dress, instead pressing his grimy hand over her mouth. With his right hand, he was reaching down between her legs, fumbling with her

94

skirt, trying to pull it up. A good portion of his weight was on her right arm, but with her left, she never stopped trying to push him away.

The man was getting visibly irritated by her struggling and he slapped her hard across the side of her head. Stunned, she was still aware of her surroundings, but her struggling ceased, and the man was able to reach down and hike up her skirt.

Suddenly, a hand gripped his shoulder and pulled him back off of her. He looked up and saw a man standing at the mouth of the alleyway. Angry at being interrupted, his face twisted into a snarl, he pulled a knife from his belt.

The interloper looked around at the articles that littered the ground. Among the trash were old discarded tools from the tool maker's shop. He quickly picked up a dull, rusty chisel, though armed in such a way, he likely knew that his best chance would be if he could get the man to run away. That chance was slim when Fiona's attacker smiled at what he was defending himself with.

The attacker lunged with the knife, and the newcomer jumped backward out of range. The knife slashed back and forth, but with a similar maneuver, the blade never reached its mark.

Fiona could feel her strength returning, and she pushed herself up into a sitting position. She wanted to get up and run home. Unfortunately, her attacker and her rescuer were between her and the opening of the alleyway.

Momentarily distracted by her movement, the newcomer was surprised by a lunge from the attacker. He tried to jump back, but tripped and went down on his back. The attacker went down, too, but the knife found a target. The blade slashed the side of the newcomer's right calf. Grunting in pain, he kicked the attacker in the face as his hand found something a little more formidable than the chisel. He gripped the handles of an equally old pair of nippers, the narrow handles a foot long.

Rubbing his bruised face, the attacker regained his feet and came toward him as he struggled upright. The attacker gripped his knife tightly, probably feeling confident over having drawn blood. He lunged again, and again, the newcomer jumped backward, jarring his back against the wall.

95

Suddenly, uttering a sound something like a roar, the attacker leapt toward him, swinging the knife in a downward arc. The newcomer jabbed forward with the nippers, both of the long, slender handles piercing the attacker's left shoulder just below the collar bone.

Taken by surprise, the roar ended with a gasp and a whimper. He pulled back, the nipper handles making a wet sucking sound as they came out. The newcomer, still holding on to the tool, seemed as shocked as the attacker. The wounded man, gasping in pain and likely knowing he couldn't fight in that condition, ran out onto the street and disappeared to the south.

The newcomer turned to Fiona now. She was sitting up, rubbing the side of her head, still dazed from the blow.

"Are ye alright?" he asked.

"I think so," she nodded. She reached up to the hand he offered, and she got unsteadily to her feet. It was only then that she realized that the top of her dress was torn and hanging down, exposing her chemise. She gasped as she pulled the ripped bodice up to try to cover herself, but the man was already slipping off his jacket and, putting the nippers down, placed the jacket around her shoulders.

"Thank you, Mr. –"

"Loganach," he replied. "Caden Loganach."

"Thank ye, Mr. Loganach. I'm Fiona MacGregor."

"I'm very pleased tae meet ye, Miss MacGregor, althoo I'm sorry it had tae be under these circumstances."

"I'm just glad ye happened along."

"I didnae just happen alang," he said. "I was in the area lookin' fur a pair o' nippers." He picked up his weapon. "I'd say these performed quite nicely."

Fiona looked at the nippers, the slender handles sticky with her attacker's blood. She seemed a little squeamish about it, but she smiled weakly at his joke. Caden noticed her struggle, and he dropped the nippers on the ground, offering Fiona his arm.

"Oh, I'm sorry, lassie," he said sympathetically, "ye've been through qui' an ordeal. Please alloo me tae escort ye home."

Fiona thanked him and inserted her left arm through his. Holding his jacket closed around her ripped dress, she leaned on him a little as he helped her out onto the street, but she noticed he was limping.

"But Mr. Loganach, you're wounded yourself." He looked down at the bloody slice in his pant leg.

"'Tis not so deep as a well, nor so wide as a church door," he replied.

"Mercutio died shortly after saying that," Fiona said dryly. "Please see that ye don't follow his example."

"Nay, I think I still ha' a year 'r twa left in me," Caden said.

Fiona smiled and pointed north.

Caden, mindful of Fiona's having recently been viciously attacked, was taking his time, for her sake. Fiona, conscious of Caden's leg wound, was walking slowly, mainly for his benefit.

As the sun was slipping closer to the horizon, Fiona had stolen a few glances at Caden. He was a handsome man with dark eyes, dark hair and a dark, neatly trimmed beard. She noticed that the beginnings of a smile usually played around his lips, and it was frequently encouraged by the playful twinkle in his eyes.

"What is it ye do, Mr. Loganach?" Fiona asked as they made their way across Princes Street.

"I own a shipping company. 'Tis nae a large operation. I only ha' four ships, but I think that may be all I can handle as it is." A bit of a smile brushed his lips. "I mainly traverse the North Atlantic, takin' Scots emigrants tae Nova Scotia and bringin' back timber for construction."

"That sounds like a profitable venture."

"'Tis a small one, but it puts food on me table. And I feel like I'm doin' a good deed, helpin' folks displaced by the Highland Clearances. I dinnae make a profit off o' them. I only charge what it costs me tae feed 'em on the journey there. Me main income is fae the timber I transport back here."

Having become so aware of the circumstances of the poor through her association with Lachlan Mac an Léigh, Fiona felt her heart go out to Caden when he expressed his concern for those less fortunate.

"Where are ye from?" Fiona asked. "Ye have the sound of a Highlander."

"Aye, me family hails from Fort Augustus, near Loch Ness. We were fisher folk, but I felt the need tae move away after me parents died."

"I've never been up there."

"Och, lassie, ye must go. 'Tis bonny country indeed!"

"Perhaps ye can show me someday."

They had just crossed into Saint Andrew Square when Fiona felt Caden's step slowing.

"Och, me goodness," Caden said as he stopped and turned a little. "Would ye look a' that!" Fiona turned to see him looking at the sky, blazing magenta overhead and burning to darker hues near the horizon.

Something caused them both to look at each other at the same moment. Fiona's upturned face was bathed in the gold and rose light of the sky above, while Caden's face, backlit by the crimsons in the west and south, appeared violet.

Caden looked at Fiona as if she was was one of the most beautiful sights his eyes had ever seen.

He didn't realize that Fiona was thinking similar thoughts of him.

§

When Murdoch opened the door, Taran MacGregor was directly behind him, his face drawn with worry. When he saw his daughter, he pushed past Murdoch to help her in.

"Good God, child, where have ye been?"

"I'm alright, Father," Fiona assured him. MacGregor looked suspiciously at Caden as he took Fiona from his arm and, not wanting him to be ignored, Fiona stopped, making her father stop as well. "This is Caden Loganach," she said.

"I'm very pleased tae meet ye, sir," Caden said with a polite bow.

"Mr. Loganach," MacGregor replied in a gruff tone. "And who are ye? What are ye doing out alone with me daughter," he looked at the disarray of Fiona's dress, "and with her in such a condition?"

"Father," Fiona said with a reprimand in her voice, pulling the jacket tighter around her, "Mr. Loganach saved me from an attacker. The least ye could do is speak politely to him."

"'Tis alright," Caden said diplomatically. "I dinnae blame 'im for bein' worried aboot his daughter."

"I'm sorry, young man," MacGregor replied. "You're right, I was worried, but I shouldn't have spoken to ye like that." Fiona smiled approvingly at her father.

"Please come in," she said.

"Thank ye, but nae. I dinnae wish tae bleed on yer floor."

Fiona looked down at his leg. His pant leg below the wound was dark with blood, though it didn't seem to be drying.

"You must have that looked at," Fiona said.

"Aye," Caden said with a wave of his hand, "I'll tend t' it when I get tae me home. Noo is the time for your family t' rally 'roond ye, nae 'roond some stranger."

"You're not just some stranger," Fiona replied indignantly. "You're the man who saved me dignity and me chastity, if not me very life."

Caden bowed again, humbly.

"'Twas little sacrifice on me own part," he said, "if it gained me the esteem of one such as yerself. If ye don' mind, perhaps I could call on ye in a day or twa, t' see how yer farin'."

"I should like that very much," Fiona said.

"And I'll collect me jacket from ye then."

Fiona looked down at his jacket, and remembering the condition of her dress under it, her face flushed a bit.

"Thank ye, Mr. Loganach.

Caden limped up to the door the following afternoon. Murdoch led him to the parlor where Fiona met him a couple of minutes later. She carried his jacket over her arm.

"I was hoping you wouldn't wait two days," Fiona said a little breathlessly, surprised by her own directness.

"Were ye, noo?" Caden replied with a smile, but then his expression softened. "Well, to be honest, I dinnae want to wait that lang meself."

"How is your leg?"

"'Tis fine. I cleaned it and wrapped it tight last night." He bent his leg at the knee and moved it around a little to demonstrate. "Give it a few weeks an' it'll be good as new."

"And it hasn't hampered your movement?"

"It weren't enough tae keep me from comin' 'ere." Fiona's cheeks pinkened a bit.

"I'm so glad."

"Aye, I'm verra fond o' that jacket."

Fiona's smile widened and, remembering she was holding it, she handed it to Caden.

"I had the dirt from the alleyway brushed from it for ye."

"Thank ye, miss. And how are ye? I hope ye're nae sufferin' any ill consequences from your adventure last night."

"None that show," she replied quietly. "Only fear and anger and a bit of embarrassment."

"The fear an' anger I understand, but ye've got nothing tae be embarrassed aboot."

"Nevertheless, I'm awfully grateful for your assistance last night, Mr. Loganach. I've never found meself in the position of needing someone to save me life. I'm just so very glad ye were there."

"I am too, miss," Caden replied, his voice softening to little more than a whisper.

Three weeks and three days after their fateful encounter in Old Town, as the first hint of autumn started chilling the air, Fiona and Caden were sitting on a bench in Saint Andrew Square. He had visited her almost every day since then, and on the days that he didn't, Fiona visited him, accompanied by her older sister, Aileen. Sitting in the square, in public and in sight of her home, she was unchaperoned.

Fiona noticed that Caden seemed quieter than usual.

"Me dear," he finally said, "I ha' somethin' tae ask ye."

"Yes?" she replied curiously.

"Since we first met," he continued nervously, looking down at his hands, "I've been hard-pressed to think of anythin' else but ye. Ye're the first thing I think of in the mornin' and the last thing I think of as I fall asleep." He took a deep breath and looked up at Fiona. "Me memory's nae as good as me eyes, though. I'd rather see ye when I wake up and afore I fall asleep."

Fiona kept quiet and waited. She had a feeling she knew where this was leading and, though she didn't realize it, she was holding her breath.

"Fiona, would ye do me the great honor o' becomin' me wife?"

*Exhaling the breath, she smiled at him and put her hand on his. She looked at him for a few seconds before responding.*

*"A few weeks ago, I replied to a suitor, never mind who," she smiled, "that I couldn't make a decision about marriage after only knowing him for two months. I find, though, that with ye, dear Caden, I feel as if I've known ye all me life. What I don't yet know about ye, I look forward to spending the rest of me life learning.*

*"Yes, me love, I'll happily be your wife!"*

*The smile that overtook Caden's face warmed Fiona's heart, and they fell into each other's arms, their lips pressed tightly together, oblivious of the people in the square around them.*

## 19

A heavy overcast hung between Suzy and the waning sunlight outside. After emerging from this latest episode from Fiona, Suzy had sat quietly on the loveseat for a while, fatigued from the experience and deep in thought. Finally, she got up and wandered into the living room, looking out the window across the harbor.

Seeing Fiona and Caden's meeting and short courtship, after thinking so strongly about Mark and Emma, left her feeling confused. Their happiness at the beginning of their relationship, and knowing that she eventually lost him mixed with the conflicting feelings Suzy had experienced earlier. Her attraction to Fin and the resulting guilt and sorrow connected to Mark left her head and her heart a churning maelstrom of emotions.

Seeing herself descending into an unhealthy pattern, she decided she needed to talk to someone. She thought about Leanne, the pastor at the Church of Spiritual Science. Part of what she wanted to talk about was more in Leanne's realm of knowledge. She pondered a few moments longer, then pulled her phone out of her sweater pocket.

She called Rachel's number.

"Hey, sweetie," Rachel answered, "how you doing?"

"Not great," Suzy sighed. "Are you busy?"

"Are you kidding? It's a 'school night.' I'm holed up at home."

"Do you mind if I come over for a while?"

"Of course not, honey. I have lasagna in the oven. You're welcome to some of my would-be leftovers."

§

Rachel had an administrative position at the State House in Boston. She liked the excitement of the city, the way the modern stood side-by-side with the historic. But she liked getting away from the excitement, too. She lived in a small barn-shaped house near the southern Marblehead city limit. The house reflected Rachel's love of early American kitsch. Practically every square inch was decorated with old – or old looking – Americana, particularly from New England, and especially from the colonial era.

Suzy shuddered to think about how long it would take to dust everything, but she always felt comfortable in Rachel's home.

The smell of the lasagna enveloped Suzy when Rachel opened the door, and it reminded her of one of her early dates with Mark. Seeing the emotion of the memory suddenly etched on Suzy's face, Rachel hugged her and pulled her inside.

"Thank you for letting me come over," Suzy said, a little more emotionally than she had intended.

"Oh, sweetie, you know I'm always here for you."

"I know you are. Thank you."

Rachel brushed it off with a shake of her head. She helped Suzy out of her coat and hung it on a distressed coat rack with a gold-painted star above each peg.

"Dinner's ready," she said. "I hope you're hungry."

§

"What were you looking so sad about when I opened the door?" Rachel asked. Suzy looked up at her, then back down at her lasagna, which she pushed around a couple of times with her fork.

"It was our third date," she finally said. "Mark was a big history buff, one of the many things that attracted me to him. So we started out early on a Saturday morning. We started at Boston Common and walked the Freedom Trail, stopping at most of the historical sites.

"Being a history major myself, I've always been interested in history, too, of course. And especially recently, I've become a little more so, but it wasn't just that. Mark's love of it made it more fun. I almost didn't have to read the plaques at the sites.

"And walking hand-in-hand through the city was, well, you know me. I'm not usually one to gush, but it was a magical morning."

"I love the Freedom Trail," Rachel said.

"Well, having started so early, we were coming back across the Charlestown Bridge from the USS Constitution right around noon. As we got back into North Boston, the air was absolutely thick with the smell of Italian food. All we had to do was decide which Italian restaurant to have lunch at.

"That memory washed over me as you opened the door and I smelled the lasagna."

"Aw, Suzy," Rachel said softly, shaking her head. "How did you two meet?"

Suzy smiled at the memory.

"It was at Judy and Brian's wedding. I was Judy's maid of honor, and I guess I took the responsibility seriously. At the reception, there was this guy hovering around the food table, and I didn't recognize him. I went up to him and asked, 'Who are you?'

"In answer, he sang, 'Who, who, who, who?'" Rachel looked confused. "From that old song, *Who Are You?* by the Who." Rachel nodded as if she understood, but didn't seem very convincing.

"Well, having evaded my question, I became even more suspicious. 'Are you a friend of the bride or the groom?' I asked.

"'Neither,' he said.

"'What are you doing here?' I asked. I was starting to get a little annoyed, and looking around for a couple of guys who could throw this wedding crasher out.

"'Jeez, lady,' he said, 'lighten up. You're probing me like an alien abductor.' Well, that remark, and the way he said it, made me laugh, but at the same time, it made me angry. And laughing at his joke despite being angry at him just made me angrier. I suppose I was being kind of ridiculous, so serious and hardheaded. But anyway, he finally answered me.

"'If you must know, I'm here with Michelle. She's a friend of Brian's.'

"'You mean you're somebody's date?' I asked, exasperated. 'Michelle's,' he repeated."

"Wasn't that when Brian's mom caught Michelle making out with Brian's married best man in the coat room?" Rachel asked.

"Mm hmm," Suzy replied. "Michelle left fairly abruptly, and her date and I spent the next few hours getting to know each other."

"A smartass from the start," Rachel said with a wistful smile. Suzy nodded and sighed.

"Okay," Suzy said, with a marked change of tone, "so how long do you think is long enough to wait before 'getting back out there'?"

Somewhat startled by the shift in conversation, Rachel squinted at Suzy, and took a deep breath to gather her thoughts.

"I think it varies with the individual. Why?"

It was Suzy's turn to take a deep breath.

"I met someone this morning." Rachel's eyebrows rose, but she waited to hear more. "We actually met earlier, online, through that genealogy site I use. I was following your advice last week about getting back into my family tree."

"Wait," Rachel said, "he's a relative?"

"No, there's no relation, but there's a connection. My ancestor sued his ancestor a long time ago. Anyway, we had exchanged a few messages through the site. He was in the area and thought we should meet. Since there have been some major developments in my search, I agreed.

"We met in Boston, near the airport. And get this: he's Michael Jones, author of *TimePlex*. Except his real name is Fin MacKinley." Suzy thought to herself that it was odd that she would pass up an opportunity to make fun of his full name, Finley MacKinley.

"Oh my god," Rachel said with quietly building excitement, "you went on a date with Michael Jones?"

"No, it wasn't a date!"

"Sorry," Rachel replied contritely. Suzy stopped and took another breath, getting her irritation under control.

"But the thing is I was attracted to him, and I think he's attracted to me. And I came back home feeling like shit. I felt like I'd betrayed Mark."

"Well, sweetie, I guess that's your answer right there." Suzy looked at her quizzically. "If you're feeling like shit about just being attracted to someone, then it's probably still too soon for you. At least to be *actively pursuing* a relationship." Rachel looked at Suzy, in thought for a moment. "Have you thought about getting a job or something?" she asked.

"You think I'm strapped for cash?"

"No, but I think you might need to get out of the house more, be around people."

"I just got out this morning, to be around a person."

"I'm talking about a social life," Rachel said exasperated. "Sitting around in that house all the time can't help you in working through your grief."

"Maybe. I don't know. I'll think about it."

"In the meantime, what if you just put relationship stuff on the back burner for a while and see if anything actually develops between you two, and if the bad feelings go away?"

"That makes sense," Suzy nodded thoughtfully.

"So," Rachel said curiously, "what's he like?"

"Fin? He's very nice, kind of quiet. Very geeky. He was just in New York at the Comic Con."

"Ah, did you tell him about your sexy Wonder Woman costume?"

"No, I did not."

"Damn, girl, you were the hit of my Halloween party a couple of years ago. I was kind of jealous of all the attention you were getting. I think Mark was a little jealous, too. Most of the guys couldn't keep their eyes off of you. A few of the women, too."

Suzy smiled.

"I don't think I want to talk about Fin right now. Or my Wonder Woman costume."

"Okay," Rachel agreed. "You said there have been some major developments in your genealogy search. Tell me about that."

Suzy looked at Rachel for a few moments, trying to determine how much she should say. They had never shared their respective thoughts about the afterlife before, and Suzy realized she didn't know anything about Rachel's belief system, aside from her background as a 'recovering Catholic' as she called it. Finally, she decided to just spill it.

She related to Rachel about opening up the carriage house and about the décor, which she knew would appeal to her, about finding the mummified baby, about the feeling that she was being watched as she unwrapped it.

She told her about 'meeting' Fiona in her dreams, and about the visions she had been having of episodes in Fiona's life. And she described the scary encounter in the carriage house three days before. The whole time, Rachel's eyes became progressively larger and rounder.

"Oh my god!" she said when Suzy had finished. "All this happened in the past week and you're just now getting around to telling me?"

"Sorry," Suzy replied with a sheepish smile, "I've been a little busy."

"I guess! Wow, with your yoga and meditation and all that, I always knew you were kind of a spiritual person, but I never realized it went that far."

"It never did. I've never communicated with a dead person until just last week. Do you have any idea how many times I wished I could a year ago? How I wanted to apologize to Mark and Emma, and how I wanted so badly to hear them forgive me?"

"I know, honey," Rachel said sympathetically, seeing the tears building in Suzy's eyes. "I'm sorry." She wanted to get the conversation back to where Suzy was excited. "So, tell me about Fiona. What's she like?"

"She's very pretty," Suzy said, wiping her eyes, "very sweet. Young Fiona, in the visions, is vivacious and the belle of the ball. Older Fiona, who's talked to me in my dreams, is quieter and more somber. She misses her husband terribly which, of course, I identify with."

"And Sir Walter Scott! Wow!"

"Yeah, and I got a signed first edition out of the deal!"

## 20

Fin was amazed. Having spent a good portion of the past weekend at one of the largest Comic Conventions in the country, having actually been one of the celebrity guests invited there to talk about his best-selling novel and the movie being made from it, having spent part of that time with two A-list Hollywood stars, having sat next to Jennifer Lawrence, his leg brushing against hers, and having her even put her arm through his and lean against him, and even exchanging a quick Hollywood kiss with her, Fin couldn't get his mind off Suzy.

With the sun streaming through his bedroom window, he plopped his suitcase on his bed and unzipped it. As he unpacked and put things away, he thought back on the time he had spent with her that morning. The tales she told about their ancestors, having seen them in visions, he didn't know if he believed that or not. After sitting across from her for a while, he happily admitted that she didn't seem like a crackpot, but still, what a story!

In the bathroom, as he was putting toiletries away, he looked up in the mirror. Suzy had said that Lachlan resembled him in some ways. Lachlan's blondish hair was longer, his face a little fuller, but she could definitely see a family resemblance. He tried to imagine his face a little fuller, his hair a little longer.

Suzy's face quickly supplanted his, though. What a beautiful lady! He remembered things he had noticed about her, the way the left side of her mouth went down slightly when she smiled, the way her eyes squinted a bit when she was making some smartass remark, the way her right eyebrow rose when she wasn't sure she believed what he was saying.

Then, he remembered a couple of times when her eyes clouded with tears and she put her head down a bit, her dark hair falling forward over her face. He remembered how, both times, she waited a few moments for the tears to subside before pushing her hair back. And he remembered how his heart went out to her at those times.

*Your heart is broken,* he thought. *Please, take mine.*

He paused and thought for a moment. Then he opened a text app on his phone and made a note of the line he had just thought.

Putting his phone away, his mind went directly back to Suzy. He felt as if he knew a fair amount about her already, and he liked what he knew. But he couldn't wait to get to know her better!

uzy sat down on her yoga mat. The lasagna had been good, but she had eaten later than she was accustomed to. The lasagna was followed by a slice of pecan pie with real whipped cream. It was all sitting heavily in her stomach.

Her visit with Rachel, though, had been beneficial. Parts of their conversation seemed to help her to clear some of the cobwebs that had been dulling her mind, particularly where Mark and Fin were concerned.

So many people, she realized, try to steer the conversation away from the difficult subject of a lost loved one, to avoid causing more sadness. Rachel, though, had asked about Mark, about how they met, and the resulting conversation of a happy memory, focused on the subject of her grief, seemed to help her to think about what was bothering her.

Fin, and Suzy's attraction to him, wasn't the real problem. She and Mark had always enjoyed a healthy sex life. Now, though, she had been celibate for a year. Fin was the first person she had felt any sexual attraction to in all that time. The feeling of guilt, of unfaithfulness to Mark, was troublesome. So, this evening, she had decided to put a relationship with Fin on the back burner, as Rachel had suggested.

But the fact that she was feeling attraction to someone else, despite the uneasiness it caused, could be a good thing. Maybe, in time, . . .

Now that she was back at home, she felt relieved. The burden on her shoulders felt lighter, though her stomach was still pretty heavy. Even though it was late, she wasn't sleepy yet.

She sat down on her yoga mat and lit a candle, concentrating on her breathing. This was followed by about fifteen minutes of yoga. Then, just in case Fiona was around and willing to show her another episode, she sat there focused on opening her mind. Watching the steady candle flame, it only took her a few moments to reach a relaxed, receptive state.

## 22

Ye're being irresponsible, child," Taran MacGregor said.

"I'm not a child, father," Fiona replied irritably. "I'm a grown woman who knows her mind better, I think, than most women me age."

"Ye've known this man for less than a month. Ye know nothing about him."

"I've seen him every day since I met him," she said, her eyes blazing. "During that time, I learned everything I need to know about him to make a decision of this magnitude. Whatever I don't yet know will be learned every day I spend with him, for the rest of me life."

"That's not near enough time to know everything about someone!"

"I hope I never know everything about him. I want to learn something new about him every day."

"Ye know what I mean, girl," Taran said, a little exasperated. "Ye can't know enough to make a wise decision."

"Wattie knew Charlotte only three weeks before he asked her. Obviously it's enough time to know enough about him to make an informed decision."

MacGregor sighed, but before he could say anything else, Fiona continued.

"Father," Fiona said, her voice changing to a more passionate plea, "Caden risked life and limb to save me own life. That speaks volumes about his character. Please believe me when I say that Caden and I are in love. And in our love, we feed each other. The more I give to him, the more I have. He is the god of my idolatry."

"Oh, for heaven's sake, girl, ye're quoting Shakespeare now?"

Fiona smiled and shrugged her shoulders helplessly.

§

Fiona and Caden were married in the MacGregors' garden on a Sunday afternoon, when the air was warm but a gentle breeze carried an autumn crispness. Her sister, Aileen, was her bride's maid, while Caden's friend, Timothy, stood beside him.

Lachlan was in attendance but, though he was invited, Charles Scott had not made the trip. Through his father, he sent a fairly stiff message of congratulations. Lachlan, ever the gentleman, wished them all the happiness in the world. Sir Walter smiled warmly at Fiona after the ceremony was over.

"I understand you invoked me example in pleading your case with your father," he said.

"Aye, Wattie," Fiona replied with an answering smile, "I did. And it was a winning argument!"

Scott leaned forward and kissed Fiona on both cheeks.

"Please give Charlotte our love," she said.

"Indeed I shall," he replied. Shaking Caden's hand, he said, "Congratulations, son. Take good care of her. Me Fiona's a special one."

"She truly is, sir," Caden replied. "Thank ye."

MacGregor was more emotional. His eyes were watery when Fiona and Caden approached him to say goodbye.

"I love ye, child," he said as Fiona kissed his cheek. "Ye know I want nothing but the best for ye." His glance at Caden was quick, but the rebuke was delivered.

"I do know that, father." MacGregor's hands were on her shoulders, and he pulled her to him and hugged her. When she pulled away, MacGregor turned to Caden.

"Son, I only hope ye can prove to be even half the man she sees in ye."

Caden smiled briefly at Fiona, but then turned his smile full on MacGregor.

"I dinnae suppose that I can ever be fully what she deserves, but I promise ye that I will have a go. And please ken, sir, that I recognize that Fiona's th' wonderful lassie she is noo mostly because o' ye."

That seemed to appease MacGregor a bit, and as they walked away, he wiped his eyes on his sleeve. Fiona wiped her own eyes as she leaned against Caden's shoulder.

§

Caden had arranged for one of his ships, The Kirstine, to cruise around Scotland, Ireland and England for their honeymoon. Fiona was excited for the experience, though she was anxious about their first night. Caden, limping down the steps, led her to their cabin.

Outside the door, Caden paused.

"I believe 'tis customary tae carry the bride o'er the threshold." Fiona smiled as he bent over and lifted her in his arms. He turned sideways to pass through the door, and as he did, his leg bumped against the doorpost. He grunted in pain and staggered slightly, but he continued into the cabin.

"That's not a sound a woman wishes to hear issuing from a man struggling with her bulk," Fiona said with a somewhat concerned tone.

"I assure ye, lassie, 'tis nae your bulk that's the cause o' the struggle."

He put her down on her feet and closed the door. He turned back to Fiona and, reaching for his belt buckle, his face flushed a bit as he looked up at her.

"I apologize, me dear, for me indelicate way of approachin' this," he said. He unbuckled his belt and undid his trousers, pushing them down to the floor.

"Caden!" Fiona said, pointing to his calf, which was fully wrapped in a bandage. There was fresh blood oozing through it now.

"Aye," he said, "I've been keepin' it wrapped tight tae keep it clean. But I felt it break open when I bumped it on the doorpost just noo."

"But Caden, that was a month ago."

"I know, lass. 'Tis healin' slow."

"Come here, me dear," Fiona said, motioning toward the bed. "Let me have a look at it." Caden pulled his trousers back up to walk to the bed. Sitting down, he took off his shoes and the trousers and put his leg up on the bed.

As Fiona unwrapped the bandage, she could smell the infection. The last layer of bandage came off and she saw the slash in his skin, gaping open again, the surrounding skin red, swollen and inflamed, oozing with blood and other matter. She turned to the bureau which had a pitcher and bowl on it. She poured water into the bowl and soaked the towel, gently bathing the wound.

"Ye probably should have had this stitched up," she said, her voice straddling the line between scolding and concern.

"Maybe so," Caden sighed. "But I thought keepin' it bound up tight would do the trick."

"Have ye any alcohol?" she asked.

"Aye, lass," Caden replied with a crooked smile, "there in the cabinet. But I dinnae think noo is the time for ye tae start swillin' whisky."

Fiona looked askance at him as she turned to the cabinet he indicated. Opening the door, she found the bottle of whisky and pulled out the cork.

"I'm sure this will burn, me love," she said. Holding the towel under his calf, she dribbled whisky into the open wound. Caden flinched a little, but didn't seem to feel much beyond the initial burn.

She soaked the towel with whisky, as Caden watched dolefully at the waste of good liquor, and she tied it around his calf.

"I'm so sorry, me love," she said, looking up at him. "'Twas because of me that your leg is in this condition."

"Nonsense, lassie," Caden replied, "it weren't your fault that a worthless bounder attacked ye. I'm just glad I was there tae help."

Fiona moved up on the bed and took his face in her hands, looking tenderly into his eyes.

"I am too, me dear one," she said as she kissed him lovingly.

§

Early in the morning, Captain Fergusson guided The Kirstine away from the pier and out the Firth of Forth toward open sea long before Caden and Fiona woke. It was nearly ten o'clock when they made their way up on deck. Aberdeen was off in the distance on their port side.

"So," Fiona said with a sly smile, "who's Kirstine?"

"She was me mother," Caden replied with a slight reprimand in his voice, but softened by a smile. He rubbed his hand along the smooth worn wood of the gunwale. "This was me first ship, and I wanted to honor me mother when I named her. I did the same when I acquired me other ships."

"You named them all Kirstine?" Fiona grinned. Caden smiled back at her joke, but continued seriously.

"I named 'em after me sisters, Brenda and Flora, and me grand-mother Moire."

"Where are your sisters?"

"Both married. Brenda bides wi' 'er husband in London, and Flora's still up in Fort Augustus, where we were raised."

"Kirstine Loganach," Fiona said. "I wish I could have met her."

"I do, too." Caden looked at Fiona. "What was ye're mother's name?"

"Elspeth," she replied. "Elspeth MacGregor."

"Elspeth," Caden repeated. "What were she like?"

"She was passionate and benevolent. She cared about people and wanted to help them. I inherited that quality from her. That's why I'm drawn to people like ye, and philanthropists like Lachlan Mac an Léigh. And even me father's support of artists. Philan-thropy is always an attractive trait to me."

They stood side-by-side for a while, silently watching Scotland slip by in the distance. Caden put his arm around Fiona's shoul-ders, holding her tightly against him, and Fiona leaned into him, indulging in the warmth of his embrace.

She stood there snuggling as close to him as she could, her hands caressing him suggestively under his coat. After a few minutes, Fiona sighed and looked shyly up at Caden.

"Can we go back down?" she asked. Seeing the twinkle in her eye, Caden smiled.

# 23

her eyes drooping, Suzy blew out the candle and pushed herself up from the yoga mat. She was finally feeling tired from the lateness of the hour, and from experiencing this latest episode, so she dragged herself up to her bedroom and did the absolute minimum preparations so she could fall into bed. Besides it being past bedtime, though, she was also feeling a little drained from the emotion in the episode.

And downright confused.

There was no resemblance between Caden and Mark, or Caden and Fin for that matter, either in physical attributes or personality. But Suzy found herself in the somewhat uncomfortable position of being attracted to him.

As she thought about it, she assumed that it was because the episodes were being delivered to her by Fiona, and experienced from Fiona's point of view, so she was likely feeling some of what Fiona felt. As if Fiona's emotions were bleeding through in the delivery.

In fact, she had noticed that she seemed to know what Fiona was thinking or feeling sometimes, even if she didn't verbalize them.

At any rate, she was exhausted. She felt like she could sleep now.

§

"Fiona," Suzy said as soon as she saw her in her pre-dream state, "these episodes you've been showing me are fascinating! I never *dreamed* that sort of thing was even possible. Pardon the pun."

"Ye seemed interested in me life, as it related to your past. I'm glad you're findin' it beneficial."

"Oh, more than beneficial. I'm getting to know you in a way I never thought possible. Photos of sepia-toned ancestors don't even hold a candle to this!"

Fiona's face expressed an emotion Suzy couldn't quite interpret. Longing perhaps.

"Ye'll know more than I do. I'll ne'er know me descendants, at least not those afore ye."

"I'm so glad I'm able to get to know you!" Suzy enthused. "You seem like somebody I'd like to have as a friend."

Fiona smiled at that, but Suzy noticed that the undertone of sadness, as always, remained in her eyes.

"Ye're very kind, lass.

"There's one thing I've been wondering about," Suzy said quietly, cautiously. "Why did you wrap up your baby and put him under the floorboards?"

Fiona's face clouded, and she seemed agitated. Suzy feared that some form of recreation of the episode in the carriage house a few days ago might be coming.

"You know what?" she quickly said, "never mind. It's none of my business."

Fiona looked at her for a few moments, her face expressing consolation. Even the ever-present sadness in her eyes seemed to relax. Suzy felt enveloped in feelings of gratitude and fondness from Fiona, and she couldn't help but reciprocate.

## 24

The sea was grey and a little choppy as the Hebrides drew near. Captain Fergusson, rather than hugging the shoreline, had been sailing in the open sea, but now, he was working the ship toward the new harbor at Port of Ness, on the northern point of the Outer Hebrides.

Neither Caden nor Fiona saw the island growing ahead of them. They were below deck in the quarters of the ship's doctor, Hamish Stewart.

For the last couple of days, Caden had been experiencing lethargy and a fever. The expression on Stewart's face earlier this morning as he examined the gash in Caden's calf was burned into Fiona's memory.

"I dinnae ken how tae tell ye this, boss," Stewart said, looking uncomfortably at Caden. He took a deep breath, then began speaking quietly, as if it would make it easier to say that way, or easier to hear. "Yer leg be badly infected, sir. I'm feart it needs tae come off."

Caden had looked at him for several seconds, as if he didn't quite understand what had been said.

"Ye want tae cut me leg off?" he finally asked.

"Ah dinnae wantae, sir," Stewart replied. "But if I dinnae take it, th' infection'll spread throo'oot yer body 'n' kill ye. I'm sorry, sir."

For several seconds, the atmosphere in the doctor's quarters was tense as Caden regarded Stewart. Feeling almost delirious under the fever, Caden looked up at Fiona, as if he was looking for guidance. Fiona closed her eyes tightly for a few seconds before looking back at Caden. Feeling chilled all over, she nodded.

Caden took a deep breath and nodded back at her.

"Do what ye think is best, Stewart," he said.

The next few minutes were frantic as Stewart got a half-empty bottle of whisky and gave it to Caden. With a hesitant expression, Caden took the bottle from him and pulled the cork, taking several swallows from it. While he was drinking, Stewart left while Fiona held Caden's hand, her face reflecting the fear and shame she felt for being responsible for this.

After a couple of minutes, Stewart returned with four other men.

"Captain Fergusson is takin' us in tae th' Port o' Ness," he had said. "We'll ha' calmer seas in th' harbor than oot 'ere rockin' on th' waves.

As the four deck hands positioned themselves at Caden's shoulders and legs, Stewart opened up a kit of tools including, prominently, a large knife and a saw.

At that point, Stewart ushered Fiona outside his quarters. The last thing she saw was one of the men placing a piece of wood in Caden's mouth, and Caden clamping his teeth down on it. Fiona nervously paced back and forth until she heard Caden start screaming. The screaming lasted only a minute or so, then went quiet. Shortly after that, Fiona shuddered as she heard the rasping of a saw. She clapped her hands over her ears and cried.

§

"Ah, there ye are, sir," Stewart said, and at the sound of his voice, Fiona opened her eyes. Exhausted from the stress and anxiety that she had been going through, she had been dozing in a chair, her head leaning back against the wall. Caden's eyes were open, but glazed. He seemed disoriented, unaware of his surroundings or of recent events.

"Hello, me love," Fiona said softly as she stood beside him and took his hand. Caden looked at her, his eyebrows puckered in confusion. As the seconds passed, though, his breathing intensified and his face began to register pain.

"Aye," Stewart said, "ye've had a rough go of it. Here, sir, drink this," as he put a little cup up to Caden's lips. Caden took a sip and his face screwed up in distaste. "I know, 'tis bitter," the doctor said, "but ye need tae drink it all."

Caden looked at Stewart as if trying to remember him. Finally, he opened his mouth and allowed the doctor to pour the rest of the liquid into it. With an apparent struggle, he swallowed.

"Tha's good. Laudanum is a fine thing. It'll take oot th' worst o' th' pain."

Caden looked up at Fiona again, and she smiled at him, keeping her head turned fully toward his face, trying hard not to notice the absence of his right leg. As the laudanum took effect, though, her husband drifted off to sleep again

§

Caden drifted in and out of consciousness over the next couple of days. Fiona left his side only long enough to deal with personal necessities.

On the third morning, Stewart started gradually reducing the laudanum dosage, and Caden was able to spend more time awake with Fiona. The pain, he said, was bad but manageable.

On the fourth day, using a pair of crutches that were acquired when Captain Fergusson put in at Londonderry, Ireland, he began hobbling around, first in the doctor's quarters, then on deck. He tired quickly and needed to rest often, but Fiona remained by his side.

"I'm sorry this hasn't been the honeymoon I had hoped tae give ye," Caden said as they stood at the gunwale, watching the rocky point of Scarborough slip past to the east.

"Oh, me love," Fiona said, squeezing his arm, "please don't. I should be apologizing to you!"

"Why, lass? What unpardonable crime ha' ye committed?"

"It's because of me that ye nearly died and lost your leg in the bargain." Fiona knew what he was about to say, so she continued quickly. "I know, it's not me fault that that awful man attacked me, but still, 'tis because of that incident that this has happened. Ye can't deny it."

"Nor would I e'en have a go at it. But the fact is if I hadn't been there, I hate t' think what would ha' happened tae ye. So for that, I'd happily lose me shank."

"Happily?" Fiona replied, looking at him with disbelief.

"Well, alright, maybe not happily. But 'tis a cost I'd pay again if I had it tae do over." He smiled at her, his first real smile since the ordeal began a few days before, and Fiona wasn't sure if it came naturally, or if he forced it for her benefit. She decided that it didn't matter. Whatever the reason, she loved him all the more for it.

123

## 25

"Oh my god," Suzy said in a whisper as she came out of the latest episode, seeing her breakfast nook re-materialize around her, blurry through the tears. Across the harbor, the lights were gradually blinking off as the sun rose, attempting to push its rays through the heavy cloud cover.

She felt as if her whole body was tense. Holding out her hand, she could see how badly she was shaking, and the candle flame was flickering in front of her from her agitated breathing. She inhaled deeply, struggling to steady her trembling breaths.

The tears in her eyes streamed down her cheeks and were quickly replaced by more as she remembered the lingering views of Fiona and Caden in the doctor's quarters. She roughly brushed them away, but again, they were replaced as she herself felt the pain and anxiety that Fiona had experienced.

She felt so bad for the young couple. Fiona was such a sweet person, tossing sunshine around wherever she went, Caden such a kind man, who loved Fiona more than anything.

She shivered and closed her robe tightly around her. She picked up her mug of tea with both hands, took a sip, then held the warm cup to her face.

Suzy had started a journal of Fiona's episodes, knowing that she wouldn't remember details of everything she had seen. This entry would be a harder one. It could wait.

She was glad that, from where she sat in her breakfast nook, she couldn't see the rocks on the north end of the harbor below Fort Sewall, but she was aware of them nevertheless. The guilt that Fiona felt over the loss of Caden's leg, and his near death, Suzy felt many times over about the death of Mark and Emma.

She knew that Mark, like Caden, would tell her that it was just an accident, that it had been a series of flukes that caused it, and that it wasn't her fault. She was sure that he would smile at her, and that she would love him all the more for it.

# 26

Fin smiled as he typed. This was good stuff. It was early in the morning, but he couldn't sleep. He had to write.

The short time he had spent with Suzy in Boston had an unforeseen effect. While he liked her on a personal level, she had also become something of a muse for him.

He knew *A Place Made of Time* still needed work on the setting, the atmosphere. And he looked forward to taking a trip to Scotland, to get a first-hand feel for the area. He had even taken a tentative look at flights to Edinburgh, though he didn't know yet when he could go. It probably wouldn't be until late summer.

But at the moment, he was doing some work on Gisele, his main female character. His comment at the Comic Con event had been only partly true. The character hadn't actually been written for Jennifer Lawrence. But once he knew that she had been cast to play Gisele in *TimePlex*, she became his inspiration as he worked on the sequel.

Now, though, Suzy had become his main inspiration.

It wasn't a total rewrite. He wouldn't be smiling about that. But he was having fun adding details, mannerisms that he had noticed in his short time with Suzy. He was altering and adding dialogue to make Gisele a little more of a lovable smartass. And while Gisele was already a strong character, Fin added just a touch of vulnerability amid the strength.

The more he read of the edits, the more he pictured Suzy.

And the more he liked it.

## 27

Suzy stood at the window of her bedroom, looking down into the back yard. Had it only been a week since she looked out there and got the idea to open up the carriage house?

Looking down at it now, she felt conflicting emotions. She felt slightly offended that, based on the result of her last entry into the carriage house, she wasn't allowed into her own property. The memory of that experience still chilled her to her core.

At the same time, she hadn't ever set foot in the carriage house in her life until a week ago, and had not missed it, had seldom even thought about it. So what difference did it make if she couldn't go in there now?

But the more she witnessed of Fiona's life, the more she liked her. The more she identified with her. The more she accepted that Fiona deserved her own space.

The heavy overcast had turned into a cold rain, intensifying some of the colors despite the murky light. But it was the kind of day that made Suzy want to stay inside and do nothing.

That complete lack of motivation, combined with how closely she related to Fiona's guilt about Caden's leg, rekindled something that Rachel had said last night.

*Maybe I* should *get a job*, Suzy thought. *Damn, I thought I was done with that.*

§

"Are you sure you're up for something as low-level as this?" asked Rachel. "I don't know that it would be making the best use of your history major. And it pays literally nothing."

Rachel was the head of the local chapter of Daughters of the American Revolution. Suzy didn't know how she found time, with her full-time job down in Boston and dusting all the historical tchotchkes in her house, not to mention coming to Suzy's rescue now and again.

Suzy's mother had enrolled her in the organization when she was a teenager, based on contributions to the war effort by Phillip Drummond and his father, Nathaniel. She hadn't been active in years, though.

"I know," Suzy replied, nodding, though the nod was lost on Rachel, since she was on the phone. "But it's not about the money. Or the degree. It's not like I'm making any use of it now, anyway, just sitting around here. And you said yourself that I needed to get out of the house."

"That's true," she replied. "But it's not really a job. I doubt you'd be busy for more than one day a week."

"Are you trying to talk me out of it?"

"Of course not," Rachel said. "Okay, well, we're hoping to get former members like yourself reactivated, and we're also involved in looking for new members, especially people of color. If you're up for it, I can have you join some of our ladies making phone calls."

"Sounds like a blast," Suzy replied sarcastically.

"Suzy, do you want to do it or not?"

"Yes, Rachel, I do."

*Jeez, some people!*

## 28

Fiona turned her head and looked toward the window. The wind was fierce, hurling sleet against the glass in a soft but persistent staccato. The window was almost completely opaque with a thickening crust of ice, snow and sleet on the outside, and frost on the inside.

She pulled the covers up a little higher, to cover her one exposed shoulder. Her other shoulder was warmed by Caden's body as her head rested on his shoulder, her dark hair billowing all about.

Listening to the chilling rhythm outside, she thought about how her life had changed in the last three months. Caden's home in Leith, near the docks on the northern shore of Edinburgh, was a far cry from the fine home she had been raised in. His entire house would probably fit in the MacGregors' entrance hall, and Caden had no staff, aside from a cook and a once a week maid, both of whom lived elsewhere. It was no wonder her father had disapproved of their union.

But Fiona had been determined to settle in to this new situation as if she had been there her whole life, calmly doing the necessary chores, though admittedly, she was unfamiliar with many of the duties she took on. Having been a bachelor for several years, Caden was accustomed to doing the daily household chores himself so, partly out of habit and partly, she suspected, out of gratitude to Fiona for not complaining, he continued doing many of them.

She was especially accommodating considering his new and unexpected disadvantage. She had not married a cripple, but she had come back from their honeymoon married to one. Again, though, she never complained, and instead, she often rushed to help him when she saw him struggling with something that, before, he had done without a thought. How could she complain? She loved him as she had never loved anyone.

After his recuperation, he had resumed his work of running his shipping company, often putting in long hours, at his office and at the docks, dealing with orders and shipping manifests, as well as caring for his duties as an employer. Yet, after a hard day at work, he would come home and, without fail, had a smile for Fiona the moment he saw her.

In the three months since their marriage, though she wouldn't have thought it possible, she had fallen even more deeply in love with him.

Warmed by her thoughts of Caden, as she usually was, Fiona turned her head back toward him and found him looking at her. He smiled when their eyes met.

"Good mornin', me love," Fiona said in a sigh.

"Ev'ry mornin'," Caden replied, "I wonder wha' I e'er did that made me so lucky tae ha' such a fine lass as ye." he shook his head and smiled. "Wha'ever it was, I'm so glad I did it!"

"Just bein' yourself is what did it," Fiona replied warmly.

Caden awkwardly turned toward her, still not accustomed to moving with only one leg. He pulled Fiona's body against his and kissed her. Fiona held him tightly, brazenly wrapping a leg around him, as he buried his face in her neck. After several seconds, aware as always of the abrupt termination of his right leg just above his knee, he pulled away and looked at her.

"I just wish I could be a complete man fer ye."

"Caden Loganach," Fiona said, "I don't think I could handle any more of a man than ye already are." Caden smiled, regretfully and supremely happily. "I only wish I could give ye a child," Fiona added.

"Och, stop it, lassie," Caden replied indignantly, "we've only bin married for three months!"

"I know," Fiona responded with a sigh, "but both me sisters found they were with child within the first month. With me, though, there's no stirrin' at all."

"Well, I'm glad of it. I dinnae wantae share ye wi' anybody just yet."

The tears returned to Fiona's eyes as she looked at him.

"What do ye suppose it's like to celebrate Christmas?" she asked.

"What made ye think o' that, lass?" Caden asked, puzzled."

"Today's December 25. I don't know why it came into me head, but I thought that a son would be nice gift for ye."

*"You're the best gift I e'er got in me life, dear Fiona," Caden said softly as one of the tears rolled from the corner of her eye onto his shoulder. "Besides, wha' if the bairn looks like me? Who wants a child wi' a fluff on 'is face and only one shank?"*

## 29

**P**uzzled, Suzy laboriously pushed herself up from her yoga mat. *They didn't celebrate Christmas? What were they, Jehovah's Witnesses?* She smiled. *Wouldn't that be ironic?* she thought. *Jehovah's Witnesses don't believe in ghosts, but I'm being visited by a JW ghost.*

Sitting down at her computer, she did a quick search for Christmas and Scotland. What she found was surprising, and a bit more involved than her initial speculation.

Centuries ago in Scotland, there was virtually no separation of church and state. In 1560, following years of enmity and political strife, Scotland broke away from the Catholic Church. In an act of religiopolitical rebellion, the Scottish Parliament abolished the Catholic faith in Scotland, making the celebration of the Mass an offense potentially punishable by death.

Under the Scottish Reformation, all holy days associated with the Catholic Church, including the "Christ Mass," and all the traditions surrounding it, were covered in this prohibition.

In the first half of the twentieth century, Christmas, if done at all, was observed very quietly. It wasn't until 1967 that the ban was officially lifted and Christmas became a public holiday.

*File that under 'things I didn't learn with my history major!'*

§

Suzy once again started wandering through the house. She couldn't remember the last time she felt so idle, almost bored. She resisted the temptation to remain in a perpetual trance, observing Fiona's life. When she came to the kitchen, she decided to bake cookies.

It was an activity that she enjoyed, but it was fraught with memories, too. Emma used to love making cookies with her, and she remembered that Mark even helped her once.

Emma would have been around five years old, and they had just gotten the DVD of *Frozen*.

She was too enthralled to be bothered with baking cookies, and to Suzy's surprise, Mark had volunteered to help her.

Emma was in the living room, laughing at something that was said or done in her new favorite movie while Suzy had Mark grease the next cookie sheet.

"Hmm," Mark said.

"What?" Suzy asked, looking up at him.

"I'm just thinking of something else I'd rather be doing with this butter." He glanced at her suggestively.

"Is everything sexual with you?" she asked, split between exasperated and flattered, as she often was with him.

"When you're nearby, babe, yeah, it pretty much is." He smiled at her, and her exasperation went out the window.

"Hold that thought," Suzy replied, sidling up to Mark and draping her arms around his waist. "Emma will be going to bed in a few hours. I'm curious to see what you have in mind."

"Oh, I think you know what I have in mind, Suzy Q."

"I can't wait." To underscore the statement, she came to him and put her arms around his waist, pulling him against her body. She mashed her midsection up against his, pressing her hips forward.

Mark responded by grabbing her butt with both hands and squeezing, pulling her sweet spots tightly against him, as she continued thrusting her hips forward and back, left and right.

Rubbing against Mark in her carnal dance, even fully clothed, the physical effect it had on him was tactually, and visibly, noticeable, and admittedly not very conducive to making cookies.

"Well, honey," Mark said a little breathlessly, "as much as I would love to continue bumping and grinding with you, I think you better get those cookies out of the oven."

Suzy sniffed the air and quickly turned away from him, knocking over a jar of mixing spoons and spatulas. Grabbing a hot pad off the counter, she whipped the oven door open and pulled the cookie sheet out. She sighed with relief when she saw that the cookies had gotten a little dark, but not burnt.

She glanced over at Mark, and she grinned as she saw him struggling to rearrange himself in his jeans.

She picked up a spatula and started sliding the cookies onto a wire rack on the counter. As she was doing that, with her other hand she gouged out a little finger-full of remaining cookie dough and put it in her mouth.

"Ah, you're one of those," Mark said.

"One of what?" she asked, looking at him quizzically.

"You're a cookie dough eater."

"Yeah, so?" She gave him her best "duh!" expression.

"I just never saw the appeal." Now her expression turned to one of disbelief.

"You don't like cookie dough?"

"I don't know. I've never eaten it."

"Haven't you ever made cookies?" She seemed almost as if she was getting indignant. It was apparently a sensitive subject.

"I've made cookies lots of times."

"Well –" She scoffed and looked at him sternly. Shaking her head, her face sported a somewhat aghast expression. "How can you make cookies and not eat cookie dough?" One would think that he had said that he doesn't breathe air.

"I could make cookies *precisely because* I didn't eat all the cookie dough," and he gave her *his* best "duh!" expression. Suzy smiled at him, but again, she just shook her head, totally bewildered.

Apparently, he was a lost cause.

After the batches she had already made, and the dough she ate, what was left made about six more cookies. As they cooked, Suzy poured some milk into three small glasses and arranged a few cookies on a tray.

By the time they carried the milk and cookies into the living room, Emma was singing *Let It Go* at the top of her lungs along with Elsa. As she saw the cookies and milk approaching, though, her face lit up with the kind of intense happiness and enthusiasm that only young children seem to be able to pull off.

"Yum!" she said as her full attention shifted to her parents and the cookies.

Suzy and Mark settled on the sofa, on either side of Emma, as they enjoyed the cookies.

After a minute or so, Suzy leaned over and whispered something in Emma's ear. Emma jerked her head around toward Mark with a shocked expression on her face.

"You don't like cookie dough?"

Mark sighed heavily. Suzy smiled.

As the memory washed over her now, her smile was more of a sad one. She decided she didn't feel like making cookies.

*Dammit, Mark, you've ruined me.*

## 30

Winter came and went, and the deciduous trees around Fin's house took on a fuzzy yellow-green look as buds began to pop out. The sky was a shade of blue that Fin had only seen in Colorado. Spring was a time of new growth, but to Fin, it seemed gloomy.

Suzy had become elusive. Shortly after their meeting in Boston back in October, they had spoken briefly on the phone, and Fin had made it known that he was interested in getting to know her better. Suzy had made it known that she wasn't ready.

Fin was naturally disappointed, but he understood the reason and told her that he was perfectly willing to give her whatever time and space she needed. Suzy thanked him, and said that she was starting a new job and would not be around much anyway. Their contact after that had become quite sparse. They had spoken only a couple of times, and it usually took Suzy a day or more to respond to his text messages.

During the last couple of months, Fin had halfheartedly started looking at MySoulmate.com again. As he was feeling discouraged about his prospects, he received an unexpected phone call.

§

"Hi Fin," said the familiar voice on the phone, "it's Kay."

"Kay," he echoed after several seconds of hesitation. "Hi."

"How are you?" she asked, and Fin noted the friendly tone, one which he hadn't heard since a couple of years before they divorced.

"I'm fine. How are you?" Fin was hoping to speed past the small talk so he could find out why she was calling.

"Fine thanks." There was another long pause before she spoke again. "Well," she finally said, her voice sounding a little nervous, "I suppose you're wondering why I'm calling after all this time."

"The thought had crossed my mind."

"Yeah," Kay said in a breathy voice that he hadn't heard in even longer. "I've just been thinking about you, Fin, and about the way we ended. And to tell you the truth, I have some regrets."

"Hmm," Fin replied ambiguously.

"Are you married? Are you seeing anyone?" Fin couldn't figure out what had prompted her to call, and he knew that asking her what she was up to would probably be counter-intuitive.

"No, on both counts."

A few seconds of silence hung in the air while he waited.

"Would you like to get together?" Kay finally asked. "I'd like to talk to you about an idea I've had, and I'd rather not do it over the phone."

*Our hero has taken a journey into a wondrous land whose boundaries are that of imagination. Next stop, The Twilight Zone.*

"Can you give me a hint?"

"Well, I've been thinking about how we ended. I know it wasn't pleasant for either of us, but I just think you got kind of a raw deal."

"I happen to agree, but Kay, you were the one who delivered that deal. You knew what I was like all along. I didn't change, you did."

She was quiet for a moment before responding.

"You're right, Fin. I was too quick to let my own personal opinions dictate what happened to you. To us. I'm sorry about that."

Fin felt as if he had been plopped into a scene from *Invasion of the Body Snatchers* and Kay was emerging from a pod. He couldn't even remember the last time she had admitted that she was wrong.

"Anyway, I'd like to try to make it up to you," she said. "Not that dinner would be enough to do that, obviously. But like I said, I just have some ideas that I'd like for us to talk about."

"Okay," he finally replied, "I'm intrigued."

§

"Damn, girl!" Fin met Kay outside the Brio Tuscan Grille near the Cherry Creek Shopping Center. It was a warm evening and, taking full advantage of the weather, Kay was wearing a slinky little low-cut black dress that came to just above her mid-thigh and swished back and forth seductively as she walked toward him. Her long, brown legs were bare, and terminated in a pair of shiny black heels, the kind Fin had heard referred to as 'come fuck me shoes.' While Fin silently kicked himself for that exclamation, Kay smiled at the compliment implicit in it.

Kay had often lamented the few extra pounds that she had sometimes carried. Looking at her now, Fin thought it looked as if she had gotten a handle on it. She looked toned and gorgeous.

"Hi, Fin," she said warmly. "It's good to see you again, under happier circumstances."

He didn't know the protocol. Never having gone out to dinner with an ex before, he wasn't sure if any kind of physical greeting was called for. Kay resolved the issue by leaning forward and placing a hand softly on his arm, lightly kissing his cheek.

*Dammit, she smells good, too!*

Fin suddenly felt a little underdressed. He had come prepared for a casual meeting over dinner. Kay looked like she was there for a date. Bitter and confused about his relationship – or lack thereof – with Suzy, he had to admit that he was somewhat receptive.

Of course, there was still the history. Their marriage had not been a happy one, and that memory came to mind. So he was still bitter about that, too, and he didn't think he was ready to just jump into bed with Kay the moment she asked.

But he really hoped she didn't ask.

As they walked through the restaurant being led to their table, his eyes were drawn, alternately, to Kay's gorgeous legs, and to the eyes of the men who saw her pass. A couple of the men were with women who seemed a little pissed at them for looking.

As they sat down, Kay's dress rode up a little higher on her thighs, and Fin was treated to a glimpse of the black lacy underwear she was wearing. He felt a momentary surge in his groin area.

*Dammit! Remember the marriage! Remember the marriage!*

The waitress approached the table almost immediately, and they ordered drinks, a dirty vodka Martini for Fin and a Manhattan for Kay. Momentarily appeased, the waitress left, and Kay and Fin looked at each other. He shook his head a little.

"What?" Kay asked with a hint of a smile.

"I'm not going to lie, Kay," he said after a few moments. "You look great!" Besides the dress and the legs and the CFM shoes, her dark hair rested in pretty, relaxed waves on her shoulders, and her eyes looked warm and sultry.

Upon hearing that remark, her smile spread wider, and it even looked as if she may have blushed a little. While he wasn't sure if he believed it or not, he was liking this version of Kay.

"Thank you, Fin," she replied. "You look good, too."

She seemed embarrassed, and even a little vulnerable.

"I'm sorry I never contacted you since the divorce," she finally said.

"That's alright, Kay. That's kind of the way divorces usually go."

"Yeah, but still, I don't really have any excuse. Except, I guess I was a little regretful."

"Regretful? About what."

"You're the one that got away. And I have to admit, Fin, you were a good one. I really fucked up with you."

Again, her face displayed that look of embarrassment. And longing.

*Dammit!*

"Where was this variant of you a few years ago?" he asked wistfully. "We probably could have actually made it work."

"You were pretty distant yourself," she replied, a little defensively at first, but then her tone softened a bit. "I suppose I should admit that I was probably instrumental in pushing you away, though." She paused in thought. She looked at Fin and shook her head. "I was just really wrapped up in my own stuff and I didn't make room for you and yours."

"I'm *still* wrapped up in my stuff, Kay" Fin said. "I'd rather read a comic book than a financial report. I'd rather watch Star Trek than a football game. I'd rather play Skyrim than softball. I'm still the same geeky guy I was back then."

Kay nodded, but the waitress returned with their drinks before she could respond. She set them down on the table and asked if they were ready to order their dinner. They ordered quickly, and after the waitress left, Kay responded.

"I know all that, and that's fine with me. I guess my main problem is that I've just always had a hard time handling defeat."

"Defeat?" Fin echoed. "You thought *I* defeated *you*? You called me every name in the book, Kay. You told me you couldn't stand me, a couple of times in front of friends."

"I'm sorry, Fin. I really am. That was wrong, and I should have handled so many things differently. But yes, I felt defeated because, well, like I said, you were the one that got away. I failed in my marriage and I lost you." She turned her head a little and discreetly wiped away a tear that had formed.

Fin sat there looking at Kay for a few moments, feeling the bitterness dissolve. He was almost at a loss for words. Almost.

"We don't even have our food yet, and already this dinner has turned out completely different from what I was expecting."

"In a good way, I hope." That look of vulnerability was back. Fin really didn't know what to make of this version of Kay. He was hesitant to jump too quickly on her bandwagon.

Still . . .

"Yes, Kay, in a *very* good way."

"Good," she smiled. "Well, let me throw you another curve." He looked at her expectantly as she shyly traced a pattern with her finger through the condensation on the side of her glass. She looked back up at him. "What do you think about you and me giving it another try?"

"Huh?" Fin was sure he looked *at least* as stupid as he sounded.

"We were good in the beginning, Fin. We just got sidetracked along the way."

Fin pondered her for what seemed like a long time, though it was just a few seconds. Physically, she looked great. In fact, she looked better than ever. Like the old saying goes, looking good is the best revenge. Kay definitely looked good, but she wasn't looking for revenge. She wanted him back.

Fin was having a little trouble with the concept, but in studying Kay's face, he was trying to see beyond the physical attributes. He was also looking for signs of deceit and artifice.

But the hardness he remembered was gone. Kay was beautiful and soft and appealing. Besides that surge he felt in the groin earlier, he was also feeling something in his chest.

He actually had the warm fuzzies!

"I am unbelievably flattered, Kay," he finally said, "but let me think about that for a while before we jump back into it." Fin was happy to note that he must be finally growing up. Instead of being led along by his penis and just saying "hell, yeah, let's go for it," he was able to keep a grasp on his common sense.

Kay smiled and nodded.

"Sure, Fin, I understand. Just let me know. But I really do appreciate you giving it some serious thought."

The rest of the dinner went very much like the first part. Kay and Fin got along great, almost like they had years ago at the beginning of their relationship. When they finally parted, it was quite late, and after a long and lingering hug outside the restaurant.

# 37

The local chapter of the Daughters of the American Revolution met in a room in Abbot Hall, the governmental center of Marblehead. Since Marblehead was such a small town, Suzy knew several of the women in the chapter, either personally or by reputation. A couple of them had been close friends of her mother.

When they met to make the phone calls, though, since there wasn't a bank of telephone lines at Abbot Hall that they could use, they would meet at different members' homes and use their own phones. There were a couple of the more introverted members who stayed at home and made calls on their own, but most of them liked the support and camaraderie of meeting as a group. And it was usually a social event, with tea and finger foods.

Suzy gave it a valiant effort. She, admittedly, wasn't a huge fan of ladies' get-togethers, especially where several of the women in the group loved to gossip. Nor did she care for making what amounted to sales calls, but she found it was work she believed in. Many people had become apathetic over the years, politically and socially, herself included. The polarization that had occurred in the country over the last few years, though, seemed to have rekindled the patriotism and social conscience of some, and Suzy found the work rewarding.

Besides the fact that it gave her a break from her house and the constant reminders of Mark and Emma. She hated to admit it, but Rachel may have been right.

As she made notes and phone calls, though, she still often found herself thinking about the visions that Fiona was still sharing with her. Over the past several months, many of them had been somewhat mundane, everyday life scenes. They were fascinating to Suzy, but someone other than a historian might have become bored with them.

Caden and Fiona were so happy together, so deeply in love, it would have been like a fairy tale if not for certain details. Details like the body snatchers, who were still in operation, and sometimes referenced in the visions. Details like the gruesome loss of Caden's leg on their honeymoon. Details like the unexpected death of Aileen's husband, Henry, early in 1825, by what Suzy suspected was tuberculosis.

After the estate was settled, with an allowance going to Aileen for living expenses, the bulk of the property was left in a trust to their young son, William. The allowance was enough for Aileen to keep up the running of the house, though with a drastically reduced staff.

Fiona had helped her sister close up unused portions of the house, and offered assistance in any other area she might need, but Aileen, in a mixed state of numbness and melancholy, often resisted the offers.

Suzy could relate.

The most recent episodes she saw, though, had been particularly noteworthy.

## 32

Fiona studied Caden as he sat in his dark red chair facing her. She liked the pose she had put him in, leaning casually on his hand. She had the basic shapes and colors blocked in on her canvas, and had begun painting several details into the background of the portrait. But something about Caden just wasn't right.

"Ye're frownin', love," Caden said.

"Aye," Fiona replied. "I'm wishing ye were wearing tighter clothing."

"Tighter clothing?" He looked down at his clothing, then back up at Fiona, confused. "Ye're just wearin' a robe. That hardly seems fair."

"Aye, but the patterns, folds and wrinkles are complicated. I don't think I'm a good enough artist to complete this painting."

"I've seen your work, love. I think ye're a fine artist."

Fiona smiled at his compliment, then became serious again as she studied him a bit longer. Suddenly, a thought occurred to her which caused her face to flush and her mouth to spread in a grin.

"What?" Caden asked. Fiona looked up at his face and shook her head, embarrassed that he had seen the change in her expression. "What?" he persisted.

"I was just thinking that I'd like to paint ye nude," Fiona replied, her face pinkening even more.

"I think I'd like that," Caden said.

"Really?" Fiona asked, surprised.

"Aye, as lang as I ha' t' sit here doin' nothing, 'twould be nice t' ha' me lovely naked wife t' look at."

Fiona sputtered at his joke and slapped a hand over her mouth. She shook her head as she looked at him. Then, still smiling, she put her brush down. She untied the belt and reached up toward her neck, pulling her robe apart, letting it fall open to expose her breasts. As she looked at Caden, and the smile playing about his lips, she suddenly became serious.

"Hold that expression!" she said. "It's perfect!"

§

*Fiona looked at the painting, hanging in its new place beside the dark red chair that Caden was sitting in as she painted it. She was quite happy with the way it had turned out.*

*Fiona turned her attention back to her chores. She was busy working on preparations for Hogmanay, the Scottish celebration of the new year. The house cleaning, she decided, was done. Black buns were out of the oven and cooling in the kitchen. All that was left was to walk through the house with a smoldering juniper branch, an ancient tradition meant to chase away disease and evil spirits.*

*It was usually a joyous occasion, but Caden seemed unmoved by it when he came in the door. Fiona smiled a greeting at him until she saw the stern lines set in his face.*

*"Caden, what's bothering ye, me dear?" Fiona inquired softly. Caden looked at her, the worry settled deeply in his face. He seemed hesitant to answer, taking the time to lean his crutches against the wall and remove his coat, hanging it on a peg by the door. It was followed by his hat and scarf. Finally, taking up his crutches again, he turned toward Fiona. He looked at her silently for a few moments as the concern built up in her eyes. Finally, as if he couldn't hold her gaze, he lowered his own eyes and sighed.*

*"I suppose ye'll know soon enough," he said. "It appears we may be in for some hard times, love." Caden sat down on the settee, stretching his leg out in front of him.*

*"How so?" Fiona asked as she sat next to him, her face wearing a worried expression*

*"I've bin hearin' rumblin's for a while. Some folks ha' been predictin' th' burstin' of an economic bubble, 'specially in shippin' companies an' textile factories. It seems as if that's happenin' noo."*

*"Aye," Fiona said, "I've overheard people talking of such things, too."*

*"A panic's settin' in, lass. Folks're withdrawin' all their money from th' banks. Some o' th' banks ha' gone under. But others are callin' in debts tae cover their losses. I'm afraid tha's happenin' tae me."*

"What do ye mean?"

"The bank wants me debts paid, Fiona. I ha' taken loans for me business, and I ha' to come up wi' the money tae pay 'em back noo."

"Can ye do that?" Fiona asked quietly, placing a hand softly on his arm. She felt a foreboding tightness building in her chest as Caden shook his head.

"Nay, love, business were good a ways back, but nae that good. Noo, other folks are sufferin' because of the panic, an' it has affected me own business. I've lost some contracts recently, an' tae pay me workers, I've had tae let some o' me own bills wait.

"I know now I should ha' been makin' larger payments on me debts, but instead, I purchased stuff, things tae make me life, and yours, easier. Nae like ye were accustomed to, by any means, but certainly more than I needed." As he talked, his voice became quieter and quivered, as if he was ashamed and embarrassed. "And I just kept takin' more emigrants tae Nova Scotia. Some of 'em were so poor, I couldnae bring meself tae e'en charge 'em for food an' lodgin'. I've been such a doltish numpty!"

"Caden, you're the most caring man I know. Your willingness to go out of your way to help others is part of what I love about ye."

"Well, noo I cannae e'en help me own wife!"

"We'll get through it, love," Fiona soothed. "When will this happen?"

She could see Caden struggling to remain calm, but despite his efforts, she could also see the tears pooling in his eyes.

"'Tis already happened, me love. They've taken me ships!"

§

Scarcely a month later, Caden came home to find Fiona almost in tears as she gathered up clothing and other necessary items, packing them into what bags she could find.

"Fiona, what're ye doin', me dear?" he asked, alarmed by the look on her face.

She looked at him for a couple of seconds as the tears accumulated in her eyes. She tried to brush them away, and she turned to pick up a letter that lay on a side table.

"Caden, me love," she said, her voice shaking, "we're being evicted."

Caden looked at the paper. It was an official notice from the bank. His house, which he had purchased less than a year before, was being repossessed. He exhaled as if he had been punched in the stomach. Fiona, seeing his hands shaking, and knowing what his day had probably been like, felt sorry that she had dumped the news on him so abruptly. She led him to the settee and helped him ease down onto it. Sitting down beside him, she took a deep breath and tried to keep her voice steady.

"Did ye have any success in your search today?" she asked softly, hopefully.

Caden looked at her, and she could see the tears collecting in his own eyes as he shook his head.

"Nay, sweetheart. There are no jobs tae be had for the likes o' me. Nobody wants tae hire a cripple."

Fiona held his gaze for a few moments. Finally, she sighed and squeezed his hand.

"I'm sorry, love. But surely not everybody feels like that."

"Well, it's that, or they're sufferin' from the panic themselves. Either way, 'tis the same result for us."

Fiona looked down at her own hands and noticed they were shaking. She clasped them firmly and struggled to steady her breathing, hoping to still the panic building inside her. She looked up at Caden and saw that his attention was engaged similarly.

"What are we to do, me dear?" she asked. Caden sighed heavily before responding.

"As ye ken, Timothy has had some setbacks of his own. But I'll check wi' him an' a couple o' other friends." He looked up at Fiona. "What about your family?"

"Aileen and me father are the only ones in Edinburgh. I know Aileen is in a state herself. She can barely take care of herself and William. And me father, as ye know, has not been himself lately. But I'll talk to them both."

Caden nodded. Having a plan seemed to help them both feel a little calmer.

§

As expected, Aileen, never having fully recovered from the death of her husband, was encased in her own grief and melancholy. She didn't fully understand Fiona's situation, or the economic circumstances that caused it, and seemed offended that Fiona would even ask her for help.

Taran MacGregor had been experiencing memory and cognitive issues lately. Having never accepted Caden, MacGregor was still displeased that Fiona had made such a poor match. As he was largely unaffected by the panic, and insulated from much outside unpleasantness by his house staff, he also did not fully understand Fiona's situation, and was outraged at Caden for not taking proper care of his little girl. In the end, MacGregor offered Fiona a place if she would "come to her senses," but Caden was not welcome.

Timothy, despite the financial troubles he had been experiencing, offered them a place to stay. After a few weeks, though, as the weather started warming a bit, he seemed uncomfortable when he sat down to dinner. He glanced at Innis, his wife, who nodded soberly at him.

"Good evenin', me friend," he started. "How have ye fared in your search for employment?"

Caden fidgeted in his seat, clearly saddened and embarrassed by the situation.

"I'm afraid me search continues tae be unsuccessful."

"I'm sorry." Timothy glanced at Innis again, then down at his hands, clenched together on the table. Finally, he pulled his hands apart and flexed his fingers, sighing heavily.

"Caden, Fiona," he said, looking at both of them, then looking away again as if he were embarrassed himself, "ye're both such good friends, so it pains me tae say this, but we cannae be puttin' ye up any longer." Caden and Fiona exchanged a nervous glance as Timothy continued. "As ye ken, me work has been affected by the Panic as well, and we cannae afford tae stay here. We've foond a smaller house tae live in."

Caden nodded somberly. Fiona felt the tightness in her chest return as her fingernails dug into her palms.

The meager dinner was eaten mostly in silence.

## 33

Fin sat in his library in front of his computer, but he wasn't looking at it. His feet were crossed on the corner of his desk as he gazed out the window. He was still in a state of shock about his sudden unexpected reunion with Kay, and about how much he had actually enjoyed dinner with her last night.

He was trying to decide what to do about her proposal. In doing so, he had dredged up a number of memories. Some of them, not surprisingly, were maddening and painful. But one of the memories was of a time early in their relationship, before they got married, when Kay broke up with him. It wasn't necessarily a happy memory, but Fin thought it could be helpful.

After they married, Fin started working for Kay's father, a building contractor. But at this time, he was waiting tables in an upscale restaurant in downtown Denver. A scheduling mix-up had resulted in him missing a holiday event that Kay had been looking forward to. She got upset, Fin got angry, words were said, and she called it off.

Fin experienced a bout of depression after that, feeling as if he had lost the perfect woman. But going to work that evening actually helped. Jeff, a fellow waiter who, Fin assumed, bathed in cologne, approached him as he was taking a break.

"*He wafted into the room wrapped in a capacious cloud of cologne,*" Fin said, speaking his literary narration a little more bitterly than he intended. "*Nearby, a canary died.*"

"Shut up," Jeff said, as Fin reached for his phone to make a note of this most recent line he wanted to save. "What's wrong with you?"

Fin put his phone away and looked dejectedly at Jeff.

"Kay broke up with me."

"Shit, I'm sorry, man."

"Me too," Fin said, lowering his eyes sadly. "She was the most perfect woman I've ever known."

"There's no such thing as a perfect woman," Jeff said shaking his head.

"I know that. I'm not saying Kay was literally perfect. I know she had flaws."

Jeff sat down across from him.

"Like what?"

Fin thought for a bit.

"Well," he was grasping at straws, "she was a little thick around the middle."

"I thought you liked 'curvy' women," Jeff replied.

"I do," he conceded, "and I did like Kay's body. But she just put on a little weight since Thanksgiving. She was working harder to take it back off, and not blow up over Christmas."

"Okay," Jeff replied, shaking his head, "well that's something pretty much everybody does, so that doesn't really count. Think hard. Did she do anything that really got on your last nerve?"

"She snored a little." Jeff nodded as Fin continued thinking about it. Finally, Fin shook his head and looked up at Jeff. "It didn't really get on my nerves, though. I thought it actually sounded kind of cute." Jeff sighed and looked away.

"You're hopeless, man."

"I know. Okay, let me think." Fin wracked his brain for anything she did that he really hated. "Alright, sometimes when we would go out to eat, she would say she didn't want fries, but then she'd end up eating mine."

"Alright, that's a good one. I've got news for you, though: Most women do that."

"She kind of nagged me about my driving."

"What do you mean? She didn't like you speeding?"

"Well, a lot of things. Like, especially if we were talking, I became a little more careless, wandering out of the lane. I guess I'm not a very good multi-tasker. I just can't concentrate on two things at once."

"Can't really blame her for that, but still, nagging is irritating. Anything else?"

"She liked country music."

"I do, too. So what?"

"I'm not in love with you. But country music just gets on my nerves."

"No accounting for some people's taste, or lack of it, but I guess we can work with that. So think about this: Chances are, her love of country music is something that will stick around, and you'd be hearing a lot of it if you were still with her."

Fin had figured on that, and had resigned himself to it when they were together. It was a compromise that he had been willing to make if it meant that Kay was with him. Now that she wasn't, though, he had to admit that he felt a little relief at the prospect of not having to listen to an endless succession of tears-in-my-beer, love-gone-wrong, God, America and pickup truck anthems.

"Oh," he said, snapping his fingers, as something else occurred to him, "she never cleaned the hair out of the drain after her shower."

"Oh my god, are you sure you're a man?" Jeff asked disdainfully. "Did you get pissed at her when she left the toilet seat up, too?" Fin rolled his eyes at him. "Okay, anyway, we've got nagging about your driving," he continued, counting on his fingers, "country music, and failure to clean out the drain." He looked disappointed. "Not a very impressive list. Maybe we should keep the weight gain issue."

"See?" Fin said. "She really was almost perfect."

"Whatever, man. Just think about those things, and how much they irritate you. And think about Kay doing them, for the rest of your damn life."

As Fin thought about it, it kind of made sense. Of course, it became a moot point when, shortly after that, she had called him up and apologized for getting angry about the whole episode. They got back together and eventually married.

Thinking back on it now, with the benefit of hindsight, he decided he could subtract the weight issue from the list, and add "soul-sucking harpy" based on the latter part of their marriage.

*Only* the latter part of their marriage, though. She sure seemed different last night.

He decided that list was no help after all.

arly in April, Suzy hosted the local chapter of the Daughters of the American Revolution at her house to make their calls. Spring was in the air, but it was a chilly evening, so Suzy lit a number of candles on the table to give an air of coziness to the dining room.

Several of the ladies had never been to Suzy's home, so she started out by showing them around, mainly the location of the bathroom, and the kitchen where she had snacks laid out. She had spent the afternoon baking cookies and making stuffed mushrooms. Others had brought food as well, and added their contributions to the selection.

"I remember when my husband remodeled this kitchen," said Helen Stewart, one of the older women in the group. Her face usually wore a stern look, her mouth rigid. She held her head up and back a bit, as if she were having a little trouble balancing the tall stiff helmet of slightly blue hair that Suzy only saw on women of a certain age. "Your parents appreciated his work and mentioned how happy they were with it every time they saw us in church."

"Yes," Suzy replied, "I remember that, too. I was a little girl then." She caught the barely perceptible emphasis that Helen placed on the word 'appreciated,' as if she was contrasting Suzy's attitude with that of her parents. She thought it was stretching it a bit to say that her parents mentioned it 'every time they saw them,' but she also knew that her parents had been only sporadic church attenders.

She looked at all the details that had changed since then, when she and Mark updated it a few years ago.

"It had just gotten a little dated," she said. Helen looked disapprovingly at her and her lips disappeared into a thin line as she left the kitchen. Suzy rolled her eyes and sighed.

"What a beautiful home you have!" said Emily Anders, a thirtyish woman who, Suzy had noticed, often gushed like an ardently enthusiastic teen. "What did you do to be able to afford this?"

"Lots of late nights in the Combat Zone," Suzy replied quite seriously. The Combat Zone was Boston's red light district during several decades in the twentieth century. Though it was no more, locals still knew what she was talking about.

"What?" Emily asked, the gush noticeably missing from her voice.

"No," Suzy replied with a smile, easily brushing away the joke, "it just took lots of scraping and careful planning. You know, getting myself born into the right family and all."

"Emily," Rachel said in an attempt to save the woman from Suzy's snark, "why don't you sit over here next to me?" She shot Suzy a reproving look, but Suzy was sure she was suppressing a smile.

With Rachel and Emily now seated, the rest of them took their phones and gathered around the table, papers, pens and literature scattered around them, and started making their calls.

§

"Thank you, Ms. Snow," Suzy said into her phone, "I'll get this information in the mail to you right away, along with a copy of the receipt for your donation. We appreciate your generosity."

She disconnected and made a couple of final notes, then clipped the papers together, placing them on top of the stack in the middle of the table. After holding her phone against her ear with her shoulder for the duration of the call, she rotated her head now to stretch her neck muscles, and as she did, she caught the nod and the complimentary smile that Rachel flashed at her.

Suzy had enjoyed a successful evening, reactivating two lapsed members, signing up a new one, and taking in three donations. But spending the evening doing what amounted to sales pitches was not something she felt entirely comfortable with, even after the last few months, so she was feeling a little fatigued.

She took a deep breath and sighed as she stared at the flame of a candle in front of her. She felt satisfaction about the success of her efforts, but being unaccustomed to talking to others for so long, she also felt the weariness settling in, and she hoped that the others were about ready to call it a night.

The candle blurred and Suzy blinked, trying to clear her vision. It wasn't until the scene started changing that she realized her mistake. She tried to stay in the present, but the colors and shapes continued to blend and shift. She had become adept at quickly entering the trance state, but aside from the very first vision, she had never tried to prevent it.

Despite her struggle to hold on to her present time and location, the scene continued to change. The only thing that remained was the candle.

## 35

Despite the near total blackness and void, the candle flickered in a draft of unknown origin. It was night. Fiona knew this, not because of the perpetual darkness, but because her husband had rejoined her some time ago. She couldn't tell if it was minutes ago or hours. The passage of the sun and moon had no meaning here. The only thing that penetrated the darkness was their candle, and those few other scattered candles and lanterns that others possessed. At this time, it was just a lantern on the other side of the small room.

Fiona remembered hearing stories about the vaults, the dark places formed by the now enclosed arches under the bridges in old town Edinburgh, years ago. She remembered discussing the plight of those poor souls living in them only last year, after her father had introduced her to Lachlan Mac an Léigh. Back then, she never would have thought that she herself would be living in the vaults.

She stared into the candle flame simply because it was something to focus on. Looking up, she could see the arch of the bridge overhead, just barely visible in the dim light, the underside of the setts curving away from her toward the wall a few feet away.

Against the opposite wall were the Fergusons, a small family of four. Fiona had visited briefly with the mother, Maddie, the day before, but Maddie was guarded and reserved, keeping her attention on her baby and her toddler. The baby had been wheezing, and Maddie was preoccupied with caring for it. Fiona felt bad for them, especially for the children, but she recognized that Maddie just wanted to be left alone. So she and Caden were keeping to themselves.

"So," she said quietly to Caden, "how did ye fare today?"

Caden looked up at her, discouragement deeply etched into his face, even in the dim, flickering light.

"There were only a couple o' jobs available," he replied, equally quietly, "and both employers decided I weren't what they were keenin' for." The discouragement on his face gave way to shame. "I took a few shillings beggin' on the wynd." He pulled off a bite of the stick of dried beef that was their dinner, chewing as he stared at the candle flame.

He coughed, at first a single hack, but after attempting to hold it back, he gave in to a long, convulsive paroxysm of coughing. He had been doing that lately, since they had been in the vaults. He pulled his plaidie around him, up around his neck. He looked with chagrin at the faded colors of his tartan. He knew the dark blues and greens could scarcely be distinguished from each other now, and the red had faded to an odd tan color. One good thing about looking at it in the vaults, he decided, was that it all just looked black.

"I'm sorry we don't have more blankets, love," Fiona lamented. She knew she had been too trusting. Most of the things they had managed to hold on to after losing their house, including blankets and warm clothing, had been taken from them a month or so back when she had left their area to relieve herself in a more private location. She had come back to find most of the things she had left there gone.

"'Tis nae your fault, me love," Caden replied.

"It is," Fiona said, "but thank ye for saying so."

Since that day, Fiona, despite the horror she felt at doing so, had taken to turning away from anyone who might be nearby, to relieve herself in a pail, adding to the already pervasive reek, and saving it until Caden returned, before she left their place and their meager possessions, to go and empty it.

They had moved a few times since they entered the vaults. Despite the filth and the stench of the place, there were more people in need than there were rooms. If both Fiona and Caden had to leave at the same time, they often returned to find their previous home occupied by new residents. At least they had learned to take their possessions with them.

Fiona's musings were interrupted when they heard a gasp from the other side of the room, and they looked up at the Fergusons. Maddie was rocking the bundle in her arms and weeping now, and her husband moved closer.

"She's gone," Maddie whispered, hugging the baby tightly, as her sobbing intensified.

Fiona and Caden looked at each other sadly, silently, allowing the Fergusons to mourn their loss in private.

§

It was morning, but time was still as indistinguishable as always in the vaults. Caden hadn't been gone very long when Fiona was surprised at his return. "We need tae leave here, lass," he said quietly. "I've found a better place for us."

The room they were in was crowded now. The Fergusons had left a few days before, but they had been replaced by a couple, a family of three, and two individuals. There was a little more light, due to the additional candles and lanterns, but even a modicum of privacy was a commodity they no longer enjoyed.

With the increase in the number of people in their room, there was also an increase in the conversations overheard. Some of them were terrifying to Fiona. The body snatchers were, apparently, still at work, not only above ground, but in the vaults.

She heard of a man who had lived on Cowgate, but who had died. Friends and family had cleaned him and dressed him, placing him in a coffin, after which they closed up his house to await his transport to the kirkyard. Sometime after that, thieves had come in through a window and removed his body, leaving stones in its place in the coffin. It was not until at least a day later, when picking up the coffin and hearing the clatter of stones shifting inside, that the theft was discovered.

She heard of certain rooms in the vaults, hidden, isolated from others, being used to store dead bodies for a day or two until they could be transported to the schools and sold. The cool temperatures helped to preserve the bodies a bit longer, especially now, during the summer. Caden confirmed the plausibility of this, as he said he had stumbled across a dead woman a few days before. She was dressed in fine clothing, not like what they saw on the denizens of the vaults, and someone had wrapped her in a blanket.

So, when Caden said he found a better place, Fiona didn't even bother to ask for details. She stood and started folding their blankets while Caden began gathering up their other possessions and stuffing them in their canvas bags. The others barely paid them any heed, other than to eye the space they were vacating.

Caden threw the bags over his shoulders, his arms through the drawstrings, then maneuvered his crutches between the other people, while Fiona followed carrying blankets. Leading her through the next room, then down a dark hallway, and finally, up a narrow stairway, they emerged into the escalating heat of a July morning.

Fiona squinted at the sunlight but, with her hands full, couldn't shield her eyes. Caden, experiencing the same, paused for a few moments to give their eyes time to adjust. As they stood there, Fiona's attention was drawn to a familiar voice.

"Fiona?" She turned and saw her old family friend, Walter Scott, limping toward her. He had a book in one hand and his cane in the other, but at sight of her, he put his arms out to her.

"Wattie?" she replied. She dropped the blankets she was carrying and went into his outstretched arms. If he was put off by the smell that she knew must be clinging to herself or her clothing, he gave no indication of it.

"Dear girl," he said warmly as she pulled away, "'tis so good to see ye, though I wish it were under better circumstances." Fiona looked down, embarrassed by her appearance. "Your father told me ye had run away."

"Me father's no longer in full possession of his faculties," she replied, disconcerted.

"Aye, I've suspected as much."

"Caden lost his business last December," Fiona explained, motioning to her husband. Scott shook his hand, nodding. "We lost our house shortly after."

"I'm so sorry," Scott said sympathetically. "'Tis been a rough time for many. I've been hard-pressed meself, after me printing business collapsed. I've resisted bankruptcy, as I can still write, so I'm hoping to be able to pay me debts. But I know too many aren't in a position to have that opportunity."

He looked down at the book that was in his hand as if surprised to be reminded that it was still there.

"Speaking of me writing," he said, "I was taking this to give to a friend, but I'll get him another one. 'Tis me latest novel." He handed it to Fiona. She looked at the title, The Fair Maid of Perth. "I want ye to have it."

He reached into his coat and pulled out a pen. He unscrewed the top and took the book from her, inscribing the title page:

To the fairest maid of Edinburgh.
With affection, Wattie.

Looking at the inscription, Fiona's eyes filled with tears. Holding the book to her chest, she looked back at Scott, smiling her thanks, not trusting her voice.

"Where are ye staying?" Scott asked. Fiona glanced at Caden before replying.

"Caden's found us a new place," she said evasively. "We're going there now."

"Ah, a new home," he smiled. "I hope ye enjoy it." He glanced around. "Well, me dear, I must be on me way. But 'twas wonderful to see ye. We must visit again soon."

"Aye, we must. Please give me love to Charlotte." Scott's face appeared pained as he looked at Fiona.

"Oh, me dear," he said quietly, "Charlotte passed away a couple of months ago."

"Wattie, I'm so sorry!" Fiona, her eyes again deluged with tears, held Scott in a lingering embrace as he patted her back.

"Thank ye, lass." He allowed her to cry for a few moments before he pushed her away. "And now, me dear, I'm afraid I really must be going. But I meant what I said about visiting again."

"Of course," Fiona said, backing away from him as she wiped away the tears, smearing the dirt on her face.

As they said good-bye and Fiona watched him walk away, she saw another familiar face down the street. This one, though, was not a welcome sight.

He was standing partially around a corner, watching her from the shadows of a building. But Fiona saw him clearly enough to recognize the man who had attacked her almost a year ago. She started to mention it to Caden, until Caden broke down in a fit of coughing. Remembering his condition, not only with the cough, but also his missing leg, she decided that it might be best to not draw his attention to the man.

She picked up the blankets that she had dropped, and she cast a quick glance down the street again. She was relieved to not see the man any longer. She put on a cheerful face as she turned to Caden.

"Alright, me love," she said, "lead the way."

It wasn't far. A minute or so later, Caden led her into a vestibule that sheltered two doors. One led into a book store which had closed up shop, possibly another victim of last year's panic. The other door led into a dark, narrow staircase, much like the others that descended into the vaults.

It was a fairly small room, as dark as the other parts of the vaults they had spent time in. There were two doors, the one they entered from the staircase, and one on the opposite side of the room. That one had a large wedge-shaped stone pressed against the base of it, so it would presumably allow no admittance from anywhere else in the vaults.

"I dinnae ken what this room was used for," Caden said. "Possibly storage for the book seller upstairs." There were a few sturdy shelves built along one wall. "But wi' the shop closed up noo, I dinnae think anybody else is aware o' this place."

"Caden," Fiona said as she looked about the room, "it's perfect."

"I think 'perfect' is stretchin' it a bit, but aye, 'tis a fair sight better than anythin' we've had in a while."

§

Caden and Fiona lay panting on the floor of their dark room which they immediately started calling their flat. There was a single candle burning on one of the shelves, illuminating the portrait of Caden that Fiona had painted. Down below, the candle illuminated Caden and Fiona's bare, glistening skin. The stone floor of the room was hard and cold through the blankets that formed a thin pallet for them and, as always, there was a chill in the air. But for now, it felt good.

Caden was lying on his side, his arm under Fiona's neck. They gazed into each other's eyes, their fingers entwined.

"Me love," Caden said, "'tis been far too lang since we've made love. Noo that we ha' this fine flat tae ourselves, let's not wait that lang again."

Fiona smiled at him, the sweet, relaxed smile that he remembered fondly, but hadn't seen in several months.

"I agree," she said. "I've missed this so."

"Ye're an amazin' woman," Caden said with a sigh.

"Amazing?" Fiona scoffed. "What have I done to merit such a sobriquet?"

"I vowed tae care and provide for ye. Since then, I've lost me business an' our home. I'm barely able tae provide any food for ye, an' our home, 'til this verra moment, has been stone cells shared wi' any number o' other inmates.

"And yet ye've ne'er once complained aboot it, but instead, ye've stood beside me through it all."

"I've stood beside ye because that's where I belong. I made vows too, Caden. I promised to love and respect ye, in good times and bad. We've had good times, and now we're having bad. We'll have good ones again, but what kind of wife would I be if I stood beside ye only when things were good?"

"Fiona Loganach, I don't deserve ye."

"Well, I agree with ye," she replied, "but likely for a different reason than ye're thinking." Caden looked at her, his eyebrows bunching together. "It's because of me that ye lost your leg," she explained, and she kept on more forcefully when she saw him start to interrupt. "That may not be why ye lost your business, but it's largely why ye haven't been able to get a job since then. So one could argue that it's me own fault that we're in this situation now. Ye certainly don't deserve that."

"Me dear, ye couldnae be further from the truth. I lost me leg because I didnae follow your advice tae have it cared for right away. And besides, no matter wha' it cost me, I'm glad I was there, because I couldnae imagine me life wi'oot ye."

Fiona sighed and moved closer to him, kissing him tenderly. Caden took her in his arms. One arm held her around her back, while his other hand softly caressed her breast. He returned her kiss hungrily, and just as the cold was starting to settle upon them, they felt the heat building again.

## 36

As the darkness of the vaults dissipated, Suzy began to see the other candles burning on the table, the one in front of her flickering from her panting. Then, she saw all the worried faces gathered around looking at her.

"Shit," she said under her breath.

"She's back," somebody said, and there seemed to be a collective sigh from most of the ladies.

"Did you see your ghost?" Emily asked.

"What?" Suzy looked at her, then shot an accusing look at Rachel. "You told them?"

"I had to," Rachel replied defensively. "They wanted to call 911."

"You were catatonic and unresponsive to external stimuli," said Jessica Forsyth. "Your breathing was shallow and your pulse was thready." When everybody looked at her, she shrugged. "What? I like medical shows."

"So?" Emily resumed. "Did you see your ghost?"

"That's not really the way it works," Suzy said uncomfortably, fighting back the embarrassment. "She's not a ghost. At least not when I see her in the visions." She related very quickly and without detail what she saw. "It's just like I'm watching a movie. Or like I'm acting out someone else's life."

"Wow, how many of those mushrooms did you have?" Jessica joked, and there was a little scattered laughter as the mood lightened.

Suzy looked at the women gathered around her, and she noticed a variety of expressions. A few, like Emily, were fascinated and wanted to know more. Some seemed doubtful, and a number of them looked stern and critical. Not surprisingly, Helen Stewart was among the latter. Standing ramrod straight a few feet away from the group, her face as icy as her blue-tinged hair, Suzy noticed that disapproval seemed to be her prevailing expression.

"You all may think this is funny," Helen said coldly, "but this is a serious thing. It's not something to be toyed with."

"I guarantee, Helen," Suzy said, "I'm not toying with it. It's not even something I sought or asked for."

"Then you should fight against it. Deuteronomy says that 'there shall not be found among you anyone that useth divination, or an enchanter, or a witch, or a charmer, or a consulter with familiar spirits, or a wizard, or a necromancer.' 'Resist the devil, and he will flee from you.'"

"Yeah, I'll remember that," Suzy replied, "if I ever see the devil. But I assure you Fiona's not Satan."

"You're so naïve," Helen said, shaking her head disdainfully. "You really believe this entity is a ghost?"

"Do you believe in an afterlife?" Suzy asked her.

"Of course."

"So, what happens to a person when they die?"

"It depends on what kind of life they've lived."

"So, heaven or hell are the only options? How can you be so certain?"

"Because I know my Bible, Suzy Drummond," Helen replied arrogantly. "Who do you think is behind these supernatural visions you're having?"

"The name is Quinn, Mrs. Stewart," Suzy said, purposely becoming more formal with her, feeling her annoyance growing. "And I've spoken to Fiona. She's a very sweet, kind person."

"Yes, 'Satan himself is transformed into an angel of light.'"

"I get it. We're all super impressed with how many scriptures you can recite. I remember one or two myself. Like 'be tolerant of one another and forgive each other.'"

"Are you asking my forgiveness?" Helen asked haughtily, standing in an almost clichéd position of looking down her nose at Suzy.

"No, Helen, I'm not asking you to forgive me, *I* forgive *you* for being such a bitch."

"Okay, ladies," Rachel intervened, "I think everybody needs to just dial it down a couple of notches." But the damage was done.

Helen took in a deep breath, her nostrils flaring widely, and her face suffused with color. Her lips turned into a severe, thin slash across her face as the tendons stood out sharply against the soft drapes of skin on her neck. She looked at two of the other members, older women who had carpooled with her, and responding to some unseen signal, they scooted their chairs back and rose to leave with Helen.

Rachel cast a pointed look at Suzy, then turned back to Helen.

"Helen, come on," she said, "Suzy's a smart aleck. I mean nobody knows that better than I do. She can be a little maddening to me, too."

"A smart aleck is one thing," Helen said coldly. "Blasphemy is another altogether. She has no excuse. Miss *Quinn* was brought up by God-fearing parents, but she's choosing to turn her back on God's clear instructions."

"This is not a religious group, Helen," Rachel implored. "We're a group of women from all different backgrounds united in a common ancestral cause."

"Do you remember what our motto is? 'God, Home and Country.' God is the first part of what we stand for. And I'll have nothing to do with someone who willfully turns her back on him."

"It's okay, Rachel," Suzy said. "As soon as this Pharisee and her zoilist ideologies take leave of me hoose, I'll ne're darken her brow again."

All heads turned to Suzy.

"What?" she asked.

§

"What the hell was that?" Rachel asked after everyone left.

"I don't know, Rachel. Maybe these nineteenth century people are rubbing off on me."

She had never heard the word 'zoilist' before in her life. She had to look it up to even understand the point she had made.

"Well, that was weird enough. But what about that whole exchange with Helen?"

"Oh, shit," Suzy said disgustedly, "she's a self-righteous asshole."

"I know that. But she's also a respected member of the community, and of the Daughters."

"About that," Suzy replied carefully, "I'm not sure this is right for me."

"What's not right for you?"

"The 'ladies' socials.' That's just not me. And the sales calls. I'm too much of an introvert to do that sort of thing on a regular basis. I mean don't get me wrong, I believe in the Daughters. I believe in their cause and their patriotism. This country could certainly use more *true* patriots now, but even more than that, it needs more tolerance. And Mrs. Holier-Than-Thou is exactly the kind of person that's tearing this country apart."

She expected Rachel to deny it. She was surprised.

"Yeah, I know," Rachel replied. "And quite frankly, I was surprised when you called me a few months ago and volunteered. I'm shocked you lasted as long as you did."

Suzy looked at her friend and felt the anger drain away.

"Thank you for understanding."

"I'm the best friend of Marblehead's number one smartass. Understanding is in my job description." Suzy smiled sheepishly at her. "So, what are you going to do now?"

"Well," Suzy said as the thought entered her head, "I think I'm going to start planning a trip to Scotland."

# 37

Beltane is an ancient Gaelic May Day festival. Celebrated on or about May 1, or roughly between the spring equinox and the summer solstice, the origins of the festival can be traced back several centuries before being shrouded in Celtic mythology.

Originally an agricultural celebration, the festival always included rituals around special bonfires which were believed to hold protective powers over the crops and livestock. In modern versions of Beltane, there came to be less of a connection to agriculture and an increased affiliation with new age beliefs of Celtic neopagans and Wiccans.

When Fin discovered that there was a Beltane festival in the Denver area, he decided he had to go.

§

"What's this called again?" Kay asked.

"Beltane," Fin replied. "It's an ancient Celtic agricultural festival."

"Hmm." Kay looked out the window as Fin drove and stole occasional glances at her legs. She had made an impression on him again when he picked her up that morning. Wearing black tights and a somewhat baggy sweater that terminated just below her hips, Kay looked sexier than ever. Fin suddenly considered staying home and exploring the curves that her clothing both revealed and suggested.

But he resisted. In the three weeks since they met for dinner that first time, they had been cautiously testing the waters with each other. Fin particularly wanted to be sure. If it happened again with Kay, he wanted it to last this time. He wanted it to be real. He didn't want it to be simply a relationship fueled by sex, or worse, a bad relationship camouflaged by sex. So they had gone out on a few chaste dates, though sometimes they stayed in for home-cooked meals and a TV show or DVD.

But they had only begun getting a bit more intimate a week before, with simple closed-mouth kisses. Kay lobbied for more, but again, Fin held back. He didn't trust his self-control if they started going *there*.

He saw a sign announcing their destination and he pulled off the road. The festival was being held on a ranch in the wooded foothills a few miles west of Denver, and the introvert in him groaned inwardly as he saw the rows and rows of cars. But he kept it to himself as he parked where he was directed.

A split rail fence separated the parking area from the festival itself, and a few ticket-takers were positioned at the gate, dressed in various old-world-style outfits. Fin took note of the costumes for possible use in his book. He also noticed that several attendees had come in costume as well. A number of warriors, complete with broadswords and battle axes, mingled with women dressed like Stevie Nicks. Men in kilts wandered around with women in filmy, flowing Renaissance-style dresses.

Like every state and city festival that Fin had attended, there were also booths featuring the food and wares of local merchants, though the ones here often had at least a hint of Celtic flavor. At lunch time, for instance, Fin tried Haggis for the first time in his life, while Kay looked a little disgustedly at it. But she loved the mead that flowed abundantly.

After her second cup, Kay made a comment after a man dressed in full Scottish regalia walked by.

"I'd like to see *you* in a kilt."

"Why?" Fin asked hesitantly, looking askance at her. "You like cross-dressers?"

"A man in a kilt isn't a cross-dresser, you moron," she scolded, but with a smile. "It's sexy!"

"What's sexy about seeing a guy's bare hairy legs?"

He watched her as she watched the man maneuver his way through the crowd. He glanced at the man as he walked away, ahead of them, and back at Kay.

"I'm not entirely sure," she pondered. "I think a man in a kilt just seems to exude a certain sexy confidence. You can see it in his swagger."

"Hmm." She seemed to have noticed that Fin wasn't completely convinced of her reasoning, and she went in for the kill.

"And it also doesn't hurt knowing that they're not wearing any underwear."

"Quick access, huh?"

"You know it, mister!" she grinned.

After that brief exchange, Fin was kind of aroused and wishing that *he* could give her some quick access, but alas, he was wearing jeans.

And they were in public.

"Don't worry, though," she said as she leaned against him, apparently noticing the disappointed look on his face, "I only have eyes for you."

Fin suddenly felt all warm and gushy. He didn't have any choice after that but to put his arm around Kay and pull her close. She smiled up at him and kissed him. And this time, they lingered, their lips open, their tongues exploring.

They spent most of the day wandering around, sampling the food and drink, listening to Celtic music, and holding hands despite how sweaty they got as the day warmed up. They explored booths dedicated to tracing one's Celtic genealogy and tartans, booths packed with crystals and tarot cards, and a couple of booth owners even surreptitiously shared shots of whisky with them.

And, of course, the ubiquitous mead. The sweetness of the honey wine was deceiving, and after a few cups of it, Fin noticed the rosy glow on Kay's face.

"Are you about ready to go?" he asked as the sun was setting. Kay looked up at him, her face showing almost disbelief that he would suggest such a thing.

"No!" she said. "Don't you want to stay for the bonfire and the dancing?" If Fin were to answer her honestly, he would have said that no, he wanted to take her home, strip off her sweater and tights, and make fevered, sweaty love to her.

Instead, they walked to a location behind a barn where cut logs, broken branches and dry brush leaned against each other six to eight feet high. A ring of torches surrounded the stack, illuminating the area.

In time, a group of men beating on drums thundered out from the barn, and the crowd parted as a procession of women, in two columns, came out behind them. Carrying fresh-budding tree branches, their faces were painted with swirling patterns, and ribbons and vines were woven and braided in their hair. They were dressed in flowing garments, though Fin was surprised to see a few of them had the top of their garments open, revealing their breasts.

The procession continued around the future bonfire, the drummers and the women interacting with some of the spectators. The rapid staccato of the drums seemed to stir everyone up, and there was a great deal of cheering and chanting as others emerged from the barn.

Fin saw a man, naked except for a loincloth, his entire body painted green, and a woman arrayed in a flowing white costume covered with leaves and flowers. They moved toward each other, weaving about in a sort of teasing dance, almost touching several times but pulling away at the last moment. As the play progressed, the green man was apparently killed, but was then reborn.

Their teasing dance began anew, with flirts and invitations passing playfully between them, until finally, they came together. As they kissed, the women from the earlier procession lit their branches on the torches that surrounded the area, then touched them to the dry brush in the center, lighting the bonfire.

As the wood caught fire and began to blaze, others came running out of the barn, men and women wearing nothing but small loincloths, their bodies painted red, their dance much more frenzied. They twirled around each other, their naked bodies glistening and reflecting the blaze of the bonfire.

Fin never saw where the drummers ended up, but the drumbeats intensified and the dancers began interacting more closely and athletically. Fin saw one of the women jump toward a man, and he caught her, balancing her body across his shoulder. A number of times, several of them came together to form small human pyramids, and a few times, Fin realized the potential embarrassment of trying to find handholds on naked bodies. The dancers seemed unconcerned, though.

As the dance progressed, a few of them beckoned toward some of the onlookers, and Fin noticed a few of the onlookers becoming participants. Men and women, perhaps fueled by mead and Scotch, lost their inhibitions and began swirling around with the red dancers. Whether they felt overdressed, or were just caught up in the moment, they started shedding their clothes, some down to their underwear, a few braver souls down to nothing.

"Come on," Kay shouted over the drums, taking his hand in hers. At first, he started moving with her, thinking she was ready to go, but then he realized that she was trying to pull him toward the dancers.

"What? No!" he replied horrified, pulling his hand away.

"Why not?" she asked, clearly disappointed.

"I haven't had nearly enough alcohol to feel comfortable doing that."

"Well, maybe we should get you some more alcohol!" Kay was moving sinuously in front of him, and he was amazed that this fully – albeit sexily – clothed woman could pull his attention away from a group of naked gyrating dancers.

Except that the fully-clothed part didn't last for long.

As he watched, Kay was swinging her hips and her shoulders in time with the drumming, working all the planes and curves that had intrigued him that morning. Though her eyes were a little glazed, she kept them on Fin as she pulled her sweater over her head.

"Kay!" he exclaimed, reaching in a panic for the sweater. He was able to grab hold of it, but Kay let go, continuing to dance sinuously in front of him wearing only her black tights, a thin nude bra and ankle-high boots. "What the fuck are you doing?"

"I'm enjoying myself, silly," she replied as if nothing could have been more obvious.

Fin tried to grasp her by the shoulders, but she laughed and backed out of his reach. As other spectators nearby saw what she was doing, they started cheering her on, and she reacted to the crowd, smiling at them as she reached behind her back and unhooked her bra. She twirled the bra over her head a few times and hurled it into the bonfire as those closest to her erupted in even louder cheers. As she put more space between herself and Fin, others filled it, and Fin could only see occasional glimpses of her now as she bent down to take off her boots and peel off her tights.

Still, Fin tried to press through the crowd to get to her, but she was already away, mixing with the fire dancers. Knowing she would want clothing, and hopefully be aghast at what she had done, when she finally came to her senses, he gathered up her tights and boots.

He watched in chagrin as Kay leaned forward and shook her breasts back and forth at a naked man who, judging by his flesh-colored flesh and exposed dangling penis, unencumbered by a loincloth, was not one of the official fire dancers, but one of the former spectators.

In some dark, private compartment in the back of his mind, Fin was turned on watching all the bouncing and jiggling breasts and penises. But he was, admittedly, quite disconcerted that Kay's breasts were among those jiggling in front of everyone.

§

"I never realized you were such a prude," Kay mumbled, quietly settling back in her seat as Fin drove toward her home.

"I'm not a prude," Fin replied bitterly, "but I never wanted a wife that I had to share with everyone else."

"You make me sound like a whore."

"I'm not saying you had sex with anyone, Kay. Not yet, anyway. But you were dancing naked with other naked people. With naked men."

"I got caught up in the heat of the moment," she said, sounding as if she felt a little sick. "Didn't you feel it? Didn't you feel anything?"

"I felt moved by the performance and the drumming. And I admit I was a little turned on by the nude dancers. But I certainly wasn't moved to strip naked and dance with them!"

"A lot of people were out there dancing naked, Fin. It was expected."

"No, it was not expected. Most of the people there were just spectators."

"Life is not a spectator sport," Kay slurred. "If you're just watching what's going on, you're wasting your life. You know who said that?" She made a scoffing sound. "What am I saying? Of course you don't know. It was a famous baseball player, Jackie Robinson."

"Women relate dancing to sex," Fin fired back. "You know who said that? Will Smith, in *Hitch*."

Kay sighed disgustedly and turned to look out the window at the darkness rushing by. She couldn't see much except for reflections of themselves from the dashboard lights. Unable to hold her head up, she let it collapse back on the headrest.

Fin let go of the steering wheel with his right hand and flexed it a few times, exhaling through his teeth at the pain. Kay saw the motion reflected in the window and turned back to him.

"You know," she said, "I think that was the first manly thing I've ever seen you do."

What finally got them away from the festival was an act of violence. Kay was dancing seductively in front of a naked man who seemed at least as inebriated as she was. When she shook her breasts at him, he responded by thrusting his hips forward and back, slapping his penis against his lower belly several times.

Kay laughed until she noticed his penis growing more erect each time. Her eyes were drawn to it, watching it with hungry fascination. Fin watched from the crowd in dismay and embarrassment as she reached for it, first letting it slap against her hand as they continued their dance. Then, she wrapped her fingers around it and used it as a handle to pull the man toward her.

The man reacted by grabbing her. He pulled her up against him and reached down in an attempt to enter her. As they were still moving to the frenzied drumming, he wasn't successful at penetration, but only managed to get his penis between her legs. Still, when he began thrusting his crotch back and forth against hers, they both seemed to appreciate the sensation.

Fin had seen enough and pushed his way through the crowd. He noticed, to his chagrin, that Kay didn't seem to be resisting the man, but he still felt obligated to defend her diminishing honor. He grabbed the man's shoulder and pulled him off of her.

"Hey," the man sputtered, his penis bouncing up and down, "leave us alone, asshole!" He staggered a little and reached for Kay, and ended up grabbing hold of her breast. Fin didn't think reasoning with the man would do any good. He punched him in the jaw. He grabbed Kay's wrist and thrust her clothes into her arms.

"If you're still so disgusted with me," Fin said, gripping the steering wheel with a little less tension, "why did you ever suggest giving us another try?"

"Because I'm fucking broke," she laboriously said as her head collapsed on the headrest again.

Fin glanced over at her and saw that she seemed to be asleep.

*Wine, the original truth serum.*

## 38

Suzy had mixed feelings. Withdrawing from the local telephone group of the Daughters of the American Revolution had been the wise choice. She didn't feel cut out for meeting regularly with what she considered typical "ladies' groups." She knew that not all of them sat around gossiping, but there were enough of them that it made her uncomfortable.

Throw into the mix the judgmental hyper-Christians like Helen Stewart, and it often made for an irritating dynamic. It didn't help that this dynamic sometimes increased the likelihood that Suzy would exacerbate the situation with her smartassery.

So she knew that leaving was the right thing to do.

At the same time, it put her right back into her previous routines, where she spent most of her time alone in her house. Being something of an introvert, she didn't mind being alone. And home was where she was most comfortable.

But it also meant she had less to distract her from her memories. Springtime, though, didn't hold as many reminders as October did. Reminders were everywhere, certainly. Photos of Mark and Emma, articles of décor that Suzy and Mark had picked out together, the toys in Emma's room.

And, of course, the two urns on the mantle.

But Suzy noticed that the difficult feelings weren't as acute. The painful memories were not as pervasive. The pain was not as sharp. They were all still there, naturally, but time and seasons had, not so much healed them, but dulled them a bit.

Maybe things were starting to look up.

§

"Hello, I'm Michelle Arthur with the *Salem Dispatch*. Is this Suzanne Quinn?"

"Yes, it is," Suzy replied suspiciously.

"Hi, Ms. Quinn. I'm calling about the reported spirit activity on your property. I may be interested in writing a column about it. What can you tell me about this ghost?"

"I'm sorry, who is this again?"

"Michelle Arthur. I'm a human interest journalist with the *Salem Dispatch*."

"How did you get my number?" Suzy was starting to feel a little pissed. "And who told you about this?"

"I'm sorry, Ms. Quinn, I can't say."

"I'm not a judge asking you to divulge your sources. I'm a private citizen wondering who the hell invaded my privacy."

"All I'm looking for is corroboration, Ms. Quinn, and some details if you can provide them. Can you confirm this haunting?"

"I will do no such thing. It's none of your fucking business."

"Ms. Quinn, there's no need to get hostile. All I'm asking for is input on your side of the story I'm writing."

"You just said you *may* be interested in writing a column. Now that I'm not giving you any information, you're *definitely* writing it?"

"Ms. Quinn, I'm giving you an opportunity here to confirm or deny the report."

"I'm giving *you* the opportunity to back off. Leave me the hell alone and I won't press charges."

## 39

I have some news," Fiona said warily. She was nervous, but Caden didn't seem to notice. He had returned later than usual to their flat.

"I ha' some news too, me dear," he replied enthusiastically. He was in an unusual mood. He seemed happy and excited, but a little shaken as well. He paused for another coughing fit, but it didn't seem to shake his mood

"What is it, love?" Fiona asked as she helped him settle on the pallet of blankets. He put his crutches aside, then held up two strips of heavy paper as Fiona sat next to him. Fiona took them and turned them toward the candle. They were tickets of passage to Boston, Massachusetts, in the United States of America.

She looked back at Caden, puzzled. He smiled and made himself comfortable to relate the story.

He had gone above ground that morning, like every other morning, to look for work. He followed leads he had heard about at shipping companies and others, but was, as usual, turned away. A man missing a leg and with a chronic cough just didn't seem like a good investment.

He spent the afternoon begging on Cowgate. It had been a hot late August afternoon, and he sought the shade from the arch of the South Bridge. As he mopped the perspiration from his face, a woman wearing expensive clothing stopped in front of him. Her face was not greatly etched with age, but her features seemed to be dragged down by a severe melancholy.

"Good day t'ye, ma'am," Caden said quietly. She didn't respond, but she opened the drawstrings of her handbag and reached inside. Caden stood there, eyes down in embarrassment, as he waited to see how much she would give him. She pulled out a wad of pound notes and looked at them for a moment, as if not sure what to do with them. Then, she handed them to Caden.

"I – are ye sure, ma'am?" Caden asked, his eyes wide. Still, she said nothing, but she saw something else in her bag. She pulled out the two tickets to America and gave them to Caden.

He looked at them, his mouth open, then looked back up to the lady's face, but she was already turning to walk away. He quickly stuffed her gifts in his pockets and fumbled with his crutches to follow.

"Ma'am, ye're too generous," he said, coming alongside her. "Are ye sure aboot this?" he asked again.

"I don't need them anymore," she said, her voice a monotone, as she turned right, walking up Blair Street. "He's gone." Caden quickly turned to follow, but was having trouble keeping up.

"I'm sorry, ma'am," he said, trying to sound sympathetic despite his panting, "who's gone?"

"'Tis over," she replied, as if she hadn't heard him. "'Tis all over." Caden heard her repeat that phrase several times as she continued on her way. Caden noticed as they passed the location where Fiona had been attacked and Caden intervened. Was it really only a year ago? He was momentarily distracted by the memory, but then he struggled to catch up to the lady.

As his breath rasped up and down his throat, he was struck by a coughing fit and he stopped, leaning on his crutches, as he tried to suppress it. When he got the cough under control, he took off after the woman again, but she was several paces ahead by now, and just turning to the right on High Street.

By the time he arrived there, he turned and went several yards, scanning the street ahead of him, but he couldn't see her. He was standing near the front of the Tron Kirk when he heard someone scream. The sound was followed by a dull thud behind him and a collective gasp from people standing nearby.

Turning around, Caden was dismayed to see the woman he had been following, face down on the street. The spire of the church had been destroyed in the great fire a couple of years before, but gaining access to what was left of it, she had jumped to her death.

Fiona looked at Caden, her eyes wide, as he finished relating the story.

"The poor dear," she whispered.

"Aye," Caden said. "In her great despair, her last livin' act was one o' such generosity that I shall e'er remember her, e'en though I ne'er knew her."

*Fiona looked at the tickets again. The ship was set to sail in a month, at the end of September. She wasn't sure how she felt about leaving her family. But as she pondered, she realized that her father, in the course of losing his rationality, had already cast her out. Aileen, lost in her grief, had done the same.*

*She sighed as she looked up at Caden.*

*"We can have a better life noo, me love," Caden said, "in the New World." Fiona smiled and wiped a tear from her eye.*

*"That makes my news even better," she replied.*

*"Och, tha's right," Caden said, "ye said ye had news, too."*

*"Aye," Fiona replied with a nervous smile. "I think I'm finally with child."*

§

*Fiona felt as if she could breathe freely as she stood in the sunshine. Having their own private vault, she often felt compelled to come outside and breathe relatively fresh air and feel sunshine on her face. There was still the chance that somebody else could discover their home, but she never went far, so she could still be in sight of the door into the vestibule.*

*This afternoon, she was surprised by a familiar face.*

*"Mrs. Loganach," Lachlan said as he stepped around to look her in the face. "I thought that was you."*

*"Mr. Mac an Léigh!" Fiona's face reflected a mix of emotions similar to when she had seen Scott, primarily joy and embarrassment. "What are ye doing down here?"*

*"I was visiting me brother," he replied, then he shrugged. "For what it's worth. He's ne'er happy tae see me. But what aboot you? How are ye faring?" No doubt he noticed the difference in her appearance and her hygiene, but he made no mention of it.*

*"Caden and I are doing as well as one can expect," she replied evasively. Lachlan seemed curious about their circumstances, but was too much of a gentleman to ask. The cellar under the bookstore, being closed off from the rest of the vaults, was not as fetid as the other sections that they had stayed in previously, and Fiona hoped that the stench was not clinging to her as before. Still, she wanted to get the discussion off of her. "Your brother does not appreciate your visits?"*

"Nay, Duncan is proud. Not too proud tae accept money when I offer it, but proud enough that it angers him tae be reminded of what he's lost. Alas, considering his choices in the way of expenditures, I've decided tae stop giving him money, so he's nae too pleased tae see me."

"I'm so sorry," Fiona replied sympathetically.

"Thank ye. I hope you're doing well."

Again, Fiona was embarrassed to tell how they were really faring, so again, she was ambiguous.

"We're abiding. Caden lost his shipping business in the panic last year, and he's looking for work now."

"I'm sorry tae hear that. I had heard that ye had run away. I'm glad it was nothing quite so philistine, but I wish your husband success in his search."

"Thank ye, Mr. Mac an Léigh."

"And now," Lachlan said, adopting a hurried demeanor, "I fear I must go. I've been invited by the Lord Provost tae speak before the city council. I'm hoping tae influence them tae do something about the vaults, and about the poor living in them."

"Oh, Mr. Mac an Léigh, I wish ye much success there!"

As he turned, Fiona was dismayed to, once again, catch a glimpse of the man who attacked her a year ago. He was watching her and Lachlan, and when Lachlan looked in his direction as he walked away, the man ducked behind a corner.

Keeping an eye on that corner, Fiona ran toward the door to the flat.

Caden's cough was finally getting better. He had gone through a rough period when he caught a cold about a week ago. The fever and other symptoms had intensified the cough, but Fiona did what she could to keep him warm and comfortable.

When the cold first took hold, Caden had wanted to continue going above ground to scrounge what food and money he could, not only for their meager meals now, but in preparation for their trip to America. But Fiona forbade it. She insisted that he get as much rest as he could, and it had paid off.

After he had come back with the tickets, they had smoothed out and counted the money. There were twenty-five brand new one pound notes, issued by the Royal Bank of Scotland. They moved the candle closer so they could see the notes better. They were amazed at the detail. Printed on both sides, which they had never seen before, they featured a portrait of King George IV.

Caden had wrapped the money and the tickets in a scrap of cloth and, lacking an abundance of hiding places in their room, hid it under their pallet of blankets. He hoped to save as much as possible to give them a decent start in their new life.

Twenty-five pounds was a far cry from what he used to have, but in their current situation, it was quite a respectable amount. Still, he didn't know anything about the economy of America, so he hoped to keep collecting as much as possible before then. He had never become comfortable with begging, but given their current goal, and the fact that it was only a temporary situation, he decided it was a necessary evil.

§

"Caden Loganach, ye'll not be going up there," Fiona said sternly, her fists on her hips, looking at him as if he were a disobedient child.

"I'm feelin' much better, noo," he argued, "And 'tis warmer ootdoors than it is in 'ere."

Fiona responded by raising an eyebrow at him.

"Ye're still weak," she replied. "Ye need to rest. Ye don't want to have a relapse before we set sail."

Caden sighed, knowing she was right.

"Try and get some sleep," Fiona suggested, her voice softening. "That's what ye need more than anything. Maybe in the morning ye can go upstairs."

"Yes, dear," Caden said with a smile and an exaggerated submissive tone. He lay down on the pallet and covered up with the brown wool blanket. "Ye goin' up for your afternoon sun noo?"

Over the last few days, Fiona had made a habit of going outside to enjoy a little sun while Caden napped in the afternoon.

"Aye," she replied. She knelt down and adjusted the blanket for him, tucking it around his neck. Caden looked lovingly up at her and smiled.

"Ah, Fiona, I'm the luckiest jimmy in th' world." Fiona raised her eyebrow again, giving him a skeptical glance, with a meaningful look around their dark, cold cell.

"Of course ye are, love," she said with a smile, and she leaned down and kissed his forehead. "Get some rest."

Fiona went up the stairs and out onto the street, keeping her eyes shaded until they grew accustomed to the light. Not only did she love the light, but the warmth was always so welcome after hours down below.

It was late in the afternoon, and the sun was starting to drop behind some of the taller structures, so Fiona walked around, following the thinning shafts of sunlight that continued to shine between buildings.

She felt as if she had to push herself. She just didn't feel as well as she used to. Her pregnancy, in the mean conditions in which she was living, was making itself known. Two months into it, her clothes had begun to feel tighter, so she had let some of them out during the hours she spent down in the flat. But beyond that, she didn't have the stamina she had before.

As always, as she was walking, she kept her eyes busy scanning the area around her, having seen her attacker twice since they had moved to this area. Her attention was rewarded by seeing a pleasantly familiar face.

"Mr. Mac an Léigh," she said, smiling at the man approaching her.

"Good afternoon, Mrs. Loganach," he replied with a smile.

"Are ye doon here visiting your brother again?"

"Aye, I was hoping tae visit him, but I couldn't find him. I'm glad now that me trip was not all for naught. Are ye doing well? And your husband?"

"We are. Caden was ill a week or so ago, but he's on the mend now."

"'Tis good tae hear. Ye know, I've mentioned ye both to me brother. I doubt he's sought ye out, but I told him I had friends living doon in this area."

"Nay, I'm afraid I've not met him."

"'Tis probably just as well. For yourself, anyway. Ye probably wouldn't care much for him, but he could certainly use the influence of decent people."

"Ye're too kind, Mr. Mac an Léigh," Fiona blushed. "And what of you? I seem to only see ye in passing lately."

"Aye," Lachlan smiled, "I have been keeping meself quite busy. But I'm happy tae say that I have a few minutes tae spend with ye now."

"Last time I saw ye, ye were on your way to speak to the city council about the vaults. Did it result in anything beneficial?"

"I've been invited tae speak again," he replied with a shrug. "I'm finding that government involves a tremendous amount of talking before any doing."

"Well," Fiona replied, "I suppose an invitation to return is a step in the right direction."

"Aye, I suppose it is, at that." Lachlan glanced around. "What about your husband? Has he had any success in his search for employment?"

"Nay, I'm afraid he has not. But we do have good news. We're going to America next week."

Surprise blanketed Lachlan's face, and Fiona decided to tell him their entire story. Lachlan was shocked to learn how greatly they had been affected by the Panic, but he was touched by the story of how they acquired the tickets to Massachusetts.

"Is Mr. Loganach nearby?" he asked.

"Aye, I forced him to get some more rest. He's probably awake now, though."

"I haven't seen him since your wedding. Do ye think he'd mind?"

"No, not at all," Fiona replied warmly. "I can take ye there. I'm afraid it's a few blocks that way. I tend to wander," she smiled sheepishly.

"That's nae a problem," Lachlan replied. "This is me coach," he said, motioning toward the carriage he had been walking toward when he first saw her.

He helped her in and directed his coachman to drive until asked to stop.

"I've not had contact with ye're father recently," Lachlan said as they got underway. "How is he faring?"

"He's not well," Fiona replied. "The last time I saw him, he was not terribly aware of circumstances, and was being sheltered by his staff."

"'Tis good he has loyal people," Lachlan replied.

"Aye," Fiona agreed. "But it's difficult being on this end of his adversity. I assume it was he who told ye I had 'run away.'"

"'Twas."

Fiona nodded and, looking out the window, motioned that they had reached their destination. Lachlan knocked on the ceiling, and the coachman pulled over to the side of the road. Lachlan opened the door, stepped out and helped Fiona down, and she approached their door.

Out of habit, she glanced both directions as she approached the door. Then she opened it and Lachlan followed her into the vestibule. Opening the door that descended to their flat, she led him down.

"Caden," she called, "we have company."

The stairway was considerably darker than outside, but the candle light ahead helped her eyes to be able to adjust once she was in the room.

Caden wasn't there. Puzzled, she looked around, but the small room was empty.

"If ye'll forgive me," Lachlan said quietly, "perhaps he's gone tae relieve the call of nature."

"But his crutches are still there," Fiona said, pointing to where they stood in the corner. And the brown wool blanket that had covered him was gone, the pallet of blankets rumpled into a shapeless wad. And his plaidie was wadded up beside the crutches. He always wore that when he went out, despite the fact that the tartan was nearly unrecognizable now.

Then, she noticed the other door, or rather she noticed the stone that had blocked it. She could see gouges in the floor, and she saw the stone sitting back against the wall. As it was obviously not as much of an impediment to opening the door as they had thought, it had been pushed across the floor, by the door itself.

"What's in there?" Lachlan asked.

"I'm not sure," Fiona replied, warily. "We've never opened it. We moved in here thinking that this room was private and separated from the rest of the vaults."

Lachlan went to the shelf that held the candle. He picked up the candle holder, and one of several extra candles that lay beside it. He lit the second candle in the flame and handed the candle holder to Fiona.

Pulling on the door, it groaned open and Lachlan stepped through into a hallway, Fiona following him. The flat was at the end of the hallway. The only way to go was to the left. Their candle flames flickered against the stone walls as they explored, looking for any sign of Caden.

They passed a couple of doors on their right, and Lachlan tried each of them. They were both locked. Doorless rooms opened on their left. Arching overhead, they were apparently rooms formed under the arches of the bridge. Illuminated by candles and lanterns, the stench that Fiona remembered from her time spent in them with Caden assaulted their noses. The inevitable dirty faces looked up at them as Lachlan and Fiona studied their features.

Continuing down the hallway, they passed numerous similar rooms, but they never saw Caden. Fiona felt a sensation of building dread, knowing that Caden would never have ventured this far on his own without his crutches.

"Maybe we should go back," Lachlan finally said. "Perhaps he's back there now."

Fiona didn't really believe that, but she nodded and they retraced their steps, finally arriving back in the flat. Still, it was empty.

"Alright," Lachlan said, "why don't ye stay here, just in case your husband returns, and I'll ask around. Surely someone has seen him."

Fiona nodded weakly, her neck muscles stiff. Lachlan took the candle holder from her and placed it back on its shelf. He blew out his candle and put it with the other extras. As Lachlan climbed the steps, Fiona sat down on the rumpled pallet, and as she leaned back against the stone wall, she slipped her hand under the blankets, feeling the cloth-enwrapped money and tickets.

§

What seemed like hours later, Lachlan returned. Fiona still sat, unmoved, where he had left her, her back against the wall. As Fiona took his outstretched hand, Lachlan helped her to her feet, but she was stiff and unsteady. Lachlan grasped her shoulders, helping to support her.

"He has not returned?" he asked, and Fiona shook her head. "I'm afraid I've not found anyone who has seen anyone of his description, but I shall keep looking. It's dark now, though, and people are sleeping. I'm afraid that I must resume me search in the morning."

Fiona nodded listlessly.

"Mrs. Loganach," Lachlan said, holding her shoulders firmly, "I must insist that ye come with me tae me home. Ye can stay in one of me guest rooms. Sleep in an actual bed tonight, and I shall resume me search tomorrow."

"Nay," she replied in a monotone. "If Caden returns, I must be here."

Lachlan looked at her, weighing the options. He was likely horrified at the thought of this well-born woman staying in this awful place alone for one more night, but at the same time, there was a logic to her reasoning. Fiona suspected that Lachlan had begun to doubt that Caden would be returning, but if he did, it would make sense for Fiona to be here. She was an adaptable woman and had adjusted to her mean life in this awful place.

Finally, he agreed and nodded to her.

"Alright," he said, "I shall send me carriage home. I'll stay here with ye, and we can resume our search in the morning. I shall direct me coachman tae return at noon. Surely we shall have discovered Mr. Loganach's whereabouts by then."

Well, damn," Suzy said as she came out of her latest vision. She had been happy for Caden and Fiona, both for their opportunity to come to America, and for expecting their child. But now, she was concerned about Caden. She knew all along that it would not have a happy ending, from her first conversation with Fiona. But having gotten to know them through the visions, and seeing how it worked out, it was becoming quite an emotional experience for her, and a physical drain.

Besides that, seeing Lachlan had reminded her of Fin, and of the way she had left their – what was it? – relationship? She knew he had been disappointed by the brush-off she had given him. But she just hadn't been in a position to be able to pursue a romance with him at the time.

What about now? More than seven months had passed since she had met – and snubbed – him. She remembered the attraction she had felt for him. He had come to mind a few times since then, and she promptly pushed the thought away. But now, for some reason, she was allowing the thought to remain. What had changed between then and now?

She didn't know, but the memory of Fin and their conversations, and especially of sitting across from him at the Dunkin' Donuts in Boston for a few hours, was causing a pleasant sensation in her chest. And it wasn't accompanied by a tormenting feeling of guilt.

*"Are ye finally loosenin' your hold on me, Caden?"* she asked. *"I mean Mark."*

§

After staring at her computer for a little while, she remembered that she had Fin's phone number. So she stared at her phone for a couple of minutes, until she finally figured out what to type and sent him a brief message.

She had just clicked "Send" when she heard her doorbell. It was Rachel.

"Suzy, I am so sorry!" Rachel said the moment Suzy opened the door.

"About what?" Suzy asked with a feeling of building dread. Rachel held out what looked like a little newspaper. Suzy took the paper and stepped aside in a wordless invitation for Rachel to enter, which she did.

Suzy closed the door and looked at the paper. It was the *Salem Dispatch*.

"Page 8," Rachel said. Suzy flipped through the pages as she unconsciously walked toward the kitchen, and Rachel followed. She found the page and sat down on a stool, distractedly motioning toward a partial bottle of Cabernet on the counter. Rachel got a couple of glasses and divvied up the wine in the bottle, as Suzy read.

"'Scottish Ghost Haunts Marblehead Home,' by Michelle Arthur." Suzy looked up at Rachel, accepting the glass she offered. She swallowed a generous portion of it and began reading.

> Suzanne Quinn of Marblehead has a problem. A non-paying tenant has taken up residence in her carriage house. According to our source, a ghost named Fiona, originally from Scotland, is taking Ms. Quinn on random and unsolicited journeys into the past.

"Oh my god," Suzy said under her breath. She downed the rest of the wine. "Who's responsible for this?"

"I don't know," Rachel replied remorsefully. "My gut reaction would be Emily, since she's an ardent believer in ghosts, and she lives near Salem. But I couldn't say for sure."

Suzy looked back down at the paper. She rested her head heavily on her hand as she scanned the rest of the article, shaking her head and sighing periodically at the sensational writing.

"Honey," Rachel said, "I am so sorry. This is all my fault."

"How is it your fault?"

"Because I'm the one who told the Daughters what was going on."

"Only to keep them from calling 911 and hauling me off to the hospital or the nuthouse."

"Still, . . ." Rachel said.

"It's not your fault, Rachel. You didn't do anything wrong. I'm the one who put myself in the position for it to happen. I should have been more careful. I should have remembered that staring into a candle flame is how I put myself into a receptive state."

"What are you going to do?"

Suzy sighed, looking at the text of the article.

"I don't know. Nothing she says is really factually wrong or personally damaging, so I doubt I have a libel case here. Invasion of privacy, maybe. I just don't know if it will be worth the time and money." Suzy closed the paper forcefully. "I guess I'll just have to wait and see what kind of offer I get for the movie rights."

# 42

**Y**our ancestor has made another appearance," Suzy's note read. That was all.

Fin read the text message a couple of times, wondering if there was anything to be read between the lines.

*It's only one line,* he thought. *You can't hide a message between one line.*

"Interesting," he tapped noncommittally into his text app. "Care to share any more information?"

He stared at his phone for a couple of minutes, but there was no response. He sighed and put the phone down on his desk. He tried to get his attention back into *A Place Made of Time*. Not that it had been there to begin with. He was still having trouble with it, and his distraction with Kay over the last few weeks certainly hadn't helped.

When he dropped her off at her house the night of the Beltane festival, he helped her to her door. She was quite unsteady, but she had enough strength and presence of mind to try to pull him inside with her.

"Come on, Fin," she beseeched, "why don't you spend the night?"

"Get some sleep, Kay," Fin replied in a monotone as he pulled away from her. He pulled the door closed and got in his car. He sat there for a few minutes, not knowing whether to cuss her out or cry.

She had called him the next morning, not to apologize, but to essentially blame him for what had happened.

"Why did you let me drink so much?" she asked.

"You're a grown woman, Kay. It's not my job to police your alcohol consumption."

"Still, that mead was like soda. I didn't realize how drunk I was until I woke up this morning with my head pounding. When did we leave?"

"I don't know. Somewhere around midnight."

"Are you mad at me?" she asked. "You sound upset."

"I'm a little pissed, yeah.

"Why?"

"Why?" he echoed, his voice hardening. "I think anybody would be a little displeased to learn that you were just using me."

"What?" She actually sounded shocked.

"You told me you're broke, Kay. You just wanted to get back together with me because I've got money now."

"Fin, I would never do that. That – that's just not me."

"Really? Is it *you* to strip naked and dance around a bonfire in front of a bunch of cheering strangers? Is it *you* to do a naked bump-and-grind routine with a naked guy in front of said cheering people?"

"What the fuck are you talking about?"

"And now you're claiming you don't remember what happened last night?"

"Fin," she said in barely more than a whisper, "I didn't really do that, did I?"

"You were the life of the party."

"Oh my god," she gasped. Fin didn't respond to her exclamation. After a pause, she continued a little shakily. "I was sure I wore a bra yesterday, but I wasn't wearing one when I woke up."

"No, your bra was the one thing I couldn't retrieve. That and your dignity. You tossed your bra into the bonfire. I'm not sure where your dignity ended up, but I sure didn't see it last night."

"Why didn't you stop me?" she asked in a horrified tone.

"I tried. But like I said, Kay, it's not my job to police you and your activities. And especially after learning the motives for your renewed interest in me, I'm just not interested in taking on the job."

She had tried again to deny her motivation, but Fin wasn't interested in continuing the ruse any further. He hung up after asking her to not contact him again.

The depression began immediately.

Fin took a sip of his Scotch and tried to purge the last couple of days, since he had called it quits with her, from his mind. Unfortunately, it just wasn't happening. They had only been seeing each other for a few weeks, but the intimacy was there. They had a history and, even though their history had initially ended unpleasantly, it had allowed the affection to return quickly.

Then, in one night, it was yanked away from him.

After a half hour of staring at his computer, he hadn't typed a single word in his book. He sighed disgustedly and stood up. In that moment, he heard the sinister opening notes of the Imperial March from *Star Wars*.

He sat back down and hesitantly picked up his phone to see who was calling. It was Suzy.

"Hello?"

"Hi, Fin," she said. "Sorry it took me so long to respond. My friend brought a crisis to my doorstep, but I'm back now. The crisis will wait, I hope."

"I hope so, too. How are you? I haven't heard from you in a while."

"Well, I'm a little disenchanted with the way one or two things have turned out recently, but overall, I'm fine. How are you?"

"I know that feeling of disenchantment very well." He was kind of surprised, though, to notice that his disappointment had dissipated somewhat with this reconnection with Suzy. "So, you have news?"

"Yeah, where did we leave off?"

"Let's see," Fin said as he raised his eyes, looking up toward the ceiling as people often do when thinking, "the last time we chatted, Fiona had chosen Caden over Charles Scott or my worthy ancestor, Lachlan, and they were about to get married."

"Okay, a lot has happened since then." She briefly explained about the marriage, the honeymoon, and the bleak episode culminating in the amputation of Caden's leg. She told him how happy they were until the Panic of 1825 when Caden lost everything, and how they eventually ended up living in the vaults.

"Anyway, in these last few episodes," Suzy continued, "Caden managed to acquire tickets to America, and Fiona found out she's pregnant. When she was above ground one day, she saw Lachlan. He had been in the area to visit his no-good brother again. This wasn't a very long or detailed scene. He asked how she was and she responded evasively."

"I suppose so," Fin replied. "Back then, I think people were a little more reserved about sharing their dirty laundry with others."

"Right. He was happy to see her, and he wished her well, but he had to leave as he was expected to speak before the city council about the plight of the homeless people living in the vaults. I thought that was pretty cool. Apparently, your ancestor wasn't a complete scofflaw."

"Good to know."

"The next time she saw him was after Caden disappeared. He's helping her look for him.

"So, you're up to date now. But it reminded me of you, and I thought you'd like to know." Fin couldn't be sure, but he thought he detected a note of warmth in her voice.

"Well, thank you for thinking of me," Fin replied. "I'm still kind of amazed, and a little creeped out, by how you can do that. Mostly, I think I'm jealous."

"Yeah, you're not the only one who's creeped out by it." She told him how she had entered her trance state in front of the Daughters of the American Revolution, and the resulting newspaper article.

Fin told Suzy about renewing relations, so to speak, with Kay, and the debacle that ended it. By the time they finished catching each other up, an hour had passed.

"So," Suzy said, "how's the book coming?"

"Ugh!" Fin grunted. "It's stagnating. I'm just not into it. I'm thinking about booking a trip to Scotland to get a feel for the place, and hopefully get an infusion of authenticity and inspiration into this story."

"I've been thinking the same thing!" Suzy exclaimed. "I want to see Edinburgh, compare it to the settings I've seen in these visions. And I *really* want to see the vaults. I kind of put my foot in my mouth, but at the beginning of all this, I told Fiona that I'll find out for certain what actually happened to Caden. But honestly I don't think there's any way, after almost two hundred years, to find out what happened to some homeless person living on – or under – the streets."

"That *does* sound like kind of a tall order. But I think it would be a fascinating exercise, and a fun vacation at the very least. When are you going?"

"I haven't made any plans yet. I've just started thinking about it."

There was a pause.

"What do you think," Fin ventured slowly, "about coordinating our plans, and maybe meet up over there?"

"I think you're overstepping your bounds, mister," Suzy replied. Fin was about to apologize, but she continued, with a smile in her voice. "And I think I'm cool with it."

## 43

There was no sign of Caden the following day, nor the days after that. Lachlan had tried insisting that Fiona come with him to his home, but still, she wouldn't be budged. He finally relented and left a dagger with her, just in case she needed to defend herself against any of the nefarious characters living in the vaults.

Fiona had never known such tension. Every muscle in her body felt stretched taut as piano wire. She held on to the merest thread of hope that Caden would return. But from the beginning, with the combined clues of the forced-open door, the pallet being rumpled as if there had been a struggle, and the blanket that covered Caden being missing, as well as his crutches being left in the room, she had feared the worst.

A few days after he had gone missing, the worst was reported to her.

§

"You have news?" Fiona asked as Lachlan came down the steps slowly. It sounded to her as if her voice was a full octave higher than usual. Even in the darkness of the room, the whites of her eyes practically glowed in the flickering candle light.

"I do, Mrs. Loganach," Lachlan said quietly, hesitantly. "I can scarcely bring meself tae tell ye, but I'm aware ye need tae know."

"What is it?" Fiona's staccato breathing and rigid throat muscles made her anxious tone unmistakable. Lachlan gripped her shoulders and looked at her face, forcing her to focus on him. Still, it took several moments for him to be able to tell her.

"I've found your husband's body." There was a hint of relief that displayed in Fiona's expression, but it was almost completely buried beneath the grief that struck her full in the chest. Her eyes glistened in the candle light, and as her body shook, the tears tumbled down her cheeks.

"Where?" she asked in a whisper. Lachlan hesitated again. He closed his eyes for a moment. Shaking his head, he opened his eyes again and looked at her.

"In the University dissecting lab."

Despite Lachlan's grip on her shoulders, Fiona fell back against the stone wall and slid to the floor, her body shaking with agonized sobs. Distressed over her grieving, Lachlan pondered what he should do. Finally, he knelt down beside her and gently touched her shoulder.

"Mrs. Loganach," he said quietly, "would ye like me tae leave ye alone for a bit?" Fiona nodded, the tears still flowing heavily. "Of course," he replied. "I shall return in a little while."

Fiona didn't see him leave.

§

Hours passed and Fiona had cried herself to sleep on the rumpled pallet of blankets. She woke up when she heard the door open upstairs. Her first thought was that Caden had returned, but then the memory washed over her, engulfing her once again in her sadness.

She sat up as the footsteps descended toward her. She smiled feebly when she saw Lachlan appear at the foot of the stairs.

"Hello, Fiona," he said softly. "How are ye feelin'?"

"A little better," she said weakly. "Mr. Mac an Léigh, I appreciate your kindness in helping me search for Caden."

"Nonsense," he smiled. "'Tis nae a problem. I'm quite happy t' be of service in any way I can." He looked around at the meager furnishings of the room. "Will ye be leavin' here noo?"

Fiona rubbed her eyes and sighed, pushing herself up. She went to the shelf where the candle sputtered. It was little more than a puddle of wax, so she lit a fresh candle. As she did, her eyes fell on the portrait of Caden, and they filled with fresh tears. Fighting to keep them contained, though, she focused on replacing the candle in the candle holder.

"I don't know where I would go, Mr. Mac an Léigh."

"Ye can come wi' me, to me home." Fiona looked up at him and smiled.

"Ye offered that once before," she said, "and I thank ye for your kind offer. But I would not want to bring even a hint of impropriety to your reputation. You're a kind and benevolent man and I don't want to besmirch your character in the eyes of others."

Lachlan started to object, but Fiona went on.

"Perhaps I should try to reconcile with me father."

Lachlan shifted nervously.

"I hope ye'll forgive me," he said, "but I took the liberty of speaking with your father. Considering what has happened, I thought he ought t' know. That's why it took me so long t' get back here."

"And?" Fiona asked anxiously. Lachlan hesitated.

"Well, he was right angry and – I'm sorry – he said he wanted nothing tae do wi' ye."

Fiona's eyes filled with tears again, and Lachlan took a step toward her, but Fiona shook her head and brushed them away. She looked at Caden's face in the portrait, thinking for several moments. She remembered his gentle voice, his soft touch.

It was only a few days ago that he held her in his arms. She remembered the last time they made love on the thin pallet on the floor. Turning, she leaned back against the shelf, only partially aware of Lachlan's presence, as she pictured Caden smiling at her, kissing her lips, holding her body against his.

Looking at the pallet of blankets, she remembered the little cloth-wrapped bundle under it.

"I suppose there's only one thing for me to do," she said. "The ship sails tomorrow for America. There's nothing left for me here. I'll stay here one last night, then I'll pack up me few belongings and set sail for a new life."

Silence filled the air in the little room for several moments before Lachlan spoke up.

"Alright," he said, "I'll go home and gather a few things and meet ye back here in the morning."

"Why?" Fiona asked, looking at him with a puzzled expression.

"Beggin' your pardon, Fiona, but ye're an attractive young woman travelin' alone. There are scurrilous fellows who would take advantage of ye. So I'll accompany ye tae the New World, as your protector."

"Nay, Mr. Mac an Léigh," Fiona protested, "I can't ask ye to do that. Ye've put yourself out so much for me already. This is too much."

"I'll nae argue with ye aboot it, Fiona," Lachlan said simply. "I'm only doing what a friend would do. Ye've got two tickets tae a country ye've ne'er been to, and where ye know nobody. I'll be your chaperone and your guardian, as I think Caden would ha' wanted."

§

Fiona collapsed on the bed in her cabin on the ship. It had been a long time since she had felt plush upholstery, and the first thing it made her think of was, oddly, Caden. Fiona had made it a point to not complain about their bad luck in the past year, as she remembered Caden thanking her for just a few weeks before.

But the whole time he was thanking and complimenting her for being such a good wife, she was wishing she didn't have to sleep on a cold stone floor, padded only with a few layers of blankets. She felt like a hypocrite. She did have complaints. She just hadn't verbalized them.

She wished that Caden was lying beside her now, enjoying the soft mattress, instead of splayed open on a dissecting table in front of a classroom of medical students. The thought brought tears to her eyes again, and a horrified shudder racked her body. She turned on her side, allowing herself to cry once more.

When she had set foot on board that morning, it was early, more than two hours before they were to pull away from the dock and set sail for America. The first thing she did was to approach the Chief Steward and explain that her husband had died, and that a friend was taking his ticket in his stead. She hoped that other arrangements might be made, since the tickets were for a first-class cabin for two.

Fortunately, the ship was not fully booked and, when he asked if they would mind trading the first-class cabin for two single intermediate cabins, Fiona agreed immediately. She thought that Lachlan seemed disappointed by the lesser arrangements, but she knew that he was used to nicer things.

The cabin was small and plain, and it was not furnished as elegantly as she had grown accustomed to growing up in her father's home. Still, after the last several months, the bed felt positively decadent.

As she lay there, luxuriating in the comfort of the bed, she drifted off to sleep. When she awoke, she felt the ship rolling under full sail, on its way to her new life.

## 44

The Dia Greine was a 200 foot clipper ship. While neither the largest nor the most luxurious ship on the sea, she was fast. The crossing from Edinburgh to Boston took twenty-four days, despite encountering three storms on the way.

It was cold for most of the journey, so Fiona spent the majority of the crossing in her cabin. She came out for meals at the communal tables shared by others in the intermediate cabins, and occasionally to visit with other passengers. But for the most part, she just wanted to be left alone.

She was finally able to read Wattie's new book, and she smiled whenever she saw his inscription on the title page:

> To the fairest maid of Edinburgh.
> With affection, Wattie.

"Not of Edinburgh any longer, I'm afraid," she said quietly. "And no longer a maid." She placed her hand on her belly, feeling the swelling of new life, and feeling sad for her fatherless child.

She saw Lachlan occasionally when she ventured out, and he often tried to engage her in conversation. She knew he was just worried about her, and she felt bad about frequently rebuffing his efforts, but without Caden, she craved solitude.

But she also noticed that Lachlan seemed different somehow. She couldn't identify exactly what it was that was different about him, but she just didn't feel as comfortable in his company as she had back home. A couple of times, he had asked to come into her cabin to spend time with her. He was concerned about her well-being and thought she shouldn't be alone so much. While she appreciated his concern, she didn't feel it was appropriate and declined the offer.

She thought that Lachlan would have given thought to the impropriety as well, but if she were honest, she realized that she hadn't really spent a great deal of time with him back home. She had met him less than two months before she met Caden. During *that interval, they had visited at each other's homes a few times, and while he had made his fondness for her known, she had not spent any extended periods with him.*

*After she met Caden, she was focused almost entirely on him, and she barely saw Lachlan again. Perhaps he had been perturbed at being replaced so abruptly by his successor, feeling that he had not been good enough. Except that he had been just as kind and gentlemanly as always when she resumed contact with him a few weeks ago.*

*Since they'd been on the Dia Greine, though, there had been several times Fiona found him looking at her with an expression that she interpreted as longing. Maybe he still had those feelings for her.*

*She didn't know. And to be honest, at this time, with the death of her husband weighing so heavily on her, she just didn't have the mental or emotional fortitude to spend time figuring it out.*

§

*"Are ye ready t' see your new country?" Lachlan asked with a smile as he sat down across from her for dinner. They were due in port the next morning.*

*"I don't know if I am or not," Fiona replied.*

*"Oh? What's the matter? Folks ha' been talkin' aboot what a big, bonny, modern city Boston is."*

*"I'm not sure I want to be in a big city again." Fiona pushed a piece of potato around on her plate, not really feeling hungry. She had been struggling with nausea for nearly the whole trip, only partly because of the motion. "I've spent me whole life in a city, and the last year on the streets. I've found it's too easy to get lost in the crowds, to be ignored if ye're of the wrong class."*

*"Where would ye want t' go?" Lachlan asked as he chewed hungrily on a piece of beef. Fiona felt her stomach turning over as she watched his fervent indulgence, and she found herself being thankful that she hadn't pursued a romance with him. She couldn't imagine having to watch him ravenously devouring his meals like this every day.*

*Then, she immediately felt ashamed about that thought, knowing it was likely a number of factors making her feel that way, not* the least of which was her pregnancy and its resultant nausea, and grieving the loss of her husband.

"I don't know. But I think a small town might be a bit more welcoming." She hesitated before speaking again, feeling a little foolish. "I think a small town might also be a bit less likely to harbor people like the body snatchers."

Lachlan swallowed the bite, and was about to take another when his hand stopped midway.

"Body snatchers?" he asked.

"I know," Fiona said. "'Tis probably silly of me. I don't even know if it's a problem in America. But having lost both me mother and me husband to them, the thought of them terrifies me."

"Of course," Lachlan replied quietly. "No, Fiona, that's not silly at all." He pondered as he chewed his next bite. He swallowed and smiled at Fiona. "I've met a few Boston people on the ship. I'll ask aroond."

§

Fiona stood at the prow of the Dia Greine, pressed on both sides by other passengers wanting to get a glimpse of Boston as they drew nearer. The sun had been up for a few hours, and its warmth was welcome on Fiona's back on this chilly morning.

They were still nearly a mile away, but the city seemed to spread out for miles in both directions. She was still experiencing that feeling of ambivalence about the city. She could already get an idea of how big it was.

She felt the people to her right shift a bit as she heard Lachlan say "excuse me." He appeared beside her with a smile on his face.

"I think I've foond the place for ye," he said. "Folks ha' talked aboot a little fishin' village a few miles up the coast from Boston called Marblehead. Supposed to be a bonny wee town, perched on the rocky shore."

Fiona looked back at the growing metropolis spreading out before her as they approached. She turned back to Lachlan, with the beginnings of a smile, the first she had experienced in a while.

"It sounds perfect."

## 45

"My name is Terri," the fiftyish woman said. She didn't bother introducing the two other women who stood a few feet behind her. "I live a few houses down," and she pointed to make sure that Suzy knew exactly which direction she meant. Suzy nodded. "We read the article in the *Salem Dispatch*. We wanted to recommend our priest. My husband and I had a problem with some demons in our house a while back. But he was able to get rid of them."

"Well, thank you for your concern," Suzy replied, careful to keep the snark out of her voice. She usually reserved full-on smartassery for at least the second meeting. "But I don't have a demon problem."

"Oh," Terri replied, confused. "But the article –"

"The article was a tad sensationalized."

"Your carriage house isn't haunted?" one of the other women asked.

"I think haunted is a bit of an exaggeration. It's occupied by a very nice ghost. She really doesn't take up much room at all."

"You may think it's nothing to be concerned about," Terri said, becoming quite stern, "but 'Satan transformeth himself into an angel of light.' You need to be very careful about this sort of thing."

"Yes, so I've heard," Suzy replied, remembering her scolding from Helen Stewart. "I will be careful. Thank you, Terri."

"It would be no problem for me to call my priest. He could probably track down the source of the problem pretty quickly. And he could definitely offer you some encouragement."

"That's okay," Suzy replied, struggling with the calm, "neither my house nor my soul are in need of saving."

"You're dealing with forces you know nothing about."

"I know more than you might realize. And I learn a little more every time I stare at a candle flame." That detail had been shared in the article, so she figured Terri would get her point.

"Young lady, this is serious. You may think nothing about toying with this yourself. But for the record, we don't want our neighborhood taken over by wicked spirits." The other two women added weight to her argument by shaking their heads.

"Noted. Thanks again." Suzy forced a smile as she closed the door, swearing under her breath.

"Sorry," she sighed, getting back on the phone.

"That's okay," Fin replied. "Who was it?"

"Just some of my neighbors wanting to do an exorcism."

"Ah. I hope you didn't vomit pea soup on them."

"No, I'll have you know I was very well-behaved. I kept my pea soup to myself."

"I love a girl who can hold her pea soup."

"Okay," Suzy said, rolling her eyes, "this was fun. Can we get back to planning our trip?"

"Absolutely," Fin replied enthusiastically.

"Oh, by the way," Suzy said, "before we get back into that, in my latest episode from Fiona, she's about to land in Boston, with Lachlan."

"Lachlan actually came with Fiona?" Fin asked, surprised.

"He did. She had just lost her husband and she didn't know anybody in America, so he wanted to accompany her as her guardian."

"Huh, that was nice of him."

"Yeah, it was," Suzy said, a little mystified. "But I'm already kind of seeing that change that you mentioned. I can't really pinpoint exactly what's different about him and, unfortunately, I didn't see anything that might have caused it, either."

"Well that sucks," Fin replied, disappointed.

"I know. But to be fair, I'm only seeing what Fiona saw. She didn't spend a lot of time with him before coming to America, so the catalyst may have occurred sometime when she wasn't with him."

"Hmm," Fin sighed. "When you started telling me about these visions, I was hoping for some kind of grand revelation, an unraveling of the mystery."

"Hey, I can't do everything for you. You'll just have to have your own visions."

"Sure, the guy who's never experienced anything even remotely paranormal."

"Right, you're the time travel guy. That's probably what you need to find out details like that."

"Don't remind me. My time machine is apparently stalled. The book's not going anywhere for now."

"Okay," Suzy said, a note of conviction in her voice, "all the more reason to get back to planning our trip. So, let's get to it."

## 46

I t was called Long Wharf, and it really was. The wharf jutted out nearly a half mile into Boston Harbor. It took some time for the Dia Greine to slowly work her way through the harbor and approach the wharf. By the time Fiona and Lachlan gathered their luggage and followed the crowd down the walkway to the dock, it was early afternoon.

Fiona hadn't been very active, having spent most of the journey in her cabin. Besides that, the nausea she experienced nearly every day left her weak and tired. Carrying her two canvas bags over her shoulders, she was winded by the time she and Lachlan reached the west end of the wharf. Here, after finding a bank and disappearing into it for a few minutes, Lachlan hired a hackney coach to take them up the coast to Marblehead.

An hour later, halfway to their destination, there was a violent bump and the coach came to an abrupt stop. Fiona was sitting in the front seat, facing backwards, but Lachlan was thrown to the floor.

"Och jings!" he exclaimed, picking himself up and pushing his hair back. He moved across the slanted floor and opened the door, climbing down as Fiona looked on, her hands on her belly, fighting to still the nausea which had suddenly returned. Finding it difficult to stay in her seat which was now facing downward, she climbed out, too.

"Sorry, folks," said Joe, the driver, who was already kneeling down looking under the coach. "Looks like the rear axle broke." The rear wheels were cocked at an extreme angle.

"Aw, what nasty luck," Lachlan replied. "Can ye fix it?"

Joe looked at him.

"In time, yes," he said, "but it'll be hours." He looked around, thinking. "I can take one of the horses back into town . . ." and his voice trailed off as his thoughts continued silently.

Lachlan and Fiona both noticed Joe suddenly focused on something behind them and they turned to look. A man was approaching them in a wagon.

Joe stepped out into the road, waving his arms, and the wagon slowed to a stop beside them.

"Looks like you've got yourself some trouble," the man said sympathetically.

"Nothing I can't take care of," Joe replied, "but that don't help these folks, I'm afraid."

"Where are you headed?" the man asked.

"Marblehead," Lachlan replied.

"I live in Marblehead," the man replied. "That's where I'm going now. Can I give you a ride?"

"Aye, that'd be grand," Lachlan replied immediately.

"What about you, Joe?" Fiona asked, not wanting to leave him in the lurch.

"That's fine," Joe replied. "To be honest, not having to get you to Marblehead would free me up to get the axle fixed. I wouldn't have to worry about you and your husband."

Fiona flinched slightly, but nobody but herself seemed to notice.

"In that case," she said to the man in the wagon, "we'd be happy to come with ye, and we thank ye for your kindness."

The man smiled and shook his head.

Lachlan pulled his luggage out of the coach and tossed the bags in the back of the wagon where a few boxes of supplies were stacked, then pulled Fiona's two canvas bags out and placed them beside his own.

Joe pulled some cash out of his pocket and counted out a few bills.

"I figure I got you about halfway," he said. "So here's half your money back." He handed the bills to Lachlan.

Lachlan took the bills from him and placed them in his pocketbook.

"That's very kind of ye, Joe," Fiona said. "Thank ye."

"Not at all," Joe replied, "I'm just glad this gentleman came along."

The man on the wagon slid over on his seat and reached his hand down to Fiona to help her up. Lachlan climbed into the back of the wagon where the luggage had been placed.

"I'll just sit back 'ere, then," he said.

Fiona nodded and smiled at Joe, who was already unhitching his horses from the coach.

"You seem a long way from home," the man said as he flicked the reins and started his horses moving again.

"Aye," Fiona replied. "We're from Scotland."

"Really? Well, that's quite a coincidence," the man replied. "I'm Scottish myself, though I was born here in America. My name is Robert Drummond."

"I'm Fiona Loganach," Fiona replied, "and this is Lachlan Mac an Léigh," motioning to Lachlan behind them. Lachlan waved a gesture of greeting toward Drummond.

"Oh," Drummond said, "I thought he was your husband."

"No, he's me travel companion. But me husband died a month ago."

"I'm so sorry," Drummond replied sympathetically.

"Thank ye, sir." Fiona sat lost in her thoughts for a few moments. Then, remembering an immediate need, she continued. "Mr. Drummond, ye wouldn't happen to know of any inexpensive places of lodging that might be available in Marblehead, would ye?"

"Well, as a matter of fact, I have a place available myself," Drummond said. "Under the circumstances, it would only be for one of you, of course," and he glanced back toward Lachlan. "But I have a carriage house that I've converted into living quarters that could be rented out to one of you."

"A carriage house?" Fiona said.

"Yes, my wife, Judith, thought herself something of an artist. She dabbled in painting pictures. To humor her, a few years ago, when I built a larger carriage house, I made the old one into a painting studio for her. But I'm afraid she died last year."

"Oh, Mr. Drummond, I'm so sorry," Fiona replied, as pained as if it were her own grief. Drummond nodded, acknowledging her sympathy.

"Thank you." He seemed anxious to get back to the other topic. "But after I lost her, I turned the studio into a small house. I was thinking I could let it out for, perhaps, two dollars a week. How does that sound?"

"I haven't much money," Fiona replied, "nor do I have a source of income as yet. And I'm afraid I don't know how much a dollar is."

"Ah, well, I can help you with that. I can take you into town and introduce you to my banker tomorrow. I'm sure he'll be able to change your money into dollars.

"Until you acquire a source of income, are you experienced in cooking?"

"I am," Fiona replied. She didn't tell him that her experience was less than a year old.

"My cook recently got married, and I've yet to hire another. Miss Ewing, my daughter's governess, has been helping out. Perhaps you can take that burden off of her, at least until I'm able to hire another cook."

"Yes, sir, I'd be happy to.

Drummond looked at her for a few seconds, studying her face.

"Very well," he said with a note of finality. "The place is yours, if you want it." He turned back toward Lachlan. "I'm afraid that doesn't help you, though."

Lachlan shook his head and waved a hand, but said nothing.

"I suppose I could put you up in my home," Drummond said, "for a night or two, until you find lodging of your own."

"That's verra kind of ye, sir," Lachlan replied. "Thank ye."

§

They continued along a trail that followed the rocky shore for the most part. Eventually, they came to a point where the trail branched off in two different directions. Drummond turned to the right.

Fiona saw what looked like an island ahead, connected to the mainland by the narrowest strip of land, which they were now driving along. Drummond saw her looking with some concern at the waves lapping against the shore a few feet on either side of them, and he smiled.

"This road washes out now and then," he said, "if we have a particularly bad storm. But I tend to like the seclusion of this area."

Fiona smiled and nodded in agreement.

The island, or the Great Neck as Drummond called it, was rough and somewhat wooded. There were a few isolated houses here and there, but for the most part, the area was unspoiled. As they continued following the trail up the west side of the Neck for a bit, the brush and trees cleared, revealing a house that would almost be at home in Europe.

The house was constructed of stone and heavy timbers, in a sprawling design with a crenelated battlement, a round turret tower in the corner, and other details that almost made Fiona feel right at home.

"My father visited his homeland in the Scottish Highlands many times," Drummond said. "He missed it a great deal, and when he settle here and built his house, he styled it after his boy-hood home.

Drummond turned off the trail toward the house and drove around it toward the back. At their approach, a tall dark-haired man came out of the large carriage house and took the reins from Drummond.

"I'll take the groceries in for you, sir," the man said.

"Thank you, Chandler," Drummond said, and Chandler nod-ded an acknowledgment. After Fiona and Lachlan retrieved their baggage from the back of the wagon, Chandler began unloading the supplies.

"Over here, Mrs. Loganach," Drummond motioned, "is the apartment." The building was smaller than the current carriage house, but it seemed to be sturdy and in good repair. "Would you like to see inside?"

"Aye, please."

"I'll be with you in a moment, Mr. MacKinley," Drummond said. Lachlan looked as if he were about to correct his pronuncia-tion, but Drummond was already leading Fiona to the door of the little carriage house apartment. The large carriage doors had been removed, the opening filled in with similar stone, leaving a door and a window in its place.

"It's really not much," he said as he opened the door. He stepped aside so Fiona could enter. She went inside and looked around. It was cozy and bright. In addition to the window to the right of the door, there were also two windows on the wall directly ahead to the left of the door. Due to the diagonal situation of the building on the property, the windows faced southwest and southeast, and the interior was flooded with light.

A small sitting room with a fireplace was on the right, a kitchen and dining area on the left, and to the right of the kitchen was a small bed chamber.

The furnishings were simple but looked comfortable, including a dining table with four very nice chairs. She looked at the trappings of the little home and placed her hand on the back of one of the dining chairs. The rail was loose, wobbling between the two delicate upright stiles.

"I'm sorry," Drummond said quickly, "I keep meaning to fix that. I promise you, I'll get that tightened up."

"'Tis but a small thing," Fiona said quietly as she looked around. She suddenly felt a little choked up when she thought about sitting in that upholstered chair by the fireplace, nursing her baby.

"It's perfect," she said quietly.

## 47

Pressing his phone against his ear, Fin smiled as he listened to Suzy enthuse about her latest episode.

"Oh my god, it was so cool! I actually saw my house when it was still fairly new! It still had an obvious design back then. Not like the mess it is now."

"Mess?" Fin asked. "Am I to understand that you're a less than stellar housekeeper?"

"Not the kind of mess I'm talking about," Suzy replied with a smartass tone, but in her excitement about her story, she didn't linger on it. "Over the last couple of centuries, a few additions have been made to the house, sometimes with seemingly little thought to matching the style of the existing structure. The original castle is still there, but it's kind of surrounded by Cape Cod and Georgian bits and pieces."

"Wait," Fin said, sitting upright, "original *castle*?"

"Yeah, the original house was built to resemble Phillip Drummond's boyhood home in the Scottish Highlands. Actually, now that I think about it, before all the additions were tacked on to it, it would probably be right at home in your novel."

"Unlike me," Fin said. "Maybe you can rub some salt in the wound, too."

"Still struggling, huh?" Suzy asked, her voice taking on a sympathetic tone.

"I'm writing the story, but it just seems dead and lifeless. I'm not getting the atmosphere I want."

"Well, our trip's coming up in a couple of months. You'll be able to soak up all that Scottish atmosphere and pour it into your story."

"Yeah, about that," Fin said sheepishly, "I got so caught up in the excitement of planning this trip that I forgot about something. I'm going to have to meet you over there a few days later than I originally planned."

"You getting cold feet, mister?"

"No, I assure you my feet are warm. But *TimePlex* is being released over the long Fourth of July weekend, and my publicist reminded me that I have a prior obligation to make an appearance at the premier in Hollywood. I'm not looking forward to it, which is probably why I was able to forget all about it."

"You're not looking forward to *that*?" Suzy asked a little disbelieving.

"I'm anxious to see the movie. It's the public appearance I'm not looking forward to. I'll probably trip on the red carpet with hundreds of cameras flashing."

"Well, maybe you can get your girlfriend to hold you up," Suzy said. Fin had never mentioned his infatuation with Jennifer Lawrence, but Suzy had picked up on it after the New York Comic Con.

"Yeah, maybe so. Of course *your* boyfriend will be on the other side of me, so I'll have plenty of support." He didn't actually know if Jennifer Lawrence and Ryan Reynolds would be there. He assumed they would, but they wouldn't necessarily be there with him.

"Well, I'll miss you those first few days," Suzy replied. The snark had left her voice, and had been replaced by that warmth that Fin had occasionally been hearing lately.

"Yeah, me too."

## 48

Ye dinnae ha' tae bide here all by yerself," Lachlan said, raising his eyebrows as if he was sharing a pearl of wisdom with her. Fiona looked at him with confusion etched into her face.

"What do ye mean, Mr. Mac an Léigh?" she asked. Lachlan had come to pay her a visit in her carriage house apartment the next morning. He was on his way out to look for a place to stay. "I've safely completed me journey," she continued. "Ye don't have to stay and watch o'er me."

"I like wha' I've seen since I've been 'ere. An' tae be completely logical, it costs less for two tae live together than apart."

"Mr. Mac an Léigh!" Fiona exclaimed. "What ye're proposing is not right!"

"Fiona, what I'm proposin' is a purely financial arrangement."

"God would not think well of such an arrangement," Fiona replied. Lachlan looked at her for a few moments.

"Of course, ye're right." He sighed. "In that case, I suppose I'll be off."

"Mr. Mac an Léigh, I'm surprised that ye've so quickly abandoned your hopes of helping those forced to live in the vaults in Edinburgh."

"'Tis a lost cause, I'm afraid," he replied sadly. "But there are unfortunates 'ere, too. As our Lord said, 'we'll always ha' the poor among us.' Me efforts can be applied 'ere as well as anywhere."

"That's true, then," Fiona replied, her face still registering surprise. "In that case, good luck to ye."

"Thank ye, me dear." Lachlan nodded a goodbye to her and squeezed her shoulder, though he seemed disappointed in the outcome of their conversation. Fiona watched after him curiously for a moment, unsettled by his unusual proposal. Finally, she closed the door and looked around her apartment.

The first thing she had done the night before was to hang the portrait that she had painted of Caden. The wall between the chair and the fireplace seemed the perfect place for it. So this morning, she took her tea, which she had started steeping just before Lachlan called, to the little table. Pouring a cup, she settled in the chair and pondered Caden's face.

"Well, me dear," she said, "I've made it. I certainly wish ye were here to share this life with me." With tears in her eyes, she quietly sipped her tea, with one hand resting on her belly, feeling the stirrings of Caden's child within.

§

"What is this?" Drummond asked, tasting the dish in front of him.

"Rumbledethumps," Fiona replied. "It was me husband's favorite."

Martha, Drummond's six-year-old daughter, giggled.

"Rumbleethumps," she echoed, then she resumed consuming what was on her plate.

The baked mixture of potatoes, onions, cabbage and cheese was one of about ten dishes that Fiona had learned to make well in the months before Caden's home was taken from him. She hoped that Drummond found a new cook before she ran out of recipes.

Drummond had invited Fiona to stay and eat with them, rather than be treated like staff. During the time she had been there preparing the dinner, Martha had taken to her, and Fiona had to admit that she liked the little girl as well.

"It's delicious," Drummond said.

"Thank ye, sir." Martha seemed to agree. She had already cleaned up her little plate and pushed it forward.

"Can I have some more?" she asked. Drummond raised his eyebrows toward her. "May I?" she corrected.

"Yes, you may," he replied. As he spooned some more onto Martha's plate, he looked at Fiona. "I haven't seen Mr. MacKinley this evening. I assume he has found suitable lodging."

"I've not seen him since he left this morning, either," Fiona responded. "But I hope he has." She hated how uncomfortable he made her feel lately. He had seemed like such a gentleman back in Edinburgh, and at the time, she had felt bad about spurning him when he made it known he wanted to get to know her better.

Now, it seemed as if that gentlemanly, philanthropic side of him had just been an act, an affectation. Had he simply been trying to appear to be a better person than he was, to be liked or admired? Fiona had a hard time believing that. 'The act' was so complete, so believable.

Anyway, since he made her uncomfortable now, she didn't want to talk about him.

"What do you do, Mr. Drummond?" she asked.

"I spend part of my time trying to follow in my father's footsteps, and the rest of it wishing I could blaze my own trail." He noticed Fiona's confused expression. "I'm sorry, I didn't answer your question, did I? I run the ship building business that my father founded before I was born. It's located on the shore of Saugus, very near where I picked you up yesterday."

"I heard the regret in your first response," Fiona said. "What is it you wish you could do?" Drummond smiled regretfully.

"Well, what I want is related to what I do. Separate from the ship building business, I also run a shipping company." He heard Fiona gasp and he looked up at her.

"That's what me husband did," she said quietly. "He had four ships, named after his mother, his sisters and his grandmother."

Drummond nodded solemnly.

"Hmm. Well, I only have three. So far." He looked thoughtfully down at the table for a moment. "But what I really want to do is to sail the seas myself, exploring and discovering." He looked up at Fiona and shook his head. "But it appears those days are over. It seems as if we've discovered everything there is to discover. We've sailed the seas, explored the continents and mapped the world. So my dreams are just that, silly dreams."

"I don't think any dream is silly," Fiona said. "Our dreams drive us to improve and expand, to become better people, sometimes even to improve the lot of mankind. Whether the dreams are attainable or not is irrelevant."

Drummond studied Fiona's face for a few moments, his eyebrows drawn together.

"You are a very wise and thoughtful woman, Mrs. Loganach."

"Oh, I don't know about that," Fiona said, her face flushing a bit. "I've just had a lot of time on me hands of late, and there's not much one can do with time but think."

Fiona was beginning to feel uncomfortable, not just with Drummond's compliments, but with the return of her nausea. She placed her napkin on the table.

"I hope ye'll forgive me," she said, "but I'm afraid I must leave. I'm not feeling well." She stood up from the table, and Drummond followed suit.

"Oh, I'm sorry Mrs. Loganach," Drummond said. "I hope you're not becoming ill."

"No, it's nothing like that," Fiona replied, her face flushing. "It's, well, I'm with child."

"Oh," Drummond said softly, "of course." He bowed his head slightly, as if embarrassed to look directly at her. He went to the sideboard and lit a candle, which he handed to her, then led her to the back door, which was only a few steps from her carriage house apartment.

"Good night, Mrs. Loganach," he replied quietly as he opened the door. "I hope you feel better."

## 49

On Memorial Day, Suzy visited the cemetery where her uncle and her parents were buried. Both her father and his brother had served in Vietnam, but only her father made it back alive.

Suzy had been born after her uncle Dave died, so she never met him, but all her life, it had been her family's tradition to visit his grave on Memorial Day. Since the accident that claimed the lives of her parents, Suzy had taken on the responsibility, and combined it with a visit to their nearby graves as well.

Her custom was a simple one. She cleared off any dead leaves, twigs and other debris that might be littering the graves, placed a tasteful arrangement of flowers before each stone, and sat for a few minutes on a nearby bench where she could see all three graves and ruminate on the lives of her loved ones.

Since Suzy had taken up yoga and meditation a few years before, her Memorial Day custom began to include a bit more of a mystical routine. Sitting on the bench with her eyes closed, her face raised toward the morning sun, she sat there quietly contemplating her family legacy. Since the death of her husband and daughter, they entered into her routine as well, even though they weren't physically buried here.

This morning, enjoying the warmth of the sun on her face, she could feel the love of her family surrounding and embracing her, almost as if they were there with her. She remembered a few years back when she had described the experience to Rachel. Rachel had joked that it sounded like the final scene in *Return of the Jedi*, when Luke Skywalker sees the souls of Yoda, Obi-Wan, and his father, Anakin, now freed from his Darth Vader accoutrements, watching over him.

Suzy had replied that that was a fairly simplistic way of looking at it, and that only someone not experienced in the ways of The Force would see it that way. Remembering that exchange now, she smiled, knowing that Fin would probably appreciate it.

She sighed, pulling her concentration back to her family members. On this sunny, spring morning, she focused her mind on achieving a state of serenity, and after a few moments, she could feel the calm descending over her.

Suddenly, her body was jarred by a mental shock, and by rapid-fire images appearing in her head. Though she wasn't able to focus on many of the scenes flashing through her mind, the emotion contained in them was tangible and terrifying. Her body shaking, she gripped the bench with both hands, her breathing quickened and intensified.

In this scene, she became a young woman running, but it was difficult to pick out details, other than bright red hair blowing in her face. What she was seeing was cut together quickly like an action movie. She could only get impressions. The young woman seemed afraid. Suzy could see the cemetery going past her, and up ahead, she saw what looked like the bench on which she now sat.

The woman threw a glance behind her, and though Suzy didn't see anything, she was immediately drenched in fear. Then, she heard a second set of footfalls, a little faster than those of the young woman. She could hear the woman panting for breath, and she could hear the panting of the second person, but the images changed rapidly, flashing by as if controlled by a strobe.

There was an abrupt thud as the second person punched the woman's shoulder, causing her to trip and fall. Rolling over, she lay face up on the ground panting, bleeding from both knees and from a fresh wound on her forehead.

Suzy saw a flash of a man's face, his mouth open from gasping for breath. She saw that he had dark hair and a beard, but little more before the picture cut away to a little red-headed boy. Another fraction of a second, and she saw a house, dark bluish grey with white trim. She saw the bench on which she now sat, from a low angle, as if viewed from the ground directly in front of it. The episode cut back to the bearded man swinging a baseball bat toward her head.

There was a blinding explosion of light, quickly followed by flashes of colors firing in all directions. The next second, everything went black.

Suzy shuddered out of the scene, her whole body tense, her lungs fighting for air. She looked down at the path in front of her, where the young woman had apparently been lying when she was killed, and Suzy shivered violently in the warm sunshine.

§

Murder was not a common occurrence in Marblehead, so Suzy remembered the killing, though she didn't remember details. So once she was able to retrieve a measure of calm, she stood up from the bench, casting a weary glance at the graves of her parents and her uncle, and she walked unsteadily back to her car.

Getting inside and closing the door, she felt warm and comforted. She sat back in the seat, put her head back and cried.

After a few minutes, taking a deep breath, she felt somewhat functional again. She wiped her eyes, started her car and drove home.

She had mixed feelings about what to do next. She wanted to get those images out of her head, but at the same time, she had to know for certain if what she suspected about the incident was true. She sat down at her computer and pulled up the local newspaper's web site. Entering a few words in the search field, she quickly found what she was looking for.

Jill Bruch, a twenty-four-year-old woman with flaming red hair, lived on the north side of Marblehead in a two-hundred-year-old house. The dark bluish grey and white house was also the home of her little red-headed boy, Bobby. A few months before, Jill's boyfriend, Doug Parrish, had moved in with her, but they had not been getting along very well. Neighbors had reported hearing numerous loud arguments between them.

On an afternoon in August, three years ago, another fight took place. Jill screamed that she had had enough, and that Doug had to leave. One neighbor who related this account in the article said that she was glad to hear Jill finally stand up to him, and thought that the neighborhood would get some peace again.

More words were exchanged, after which Jill left, slamming the door behind her. She was known to enjoy running, sometimes through the nearby cemetery which she found to be relaxing. This time, though, Doug followed her.

The same neighbor interviewed in the article saw Doug chasing after Jill with the bat, and she called the police. They were on the scene quickly, but not soon enough to save Jill. When Doug had caught up with her, he proceeded to beat her to death with a baseball bat. Doug was pretty much crazed by the time the police arrived, and he rushed one of them with his baseball bat and was shot dead.

Jill's son, Bobby, the little red-headed boy that Suzy had seen in the vision just before Jill was killed, had been with her parents at the time, and was spared the danger and terror of that afternoon, but not the loss of his mother.

Suzy realized that her suspicion was correct. Sitting on the bench in the cemetery, she had seen flickerings of what Jill Bruch had seen moments before her death. Her home, her son, and finally, her boyfriend/killer.

That led to two realizations. First, Jill Bruch's ghost was still hanging around the location where she was killed. The second, and to Suzy, the most disconcerting, realization was that she was able to see her "episodes" as well.

"hosts really aren't my area of expertise," Leanne said to Lilith, one of her parishioners, as Suzy sat nearby in Lilith's living room. "So I really appreciate you taking the time to meet with us and possibly offer some guidance."

"It's my pleasure," Lilith said, "although I don't like to use the word 'ghost.' That often has a negative connotation. I prefer the word 'spirit.'"

Lilith was a tiny woman, barely up to Suzy's shoulder. Her age was difficult to guess. Her hair was grey, her hands gnarled with age, but her face was relatively unlined. There were some creases at the sides of her eyes and her mouth, and these deepened whenever she smiled, which she did frequently. If she had to guess, Suzy would say that Lilith must be seventy, maybe eighty.

Her home, like most of the houses in Marblehead, was at least two hundred years old. *Unlike* most of the houses in Marblehead, crystals of every imaginable shape and color lined the perimeter of many of its horizontal surfaces, including the edges of her floors, and some were hanging from the ceiling.

The room smelled like a gift shop, with incense and candles burning in various locations around the dim living room. Suzy made a mental note to not stare too long at any of the flames.

"Of course," she replied, and Lilith smiled at her.

"Alright, why don't you tell me what's troubling you."

Suzy took a deep breath and started out by relating what she had been experiencing for the last several months, the visions and the dream communication with Fiona. She included the traumatic episode in the carriage house near the beginning, but was careful to point out that she liked Fiona and was, otherwise, not frightened by the visitations.

Then, she told about the experience she had that morning in the cemetery.

Through it all, Lilith sat still in her chair, her feet not quite touching the floor, listening intently, her face relaxed in the beginnings of a smile. Her face sometimes indicated curiosity, sometimes surprise, usually geniality. She was never judgmental, but always respectful.

"Fascinating," she finally said when Suzy finished.

"Okay, I agree it's fascinating," Suzy replied, "but after this morning, I have to admit I'm a little more concerned than I was before."

"Yes, that must have been frightening."

Quashing the urge to say, "No shit, Sherlock," Suzy nodded and looked down at her hands folded in her lap to gather her thoughts.

"I've figured out," she said, "that I can only receive these visions when I'm near the spirit of the person they're about. Which is why I've never had a vision of Fiona anyplace outside of my own home, because the carriage house is where she's located. After the first one, I worried that a vision might kick in when I'm driving, but thankfully, that has never happened."

Lilith nodded in agreement, her eyes crinkled a bit. Suzy continued.

"I understand that, this morning, I must have received a vision from the spirit of Jill Bruch in the cemetery where she was killed. But I'm confused. First of all, why? Why did I receive a vision from someone I don't know and have no connection with whatsoever?

"And why was it so different? I mean I picked up on the emotion, but there were so many things that I saw in those few seconds that seemed completely unrelated. I saw her house, I saw her son, and I saw the guy that killed her. But other than that, there were just flickers of images, cut together in fractions of a second, like some crazy music video. There was no discernible connection from one to the next. It wasn't coherent or, apparently, chronological. It was just a confusing jumble."

"Hmm," Lilith nodded and pondered for a few moments. "I'm sure you've heard the idea that someone's life flashes before their eyes just before they die."

"Of course," Suzy nodded.

"I would venture a guess that, if you took the time and really concentrated on it, and you wrote down every image that you remembered from that experience, and if you researched Jill Bruch's life, you would find some connection. Not a connection to her death, but to her life. *You* were seeing her life flash before her eyes."

"Wow!" Suzy said, breathless, and a little chilled at the concept.

"The difference in the style of the vision," Lilith continued, "could, I suppose, be attributed to a number of things. Maybe your family connection with Fiona makes for a more cohesive, chronological vision. Or maybe *she* controls that, and she's revealing her story to you in that fashion.

"On the other hand, it could be just a difference in Fiona's and Jill's personalities. Or their maturity. You said Fiona was about fifty-one when she died. Jill Bruch was twenty-four. Jill was also a modern woman, accustomed to a faster lifestyle, and maybe that came through in the vision.

"Or it could very likely be the terror she was experiencing at the moment. She was afraid for her life, and our minds seldom work the way we might like when we're in a life-or-death situation. Or it could be a composite of these."

"Okay," Suzy nodded, "that all makes sense. But why? Do these dead people just broadcast their visions at me? What's the deal with that?"

"I think it could be a combination of reasons. In the case of Fiona, it sounds as if she is delivering the visions to you in a logical, chronological order. You've demonstrated your interest in her life, and she's obliging by, as you said, broadcasting the visions to you as they happened.

"With Jill, I think it may have just been more random. You just happened to be in her vicinity and your ability became a conduit between her mind and yours. You picked up her thoughts when you were near her."

"I read her mind?" Suzy looked at Lilith incredulously.

"You read her mental communication."

"Why can't I do that with living people? Not that I want to."

"I couldn't say. Maybe you could if you cultivated the ability. From what I've heard today, you do seem to possess a predilection toward the paranormal, what people commonly refer to as extrasensory perception."

"That is so weird. I mean I've come to accept receiving visions from Fiona. She's family. But this vision of someone with whom I have no connection whatsoever?"

"It could be that your abilities, your talents, are sharpening. You've become adept at putting yourself in a trance state. You're more receptive to a connection with the spirit world, what I call SpiritSense, and your gift is becoming more pronounced."

"My gift?" Suzy said skeptically. "I don't know about that. After this morning, I'm not sure what I'd call it, but I don't think 'gift' would even make the list. I mean I don't think I'm ready to be a spirit medium."

"What you do with the gift is entirely up to you," Lilith said. "But you do have an open heart and an open mind, two important qualities for a lightworker."

"A lightworker?" Suzy asked, scrunching her eyebrows together.

"A lightworker is a highly-attuned being, someone with SpiritSense, who has the ability and the desire to help others, to lead them to a better place. They're extremely intuitive and spiritual, and while they are often 'loners,' they connect easily with other people, and they're usually wise and mature beyond their years, what many like to call an old soul. They often focus on self-growth, but they're also driven to help others grow, as well, and they have an uncanny ability to facilitate that."

"Wow," Suzy replied. "Well, I'm flattered that you think that's me, but I'm not so sure."

"When Leanne called me, she told me about your personality and," she paused with a hand over her heart and smiled, "as my dear husband used to call it, your 'wisenheimer' attitude." Suzy glanced at Leanne whose face reddened a bit. "But despite that," Lilith continued, "I peg you as a warm and caring soul."

"Don't tell anyone," Suzy said, but she smiled at the compliment.

"Some believe that time is not really a chronological phenomenon," Lilith said, getting back to the issue at hand, "but that that's only the way we perceive it. If that's the case, then our lives may overlap with some in the past and the future in ways most of us can't even imagine. You're developing your SpiritSense, an ability to connect empathically with some of those who are no longer on this plane of existence. Who knows? You might even be able to help them to find their way into the next."

"Hold on," Suzy said, "you mean like an exorcist?"

"Well no, dear, exorcism is for casting out the devil or demons, not spirits of those who have passed on. But some spirits, for whatever reason, may not know how to get to the next place. We're spiritual beings, but we are housed in a physical skin to allow us to live and interact with the physical world. When that skin dies, it may be a traumatic event and, being sentimental creatures, we sometimes tend to hold on to what's familiar."

"This is so crazy," Suzy said, shaking her head. "As recently as just a couple of years ago, I didn't even know if I believed in any kind of an afterlife, and now, it seems, I have a front row seat."

"More than just a seat," Leanne said, "you could be an usher."

"You told me a few months ago," Suzy said to Leanne, her face puckered in thought, "that the physical realm is ours, like Lilith just said, and that spirits have little or no influence over us."

"That's basically true, yes."

"Does that mean we can just tell them to go? Seems like a lot of haunted house movies could have been resolved pretty easily."

"Well, I'm not contradicting that thought," Lilith said hesitantly, glancing at Leanne, "but it may or may not be that simple."

"May or may not?" Suzy echoed.

"Some spirits, whether because of fear, sentimentality, or any number of other influences, may hold on tighter to what they know. So our encouragement for them to move on to the next realm may meet with some resistance. We may need to find something that exerts a greater influence over them than what holds them here."

§

Suzy approached the bench hesitantly. She cast a glance at her parents' gravestones. She didn't know whether she was looking for encouragement, or strength, or perhaps she was afraid she might receive confirmation of her own fear that she was being stupid.

If Lilith was to be believed, though, Suzy was just answering her calling. Lightworker? Ridiculous.

She sat down on the bench and looked at the spot on the path where Jill Bruch had been murdered, and she shivered remembering the image of Doug Parrish swinging the baseball bat at her head, just before Jill was killed.

Suzy took a deep breath and sat back, trying to relax. She looked around and saw a few scattered people in the cemetery, but she wasn't sure if that encouraged her or increased her nervousness. She remembered the embarrassment she felt coming out of the trance in front of the local chapter of the Daughters of the American Revolution. Realizing that she was still holding that breath in her lungs, she let it out slowly.

She closed her eyes and tried to reach the meditative state needed to make contact. Suddenly, there were lightning flashes of images that she had seen earlier, but they didn't take her by surprise as much as before. And this time, she tried to strike a balance between consciousness and the trance state.

It was difficult. Jill's emotions were strong, overpowering. But Suzy remembered occasions in the past when she experienced a nightmare, and she was able to tell herself while in the dream state that it was just a dream, and that helped her to cope with the scary or sad images, and even to wake herself up. She held on to the thought that what she was seeing now was not happening to her. As if she were her own hypnotherapist, she told herself that she was safe. She was only a spectator.

When she saw the image of Bobby, Jill's son, appear, she tried to make contact.

"Jill," she said softly, "my name is Suzy. Suzy Quinn." She hoped that she had guessed correctly, that catching Jill when her thoughts were on her son would make her more receptive, that her mind would be more calm, more peaceful.

By the time she finished her greeting, the image had already switched to the house, but it sort of blurred and flickered back and forth between the boy and the house, before settling on the boy. The image changed to a memory of Bobby playing with Jill in the back yard of her home. The 'motion picture' was a little more in keeping with what Suzy was accustomed to, instead of the blink-of-an-eye flashes of still images. It was a happy memory, and Suzy smiled as she watched the happy little boy interacting with her as his mother.

The scene dissolved into an image of Jill standing in front of her on the path, with her unmistakable red hair and her eyes, different from Fiona's, yet similar in the tangible sadness they contained.

"Do I know you?" Jill asked.

"No, you don't," Suzy replied, "but I know what happened. And I think I know why you're still here. You're worried about your little boy."

The image of Jill, though obviously no longer corporeal, showed the representation of tears in her eyes, and she nodded.

"I'm so sorry about what happened to you," Suzy said, tears filling her own eyes, though she wasn't physically aware of it. "But Bobby is fine. Your parents have taken him in. They're raising him as if he was their own."

At this news, Jill seemed relieved, yet something still bothered her.

"He'll forget about me," she said.

"No," Suzy insisted, remembering details of the news articles she read. "They speak of you all the time to him. He's surrounded by photographs and mementos of you. They make sure he knows what a brave and loving mother he had. They love you and miss you, too, and they want to make sure he always remembers his mother, and how much you love him."

Jill smiled through her 'tears.'

"Why are you here, Suzy?" she asked.

"Because I know what it's like to lose someone you love, and to wish you knew how they were." The tears tumbled down her own cheeks as she continued. "I lost my husband and my daughter a year and a half ago, and there's not a single day that goes by that I don't wish and wonder about them.

"And I want you to know that you don't have to stay here in torment about Bobby. He's being loved and cared for."

Jill stood on the path in front of Suzy, sobbing for a few moments. Then, she made a motion very similar to wiping her eyes and looked intently at Suzy.

Suzy knew that, with no body, there were no tears. So she was intrigued by the apparently reflexive action of wiping them away.

"You're a good person," Jill finally said.

"I just hate the idea of you being stuck here in distress about your little boy. I wanted you to know that he'll be alright, and that, if you want to, you can move on."

"Thank you." Jill looked at Suzy intently for a few moments. In time, the sadness that had tinged her intensity was replaced by something else. Hope perhaps? Her lips curved upwards slightly in a shaky smile.

A moment later, with no further expression, the image of Jill vanished in a flash of light. Suzy remembered the adage, 'go toward the light.' She wondered if what she saw was the manifestation to an 'onlooker' of that very phenomenon.

As the cemetery rematerialized around her, Suzy sat on the bench feeling exhausted, as usual, but also enveloped in a feeling of warm contentment. Fortunately, her flippant persona stepped in before she thought of it as a hug from Jill, or the universe.

*God, maybe Lilith is right. I'm a freaking lightworker!*

## 51

Fiona rested her head on the back of the chair as she gazed at Caden's portrait. Fatigue had become a constant companion to her lately. Fortunately, true to his word, Drummond had hired a new cook a few days after Fiona arrived, so she didn't have those duties anymore.

She had started taking in mending and sewing jobs, earning money for her personal needs, which now included fabric for new dresses necessitated by her expanding belly. Most of her time during the winter months were spent in the chair by the fire as she worked on clothing for herself or others.

In the past few months, she had seen Lachlan a couple of times. On both occasions, it was after he had come to see Drummond. The first time was a couple of days after they arrived, to inform Drummond that he had found lodging in a boarding house in Marblehead. The second time was in November when Lachlan had contracted Drummond to retrieve some of his possessions, including cash, from Edinburgh. Taking up permanent residence here, he needed his resources brought to him.

On that second visit, when he called at the carriage house, Lachlan had broached the topic of marriage. Still attracted to Fiona, he knew that she would not consider a union with him without it being legal and moral. He had been disappointed at her refusal.

"Me dear husband has been dead for scarcely two months," she replied. "Indeed I'm flattered by your offer, but I'm afraid I cannot accept it."

"But I'll be able tae care for ye in the way ye need and deserve," he replied. "Ye cannae do that on your own, by takin' in other people's mending."

"I shall manage, Mr. Mac an Léigh."

"What aboot your child? It'll be born withoot a name."

"Me babe will have the name of meself and his father."

"But I can be a real father tae your wee bairn, so it wilnae be a bastard."

"Mr. Mac an Léigh," Fiona replied, becoming exasperated, "I'm surprised at ye. Me child will not be a bastard. I'm a widow, not a whore."

Lachlan frowned and nodded.

"Aye, of course. I'm sorry."

That was nearly two months ago. It was the last time she had seen him and, given the odd change in his demeanor, she found that she did not miss him.

As she knew nobody in this new country, Fiona had become withdrawn, mourning Caden in private as she engaged in her lonely occupation. Her life developed a routine, which was shattered on a cold, snowy morning in January.

§

Fiona awoke when it was still dark, and she pulled on boots and a long coat for her trek to the outhouse behind the carriage house. Snow had been falling all night and Fiona trudged through snow up to her knees. She didn't feel well, but she attributed it to the weather. Perhaps she was catching a cold.

By the time she got back in the carriage house and climbed in bed, she was freezing and exhausted, but she couldn't get back to sleep. Tossing and turning, she couldn't get comfortable. She finally got up and stirred up the fire. After putting a couple of big new logs on the burning embers, she stirred up the embers in the stove as well, to put on some water to boil for tea.

As she stood up, she felt a pop and a sudden release of pressure, as warm liquid ran down her legs. Looking down at the floor, she saw blood mixed in the puddle.

"Nay!" she gasped in a panic. "Nay, me wee one, ye're too early!" The baby wasn't due for another three months.

She turned toward the door, embarrassed but seeing no other choice than to wake Drummond and request a doctor. She only made it a couple of steps before she collapsed on the floor in pain.

Leaning with her back against the leg of her dining table, she pulled her knees up in a position that eased the pain a bit. Seeing the blood on her legs, feeling her body convulsing in agony, she knew that something was terribly wrong.

§

She felt weak, lethargic. And so cold! Her head was lying on the seat of one of the wooden dining chairs, facing the fireplace. She raised her eyes and looked toward it and saw that the fire was out. Bright white light was streaming in the front window.

Her body felt stiff and sore, and as consciousness began seeping back into her, she was able to localize the soreness. That's when she remembered. She lifted her head and looked down between her legs. The ooze, which included blood and other matter, was still there, puddled on the floor, drying on her legs. And there in the middle of it was poor little Caden. He had come out still and grey. He never even took a breath.

The afterbirth and the cord were scattered on the floor in the muck, beside his little body. As she looked at the baby, tears streaming down her cheeks, she felt her body start to convulse again, this time with the grief of yet another loss.

She remembered Caden, her dear husband, being forcibly taken from her just four months ago, his body sold to the university to be cut open and experimented on. She remembered her mother, a few years before, being stolen from her grave, and also sold to the university.

She couldn't let that happen to her baby. She didn't know if body snatchers were active in America, but she couldn't take the chance. She had to protect little Caden.

But first, she had to get the fire going. She couldn't protect her baby if she froze to death.

She pushed herself up and turned onto her hands and knees. With a supreme effort, she pulled up on the edge of the table. Dragging a knee forward, she managed to pull it up and get one foot flat on the floor. Pushing with her leg and pulling with her arms, she got herself into a hunched and unsteady standing position, leaning heavily on the table.

Wiping her eyes, she took a few deep breaths and, concentrating to steady herself, she dragged her feet toward the fireplace. She collapsed on the floor in front of the fireplace, bruising her knees in the process, and she poked at the ashes, exposing the embers buried within. She reached for another log and, crying with the intense effort required, lifted it and placed it on the embers.

*She stayed there on her hands and knees for a few moments, feeling the heat warming her. After a couple of minutes, she felt somewhat energized and pulled herself up, finally leaning against the mantle.*

*As she leaned there, she saw Caden's plaidie folded and draped over the back of her upholstered chair. She had washed and mended it, with the hope of passing it on to their child.*

*She knew now that she* would *be passing it on, as little Caden's burial shroud.*

## 52

The police car pulled up quietly in front of Suzy's home as she watched from the front window. A couple of the people gathered out there left when they saw the police, but the rest, eight or ten of them, stayed to talk to the officer.

Suzy didn't personally know any of them. However, she did recognize one of the women who, a few weeks ago, accompanied her religious zealot neighbor, Terri, in denouncing the idea of a ghost inhabiting the carriage house. A small confrontation like that, Suzy was comfortable with directly castigating and sending home. This size group, though, could turn dangerous.

She saw a man in the group talking to the police officer, and a couple of times, he gestured toward the house, or more specifically, toward the back, the carriage house, and the officer turned to look.

The police officer shook his head and said something to the group, and after a few more exchanges, the group reluctantly broke up. After they dispersed, the officer got back in his car and drove up to the front door. Suzy was there to meet him.

"Hi, Ms. Quinn?" he asked.

"Yes," Suzy replied, relieved.

"I'm Officer Miller. Do you know what was going on out there?"

"I have a pretty good idea."

"Mr. Robb, there, told me you have a ghost in your house."

"In the carriage house, actually," Suzy corrected, "but she sometimes comes to visit me in my house. We sympathize with each other." Suzy was still shaken by the last episode. Miller reacted with a slight, apparently involuntary smile.

"A couple of them are your neighbors," he said, "but they invited some friends to come and protest the allowance of Satanic activity here." Then he shook his head and waved a hand in dismissal. "Anyway, it's not my place to criticize their beliefs. Or yours, for that matter."

"Sure. Thank you for running them off."

"Well, the fact is they're within their rights to do that. As long as they're not on your property and they're not blocking traffic on the street, they have the right to protest. But I didn't tell them that. I let them know that *you* have the right to engage in any spiritual belief system that doesn't harm or encroach on anybody else's rights or well-being."

"I appreciate that," Suzy replied. "Does that include goat sacrifices under the full moon?"

"Have a good day, Ms. Quinn," he smiled.

## 53

Fiona tried to keep her attention focused on the mending she was working on. It was a simple piece, but her attention kept being pulled back to the floorboard next to her chair.

After she had rested and regained a little strength, interrupted with interludes of sobbing, she had cleaned herself up. Then, she spent an hour or so scrubbing the floor, thankful for the distraction that the physical effort afforded. As she did so, she was glad she hadn't been able to make it back to her bed. Had this mess been made there, she probably would not have been able to clean it up to her satisfaction.

She had noticed the slight gap in the floorboards near her chair shortly after she had moved in. Now, taking a knife, she was able to pry it up. Examining below it, between the floor joists, she determined that it would serve her purpose.

The final chore was the most difficult one. She took her time, holding and carefully wrapping the little body, again interspersed with moments of tears. After the final wrapping, her husband's faded plaidie, she placed the little bundle under the floor and replaced the board, stomping her foot on it to tamp the nails back in place.

As she tried to resume a normal life, she knew she had gone a little mad. Who buries their child under the floor of their home? But she couldn't help it. Her terror of the body snatchers still haunted her, and she couldn't subject her baby to the possibility of that horrible indignity.

She jabbed her finger with the needle and, sucking on the offended digit, for the hundredth time, she dragged her attention back to her work.

§

She put her mending aside when there was a knock on her door. Her first thought was that somebody might be dropping off some more work for her.

Instead, it was Drummond.

"Good evening, Mrs. Loganach," he said.

"Mr. Drummond, please come in." He accepted her invitation and Fiona closed the door against the cold.

"I haven't seen you in a while, but –" As she turned, he saw her in the light now, and he interrupted himself. When he spoke again, his voice expressed shock. "My dear, are you alright?"

Fiona wasn't aware of the tears still staining her cheeks, or of the shadows under her eyes. Before she had a chance to respond, Drummond's eyes briefly glanced at her midsection. Fiona did notice that.

"I lost the baby," she said quietly.

"Mrs. Loganach, I am so sorry! Is there anything you need?"

"Ye're too kind, sir. Thank ye, no." She tried to smile, hoping he didn't ask about the final disposition of the body. "Was there something ye needed?"

"Oh, yes," Drummond replied, remembering the reason he called. "Well, I was just wondering if you've seen Mr. MacKinley recently."

"Nay, I haven't seen him since November, when he contracted ye to ship some of his possessions here to America."

Drummond looked disappointed.

"Yes, I'm afraid that's the last time I saw him, as well."

"Is there a problem?"

"I'm hoping it's just a misunderstanding." Drummond hesitated, obviously feeling awkward. "I wasn't there when the ship docked, but Mr. MacKinley was.

"My first mate was supervising the unloading of the ship and, according to him, Mr. MacKinley had paperwork instructing that his property was to be loaded onto his wagon, and his money to be handed over to him personally.

"But I never issued any such orders, and I have not been paid for fulfilling my agreement with him. My efforts to collect my payment have, thus far, been unsuccessful."

"I'm sorry, Mr. Drummond," Fiona replied sympathetically. "If I see him, I shall instruct him to contact ye right away."

"Yes, thank you." Drummond looked at Fiona for a couple of seconds. "Mrs. Loganach, if there's anything at all I can do for you, please don't hesitate to ask."

"Thank ye, sir," Fiona said, managing an actual smile this time, though the sadness remained in her eyes.

§

"Mr. Drummond, ye must stop this," Fiona insisted as she accepted the small casserole dish from him. Her voice, while firm, was also warm with gratitude.

"It's nothing, Mrs. Loganach," he replied, "really. It's just that Mrs. Taylor, my cook, had prepared a little more than was needed for myself and Martha, so I instructed her to cook a small batch to bring to you."

"Ye're a good man. But sir, in the last several weeks, ye've brought me soup and bread and meat and books. I appreciate your generosity, but 'tis too much to repay."

"Nonsense," Drummond said, brushing it off with a wave of his hand. "I don't expect you to repay it. The fact is I'm frugal. I don't want excess food to go to waste. And the books, well, I noticed your one book over there on the bookcase after you moved in, and it looked rather forlorn."

"Ah, so ye just wanted me lonesome book to have some company?" Fiona smiled.

"Indeed I did," he smiled in return. "Of course, I can't stop you from reading them yourself. That's between you and your book."

"I have enjoyed them," Fiona replied. "They've helped to pass the time when I'm not working."

"Good." Drummond looked at her as he thought for a moment. "Mrs. Loganach, an idea just presented itself. Perhaps you'd like to spend your evenings with Martha and me, rather than sitting out here all alone."

"That's a very kind offer, sir, but I wouldn't want to intrude on your family time."

"I assure you it would be no intrusion at all. Martha likes you and asks after you often." Sensing Fiona's hesitance, and realizing he was sounding insistent, he suddenly put his hands up in a gesture of surrender. "I'll not force the issue. Just know that the invitation is there."

"Thank ye, again, sir." As Fiona inhaled, she looked down at the dish in her hands, then back up at Drummond, her eyebrows knitting together. The aroma was enticingly familiar. "What is this?" she asked as she lifted the lid and peeked under it.

"Rumbleethumps, as Martha calls it." Fiona looked up at him with fresh tears in her eyes, as Drummond continued. "We both love it. Thank you for giving me the recipe. I have Mrs. Taylor make it every couple of weeks."

"Ye're a very thoughtful man, Mr. Drummond," Fiona replied, replacing the cover. "Thank ye so much. And I shall indeed consider your kind invitation."

## 54

That must have been quite the harrowing episode," Fin said. Suzy had just related the last couple of visions to him, and he had her on speaker phone as he continued packing for his trip to Los Angeles, to be followed immediately by his trip to Scotland.

"Yes, it was," she agreed, her voice trembling a little. Fin noticed the tremulous quality of her response, and he paused. He put down the underwear and picked up his phone, turning the speaker off.

"Are you okay?"

"I'm fine," Suzy replied. "I mean it's not like I'm just watching a sad movie. It's more like I have a connection with Fiona, and I actually *feel* her emotions concerning what she's experiencing."

"As if you didn't have enough of your own already," Fin said sympathetically.

"Yeah," Suzy agreed. "But it's good stuff, too. You know, obviously I felt her heartbreak when she lost her husband, and then her baby, which all struck a little close to home for me. But I'm also feeling the heartwarming emotions now as Drummond is showing himself to be such a kind and generous benefactor."

"Well, I'm glad it's looking up a little."

"Me too."

"Then, of course, there's *my* insufferable great-great-great-great-great-grandfather."

"That's true. I guess I better keep my eye on you."

"That's okay," Fin smiled, "I plan to keep my eye on you quite a bit when we're together in Scotland."

Suzy chuckled.

"Anyway, then I have to come out of the visions and witness the latest episode in the ridiculous saga of the ghost hunters versus the fundamentalists."

"Now what?"

"Oh, nothing major. There were just a couple of guys out front yesterday dressed like Bill Murray and Dan Aykroyd in *Ghostbusters*."

"How cool is that!"

"Yeah, really cool," Suzy responded in a tone that implied that she was somewhat less impressed than Fin was with her visitors. "So, are you ready?"

"For my trip? Almost. I'm finishing my packing now. What about you?"

"We're not leaving for a couple more days," Suzy said with a 'no problem' tone. "I've got loads of time."

"I guess I need to work on my procrastination."

"My motto is, 'Procrastinate now! Don't put it off!'" Fin chuckled at that. "How are you dealing with the red carpet thing?" Suzy asked.

"I think I've come to terms with it," Fin said thoughtfully. "I'm anxious to see the movie. The red carpet is just how I get there. But I've realized that I'm basically a nobody. I doubt I'm going to be stopped for photos and interviews like Ryan Reynolds and Jennifer Lawrence. Nobody's going to care 'who I'm wearing.'"

He sighed.

"I'll tell you one thing, though. I'm definitely not looking forward to thirteen hours on a plane."

"Bring a long book," Suzy suggested. "I hear *TimePlex* is pretty good."

## 55

The seasons came and went, and Fiona took note of the characteristics of each. Despite the heartache she experienced in the middle of winter, when her mood was more observant, she noticed how beautiful the snow was on this wild island. During these cold months, Drummond frequently brought her hot dishes and freshly-baked bread.

The spring flowers were lovely, and Fiona was particularly taken with the vivid blossoms of the cherry trees. Drummond brought her fresh vegetable soup and strawberry pie.

Summer was warm and humid, and the Great Neck turned a vibrant green. This was when Drummond brought fresh blueberry muffins and apple cobbler.

Now, at the beginning of autumn, she was starting to see the beginnings of the warm colors that were prevalent last year when she moved here. Drummond had already brought her roasted potatoes and pumpkin pie.

Not to be outdone, Drummond's daughter, Martha, frequently painted pictures for Fiona, or wrote simple little childish poems. Fiona treasured all of them.

On one of these early autumn days, as the crisp afternoon gave way to the chill of early evening, there came a knock on her door. She knew who it was before she opened it.

"Mr. Drummond," she smiled. "Please come in." After closing the door, she turned to see today's offering.

"It was my desire to bring you something that was truly from me, instead of Mrs. Taylor," Drummond said, holding a lopsided cake. He looked at it a little critically. "I found a recipe that my wife used to make, and I followed the instructions precisely. I don't know why it looks the way it does, but I hope it tastes good."

Fiona smiled at him, having become accustomed to his gifts.

"Mr. Drummond, your very thoughtful gifts, while always greatly appreciated, are certainly not necessary," she said. She uttered a similar sentiment every time he brought her something, but it didn't deter him.

"I'm aware, Mrs. Loganach, that you're a very capable woman, and that my ministrations are not something you require." It was similar to the response he gave her every time. "But it is something that I desire to do for you." He handed the cake to her.

"Please sit down," Fiona replied as she set the cake on her table. Drummond pulled one of the chairs out and felt the wobbling back.

"Mrs. Loganach," he said, "I'm so embarrassed. I still haven't fixed this chair." He sat down but didn't lean back.

"I assure ye, Mr. Drummond, 'tis not a problem," Fiona said as she sat down across from him. "Another 'thank ye' seems so insignificant for everything ye do for me. Not just these gifts, but ye've been feeding me dinner most evenings as well. In fact, ye've practically made me a part of your family."

"Martha certainly loves you," he replied with a warm smile. "Every morning, she asks if Mrs. Loganach is coming for dinner. I'm happy when I can tell her 'yes.' But really, it's enough for me just to know that you appreciate the things I do."

"Oh aye," she said, leaning forward, folding her hands on the table, "I do ever so much!"

"And if I ever do something you don't like, or give you something you don't want, please let me know."

"If the past several months provide any clue, Mr. Drummond, I can't foresee that being a problem."

"Good. There is something that I would like from you, if you wouldn't mind." He paused nervously. "I would like for you to call me Robert." Fiona looked at him, a little surprised. "You've been living in my carriage house for nearly a year now. I think we know each other well enough to not be quite so formal."

"Very well, Robert," she agreed with a smile, "then ye may call me Fiona."

"Splendid!" Drummond beamed at her. He sat rooted in place as if he was casting about for something to say.

"Is there anything else, Robert?" Fiona asked curiously.

"Yes, Fiona, there is," he said as he breathed restlessly and his smile faded, replaced with tense lines around his mouth. Impulsively, he reached forward and took her hands in his. Startled, she sat up, but Drummond held on to her hands. "As you yourself said, we've practically made you a part of the family. That is only partly a matter of convenience. The fact is I've grown quite fond of you. We both have."

Fiona licked her lips, feeling suddenly very dry, but before she could say anything, Drummond pressed on.

"In my estimation, 'practically part of the family' is not quite enough. I think that can be improved on. Over the past year, I've learned what a fine woman you are, Fiona, and it would make me very happy if you would agree to be my wife."

"Mr. – Robert," Fiona flushed, "I don't know what to say. I don't know if I'm ready for that. Earlier this year, I lost me baby. A few months before that, I lost me husband."

"I know, Fiona. You're due some happiness now." Noticing her skepticism, he continued. "I don't expect to be your best love. I know you loved Caden, and you lost him through no fault of your own. I loved Judith as well. But as I said, I've grown fond of you and, unless I'm misinterpreting your responses, I think you feel similarly toward me."

Fiona smiled softly and nodded.

"Our former spouses have passed on. Finding someone else is not being unfaithful to their memory. We've been left to find happiness again. These past few months, Fiona, I've been discovering that I've found it."

Fiona's soft smile turned into a full-faced grin, and she nodded again.

"I think I have too."

They were married on a crisp October day in St. Michael's Church on the Marblehead mainland. The wood frame church was 113 years old, a fact which Drummond spoke of proudly. Fiona smiled as she remembered St. Giles Cathedral, a few blocks from her family home in Edinburgh, 600 years old when St. Michael's was being built.

But she allowed Drummond his boast. He was her husband, after all.

## 56

This was the first actual vacation that Suzy had taken since losing Mark. While the thought was a poignant one, she was a little surprised that it didn't bring on the depression that had been her companion for so long.

She had never taken a long trip by herself before. She realized that she wouldn't actually be alone, since Fin was going to join her in Edinburgh. But for the flight and the first few days, she would be entirely on her own. She felt a bit of reticence, but no melancholy.

She thought about Fiona leaving Scotland for America after losing everything. Her trip wasn't totally by herself, either, since she traveled with Lachlan, but still she kept pretty much to herself. The fortitude required for an endeavor like that, in an age when travel was measured in number of days or weeks instead of hours, was amazing to Suzy. Her own crossing would be done in about ten hours.

Suzy had told Fiona that she was going to Scotland for a visit, and that she was still determined to find out anything she could about Caden. She also warned her that, after almost two hundred years, she didn't have her hopes very high.

Fiona had smiled at her, the most complete smile that Suzy had seen from Fiona.

Suzy looked out the window at the ocean six and a half miles below. Aside from a few wispy clouds, there was nothing to be seen but the expanse of blue stretching out for miles in all directions, eventually blending with the blue horizon.

Looking to her left, she imagined what it would be like to see Fin sitting there. She even imagined at some point reaching over and putting her hand in his. She didn't know if it would get to that point or not, but some of their banter on the phone had begun to lean in that direction. She had a pretty good idea where it was heading when at least some of her remarks were not of the smartass variety.

She looked back out the window and sighed, and in doing so, surprised herself. She was becoming quite the softy.

She figured it was time to occupy her mind with more than daydreams. She opened the book that she had brought with her. She had decided to check out Fin's, aka Michael Jones' other work and decided to get the two novels that he published after *TimePlex*. She had already reread *TimePlex* a few months ago, after she met Fin, and she found that the story held up well. She was impressed by her friend's ability to tell a story.

He had told her that, while neither of those later novels sold as well as *TimePlex*, one of them, *DragonCache*, was his favorite. Inspired by Tolkien and Le Guin, it was a sword-and-sorcery adventure novel that he fantasized being discovered by Peter Jackson.

So far, no such luck.

After the first couple of pages, though, Suzy was hooked.

uzy felt a little lonely at first. Being so far from home, she hadn't experienced a vision from Fiona for a couple of days. She and Fin had exchanged a few text messages, but that had been intermittent, as well, since he had been busy getting ready for his trip to LA.

Suzy's flight had been long but uneventful. She had spent it, mainly, dozing and reading. Halfway through *Dragon-Cache*, she had determined that Fin was one of her favorite writers.

Her flight had taken off from Logan at 5:00 pm and, with a brief stop in Reykjavik, arrived in Edinburgh at about 9:30 the next morning. She had never been able to sleep well on airplanes, though, so by the time she reached her hotel, she was jet lagged and exhausted. She spent a few hours sleeping until nearly noon.

But after that, she had spent the rest of the day exploring Old Town Edinburgh, particularly in the vicinity of South Bridge and the Royal Mile, one of the main commercial and tourist arteries in Old Town.

Being a history buff, one of the things she loved about Boston was how it preserved so much of its history. Here in Edinburgh, that was even more the case. At least in her vicinity in Old Town, every one of the stone buildings around her looked to be at least two hundred years old, and she couldn't help wondering what stories they might tell.

She took special delight in the occasions when she recognized something she had seen in one of Fiona's visions, a building or a bridge. One of the most moving, to Suzy, was where Cowgate passes under the South Bridge arch, where the distraught woman had given Caden the money and the tickets. In that area, some of the buildings nearby were newer, some were the same but with updated façades, but it was still easily recognizable.

The next day, once she got down to business, she started by visiting the National Library of Scotland, located just off the Royal Mile. After filling out a form and getting her picture taken, she was given a library card which granted her access to the reading rooms, books, and other collections of the library.

She spent nearly the whole day researching the vaults and cellars of the town, studying whatever books, maps and diagrams she could find, and making copies of what she thought might be useful in her search. She did a genealogical search for Caden Loganach but, not surprisingly, found nothing. However, she did take numerous copies of information about Edinburgh's underground to the hotel with her at the end of the day.

§

Suzy sat on her bed, poring over the copies she had made. Some of the maps were fragments, to illustrate something about whatever was being discussed in the book it was taken from. Others were more extensive.

She had them arranged on the bed as she discovered the location, trying to place each of them in their correct relative position. They were all in different scales, but as she located where one of the puzzle pieces fit, she added it to the drawing she was making in a large notebook. After a couple of hours, she had laid out where several of the vaults were located in relation to the streets above.

Her map was still very incomplete, but she was mainly focusing her attention on the general area where she knew Fiona and Caden had lived. Having spent her first afternoon here exploring, she had compiled a usable list of locations that she recognized.

Obviously, a project of this magnitude wasn't going to be done tonight. She was feeling hungry and decided to go get dinner. Last night, she had eaten in the hotel restaurant and, still wiped out from travel, had gone to bed early. Tonight, she decided to see what there was out on the town.

The Royal Mile is actually a series of five short streets, Castlehill, the Lawnmarket, the High Street, the Canongate and Abbey Strand. These five streets, though, were one continuous thoroughfare and made up the busiest street in Old Town.

Joined together, the street is almost exactly a mile long. Stretching from the Edinburgh Castle, perched high on the Castle Rock on the west end to Holyrood Palace on the east, the mile in between is filled with shops, restaurants and pubs, many of them obviously aimed toward tourists. Among them was a company that gave tours of the vaults. Suzy would be taking the tour tomorrow.

As she walked out of her hotel, she was surprised by how light it was. It was nearly nine o'clock, but it seemed like late afternoon. She had learned when researching the weather before her trip that Edinburgh was about fourteen degrees north of Boston. Those fourteen degrees must make quite a difference.

Out of curiosity, she got out her phone and did a quick comparison. Sunset in Edinburgh was at 10:00, an hour and a half later than in Boston.

"Weird," she concluded. Her stomach growled, pulling her back from her distraction. She walked for a block or two, looking at restaurants located on the Royal Mile and decided on one that had an outdoor patio where she could people-watch while she ate.

She was too hungry to peruse the menu for very long, so she settled almost immediately on the fish and chips and a local ale. She checked text messages and Facebook notifications while she waited, but there wasn't much to see, not with Edinburgh surrounding her. She put her phone down and watched the people passing by.

The service was fast, and within minutes, she was enjoying her late dinner. As she ate, one little girl caught her eye. She was perhaps seven or eight years old, with blonde hair and blue eyes. She reminded Suzy instantly of Emma. She was walking along the three-foot metal fencing that separated the dining area from the street, just looking around. She seemed curious about the people eating there.

As she came in front of Suzy's table and looked at her, Suzy smiled at her.

"Hello," she said.

"Good forenicht, ma'am," the little girl replied with a heavy accent, apparently a little surprised to be addressed by one of the tourists. Separated by the fence, Suzy thought it would not be objectionable to engage the little girl in conversation.

"What's your name?"

"Me name's Catriona, ma'am." The girl was quite personable. "What's yers?"

"I'm Suzy. Where's your mother?" she asked, looking around.

"Me mum's in th' neist steid," Catriona replied.

"Where?"

"She went ahead o' me." Suzy had to listen carefully to understand the dialect. She looked around again, but didn't see anybody who looked to be in a panic, searching for her little girl.

"Isn't she afraid somebody might take you?"

"Who'd wantae tak me?"

Suzy smiled a little wistfully. *How different Edinburgh must be from virtually any big city in America!* Still . . .

"Maybe you should find your mother," Suzy said. "She might be worried." The little girl smiled and wandered away.

After she finished her dinner, she started wandering back toward the hotel while perusing some of the shops along the way. She remembered that the next morning was the Fourth of July. Considering the patriotic fervor with which it's observed in America, she found it mildly disorienting that, here, it was just another day. She looked down at her phone and opened her contacts.

"Hey, you," Fin answered right away. He sounded out of breath.

"Hey, yourself. How's it going?"

"Good. I'm just finishing up some last-minute packing. I'm leaving for the airport in an hour."

"Okay, I won't keep you. But I figured you'd be pretty busy tomorrow, getting ready for the big premiere, so I decided to wish you good luck tonight."

"Well, I'm glad you did. Thank you. Are you enjoying Edinburgh?"

"Very much. Everybody talks like Montgomery Scott. You'll love it."

"I love that you know his name," Fin replied with a smile in his voice. "Everybody knows him as Scotty. Only a true aficionado would know his full name."

"Whatever, nerd boy," Suzy replied, smiling back at him. "Anyway, I know you're busy, so I'll let you go."

"Okay, Suzy, thanks for calling. I can't wait to see you." Immediately recognizing his moment of weakness, he uttered a light gasp and nervously tried to cover it up. "I mean I can't wait to see Edinburgh. Well," he paused, "I can't wait to see you, too."

"Say good-night, Fin."

"Good-night, Fin."

As she slipped her phone in her purse, Suzy smiled and sighed. Then, she shook her head.

*Shit, girl, you're losing it.*

## 58

I f Fin could have had only one wish granted about the world premiere of the movie based on his book, it would be to have it at the legendary Chinese Theatre, on Hollywood Boulevard. His whole life, though he had never been there, he remembered being enthralled by the idea of all the handprints and footprints and otherprints of various movie stars in the cement in front of the world's most famous movie theater.

Now, he was one of the stars approaching it. Granted, he knew he was not as well-known as Clark Gable or Mel Brooks or Jennifer Lawrence, or any of the other stars who had something imprinted in a square in front of the theater. But he was the author of the book that was the basis of the summer blockbuster that was making its world premiere here.

He had to admit that the approach, at least, was a little less glamorous than he had imagined. The walkway was lined on one side with metal barricades holding back the paparazzi. On the other side, behind the red carpet (which was actually dark blue, the color of the book cover), was the backdrop featuring the large *TimePlex* logo, interspersed with smaller logos of corporate sponsors. Still, he felt important, being stopped by some of the photographers and asked his thoughts about the movie (which he, obviously, hadn't seen yet) or about the stars of his story.

Fortunately, nobody asked him whose tuxedo he was wearing. He didn't remember the brand.

He was just tossing off a brief response to the smiling and enthusiastic *Entertainment Tonight* correspondent who had recognized him from his author photo when he felt somebody grab him by the left shoulder. He hadn't even noticed anybody approach. He turned and was surprised to see a familiar face.

"You're up for a promotion, buddy!" Ryan Reynolds blustered to the reporter. "You've cornered the puppet-master, Michael Jones himself, the originator of our thought and expression."

He felt other hands grab his right arm, and he looked down to see Jennifer Lawrence on his right side.

"Yeah," she affirmed, then looked confused. Looking up at Fin, she said, "Wait, what do we say now?" That was followed by her signature guttural laugh, and Fin was happy to be saved from facing the reporters one-on-one. He also remembered the teasing banter he and Suzy had engaged in a few days before, in which he joked about having Ryan Reynolds and Jennifer Lawrence flanking him on the red carpet. If he had to miss out on being with Suzy the first few days in Scotland, he was glad it was like this.

With the camera rolling, the reporter seemed overjoyed with his good luck at snagging the main stars of the movie, along with the author. He asked a couple more questions, which Fin was happy to let Ryan and Jennifer handle.

After they finished off the reporter, to his delight, they started to continue toward the entrance to the theater, with their arms through his, but Ryan stopped.

"Hold it," he said in his familiar soft voice, "I'm sorry, man. You're a nice guy and all, but I kind of like my wife a little better." It was only then that Fin noticed Blake Lively standing in the background, smiling, allowing her husband his moment of silliness. Ryan continued in a taunting tone. "Jennifer doesn't have anybody. Maybe she can stay with you."

"I *do too* have somebody," Jennifer shot back in her best spiteful, junior high voice, "he just couldn't come tonight." She looked up at Fin. "But yes, I'd be happy to stay with you this evening."

As cameras flashed, the two pairs entered the theater together.

§

The theater was beautiful, one of the last of the great movie palaces. Like nearly all theaters nowadays, it was part of a multiplex, but the premiere, *his* premiere, was in the main auditorium.

If Fin was star-struck at the New York Comic Con, he was absolutely enraptured here. For him, the highlight of the time spent milling about before the movie was when he met Patrick Stewart and Ian McKellen, the stars of three of his favorite sci-fi/fantasy franchises. Fin was barely able to utter two words, but both actors were gracious and funny.

He couldn't wait to tell Suzy about it.

As the time approached, Janek Laar, the director (Fin made a point of remembering his name this time) walked in front of the auditorium, dwarfed by the enormous red and gold curtain.

Everybody settled into their seats, Ryan and Blake on his left, and Jennifer on his right. The auditorium quieted down and Janek spoke briefly.

"I'd like to thank all of you for coming tonight. As many of you know, this is my first major motion picture, and I've poured my soul into it. Fortunately, I had the support of many fine people, on both sides of the camera. We're all very proud of this picture, and we hope you enjoy it."

There was applause as the lights dimmed, and the curtains were swept aside. The movie started immediately.

Fin was a little startled. It made sense, but he had never gone to a movie that didn't have at least fifteen minutes of previews preceding it.

Fin was hyperaware during the movie, of so many things. He was curious about how his original story had fared, but he tried to separate the movie from his novel, viewing it as an independent entity. He was attentive to the adaptation of his characters to the screen. He took note of the audience's reaction to virtually everything in the movie, but particularly to the dialogue and scenes that had survived from the original novel.

By the time it was over, he had to admit that, given the limitations of a screen adaptation, Laar had been pretty faithful to the original material. The movie had lived up to the moniker "Summer Blockbuster."

After the applause, the lights came up and everyone rose, as did the din in the auditorium.

"Nice job, guys!" Fin said to his companions, and they both smiled. "Well, nice job Jennifer. Ryan, I noticed a few things you could work on." Ryan cast his eyes downward in a contrite manner, but he smiled afterward.

Others started crowding around them, congratulating Ryan and Jennifer, and a few of them included Fin in their conversations. Somebody mentioned the afterparty, and Ryan turned to Fin.

"You're coming to the afterparty, aren't you, Michael?"

"I'm afraid I can't," he replied. "I have to catch a plane to Edinburgh."

"Oh, that's too bad," Ryan replied, apparently genuinely sorry. "Jennifer will be so distraught."

"Stop trying to get me in trouble, Ryan," Jennifer shot back. "He trusts me!" Fin could see the concealed smiles behind their faces, so he wasn't concerned.

Suddenly, Ryan perked up. "Wait, Edinburgh? That's research for the sequel, isn't it?"

"It is, partly," Fin replied.

And suddenly, he couldn't wait to get on that plane.

## 59

Suzy planned on spending July 4th doing more re-search, both at the library and by walking around on a self-guided tour of the area. In doing so, she hoped to fill in a few more details on her map.

It was also the day of her vaults tour, and she could hardly wait. The tour was conducted by a young woman wearing a black hooded cloak, meant to be creepy, she understood, but Suzy thought it just looked like a cheap, and rather silly, Halloween costume.

The starting point was a kiosk located, naturally, on the Royal Mile, near the Mercat Cross, a small stone structure where, in times past, important civic announcements were made and punishments were meted out. The tour began with a bit of interesting history and silliness about life in eighteenth- and nineteenth-century Scotland. It included information on the brutality that was sometimes a part of life at that time (*interesting*), including crime and punishment (*sometimes cringe-worthy*), and a mock whipping of a "volunteer" the tour guide pulled from the group, barely touching him with the coiled whip (*silly, and mildly BDSM*).

There was information about the sanitation habits of the time, which Suzy already knew about from her visions and research. Walking through the streets and closes, more history was related. One such tidbit was Mary King's Close, supposedly one of the more haunted locations in the city. It's rumored that, during the plague epidemic in 1645, the close was bricked up to contain the spread of the disease by enclosing the infected inside, leaving them to die. The tour guide didn't affirm that it was simply an urban legend, though, leaving it open for personal interpretation and sensationalism (*silly*).

Suzy was relieved when, perhaps a half hour later, they finally began their descent down an exterior stone stairway that seemed to follow the contours of the natural hillside. During the tour, she tried to make mental notes of locations, turns, and so on, but the tour was so meandering that she quickly lost her bearings. By the time they actually entered the vaults, she was completely lost.

But once she was there, she was enthralled. There was nothing recognizable about the three or four rooms that they actually visited, but still, being in the general location where Fiona and Caden lived for a while was particularly touching for Suzy.

All of the rooms had vaulted ceilings, which she knew were the underside of the arches of South Bridge overhead. There were stories associated with each of the rooms about legendary denizens, including a cobbler who made shoes for inhabitants of the vaults. Supposedly a friendly person, he has been known to smile at people in the tours as they passed through.

Another famous one was 'Mr. Boots' who was reported to have murdered a woman and kept her body in the room that his ghost still inhabits. He stands guard over the location where he kept her body, becoming angry and aggressive toward anyone who invades his space.

Nobody in Suzy's group indicated any type of contact with these or any other ghosts, nor did Suzy sense their presence.

Before she realized it, her group was already heading back up to the surface. They emerged about a half block south of the Royal Mile, and it took a few moments for Suzy to get her bearings.

She decided she would need to take the tour again.

§

After lunch, Suzy went to the tour office, near where the tour had ended that morning. Unfortunately, the next two tours were already full. She mentally kicked herself for not thinking to get a ticket before, and she booked the next available one. That meant she had almost an hour and a half to kill. She decided to do a little more exploring until the next tour began.

She ventured off the Royal Mile and headed down South Bridge to explore, as well as the parallel streets on both sides of it, Niddry and Blair. While she was looking at the sights, she was also aware of the buildings, examining the architecture for familiar locations, sites that she may have seen in her visions. Thus, about a half hour after she began her wandering, she stopped short, looking at a grouping of newer storefronts, and at the venerable old architectural details that showed above them.

*I found it, Fiona.*

The storefronts were completely different, as she had expected. Set into the old stone building now were a drug store and a little coffee shop called The Royal Grind. But the architecture above them was the same as she remembered from her visions, except for a heavier aging of dirt. The doors to the drug store and the coffee shop were close together, perhaps a foot and a half apart where, two centuries ago, there used to be a vestibule. Suzy snapped a couple of pictures on her phone, of the two doorways, and of the old building they were now in.

She went to the entrance to the drug store, examining the area by the door as she did. Not surprisingly, there was no indication of where a two-hundred-year-old staircase used to be. The drug store was where the old closed up book shop used to be, so the stairway down to Fiona and Caden's flat would have been approximately where the current door to The Royal Grind was located. She went inside.

The warm smell of coffee enveloped her. That, and the greetings of the barista, convinced her to go to the counter and order a cup. The barista was an older bearded man, and the woman at the cash register, Deòiridh, according to her name tag, seemed roughly the same age.

"How long have you been here?" Suzy asked as she paid. There was only one other person in the shop, and he already had his coffee, so Suzy didn't feel as if she was taking them from their customers.

"Och, we've been 'ere in this same steid for nearly thirty years. Me husband, Kirk, started up this place aboot the time 'e got laid off from his accoonting job. Best thing that e'er happened tae us."

Suzy looked at the one other customer. Must be busier in the mornings, she thought. She smiled at the barista, Kirk, according to his name tag, as he set Fiona's coffee on the counter.

Suzy paused as she tried to think of a segue that wasn't quite so jarring. Failing that, . . .

"Before you opened your shop, was there a stairway over there by the front door that led down to the vaults?"

"A stairway?" the man asked. "Nay, we dinnae even have a cellar 'ere. Th' vaults, ye say?"

"Yes," Suzy answered absently. Then, she smiled and shook her head at them, waving away her question. "Never mind. Thank you."

She took a sip of her coffee as she walked toward a table and decided to put some cream and sugar in it. Being more of a tea drinker, she marveled at how coffee often smelled better to her than it tasted.

Sitting down at a table by a window, she pulled out a pencil and the map that she had been working on. Locating where she was now, she marked it on the map, drawing a light outline of where the stairs had been, noting their position relative to where the vaults tour ended.

Sipping her coffee, she perused the map while occasionally looking out the window. She wondered how many of the people walking by were locals and how many were tourists. A few years back, the usual tell was a camera slung around someone's neck.

She mused that she didn't see as many people with cameras anymore. She did see a number of people taking selfies and photos of the interesting sites with their phones, and she realized that she saw this activity now more than she ever used to see people with actual cameras.

Was that a phenomenon primarily among Americans? She had heard it said that Americans were becoming more narcissistic. What about the rest of the world? Could some of those people taking selfies on their phones be locals, Scots who wanted to document their daily life on Facebook or Twitter or Instagram?

Looking at her watch, Suzy saw that it was almost time for the tour to start. She looked at the map again, then put it away in her purse. She finished the last of her coffee and placed the cup on the counter, thanking Kirk and Deòiridh, then she went out the front door, almost running into Catriona.

"You again!" Suzy said, surprised.

"Aye, ma'am, 'tis meself," the little girl replied with a smile. She was wearing the same clothes she wore the last time Suzy saw her, and now, in the full overhead sunlight, Suzy could see that the girl's face was dirty. She wondered if Scotland had as much of a problem with homelessness as many cities in America.

Then again, she was a seven-year-old child. They tend to get dirty.

"It's good to see you again," Suzy said as she started walking, "but I'm afraid I have to go. I have a tour starting in a couple of minutes."

"A'right, ma'am, I'll donder alang wi' ye," the girl said as she walked alongside Suzy. Her legs were pumping hard, taking two steps for each of Suzy's, but she seemed fine with that, smiling all the way.

"What do you do around here?" Suzy asked. "Are you on your own all day?"

"Aye, ma'am. I watch folk, I blether tae ye, I play wi' me mukker."

"Your mukker?"

"Aye. Me friend."

"Oh, well, I'm glad you're not alone all day."

"Nay, ma'am, I'm wi' folk all th' time."

The group was already gathered for the tour at the kiosk, and Suzy pointed at them.

"Well, that's where I'm going, so I'll have to leave you here."

"That's braw, ma'am. Mebbe I'll see ye again."

"I hope so, Catriona. Be safe."

The little girl smiled at her and waved as Suzy walked away.

§

She joined the group, ignoring a woman who had been staring at her as she approached. A young woman arrived wearing a black hooded cloak, signaling that the tour was about to start. Suzy got out her ticket, ready to present it to the guide, when she noticed the woman in her group was staring at her again. As Suzy looked at her, the woman looked away, and Suzy wiped her lip, thinking that she probably had a coffee mustache or something like that.

She was accustomed to having young men stare at her. She didn't like it. It made her uncomfortable, but apparently it was something that attractive people had to come to terms with. Having other women stare at her was less common, and the expression on this woman's face was not one of admiration. When the woman glanced over at her again, Suzy spoke up in a sarcastic tone.

"Why are you staring at me? Did I spit on you or something?"

*Yeah, I've got SpiritSense up the wazoo! Some lightworker, huh Lilith?*

The woman sneered disgustedly as she looked away, mumbling something to her friend, who also looked over at Suzy.

Self-conscious now, Suzy glanced down to be sure her jeans weren't unzipped or that she hadn't missed a couple of buttons on her blouse.

265

The tour guide was making her way through their cluster. As she approached Suzy, she took her ticket which, thankfully, got Suzy's mind off the ill-mannered wench in the group.

Suzy paid little attention to the early part of the tour, including the mock whipping. Even the history didn't interest her this time. That's not why she was there. By the time they started moving, though, she had her map out and noted every turn they made.

Once they descended into the vaults, she lagged behind at the rear of the group. Besides the turns, she also made annotations about doors and hallways not taken, counting steps between rooms, and noting anything else that occurred to her.

When they came up the stairs and out onto the street, she made a quick note of that location as well, then she put the map in her purse and left the group, not sticking around for the final words of the guide.

She couldn't wait to get back to her hotel and compile all the information she had gathered.

uzy had spent the day tracing her original drawing onto a fresh sheet of paper, adding new details she had gathered after taking the tour yet again. It still wasn't a complete picture. There were gaps here and there, but the gaps were filling in, and she felt as if she could interpolate from the existing data.

It was nearly 7:30 when she was interrupted by a knock on her door. She opened it to find Fin standing there, trying to look irritated, but a goofy grin kept creeping onto his face.

"Hey, why don't you answer your phone?" he asked.

"You're here!" Suzy exclaimed. "God, I lost all track of time. Come in!"

Fin stepped into the room and Suzy closed the door, after which they clumsily fumbled about with a greeting. They settled on a hug. It lasted a little longer than either expected, though neither complained.

"I didn't realize it was so late," she said.

"I'm glad I didn't have to rely on you for a ride from the airport," Fin said, still half-heartedly sporting his aggravation.

"Sorry," Suzy replied a little contritely. "I turned my ringer off this afternoon during the vaults tour. I guess I forgot to turn it back on."

"It's okay," Fin insisted, letting the smile take over his face. He looked at the guidebooks, maps and other papers scattered across the bed. "What are you doing over there? It looks like you're planning some kind of bank heist."

"Come here! You've got to see this." Suzy took Fin's hand and he allowed her to pull him excitedly to her bed. Under other circumstances . . . .

He pushed the thought from his mind as they both sat on the edge of the bed and Suzy picked up her hand-drawn map.

"I found it," she said. "There's a coffee shop and a drug store there now, but I found it!"

"Fiona and Caden's flat? That's great!"

"Well, no, I didn't find the room itself. Or the stairs to it, for that matter. But I found where it used to be."

She fished her phone out of her purse and, after turning the ringer back on, pulled up the pictures she took yesterday afternoon of the storefronts and the building.

"There used to be one door here," she said, pointing to the two doorways, "which led into the vestibule. The drug store is where the old closed book store was. This door into the coffee shop is roughly where the door to the stairs used to be."

"No stairs now, though?"

"No, I'm afraid not. I went in and had some coffee, and talked briefly to the owners. They've been there for thirty years, but they didn't know anything about stairs down to the vaults. The stairway would have been filled in long before they came along."

"Filled in?"

"Yeah," Suzy replied as she sifted through some of her notes on the bed. Finding the paper she was looking for, she scanned the details. "Nobody knows for sure when, but at some point, tons of rubble were dumped into the vaults, closing them off to the public. Some areas were probably even bricked over. There were virtually no written records about the vaults, so people eventually forgot all about them. Most people in the latter half of the twentieth century probably never even heard of them.

"It wasn't until sometime in the 1980s that they were rediscovered by a Scottish rugby player, of all people, Norrie Rowan."

"A rugby player? How did he find it?"

"I'm not sure. He's retired now. In fact, he ran for a position in Parliament a couple of decades ago. But I guess after his retirement from rugby, he ran several pubs. Maybe it was on one of his properties that he discovered an entrance to the vaults.

"He and his son excavated hundreds of tons of rubble and artifacts during the 1990s. So it's only been since then that modern people know about the vaults.

"Cool."

"Even cooler, in 1989, Norrie Rowan used the tunnel he excavated to help Cristian Raducanu, a rugby player from Romania, escape the Romanian secret police and seek political asylum."

She picked up her newly updated map and spent the next few minutes showing Fin everything that she had learned and pieced together over the last few days. Finally, she realized that he was just looking at her, smiling.

"Waddayoo lookin' at?" Suzy said, assuming a tough New York accent.

"You sound like Marisa Tomei in *My Cousin Vinny*," Fin replied with a chuckle.

"You didn' ansah my queschun," Suzy said, still in character.

Fin smiled and shook his head.

"I'm just happy to be here."

Suzy returned the smile and, placing her hand on top of his, dropped the act.

"Me too. Oh," she looked at her watch, "you're probably exhausted, and hungry."

"Yeah," Fin replied, "I haven't had lunch yet."

"You still won't. It's dinner time."

§

They sat at a table in a dim little pub that was probably aimed directly at tourists, but they didn't care. Fin ordered Haggis, Neeps and Tatties, wanting to compare it to the version he had at the Beltane festival in Colorado, on that ill-fated last day with Kay. Suzy was excited to see Rumbledethumps on the menu, and she ordered that.

"Rumbledethumps?" Fin asked incredulously.

"It was Caden's favorite dish, and Fiona made it once for Robert Drummond. He and Martha loved it, too."

"Hmm," Fin replied, happily studying Suzy's face.

"Hey, buster," she said, "keep your eyes to yourself." Despite her smartass tone, she couldn't keep the warm smile from her face.

"I can't help it," he mused. "I'm just so happy to finally be here with you."

"Well, don't get ahead of yourself," Suzy said, trying to remain balanced. "We don't even know if we like each other yet."

"Yeah, we do," Fin replied, surprising himself with his confident attitude.

Before Suzy could reply, the waiter returned and set their drinks on the table. Fin picked up his Ben Nevis and held it up in preparation for a toast. Suzy responded by picking up her glass of Scottish raspberry wine, a novelty she felt she had to try.

"To us," Fin said, "as we embark on our first date, which has been a long time coming."

"Wait, what about Dunkin' Donuts?"

"You stated in no uncertain terms that that was not, under any circumstances, a date."

"Hmm," Suzy replied, twisting her face into a look of chagrin, "I guess I was kind of an asshole."

"No, you weren't an asshole. You just weren't ready yet. Now, nine months later, I'm *really* glad you're ready."

"So am I." They clinked their glasses together and drank. "Oh!" Suzy exclaimed, "and to you! How did your first world premiere go?"

"Oh, honey, it was so cool!" Fin became extremely animated and roughly set his glass down as his inner geek emerged. "The movie was really good. The screenwriter and the director did an amazing job with my material. And Ryan and Jennifer were great as Spencer and Gisele. They embodied the roles as if they were written for them."

"So, you're on a first name basis with them?" Suzy asked with a grin.

"We sat together in the theater."

"You did not!"

"I swear on the life of Jean-Luc Picard, whom I also met. They saved me from a reporter. Ryan's wife was with him, but Jennifer was there alone."

"So, you were Jennifer Lawrence's date?"

"I was. Don't worry, she was well-behaved."

"She was? What about you?"

"Are you kidding? I could barely form coherent sentences. I was the idiot they felt sorry for."

Suzy didn't respond, but just sat there smiling at him.

"What?" Fin asked.

"You called me 'honey.'"

"I did? I'm sorry. But it'll probably happen again."

"I didn't mind."

"Ah, so you *do* like me. See? I knew it!"

"Okay, Maverick, don't get cocky."

§

Both of their dinners met with their satisfaction taste-wise, each of them agreeing on the term "Scottish comfort food." They followed them up with delicious Scottish desserts. Suzy ordered Cranachan and Fin had Tipsy Laird. By the time they finished, they were both quite satisfied, though Fin felt as if he was dragging.

He had reset his watch to reflect local time. As they walked out of the pub into the light, he looked at it again.

"Nine forty-five," he said, looking up at the sky. The sun couldn't be seen over the buildings, but it hadn't set yet. While it was still light out, it was beginning to look like early dusk. "That is so weird." They started walking toward the hotel.

"I know. I haven't gotten used to it yet, either."

"Well, the night is young." Fin looked at Suzy. "Apparently. I can't believe I'm so tired."

"Did you sleep on the plane?"

"Not really. I don't sleep well on planes."

"I don't either," Suzy replied. "So, there's your answer. You're suffering from jet lag. So why don't we get some sleep, and we'll meet up in the morning and do some site-seeing."

"That seems like kind of an anti-climactic end to our first evening together," Fin said, "but I have to say it sounds pretty good."

They separated in the lobby of the hotel, after a lingering hug, and went to their respective rooms.

## 61

Suzy was surprised at how relaxed she felt. The last several nights, she had felt a little tense, she assumed because of her earlier reticence about traveling to a foreign country alone. Tonight, though, she felt completely calm and composed.

Having a somewhat independent nature, she had a hard time believing it had anything to do with Fin being in the hotel, on the next floor down. But still the calm was unmistakable.

As she lay in bed in that totally relaxed state just before deep sleep, she felt a presence. Since she had been away from home, she had missed Fiona. Now, she welcomed the familiar feeling, as it was similar to Fiona's visitations, and she allowed herself to be drawn into that early dream state.

"Ye dinnae seem like ye'r fae aroond 'ere," the man said in a very heavy accent, even before Suzy saw his face. When he finally appeared, she saw a young man with a headful of black, curly hair and a careworn face. He was wearing knickerbockers, boots and a plaid vest, and he was actually wearing a tam o' shanter on his head.

"No," Suzy replied, "I'm from America."

"America? Ye'r a lang wey fae hame, lass."

"I am. What about you? Why are you here?"

He looked down, deep in thought.

"I've pondered it fur a lang time. I came 'ere wi' me bride, Allison, a few days afore I was tae ship oot tae th' Somme, in France. I was aff tae rammy in th' war tae end all wars. Bit I dinnae think I made it oot o' 'ere."

The 'war to end all wars,' Suzy knew, was a name applied naïvely, and much too optimistically, to World War I. The Battle of the Somme took place in 1916. This young man must have married his sweetheart in advance of going off to war, but died before the honeymoon was over.

She couldn't help wondering about, and feeling sorry for, his young bride.

"What's your name?"

"They call me Jimmy, ma'am. Jimmy Campbell. Whit's yers?"

"I'm Suzy Quinn."

"Nice tae mak yer acquaintance, Suzy Quinn. Howfur is it ye'r able tae blether tae me? Nobody has chatted wi' me in ages."

"Kind of a long story," Suzy replied a little diffidently. "Some have called it a gift."

"'Tis certainly a gift fur me. Ah haven't hud a' body tae speak wi' in a lang time."

"Why haven't you moved on?"

"Moved on?"

"You don't have to stay here in this place, where there aren't others like yourself."

"I've bin worried aboot me Allison. I'm wantin' tae ken she's a'richt."

"Well, Jimmy, are you aware of the passage of time?"

"A little. I ken 'tis been a while."

"The Battle of the Somme was over a hundred years ago." She hesitated, trying to figure out how best to break it to him. She couldn't think of an easy way to say it. "Even if she lived a long life, Allison would be dead by now." Jimmy looked pained. "I don't know anything about Allison, so I can't make any promises. I don't know what her life has been like, but it's possible she could be in the next place waiting for you. But I'm sure she's not here, or you would probably have come across her in the last hundred years. I think you should move on."

Jimmy looked at Suzy for a while, pondering her suggestion. Suzy couldn't quite figure what he was thinking.

"Ye'r richt," he finally said with some resignation. "Ta, Suzy Quinn." He paused. "Howfur did th' war tae end all wars turn oot?"

"We won," Suzy said with a smile. She couldn't bring herself to reveal how much of a misnomer that name ended up being.

Jimmy smiled for the first time in their conversation. He looked at Suzy for a few moments, then nodded, disappearing in a flash of light, just like Suzy remembered Jill Bruch doing.

Suzy smiled herself, despite seeing Lilith in her mind nodding at her, confirming her hypothesis that Suzy was a lightworker. In spite of her lingering misgivings about that theory, Suzy put her SpiritSense on the back burner and drifted off into a deep and satisfying sleep.

## 62

"There was a ghost in the hotel?" Fin asked alarmed, over breakfast in the hotel restaurant. "And you just sent him away? Just like that?"

Suzy shrugged as if it was no big deal. Inside, she recognized that it was a *huge* deal. But she wasn't prepared, yet, to expose her nerdy underside and let on to Fin that she thought it was actually pretty cool that she was able to do that.

"I told you back in Boston that this is our realm, and that if we tell ghosts to move on, they have to do it."

"Simple as that?" Fin asked incredulously.

"Well, apparently. I've done it twice now." Suzy didn't tell him what Lilith had said, that some spirits hold on tighter to their places here. So far, though, that hadn't been her experience.

"What if they don't want to move on?" Fin asked, as if he had read the thought that Suzy was holding back. "Are there ghost police to enforce it?"

"I don't know, Fin. It's not an exact science."

Fin looked at her skeptically, thinking it's not *any* kind of science. He was reluctant to be too contradictory, but he wasn't sure whether he was convinced or not.

"How do you know it wasn't just a dream?"

"Have you ever heard the word 'rammy'?"

"No."

"Neither have I, but I understood him. This morning, I looked it up. It took quite a bit of searching, but I found a reference. It's a Scottish word meaning 'fight.' How would I dream something using a real word that I'd never heard before?"

"Well," Fin said hesitantly, "the brain stores things all the time, things that we don't remember ever hearing. It can call them to mind when we least expect it."

"With correct meaning and usage?" Fin shrugged non-committally. "You don't believe me."

"I believe *you* believe what you saw. But Suzy, I've never experienced anything supernatural before. I guess I'm just not entirely convinced yet about ghosts."

"And what about Fiona's story? Between the two of us, I'm not the storyteller here. I don't have that vivid of an imagination."

"I have to admit that is a fairly convincing point."

Mollified a bit by that concession, Suzy fought her first instinct to become offended by Fin's disbelief. She knew she had felt the same way years before.

"Okay," she nodded, "fair enough."

Fin sighed, then he hoped it hadn't been a visible reaction. Suzy saw it, though, and smiled.

"Did you think I was going to be pissed at you?"

"Wouldn't be the first time I did or said something that pissed someone off," Fin replied.

"So," Suzy said, deciding to change the subject, "what do you want to do today?"

"Well, I have to say that castle up on the rock looks rather intriguing."

"I haven't been up there yet. Let's do it."

§

Yesterday, when she was above ground, anyway, Suzy had been a little warm wearing jeans. Today, she wore shorts, and Fin was very glad she did.

He found himself admiring her legs frequently. Suzy caught him looking a couple of times, too, and she smiled. It had been nearly two years since she cared what anybody thought about how she looked. With the right person, she remembered, it felt good.

After breakfast, they took a long, grueling hike up the hill. Once there, they toured several of the buildings on top of Castle Rock, including the oldest building in Edinburgh, St. Margaret's chapel, built around 1130 AD, and the aptly named Great Hall. Built in 1511, it had high, heavily-timbered vaulted ceilings and enormous fireplaces, and was lined with gorgeous suits of armor and intriguing arms from times past.

Fin was beginning to get a feel of the area. The atmosphere of the past still hung heavy in the air. He had begun to notice it down on the Royal Mile. Even though it was crowded with modern tourists, he could easily imagine the settings, the streets and closes, the old stone buildings, populated with denizens of the nineteenth century. Some areas, like up here on Castle Rock, could take him back even further, to the Middle Ages.

He allowed the history to seep into his consciousness, and he was already thinking of descriptions he could add to his story to make it feel more authentic. And not just the sights, but the sounds and the smells. Old places gave voices a distinctive sound, the stone and hard woods reflecting it back differently. He was also noticing that they absorbed the odors of the ages. Fin wasn't able to distinguish specific smells as he stood near the walls and doorways, but they had melded into a singular aroma of antiquity.

A little after noon, they made their way back down the hill toward the Royal Mile. Tucked up into the shade of one of the buildings was a bagpiper in full Highland dress, belting out *Scotland the Brave*. As they approached, Fin felt the familiar feeling, the hair rising on the back of his neck, the goose bumps appearing on his arms, the seductive tightening sensation in his chest. It was all he could do to keep the tears from his eyes.

Suzy slipped her hand into his. Closing his hand around hers, he looked at her and smiled. She looked back at him a little vacantly. She just shrugged as if it was inevitable and there was nothing she could do about it.

§

"So," Fin said, leaning back comfortably in his chair as they sat at a little table on the patio of an outdoor café, "did you happen to come in contact with any ghosts up there at the castle?"

Suzy looked askance at him.

"Are you making fun of me?"

"No," Fin answered quickly, "I'm serious. I'd love to believe. I just need a little more proof."

"No, I didn't encounter any spirits up there."

"Do you think that's odd? I would think a lot of people have probably died up there over the centuries."

"Yeah, I imagine that's probably true," Suzy replied thoughtfully. "But as I've said, this isn't an exact science. It's been about nine months that I've had this ability, and I'm still coming to terms with it. I don't really understand it myself." She looked at Fin. "What about you? Do you feel like this is helping at all with your book?"

"I do!" Fin said excitedly. "I'm beginning to feel like the title I've tentatively chosen, *A Place Made of Time*, is spot on. In the short time I've been here, I'm already getting a feel for ancient Celtic culture."

"Ancient?" Suzy asked.

"Well, maybe not medieval, except for up there on the rock. But even down here, the age is so apparent. I mean look at that," he said, gesturing to the row of stone buildings across the street from them. Even though they were built up against each other in a block, each building was distinct and individual in style. He chose one of them.

"That one, for instance. They just don't make big stone arch entryways like that anymore. Those decorative architectural details above them are unheard of these days, too. Look at the almost rusticated sandstone, and how it's absorbed the dirt and soot of the centuries, and the tracks it's made under the windows from rain and other runoff. I suppose some people don't care for that much, but I think it tells the story of the city's antiquity.

"And then contrast that with the building butted up right next to it, and its rubble-style wall. That's a fairly ancient style of masonry. And the tooling on the stone window sills over there. Nobody takes the time to add details like that anymore."

He looked at Suzy who, he realized, wasn't looking at where he was pointing. She was looking at him and smiling.

"What?" he asked.

"I'm just enjoying your enthusiasm," she said. "I never realized you were such an expert on architecture."

Fin shrugged and smiled a little shyly in response to her compliment.

"A writer tends to become an expert on a lot of things, in theory, anyway. I spend at least as much time doing research as I do actually writing."

When their lunch arrived, they spent a little less time talking, and enjoyed the food, watching the people walking by. Through the summer crowd, Suzy caught a glimpse of Catriona across the street. Standing in the shadow of one of the stone arches Fin had earlier been expounding on, the little girl looked at Suzy, but didn't make any moves to cross the street toward her.

Suzy waved, but when Fin noticed and looked up, the girl backed deeper into the shadows.

"See someone you know?" Fin asked.

"A little girl I've seen a couple of times, Catriona. She's a very sweet girl, but I've never seen her with her mother. Or her father, for that matter. I've wondered if she might be homeless. Considering the way she backed into the shadows when you looked up, I'm wondering now if she has had issues with men." Suzy looked at Fin and sighed. "She kind of reminds me a little of my daughter, Emma."

Fin smiled sympathetically and placed his hand on hers. Suzy turned her hand over and their fingers interlocked. She was a little surprised at herself, allowing this moment of vulnerability in front of Fin.

She looked back across the street, but Catriona was gone.

# 63

At the base of Castle Rock, just north of the west end of the Royal Mile, was Princes Street Gardens, a big, beautiful, peaceful park. It was a good place to ponder, with few distractions. As Fin and Suzy wandered through the park, their hands had remained locked together most of the time since lunch. At the same time, they hadn't spoken much since then, each lost in their thoughts.

Mostly about each other.

Among the sights, natural and otherwise, Fin was excited to find the small, modest Robert Louis Stevenson Memorial. Standing among a small grove of young birch trees, several yards off the path, was an unassuming stone resembling a grave marker, which simply said:

A MAN OF LETTERS
RLS
1850 - 1894

*"The Strange Case of Dr Jekyll and Mr Hyde* was an early literary inspiration for me," Fin said quietly. "I was fascinated by the way he wrote about the characters, one good and one evil, but both dwelling in the same person."

Suzy looked up at him and smiled, leaning a little closer to him.

From there, they meandered back to the path, finding an unoccupied bench that was shaded by a large tree. With a glance at each other, they headed for the bench and sat down. It felt good to get off their feet.

"So, when are we going to tour these vaults you've been talking about?" Fin asked.

"I got tickets for tomorrow," Suzy replied quietly. "The early tours were already booked. Ours is late morning, just before lunch."

"Sounds good."

A few more quiet minutes passed before Suzy broke the silence.

"I hope you realize how crazy it is that I'm sitting here, holding hands with you."

"Why is it crazy?" Fin asked.

"It's been almost two years since I lost my family," Suzy replied, visibly holding back the tears. Fin wanted to put his arms around her and comfort her, but he waited, allowing her to speak. "Since then, I haven't really let anybody in. I had to protect myself. Really, my best friend, Rachel, is the only one who truly knows me anymore.

"I have a few other friends that I get together with occasionally, but they don't ask how I'm doing about it anymore. It's been almost two years so, you know, I must be over it by now. It doesn't affect them, so it's not on their minds." Suzy looked up at Fin. "I know I can be a smartass, but I didn't mean for that to be a smartass remark. It's just the truth. We don't tend to think too much beyond our own little sphere."

"I can't imagine what that's like," Fin said. "Is it always on your mind?"

"Not always, but it's always there." She looked across the grassy expanse ahead of her and sighed. "A therapist I saw for a while once told me that you never get over it, you just, eventually, get through it. I think I'm finally coming through it, but it's still there." She looked up at Fin.

"So that's why I say that this is so crazy. We've known each other for such a short time, but despite those barriers I've built, I'm here with you, holding your hand, and actually feeling comfortable with it."

Fin smiled and let go of her hand, putting his arm around her and pulling her close.

"It hasn't really been such a short period of time," he countered. "We had some basic correspondence through FamilyLine.com for a while, and started communicating in earnest about nine months ago. And we actually met face-to-face," Fin stopped and thought for a moment, "well, it was *exactly* nine months ago today."

"Hmm," Suzy replied, leaning comfortably against him, "yeah, I guess that makes sense. It's not like we're total strangers who just met yesterday, and today I'm in your arms."

Fin nodded, contentedly caressing her shoulder.

"It's kind of weird for me, too," he said. "I mean I think it would be a lot easier for me if your husband had been an asshole and you divorced him. Then I'd know that you didn't have feelings for him anymore. But I assume you loved him when he died." Suzy nodded. "So I feel like I'm always going to be compared to him in various ways, and probably not in a complimentary way. And, of course, that doesn't even take into account your daughter." He looked out across the grass and sighed, as Suzy had just moments before. "God! What a strong woman you must be!"

"Right!" Suzy scoffed. "For the first several months, I had to practically force myself at gunpoint to get out of bed and go about my life."

"And you did it! That's proof of your strength, doing what you need to do when you don't feel like it."

"Are you okay with strong women?" Suzy asked. Fin chuckled.

"I think you'll find I'm not a typical guy. I don't care for their ideal fifties-version of silly, fawning, empty-headed women who rely on men for everything."

"I'm not sure that's really a *typical* guy," Suzy replied, "but I get what you mean."

"Well, it's kind of been my experience more often than not. But the point I'm making is that I *like* strong, intelligent women. I'm not intimidated by them. And I'm *really* not intimidated by you." He realized belatedly that that didn't come out the way he had intended it. "What I mean is that you, well . . ."

"Shut up," Suzy said as, impulsively, she leaned toward him and kissed him.

## 64

Their excitement about the things they had seen during the day was tempered by the closeness that had developed between them during the afternoon. They ate their dinner in the hotel restaurant in relative silence, punctuated primarily by smiles, warm glances, and occasional hand-holding across the table. Suzy studiously avoided looking for too long at the candle that burned on their table.

They both declined dessert, and when the waiter put the check down on the table, they both reached for it. It had been placed closer to Fin, so he had it in his hand before Suzy could pick it up.

"I'll get it," he said.

"I'll pay for mine," Suzy replied.

"Suzy, I assure you, I can certainly afford to pay for both of our meals."

"I can too. If we actually become 'a thing,' then you can pay for some of *our* dinners. But until then, I'd like to pay my own way."

Fin looked at her for a moment. Hoping to not spoil the moment, and not wanting to be like the 'typical guys' he had distanced himself from earlier, he agreed. And he noticed a look in her eyes which he interpreted as approval.

After they paid, they stood and their hands, as if magnetized, instantly found each other as they walked out. They climbed the stairs to the third floor, Suzy never letting go of Fin's hand. They approached her room and she inserted the key, pulling him through the door with her.

Once the door was closed and they were tucked away in the privacy of her room, Suzy turned and was enveloped in Fin's arms, their mouths hungrily exploring each other.

*They came together slowly,* Fin thought, *and his lips found hers like a heatseeker finds, well, heat.*

Fin decided to keep that one to himself as he focused on Suzy's lips, reveling in the warmth and softness of her body in his arms. They came apart for a moment, looking into each other's eyes, and Suzy pulled Fin toward the bed. She reached down and pulled the covers away, and they sat on the edge of the bed, resuming their oral exploration.

Fin's hands were caressing Suzy, and as he placed his hand on her breast, he felt her stiffen a bit. He stopped, and moved his hand down to her side. She pulled away and looked at him, the expression in her eyes a little inscrutable.

"What is it?" he asked.

"I'm so sorry, Fin," Suzy replied softly, tears in her eyes, "I don't think I'm ready."

"Oh, honey," Fin replied sympathetically, placing his hand on her cheek, "that's okay. Just tell me what you want me to do."

She looked at him for a few moments, her eyes peering deeply into him, while her hands still gripped him tightly.

"Just lie beside me," she finally said.

"Of course." He stood and walked around to the other side of the bed, ignoring his erection, as Suzy lay down where she sat. He pushed the covers down on his side and kicked his shoes off, lying down beside her.

"I'm sorry," Suzy repeated, laying her head on Fin's shoulder as he wrapped his arm around her.

"Don't be," Fin said. "It's okay. Really." She looked at him, her eyes crossing a little from two inches away. Fin smiled and kissed the tip of her nose.

"How did you get to be so nice?" Suzy asked.

"I don't know," Fin shrugged. "Good genes, I guess."

"Remind me to thank your parents."

Fin smiled. They just looked at each other for a few moments before Fin spoke.

"So, tell me about Mark and Emma. What were they like?"

"Oh, Fin," Suzy said, "are you sure?"

"Absolutely! They're a part of your life. I want to know about them."

The first thing that came to her mind was Christmas morning, about four and a half years ago.

Mark, Suzy and Emma were opening their presents. Colored paper and bows were strewn all across the floor as evidence of the gift-giving orgy that had just occurred.

Emma was oblivious to Mark and Suzy as she played with the plush stuffed squid Mark had given her. It was one of the most bizarre looking toys they had ever seen, so naturally it appealed to Mark. He was quite happy to see that it appealed to Emma, as well. He had named the squid Pro Quo.

"Mark, what did you do?" Suzy asked quietly, looking at the black velvet-covered box she was holding in her hand.

"Well, I'm trying to give you a present, Suzy Q," he replied casually. "All you have to do is open it."

She took a breath and slowly opened the hinged lid, looking at the diamond ring inside. She looked back up at Mark quizzically.

"I remembered that, when we first got together," he explained, "I couldn't afford an engagement ring for you. You even offered to pay for our wedding rings, which I wouldn't allow, and I added to my college debt to buy them myself.

"But the engagement ring was always there in the back of my mind. Now," he took the box from her and slipped the ring out of it, "it can be off my mind and on your finger."

Suzy admired the engagement ring against the wedding band, turning her hand to catch the light from different angles.

"It's beautiful," she said, barely over a whisper. "Thank you." She turned and looked at Mark's face. Keeping her voice down so that Emma couldn't hear, her face took on a bit of a sardonic expression. "I think you might just get lucky tonight."

"I got lucky eight years ago."

"Good answer," she smiled, looking back at the ring.

Mark had saved that gift for last, so they spent a little time just enjoying the closeness of each other, and watching Emma play with her bizarre stuffed toy. After a while, Suzy pushed herself up off the sofa and began gathering up the paper and bows. They had some neatening up to do before Mark's parents arrived for Christmas dinner.

Any large, reusable pieces, Suzy placed in a plastic grocery bag while Mark stuffed a larger box with the much more plentiful collection of ripped and shredded paper and ribbons. To a Christmas present in the hands of a six-year-old child, Christmas morning was a grisly bloodbath.

They carried their loads into the kitchen, and Mark dropped his box outside the kitchen door, to take out to the trash later. He stayed there for a few moments, looking at the sparkling snow. Fresh snowfall overnight had produced a white Christmas, the snow blanketing the ground and clinging to the bare branches of the trees, but the sky had cleared to a brilliant blue. Miniature rainbows could be seen here and there in icicle prisms, and over Mark's shoulder, Suzy could see a layer of mist hovering over the gentle waves in the harbor.

Suzy was admiring her ring again, now in the sunlight coming through the door that Mark was now closing.

"You know we still have a lot to do before my folks get here, right?" he said, scooping her into his arms.

"Then you shouldn't have given me something so distracting, buster," Suzy replied. "You'll not make me a scapegoat for bad impressions on your parents."

"I want a scapegoat!" Emma said. They hadn't even heard her come into the kitchen, but she was still holding and petting her fuzzy squid.

"A scapegoat's not an animal, honey," Suzy said, pulling away from Mark and looking down at Emma. "It's just a figure of speech."

Mark took her left hand and looked at the ring.

"Do you remember how you kept putting me off back then?" he asked.

"I remember being cautious," Suzy countered. "I had to protect myself. You were this flighty guy who left his girlfriend to be with me. I wanted to be sure you wouldn't do the same when you met someone else."

"There was *never* anyone else. There was always only you. I just had to find you."

"Dammit, stop that," Suzy said with an involuntary sigh.

"It's true," Mark continued. "I always knew exactly what I wanted. That's why I kept after you. And *finally* you saw the wisdom of agreeing to the perfect match."

"Okay, slick," Suzy said, kissing him and pulling away. She was happy for the glib remark which served to at least weaken the spell he had cast over her, so she could pull herself away from him. "Whatever you say. Remember, we still have a lot to do." But she was still flushed with romance.

She went to the stove and turned the oven on as Mark opened the refrigerator and pulled out a foil-covered pan. They had seasoned the tenderloin and gotten it ready to go the night before.

He turned back toward Suzy who was now wiping the countertop. Her head was down and her hair separated in the back, with some hanging over her left shoulder and some over her right. Her neck was exposed and apparently offered an enticing temptation he couldn't resist.

He came up behind her, put his arms around her and kissed the back of her neck. Hearing the quiet but sustained "Mmm" sound coming from her throat, he was encouraged to continue, moving around the side of her neck as he pulled her hair out of the way, and ended up nibbling her ear.

Moving as if she was strenuously trying to swim through maple syrup, she slowly and laboriously turned herself around to face Mark, bending her arms and tucking them snugly between them, her hands against his chest. She looked into his eyes and smiled.

"We don't have time for this, Mark," she said quietly.

"We still have to wait for the temperature to rise."

"I'd say it already has."

"I'm talking about the oven," he said in a quiet but stern voice. "What are you talking about?"

"Besides," she said even more quietly, barely above a whisper, "Emma's right here!"

"You know, I'm sure this isn't the first time Emma's witnessed a little affection between us. And it won't be the last." To prove his point, he planted an exaggeratedly noisy kiss on Suzy's lips, which was followed by a giggle from Emma. "I happen to be in love with you, Suzy Quinn," Mark said as a little seriousness settled back over him.

Suzy smiled and sighed as their eyes locked.

"So, you're happy?" she asked.

"Honey," he replied, "I passed happy years ago. In fact, if anybody ever asked me what my favorite feeling is, I'd have to say, 'Suzy.'"

Suzy smiled and blushed. "Suzy's a feeling now? Not happiness?" she asked.

"Potayto, potahto."

She sighed again and kissed him.

Once again reminding them of her presence, Emma walked out of the kitchen quietly singing "potayto, potahto" to the tune of *Hakuna Matata*. Suzy and Mark collapsed against each other in a mutual snort fit.

After Suzy related the memory to Fin, minus some of the intimacies, he smiled.

"No wonder you loved him. I kind of love him, too, now."

Suzy looked at Fin, her eyes a little dewy. Again amazed at the vulnerability she allowed herself with him, she held him close.

"Is there anything I can do to help?" Fin asked, seeing the tears in her eyes. Suzy looked at him and sighed.

"Don't give up on me," she whispered.

"Oh, come on," he replied, "give me something difficult."

Suzy smiled, snuggling against him. As he held her close, she eventually fell asleep in his arms.

## 65

Suzy was the first to wake, and she did so with a feeling of embarrassment. She wasn't accustomed to exhibiting weakness in front of others. Rachel would have countered that it wasn't weakness, but Suzy didn't want to argue with someone who wasn't even there.

Fin was still lying beside her, though his arm was no longer under her neck. He was lying on his side facing her, his hand resting gently on her shoulder.

She turned to face him, and the movement caused him to stir and reposition a bit, but he quickly settled back to sleep. Peering at his face, Suzy pondered the previous night. She had fully intended to make love to him. They were barreling full speed ahead, when *the feeling* kicked in.

Yet Fin had dealt with it admirably, graciously. No attempts to coerce or guilt her into going ahead with it. He was completely understanding and accommodating. *And asking her to tell him about her late husband!* What man who had just had a roll in the hay snatched away from him would do that?

As she lay there watching Fin, his eyelids fluttered a bit and opened. As his eyes focused on Suzy's face, his expression softened, warming her heart.

"Hey, you," he said. Self-conscious, he quickly wiped his eyes and felt the side of his face, hoping he hadn't been drooling.

"Hey yourself," Suzy replied with a relaxed smile.

"How are you feeling?"

"A little embarrassed, but otherwise, fine."

"Embarrassed? Why?"

"I wanted to make love to you last night. I really did. I didn't mean to lead you on."

"Oh honey," Fin said, placing his hand on her shoulder, "it's okay. You didn't lead me on. You've been through something horrible. It's not my place, or anybody else's, to say when you're going to be ready. That's entirely up to you. I'm just so happy to be here with you." Suzy narrowed her eyes and shook her head, though her expression remained affectionate.

"God, where the hell did you come from?" she asked.

"From a family who still believes in courtesy and manners and a woman's right to say no."

"You better watch it, Fin. You just might make me fall in love with you."

"Whenever you're ready," he smiled. Suzy sat up and rearranged her pillows, leaning back against the headboard. Fin followed suit.

"I really do appreciate your thoughtfulness," Suzy said. "Thank you."

"You're welcome."

Suzy leaned against his shoulder and Fin took advantage of her closeness by kissing the top of her head.

"So," he said, "what's on the agenda today, besides the tour of the vaults?"

"What would *you* like to do?"

"Well, to be perfectly honest, this is pretty nice. But," he sighed, "I know I didn't fly five thousand miles to sit in a hotel room. So I'll just say that wandering around the city with you sounds wonderful."

Suzy turned her head to look up at Fin, and she kissed him.

"That does sound good," she said. "But first, breakfast!"

§

Suzy and Fin walked out of the Elephant House, the cafe where they had breakfast. Known as the birthplace of Harry Potter, where J.K. Rowling conceived and wrote part of her series, Fin particularly enjoyed the literary connection.

Standing in front of the red façade, they looked around at all the people.

"Popular place, huh?" Suzy said.

"Yeah, it's a good thing we got here early."

There was usually a line for a table, and several people could often be seen crowded around the front to read the sign in the window telling about the café's connection to one of the world's most popular and successful literary series.

Among them was a family of four, parents with twin girls around twelve years old, Americans from the sound of their speech. Of the four of them, the mother seemed to be the most excited to be there, and she was trying to take a picture with her family standing beside the sign.

She backed up to the curb and waited for a few other people to clear out of the shot. Looking at the picture in her phone, she checked for traffic to her right and backed off the curb, apparently forgetting that traffic in the UK traveled on the opposite side of the street.

The shock on the faces of her family, as well as the gasp that arose from several onlookers, made her hesitate and look around, so the UPS truck only struck a glancing blow. Still, it knocked her down against the curb where she lay completely still, her phone lying shattered on the sidewalk at her side.

She never heard the screams of her daughters.

"Oh my god!" Suzy exclaimed, her hand over her mouth. Fin already had his phone out, but he hesitated. He knew 911 was the American emergency number. He didn't know what it was in Scotland. He saw a few other people making the call on their phones, so he put his away.

"In the name o' God," the UPS driver said in a panic as he came out of his truck, "she joost stipped right oot in front o' me!"

Nobody paid him any mind, though, as a crowd gathered around the family kneeling next to the woman, the girls crying over her.

"Lemme through," a man said urgently, pushing his way through the people crowding around. The woman's panic-stricken husband looked at him. "Lemme have a look. I was a medic o' the British Army in Afghanistan." The crowd parted and the man knelt down beside the woman.

Suzy and Fin watched, barely breathing, as the man quickly examined her, then began administering CPR. Over the muttering voices of the crowd, though, Suzy clearly heard the voice of a woman.

"Stupid! Stupid! Stupid!" the voice kept repeating.

Suzy looked around at the faces in the crowd, and was shocked to see the victim of the accident standing there watching. She was wringing her hands, looking in anguish at her daughters.

"Oh my god," Suzy repeated, barely over a whisper. Fin heard her and put his arm around her in an attempt to calm her. The woman heard, too, and looked up. Their eyes locked instantly. At the same time, they both looked down at the unconscious woman on the sidewalk as the medic frantically pumped her chest.

"You can see me?" the woman asked, and Suzy looked back up at her. She didn't actually hear the question, but sensed it.

"Yes," Suzy replied.

"Yes what?" Fin asked, but Suzy was entirely focused on the woman. Before she could ask the woman's name, the woman answered.

"Jenny Mitchel. How – how can you see me?" Suzy realized that she had made a mental link with her, a psychic connection, as she had with Fiona, and she didn't have to speak out loud.

"It's just something I can do, apparently," Suzy thought. Jenny nodded and looked back at her daughters, embraced now by their father, her heart breaking for them. "I'm so sorry," Suzy told Jenny. "But it's going to be alright. They're in good hands."

"I know," Jenny replied, attempting to hold back the tears. "Jack loves them so much. But I do, too! I don't want to leave them."

"Of course you don't." Suzy wiped a tear away and looked back down at the medic as he finished giving mouth-to-mouth and began another round of chest compressions. There was a gasp, first from the woman on the ground, followed immediately by the crowd. Jenny opened her eyes wide and looked around, and Suzy looked up to find that Jenny, or Jenny's spirit, had vanished.

As the medic stood up, Jenny's husband knelt beside her, his own tears coming now, as she tried to sit up.

"Don't move, honey," he said. "An ambulance is coming." Already, Suzy could hear a distant siren approaching. As the girls sat down on each side of Jenny, gingerly holding her hands, Jack stood up and turned to the medic.

"I can't thank you enough!" he said, shaking his hand. "You saved her life!"

The medic smiled and muttered something that Suzy couldn't hear. She suddenly felt dizzy and leaned hard against Fin.

"Suzy!" he exclaimed, turning to hold her up. "Are you alright?" Suzy was holding her face in her hands.

"I saw her," she said.

"Oh, honey," Fin said sympathetically, "I know. We all saw it. But don't worry. She's going to be fine."

"No, I mean I *saw* her. I saw Jenny. She was standing right over there."

"Who's Jenny?" Fin asked, confused.

"Jenny," Jack said at that moment, getting back down on his knees as Jenny was trying to sit up, "I wish you'd just stay there. The ambulance will be here in a minute."

Fin heard his remark and looked at him, and at his wife, Jenny, and he immediately realized who Suzy was talking about.

"I just want to sit up," Jenny replied. She sat back against one of the short conical concrete pylons standing in front of the building.

"We spoke to each other," Suzy said.

As the crowd began dispersing, and Jenny was sitting somewhat upright rubbing the back of her head, she looked around, and through the milling crowd, she saw Suzy. Just like before, their eyes locked, and a look of recognition showed on Jenny's face.

The deafening sound of the siren stopped as the ambulance pulled up and parked near Jenny, in front of the UPS truck. The EMTs got out and began examining her, talking to her, to her husband, to the UPS driver, and to the medic who administered CPR. But Jenny kept looking over toward Suzy between responses.

"Come on, sweetheart," Fin said softly, "let's go." Suzy let him guide her away, but she kept looking back at Jenny until she was lost behind the people milling about between them.

§

"You're telling me you saw her ghost standing right there with us?" Fin asked sitting next to Suzy on the steps of a church.

"Well, across from us," Suzy replied, "but yes. Although, technically, I don't know if it's a ghost if her body wasn't completely dead yet." Her voice had a somewhat faraway quality to it.

"Oh, so she was 'only mostly dead?' Sorry, I don't think I'm up for *Princess Bride* references right now. I'm kind of creeped out."

"No," Suzy said, shaking her head, a distant smile on her face, "it was beautiful!" She looked at Fin. "So, are you saying you believe me now?"

Fin looked at her and pondered.

"I don't know. I mean it's possible her husband said her name earlier and it registered in your subconscious." He shook his head and sighed. "I'm sorry, I don't mean to be so negative. It's just that, well, this is huge!"

"She mentioned her husband, Jack, and her daughters. She didn't want to leave them."

"What, that's all it took?" Fin asked incredulously. "So if I'm just not ready to go, I can live forever?"

"No, of course not," Suzy said with a smile. "But Jenny's injuries didn't turn out to be fatal. And it's fortunate that the medic was nearby to bring her back. Some people don't get that chance."

"No shit!" Fin remembered what had happened to Suzy's husband and daughter, and he turned to her with a sigh. "I guess you know that better than anybody. I'm sorry, honey. I didn't mean to sound angry. I just don't know how to react to this."

"It can be difficult to let go of long-held beliefs."

"Yeah, I suppose so." He sat with his head hanging down for a few seconds, then he looked back over at Suzy. "You're not still dizzy anymore, are you?"

"No, I'm fine." Her voice still sounded kind of hazy.

Fin squinted as he looked at her. "Why are you being so understanding? Why aren't you making smartass remarks about what a baby I'm being?"

"I don't know," Suzy replied with a smile. "I just feel really calm and relaxed. I feel like I've had too much to think." She gave a tipsy-sounding laugh as she thought about what she just said. Then, she frowned at Fin. "That *is* kind of out of character, though, isn't it? I promise I'll get back to ripping you a new one soon."

§

"Justice in old Edinburgh was harsh," the tour guide was saying. Suzy glanced to her side at Fin. He seemed interested in the information being presented, though he had already expressed thoughts similar to Suzy's about the Halloween costume the guide wore. "Even stealin' a loaf o' bread could get a person hanged. Crimes that didn't warrant a hangin' might get the criminal dragged 'ere tae the Mercat Cross in chains, both for 'is punishment, and tae serve as an example tae others who might be tempted tae commit the same heinous crime.

298

"You, sir," she said, pointing her coiled whip at Fin, "could ye step up 'ere, please?"

"No," he said, shaking his head, and he glanced at Suzy. Suzy placed her hand on his back and nodded at him with an expression that seemed to say, "Trust me."

"Come on, sir," the guide coaxed, "don't make it harder than it has tae be."

He figured he probably had more attention on him as he fought the attention than he would if he simply went along with it. With a heavy sigh, he stepped forward to the little castle-like structure of the Mercat Cross. The tour guide smiled at him.

"Step up here," she said, instructing him to stand on the upper of two steps in an inset arch in the structure. "What's yer name?"

"Fin."

"Where ye from, Fin?"

"Denver."

"Denver? Colorado? Ye're an American, eh?"

"Yes."

"Ye seem like ye'd rather be somewhere else."

"At the moment, just about anywhere." A few people in the group laughed. A couple of them seemed to understand, as their expressions looked sympathetic.

"Well, Fin, that's too bad. Ye ha' tae be here tae accept yer punishment, and tae serve as an example tae others.

"Ye've been foond guilty of assaultin' a twelve-year-old girl. Admittedly not as bad as stealin' a loaf o' bread," the guide added in a tone she thought sounded ironic, and there were a few uncomfortable chuckles from the group, "but nonetheless serious enough tae get yerself publicly flogged.

"So, we've dragged ye from the magistrate to the Mercat Cross in the public square. Turn aroond," the guide said. With another sigh, Fin turned and faced the Mercat Cross, trying to keep his nose from actually touching the stone. "Ye've been sentenced tae forty lashes," the guide said, as she began tapping his lower back with her rolled up whip, as if lightly spanking him. With his back to the crowd, Fin was hoping he hadn't sat in anything dirty on those church steps a few minutes before. He wasn't really paying attention to what the guide was going on about after that.

"From 'ere," the guide continued, "ye'll be dragged in yer chains through the city streets, bleedin' an' staggerin', tae further serve as an example, and tae impress upon ye the seriousness o' yer actions. Unfortunately," she glanced at her watch, "we dinnae ha' time fer that so, this time, I'll let ye off wi' a warnin'. Ye can go now." She touched his arm and directed him off the steps. "Thank ye, Fin," she said, clearly pleased with her cleverness.

Suzy was grinning when he came back to her side.

"I hate you," he said under his breath. Suzy put her arms around him and buried her face in his side to muffle the chortle issuing from her mouth. Suddenly, with Suzy holding him close, Fin thought it hadn't been so bad after all.

Following the guide, the group started moving, and Suzy got out her much-altered-and-notated map to follow along, and hopefully add to. Fin thought the history related was interesting, as Suzy had, but after the third stop in one of the closes, Fin leaned toward Suzy.

"So," he whispered, "does this vaults tour ever actually go into the vaults?" Suzy nodded understandingly.

"Almost there."

Finally, they started descending underground, and Fin began to perk up. He had never heard of the vaults until Suzy told him about her episodes with Fiona, and he hadn't really been able to picture what she was relating to him. So actually being there, walking through the rooms and seeing the shape of them, made it real to him.

He gave skeptical attention to the stories the guide related about the ghosts haunting the vaults, and he noted that nobody in the group seemed to sense or experience any kind of 'presence.'

Suzy was, once again, lagging behind, comparing earlier notations on her map, and making new notes, so Fin was with her at the back of the group. He was surprised at how quickly the tour went, when the rest of the group began ascending a narrow stone stairway back up to the surface.

"Fascinating," he said, raising one eyebrow, as he gave his best impression of Mr. Spock.

Suzy didn't catch it, though. Climbing the steps, she was immersed in her map and notes. It was only the sudden blast of sunshine that broke her attention.

"I think I know where it is," she said.

## 66

"Alright, Suzy," Fin said over lunch, "I have a confession to make." Suzy looked at him guardedly. "I took the liberty of booking a little side trip for us in the Highlands."

"Huh?" Suzy asked, puzzled.

"Okay," Fin said, beginning to get a little excited, "I remember you telling me that Caden was raised in Fort Augustus, and I thought it might be nice, since you're partly doing this trip for Fiona, to check out where he came from. Especially since she said she'd never been there."

"You are so thoughtful!" Suzy enthused.

"Well, I'd like to agree with you," Fin said hesitantly, "and maybe I am, but I'm afraid there's a little more to it than just thoughtfulness."

"What do you mean?"

Fin looked at Suzy for a moment before plowing ahead.

"What you're wanting to do is more than a little crazy," he finally admitted. "You must see that."

"It's not crazy," Suzy argued. "It's necessary."

"Well, we apparently have differing views on what constitutes a necessity. Regardless, honey, please give it a little time. Put it on the back burner for a couple of days. See if you still feel as strongly about it then."

"I've felt this strongly about it for nine months. I don't see how a couple of days is going to change anything."

"Then do it for me." Fin didn't know how strong an argument that was, considering the newness of their relationship, but he had to try it. "I'm extremely apprehensive about this. Let's go up into the Highlands, spend a nice relaxing day at Loch Ness, and see where Caden grew up, and just see if you're still this motivated after that."

Suzy looked at him hesitantly. Finally, it seemed to Fin as if she might be giving in.

"When did you do this?" Suzy asked.

"I booked it yesterday. I just wasn't sure how to bring it up. But then, we spent the night together without any apparent repercussions, so I figured I might as well just spill it. But," he was quick to add, "it's a suite, so I can sleep on the sofa in the living room if you prefer."

"When do we go?" Suzy asked, feeling herself starting to give in.

"We'll leave after breakfast tomorrow."

"And after you've gotten this out of your system, we'll carry out my plan?"

"If you're still hell-bent on doing it," Fin sighed, "then yes, we'll do it."

"Okay, then."

§

They had spent the night in their respective hotel rooms. Fin said he didn't want to try to force anything physical so soon on the heels of Suzy's reaction the night before. Suzy smiled and kissed him tenderly before he went down to his own room.

After breakfast, they walked together to the Enterprise Rent-A-Car near the train station just north of the Royal Mile, and Fin signed the paperwork on the car he had rented a couple of days before.

It had taken him a little while to get used to driving on 'the wrong side' of both the car and the street. But he felt a little more comfortable once they got out of the city and onto the divided highway.

During the trip, the temperature dropped at least ten degrees. The three and a quarter hour drive had taken them a little over four hours, since they had stopped a few times to take photos on the way. Suzy was rather taken with the shaggy cattle they had seen occasionally, and the sheep. Emma had always loved sheep.

"Well, the Highlands are nothing like the Rocky Mountains," Fin said, looking at the burgeoning clouds hanging low over the hills and peaks, "but it certainly is a beautiful and rugged country." Suzy reverently agreed.

Finally, as they drove through the little village of Fort Augustus, Suzy was looking eagerly at any building that might have been there when Caden lived here. But she was confused when Fin pulled up in front of what looked a little like a grey stone castle and shut the car off.

"What is this?" she asked, awestruck, leaning forward to peer up at the façade of the stone fortress through the windshield.

"This is where we're staying," Fin said, clearly proud of himself. "It's a former Benedictine abbey that's been converted into apartments and vacation units. And the southern shore of Loch Ness is right on the other side of it."

"It looks positively medieval!" Suzy said, pointing at gargoyles protruding out from the battlement.

"Well, it's not quite as old as it looks. It was originally a fort, built in the early 1700s. The monastery was built from dismantled pieces of the fort in 1879. Still, even though the abbey's less than 150 years old, I figure the setting could make up for its lack of maturity."

"Fin, it's beautiful!" She put her hand on his and smiled at him. "You done good!"

Fin sighed and smiled back at her.

§

Checking in took longer than either of them had hoped. The, apparently, sole manager on duty was not in the undersized office, and it took some waiting and some searching before he could be located to check them in and take them to their suite. He seemed a little breathless, but was friendly and personable.

The unit that Fin had rented was a little ground-level octagonal turret, the former scriptorium of the abbey, and they fell in love with the place immediately. After the manager quickly showed them around, he left them to explore the unit on their own.

The main floor of the Scriptorium was made up of the small living/dining area, and the kitchen (which they didn't plan on using), with a tall, narrow window on each of the external planes of the octagon. The bathroom, a little jarring with its modern décor, but still nicely appointed, was off the foyer in the rectilinear portion of the building next to the turret.

Up a curved stairway around the back side of the turret was the bedroom, which comprised the upper floor of the Scriptorium. The main furniture was the old fashioned iron queen-sized bed. It stood prominently below the dark exposed rafters of the high conical chapel ceiling, and there was a small stained glass window set into each of the front planes of the octagon.

"It looks like the perfect room for a positively religious experience," Suzy said.

"I'm glad *you* were the one to say it," Fin grinned back at her. "I was definitely thinking it."

They were both drawn to the legendary lake behind the abbey, but considering the time, and their appetites, the first thing they did after checking in was have lunch in one of the quaint old restaurants within easy walking distance. Before they were finished, though, the clouds opened up as they had been threatening to do for most of their drive.

"I didn't even think to pack a rain coat," Fin said, as they stood looking out the door of the restaurant.

"What's the matter," Suzy replied, "you think you're going to melt?" Holding her head up as if striking out on a heroic quest, she stepped out the door and into the rain and began walking toward the abbey. Fin shook his head and smiled, and took off after her.

"Are you just going to walk?" Fin asked as he quickly came alongside her.

"Well, you didn't think to bring the car, so yeah, I think that's our only option."

"I was thinking we could run, smartass," Fin said.

"Sorry, princess, but the *Mythbusters* proved without a doubt that running in the rain doesn't keep you any dryer than walking. In fact, if anything, running makes you even wetter."

"I loved that show!" Fin replied enthusiastically.

"I figured you probably did," Suzy said as she smiled up at him. "I did, too."

Rivulets of rain were streaming down her face from her already soaked tresses, but aside from squinting her eyes through the water, she seemed to not mind at all.

Fin smiled back at her, as they crossed the road and walked past a little stone church, which looked as if it had been built from the same stones that formed the monastery. They turned onto the path that skirted the large expanse of grass in front of the abbey, still nearly two hundred yards ahead of them.

Taking note of the rosy quality Suzy's face was taking on, both from the rain and from the dropping temperature, Fin slowed. Suzy was puzzled by the look on his face, and she stopped.

"What is it?" she asked. Fin looked at her and shook his head.

"I just think you're the most beautiful thing I've ever seen."

"*Now* you say that?" she said with a sarcastic tone, tempered by a smile. "I must look like a wet dog."

"No," Fin said quietly, "not a dog. Not even close."

In response to his words and his expression, Suzy's face softened. She looked at him for a few seconds, examining her feelings, and she reached her hand out tentatively. Fin took it decisively and pulled her to him. Wrapping his arms around her, he held her close, feeling the warmth of her body through her cold, wet clothes.

Suzy was taken somewhat by surprise, but as she let herself be engulfed by Fin's arms, she realized it was exactly what she wanted. She molded her body against his and put her head back, her wet hair hanging down heavily behind her, as Fin crushed his lips against hers.

Her mind was brushed with the thought of how, during the last couple of years, she had learned to be alone. She had to be strong, to handle everything on her own. Now, she was reminded of how good it felt to let someone else be the strong one, to allow herself to be held, cuddled and kissed.

Feeling the passion in Fin's kiss, it seemed to her as if her heart was beating against her eardrums. Blinking the rain out of her eyes, she looked up at Fin for a moment, almost surprised that he didn't seem to be wondering what all the pounding was. All she saw was the ardor and the yearning emotion in his eyes.

Her arms, at first a little guarded, now clutched at Fin desperately.

§

Once they separated, they ran the rest of the way to the abbey, and through the hallway leading to the Scriptorium. Coming inside and closing the door, they looked at each other, still panting from their run and from their arousal.

"I'm cold," Suzy said.

"I know," Fin replied. "As they say in the movies, we should get out of these wet clothes."

Still staring into Fin's eyes, Suzy leaned forward to kiss him, reaching up to unbutton his shirt. Fin fumbled with Suzy's blouse, which was clinging stubbornly to her body and to the top of her jeans.

As Suzy tried to push Fin's soaked shirt back over his shoulders, she found it was resisting her efforts. She ended up pushing him back against the wall and away from her lips, but then she couldn't get the shirt down, because she had pushed him back against it.

"I guess when they rip each other's clothes off on TV," Fin said, "they're not soaking wet."

"Yeah, I guess not," Suzy replied, as her teeth chattered a bit. "Or freezing!"

"Let's just get our clothes off and get dry. But don't forget where we left off!"

They each laboriously peeled off their clothes, laying them out on the tile floor of the large entryway, each of them stealing glimpses at the other, but too miserable to do anything about it. Fin retrieved a couple of plush bath towels from the bathroom. As they dried themselves off, they ran up the stairs and jumped into bed.

"I have to admit this is not exactly the way I pictured our first time," Fin said as they lay there shivering under the covers.

"Oh, s-stop b-being such a b-baby," Suzy stuttered, "and share s-some of that b-body heat with m-me!"

Fin slipped his arm under Suzy's neck and pulled her shivering body against him. Her skin was cool to the touch, but he figured his probably was, too. He couldn't help but notice the odd incongruity of holding a naked woman that he was wildly attracted to against his own naked body, and their main consideration was just getting warm.

"So," Suzy said, her cheek pressed against his, feeling a little self-conscious, "how 'bout them Patriots, huh?"

Fin snickered.

"I suppose now is as good a time to tell you as any. I'm not into sports."

"Practically perfect in every way," Suzy sighed.

"Yeah, me and Mary Poppins," Fin replied, hoping his Cockney accent was as bad as the one Dick Van Dyke used in the movie.

They stayed there in each other's arms, contentedly listening to their breathing, and the rain on the roof twenty feet above them. After a couple more minutes, they started warming up, so Fin let go of Suzy and they awkwardly scooted apart a bit. Keeping the covers pulled up tight over them, they turned to face each other.

"So, what do you think of Fort Augustus, so far?" Fin asked.

"Wonderful!" Suzy replied sarcastically, with a wry expression. Then, her face softened. "Actually, it really is beautiful here. I just wish we had been prepared for the weather."

"I'm sorry about throwing a monkey wrench in your vacation."

"No, don't be. I'm so glad you did. I meant what I said yesterday. This really was very thoughtful of you." Fin smiled and nodded an acknowledgment. "I'm amazed you remembered the name of the place. It was months ago that I saw that episode where Fiona met Caden."

"I made notes now and then. Besides, it wasn't that long ago you told me about it. You had kind of cut it off with me back when you saw that episode." Suzy looked a little chagrined at the reminder. "It was only after you contacted me again that you caught me up on everything that had happened. I made a note of the location at that time, to look it up."

"Still, *very* thoughtful!"

"Thank you, I'm glad you're enjoying it so far."

"And besides, if we had to get rained in somewhere, what more beautiful place could we be stuck in than this?"

"And what more lovely person could I be stuck with?" Fin said softly. He reached over to her face cradled in her pillow and brushed a lock of hair out of her face. Her hair was still damp and cool, but her cheek was warm again when he placed his hand on it.

Suzy sighed and shook her head a little.

"Fin," she said quietly, "please don't hurt me."

"Oh, honey, I wouldn't dream of it!"

"I know I'm a smartass, but I'm not as tough or strong as I try to make myself out to be. I'm broken. I mean I'm not trying to sound like this poor, helpless, oppressed little lady. I know I've had a decent life. Sure, I've had my share of broken hearts, like anyone else, but this last one was the toughest."

"I know, baby," Fin said. "You are anything but helpless. I don't know how you got through that. But I think I can honestly say that, from this point on, hurting you would hurt *me* more than you could imagine!"

Suzy felt a tear roll over the bridge of her nose onto the pillow. She looked at Fin's face for a moment, peering into his eyes. Mustering up strength, and a little bravery, she reached out to Fin and scooted closer to him. He smiled gently and pulled her body against his, pressing his lips to hers.

Feeling his kiss, she felt her strength and bravery skyrocket. She held him and allowed her hands to explore his body under the covers, while Fin, taking his cues from her, began doing the same.

Suzy stiffened momentarily when Fin touched her breast, caressing her nipple which was still hard and cool. He pulled back a bit to look at her face, to make sure it was alright that he was doing that. She exhaled and nodded and Fin smiled, kissing her again.

Her hand was resting on his hip, and she tentatively moved it downward across his upper thigh, until she felt the coarse hair. Fingering it for a few moments, she hesitantly slipped her fingers a little lower, and then she felt it. He was already nearly erect, and when she wrapped her fingers gently around it, it responded quickly.

It had been almost two years, and she savored the feeling of him in her hand. She looked at Fin's admiring, appreciative face inches from hers. She smiled at him and sighed, and she gave herself fully, willingly, to him.

## 67

"W ouldn't it be cool if we were the ones to finally see Nessie again, after all these years?" Fin asked. They had decided to go for a walk after breakfast. They chose a path on a short, narrow peninsula, barely twenty feet wide, which stuck out into Loch Ness behind the Abbey. The sun was back out this morning, but there were more clouds on the horizon. There were still some scattered puddles on the muddy path from the previous day's rain, but having survived their first encounter with the storm, they were unconcerned.

"Yeah," Suzy replied, looking askance at him, "you do know that famous photograph has been proven to be a fake, right?"

"Hey, don't harsh my buzz," Fin said, sounding a little less cool than he had hoped.

Suzy chuckled at him, but despite the uncool factor, she kept a tight hold on his arm.

"So," she said, "you don't talk much about your family. Tell me about them."

"My parents and my sister live in Kansas," he replied a little distantly. "We don't talk much. They're very religious. When I started writing stories that had explicit scenes in them, they were horrified and shocked and absolutely embarrassed. When I got divorced from Kay, that was just another nail in my coffin. I've resigned myself to spending eternity in hell."

His casual attitude and tone belied the terror of his eternal destiny.

"I'm sorry," Suzy replied sincerely. "I mean not about hell. Chances are I'll probably be there with you. But I'm sorry about your disconnect from your family. I'd give almost anything to be able to spend some time with my parents again."

"Yeah, I miss them, but I guess I've come to terms with it." Fin pondered a few moments. "I think it would have been a lot harder for me if I wasn't an introvert. I've always been accustomed to being happy by myself."

Suzy turned her head to look up at him, and seeing the motion, he returned her gaze.

"It's really too bad," she said. "They're missing out on so much!"

"You really think I'm that phenomenal, do you?" Fin asked, his face taking on a haughty expression.

"Don't push it, Keypoke," Suzy replied, looking away and trying to sound indifferent, but not quite pulling it off. "Yeah, I guess I do," she said under her breath. She turned her attention to him again. She pondered for a few steps before she finally spoke, and when she did, her tone was introspective.

"You know, I think I started falling in love with you a few nights ago, in my hotel room."

"You have no idea how many other women have been similarly grateful to me for *not* making love to them," Fin said.

"I'm being serious," Suzy said, then smiled slightly, "for a change. It really meant a lot to me that you were concerned enough about my feelings to not keep pushing me to have sex with you. A lot of men would have been really pissed. And then to ask me about my late husband!" She sighed and shook her head. "That was when I realized how much you really cared about *me*, and not just about getting in my pants."

Fin lifted his arm and placed it around her as they came to the end of the peninsula, and Suzy snuggled up to him. They stood quietly looking at the hills on both sides of the lake. Loch Ness was less than two miles across at its widest point, but a little over twenty-two miles long. The hills on both shores eventually converged on the distant horizon to the northeast. It was still early, and not many people were out yet. The only sound they heard was the gentle lapping of the waves on the rocks.

"Well," Fin said, "Caden was right. This is beautiful country."

"It sure is. It's too bad Fiona never got to see it, but I'm glad I can see it with you."

Fin didn't need any more of an invitation than that. He turned to Suzy and took her face in his hands, kissing her lips, gently at first, then urgently, desperately.

Without a word spoken between them, they turned and walked back up the path, toward their suite.

§

They spent most of the day in the Scriptorium, alternately making love, talking, and quietly studying each other's faces. They came out a couple of times to stretch their legs and eat and explore the Abbey, but they always seemed to find their way back to the bed.

Suzy was a little surprised when the next morning arrived and she realized that she wasn't ready to leave. Still, she was looking forward to getting back to Edinburgh and continuing her quest.

## 68

Y ou haven't given up on that crazy idea, huh?" Fin asked, disappointed. They were still about a half hour from the rental car office, and Fin had hoped that Suzy had, somehow, forgotten about it.

"It's not a crazy idea," Suzy replied indignantly, "and no, I haven't given up on it."

Fin caught the irritation in her voice and, with their romance still so fresh and new, he decided to keep quiet. Suzy didn't speak again until they were on the Queensferry Crossing Bridge.

"You don't have to go along with me, you know," she said. Fin briefly pulled his attention from the road, and the rhythm of the massive white cables gliding by on his right. He glanced at Suzy, then back to the road. "I never said *you* had to do it," Suzy concluded.

"I know," Fin replied. "But I said I would. I'm not someone who goes back on my word."

"Well," Suzy said, then she paused as she pondered what he said. "Actually, you have no idea how much I appreciate that. But still, if you don't feel good about it, I don't want you to feel like you have to follow through on it."

"I understand, but *someone* has to look after you." He glanced at her and smiled to let her know his remark was meant to be tongue-in-cheek. She smiled back at him, and they made the remainder of the journey in silence.

After checking the car in, they walked back to the Royal Mile with their overnight baggage in tow. They both went to Suzy's room and Fin sat quietly while she used her phone to purchase tickets for the last vaults tour of the day.

They still had a couple of hours until then, and they had skipped lunch while they were driving, so they were both hungry. They decided to go to the little café where Suzy had dinner on her second evening in Edinburgh, sitting on the patio. It was the middle of the afternoon, so they didn't have to wait for a table.

"So," Fin said as they ate, "did you make contact with any ghosts at the Abbey?" He had a hint of a smile on his face, unlike when he asked the similar question after their tour of the castle. Suzy wasn't sure if that gave evidence of his skepticism, or if he was just making light conversation.

"If I had, don't you think I would have told you?" Suzy asked with a quizzical smile. "In fact, we were together the whole time. You probably would have noticed."

"Is that unusual?"

"I haven't been doing it for very long. It's *all* unusual."

"Maybe so, but I would have thought that, over the last century and a half, somebody must have died there."

"It's not just the fact that somebody died that makes a place haunted," Suzy explained, "but that they died suddenly and violently, or died with unfinished business, or something like that.

"Besides, I don't think I was very open to making contact with spirits the last couple of days. I was pretty focused on you."

"Hmm," Fin nodded in agreement, "likewise."

They smiled at each other and Suzy took a sip of her drink. As she looked out at the people on the Royal Mile, she saw Catriona. She was watching from across the street but, like last time, seemed to be hiding behind the corner of a building.

"What's the matter?" Fin asked, noticing Suzy's puzzled expression.

"It's that little girl again, Catriona." Fin followed her gaze across the street, and again, Catriona backed out of sight.

"I don't see her."

"No, she backed away again." Suzy contemplated the corner. "I wonder what her story is."

"I can tell you," Fin said. Suzy looked at him, confused. "It's my job," he shrugged, "I make stories."

"Okay, Steinbeck," Suzy said, "tell me her story."

Fin turned his eyes upward, thinking.

"Catriona Stuart, distant cousin of Bonnie Prince Charlie, makes one last attempt to take the Scottish throne. But she and her ragtag army of ragamuffins and gutter snipes are distracted from their righteous cause when the Queen presents hot tea and crumpets absolutely dripping with butter. Reluctantly admitting defeat, Catriona is forced to wander the streets looking for someone, *anyone*, willing to create a diversion sufficient for her to gain access to the palace and reclaim the throne, thus taking her rightful place as monarch over her faithful subjects."

"I like it," Suzy nodded, smiling. She looked back across the street, but Catriona was gone.

§

Suzy grinned when Fin insisted on standing on the fringe of the group. Some other poor bastard near the front was chosen as the 'volunteer' to demonstrate the crime and punishment portion at the beginning of the tour. Staying at the edge served Suzy's purpose anyway. She noticed that the guide this time was a young, pretty girl, who was already interacting and flirting with a couple of young guys at the front of the group. Suzy hoped that might end up serving her purpose as well.

It was a pretty large group, probably a sold-out crowd, which Suzy thought would probably help. As they moved about aboveground on the streets and closes, Fin listened attentively to the history that the guide related, thinking the stories might possibly provide some inspiration for his current story, or a future one.

Suzy only gave partial attention, this being her fifth time hearing it. But she had gotten out her map and was double-checking her recent edits and additions, following the turns that the group made. Her pulse was racing by the time the guide unlocked the door that led to the stairway down into the vaults.

Fin was nervous, too, but noticing Suzy's apparent fear-lessness, he tried to focus on the narration of the guide up ahead at the front of the group, and on not tripping down the steps.

They came into the first room, where the group was al-ready crowded in and the guide had already started telling her stories about it. Fin was as fascinated as he had been the first time he heard it, although after a couple of minutes, the guide's voice faded away as Fin became lost in his own thoughts.

He tried to imagine the room without the modern people milling about, without the dim electric lights. He tried to picture the poor denizens in the past huddled around a can-dle or lantern, and the helpless desperation that must have permeated every waking moment of their lives.

He thought of Dante's often misquoted words of the in-scription at the entrance of hell, "All hope abandon ye who enter here." Caden and Fiona's ticket out of here notwith-standing, absolute hopelessness must have been the lot of the vast majority of those forced to live here.

As the group started moving on to the next stop, Fin felt Suzy's hand on his arm, and they hung back, being the last ones out of the room. The tour group continued down a hallway and into the next room.

Due to the size of the group and the room, Suzy and Fin stood just inside the doorway. After the guide finished tell-ing her stories about this room, and flirting with the young guys who were staying up front near her, Suzy and Fin let everyone file past them while they stayed behind under the guise of wanting to take pictures of the room without all the people in it. Then, they followed the group to the next room, and repeated the performance.

At the last room on the tour, as everyone was still filing through the doorway, Suzy was counting on the group be-ing distracted with getting into the room, finding a place to stand and waiting for the guide to start her spiel. Before the group was settled, Suzy and Fin quietly walked past the door.

They also went past the next doorway, the one that led up to ground level, where Suzy knew everyone would be filing out in a few minutes, and found the next room, one which was not on the tour. It was dark, only barely illuminated by light from back in the tour area, reflecting off the stone walls. Fin couldn't even see Suzy standing right in front of him. Her form was just a slightly darker darkness in the room.

After a few minutes, they heard the sound of many footsteps on the ground, and a few hushed voices. Why did people always seem to talk quietly in the dark? Finally, the group followed the guide up the stairs back to ground level. At that time, the room they were in was suddenly bathed in light as Suzy switched her little flashlight on. She fished another one out of her purse and handed it to Fin.

"Okay," Fin said once the danger of being overheard by the tour group had passed, "I understand why you wanted to take the last tour of the day. You didn't want to be interrupted by the next tour and have your plan thwarted. But have you given any thought to how we're going to get out of here once you've gotten this out of your system?"

"One thing at a time, Captain Negative," she replied. The thought did make her pause for a moment, but she didn't want to reveal that to Fin. She shined her flashlight on her map, turning it so that it was oriented to their position. "Okay," she said, "this way."

Fin took a deep breath and followed her out the door.

§

"This has to be it," Suzy said. They had passed several doorways until they reached this one. Most of them had been simple arched doorways, without a door, like those on the tour. A few had doors hung in them, and this was one of them. Suzy gave one last look at her map, then stuck it back in her purse. She pushed on the door. It moved.

The door creaked and groaned on its ancient hinges and Suzy leaned against it to swing it in, and she and Fin went into the room. She recognized the room at once. It was, without any doubt, the room that Fiona and Caden had occupied.

She shone her flashlight around, looking at the sparse but familiar features of the room, the shelves on the wall on her right, where there were still some old, dusty candles and a candle holder. She almost expected to see Fiona's portrait of Caden standing there on the shelf, except that she knew it was now hung on the wall in her carriage house back in Marblehead.

Beyond the shelves was the stairway, now filled in with dirt and rubble. Suzy turned her flashlight, glancing into the corner where she had last seen Caden's crutches standing but, of course, they weren't there now.

She looked down at the floor near the door. The stone that had been used as a doorstop was not there, but she could see a gouge in the floor where it had been pushed in an arc when the door was forced open in Caden's day. The gouge was rounded and worn now, but still visible.

"This is it!" she exclaimed with tears in her eyes. "This was the room that Fiona and Caden lived in!"

"You're sure?" Fin asked, a little amazed at Suzy despite his apprehension about being stuck in here all night.

"Absolutely." She trained her flashlight on the floor to their left. "This is where they had their bed, the pallet made of blankets. Caden stood his crutches there in that corner when he wasn't using them. And over here on these shelves," she swung the beam to the right, "just behind the candles, stood a little framed portrait that Fiona had painted of Caden, a portrait that now hangs in my carriage house."

"Wow," Fin said, remembering the scenes that Suzy had related to him.

Walking to the shelves, Suzy shone her flashlight in her purse and pulled out a lighter. She lit the candle in the holder, which sputtered and smoked, burning the thick coating of dust before settling into a steady flame. Suzy and Fin turned off their flashlights and looked around at the meager but warm illumination.

"So," Fin said, "what now?"

"Now," Suzy replied quietly, "we say goodbye."

§

After dripping some of the greasy melted wax from the burning candle onto the shelf, Suzy stood two of the other candles there, holding them until the wax hardened. She had brought her own candles to use in her ceremony, but since these were here, she thought they would be more appropriate.

Fin didn't really understand what she was doing, aside from the rough draft of an idea she had in America, but he stood at the side, watching respectfully.

Suzy picked up the candle holder again and lit the two candles now standing side-by-side. Like the first one, they sputtered and smoked at first, then burned steadily. Suzy looked at Fin.

"I thought this would be a fitting symbol," she said, "to represent Caden and Fiona's deep love for each other." Fin smiled and nodded. With three candles burning now, the room was awash with warm light, casting deep, flickering shadows.

Next, Suzy pulled a folded sheet of paper out of her purse and opened it up. Facing the candles, in a quiet and steady voice, she read from the paper:

> True love's the gift which God has given
> To man alone beneath the heaven.
> It is not fantasy's hot fire,
> Whose wishes, soon as granted, fly;
> It lieth not in fierce desire;
> With dead desire it does not die.
> It is the secret sympathy,

The silver link, the silken tie,
Which heart to heart, and mind to mind,
In body and in soul can bind.

"That's beautiful," Fin said. "Who wrote that?"

"Sir Walter Scott, a personal friend of Fiona's. He was at their wedding and wished them well."

"Right, I remember you telling me about it."

"I originally started thinking about making this trip," she said, still looking at the candles, "because I had come to love Fiona, and I wanted to honor her. And I wanted to pay tribute to Caden, the love of her life, and to say goodbye to him on her behalf."

With that, she placed the paper on the shelf in front of the two candles. She blew out both flames, leaving just the candle in the holder burning.

She heard a gasp and turned to look at Fin. He seemed panicked, his head swiveling around frantically.

"What is it?" Suzy asked.

"I–" He hesitated, looking embarrassed, his breath a white cloud. "It felt like somebody touched me."

"Somebody touched you?"

"I don't know," he said panting, "it just felt like someone came in the door and brushed past me."

The light fluctuated briefly, and Suzy looked at the candle. The flame flickered a bit, then settled back into a steady burn. Suzy suddenly felt cold and, like Fin, sensed the presence of somebody else, and she spun around.

"What the fuck!" Fin exclaimed in a tense whisper, stepping backwards against the wall.

"You see them, too?" Suzy asked quietly, rubbing the goose bumps on her arms, as she looked at a number of apparitions standing before them. There were male and female, young and old. "So it's not just me."

"Yeah, Suzy, I see the ghosts packed into the room. No wonder this wasn't on the tour!"

As Suzy looked at the spirits, she caught her breath. She recognized one of them in front. A little blonde girl, in familiar clothing. It was Catriona.

As she looked in dismay at the little wraith, the girl looked up at her. The movement spooked Fin even more.

"Shit!" he exclaimed. "Shit! Shit! Shit!"

Once she got past the initial surprise, Suzy felt as if her heart was being squeezed mercilessly. She remembered how Catriona had, from the beginning, reminded her of Emma. She remembered her dreams in which she saw Mark and Emma being pulled out of the water by the Coast Guard back at Marblehead and how, in her dream, Emma opened her eyes to look imploringly at Suzy.

Suzy couldn't take her eyes off of Catriona. The little girl seemed ethereal, vaporous. Despite how solid and alive she had seemed up above, down here, Suzy realized that she was little more than a mist, surrounded by what appeared to be a wavering glow or aura.

"Catriona!" Suzy said under her breath. "You're – you're dead?"

"Aye, ma'am," the little girl replied, her voice a little colder than she remembered it. "I were murdered 'ere."

"Oh, my god," Suzy squeaked, wiping a tear from her eye. "I'm so sorry, baby."

"'Tis nae yer fault, ma'am," Catriona said in a matter-of-fact tone, "ye didnae ha' anythin' tae do wi' it."

Suzy's attention was dragged away from Catriona by the heavy breathing on her left. She looked at Fin and saw what a hard time he was having. She remembered her chats with Leanne and Lilith about ghosts, or rather spirits.

"Relax, Fin," she said in a level voice. "Just concentrate on breathing slowly. They're just people."

"Yeah," he panted, "dead people!"

"Yes, but they're people with personalities and feelings. They're just like us."

"Except we're not dead!"

Suddenly, Catriona looked timorously at Fin. Her eyes showed distrust, and Suzy noticed that she was standing between the spirits of two women.

Suzy didn't notice Fin's reaction to the little girl's stare, as he flattened himself against the wall. Focused as intently on the little girl as Suzy was, she felt the familiar beginnings of one of her episodes. Her vision blurred and she felt the familiar tingling sensation.

Suzy sat, as Catriona, in the lap of her father. They were in a room similar to this one, illuminated by candles, and they looked down at the emaciated body of a woman. The body was still, and there was reddish foam dried around her lips.

"Is me mum feelin' better noo?" Catriona asked.

"Aye, child," the man said, "she's in a better place."

Suzy, in her vision, felt Catriona's thoughts. *Why did me mum go tae a better place an' leave me 'ere? Why dinnae she tak me wi' her?*

As Suzy watched, the man slipped his hand under the child's dress and between her legs.

"Nay, da," Catriona whimpered quietly, twisting in his lap and trying to push his hand away. "Please, dinnae do that."

"Ye're in me care, noo," he replied harshly. "Ye ha' tae do as I say, child."

Suzy struggled against the vision, and mercifully, the scene changed, though as it turned out, it was not necessarily a better one.

A different man was carrying Catriona under his arm like a sack of potatoes down a dark hallway. Her last memory was of her father pocketing the few coins that the man had given him.

She had stopped struggling a few moments before. The man's hand was held tightly over her mouth, and once he entered this room, he deposited her roughly onto the floor. Her eyes registered her surroundings, and the man who had put her here, but she was barely conscious and couldn't move. The man had held his hand over her mouth and nose for most of the walk down the hallway, and she had struggled initially, but she had felt her strength depleting before he had even pushed the door open.

Once she was lying on the floor, the man knelt down, pressing a wadded blanket over her mouth and nose, to finish the job.

As Suzy watched, the viewpoint gradually changed to outside the little girl's body, watching the scene around her. She looked down at the little girl lying on the floor, her body completely still now. The man pulled the door closed as he disappeared back into the hallway.

Suzy felt the similarly familiar feeling of the episode ending, with the residual exhaustion, as the scene blended into the current one, although in this case, there was little change. The setting of the episode was identical to their current location, with the addition of the other spirits gathered in front of her.

Upon her return to the present, the other spirits began turning their eyes to her as well. Suzy, tears streaming down her cheeks, braced herself weakly on the heavy shelf as she started seeing one episode after another of how the unfortunate souls ended up here. Their final scenes were all similar, as they were smothered by either the man who had killed Catriona, or by his accomplice.

As the ghosts stood before her, Suzy wiped the icy tears from her face. But there was one behind them, leaning against the wall, who had yet to turn his attention to her. As he moved around them and looked at her, Suzy gasped as she saw his face, and his one leg.

"Caden!"

§

Fin, his eyes like saucers, watched the tableau, fascinated but terrified. His heart was racing, pumping a massive bolus of fear through his veins. The thought that came to his mind was of the climactic scene in *Poltergeist* when all the rotting corpses and skeletons started bobbing to the surface of the swimming pool around JoBeth Williams, as she screamed and fought to get away from them.

Okay, these bodies weren't surrounding him, but they were animated, *somewhat* animated anyway, standing there and speaking. Dead people weren't supposed to do that!

He could see that they didn't seem to have any real substance. They weren't quite transparent, but translucent. The flame from the candle seemed to illuminate them, but he noticed that their bodies didn't impede the light. The candle light continued beyond them, flickering against the wall, but they didn't cast a shadow.

Then he noticed that it looked almost as if they were glowing from within, so maybe it wasn't the candle illuminating them after all. An irregular, undulating glow seemed to emanate from their bodies, giving an appearance similar to that of waves of heat around embers. Fin had heard new age people speak about auras, and he wondered if the effect he was witnessing might be the aura of the ghosts, or if ghosts even have auras.

His heart was pounding a staccato rhythm in his chest when he heard Suzy address Caden, the last dead person to come forward. Having heard Suzy's tales about Fiona and Caden, seeing someone whom he had become somewhat familiar with, through her stories, actually seemed to calm him a bit.

Fin called to mind Suzy's suggestion a few minutes ago, and he concentrated on breathing normally. To help with that, he paid special attention to Caden, taking note of his 'physical' features.

The man seemed to be around thirty, although the thought occurred to Fin that it might be difficult to judge the age of someone from two hundred years ago, when life was harder and life expectancy was considerably lower. And, of course, it wasn't a body, but a ghost. Who knows how well a ghost reflects the age of its former body? But he was a handsome man, with dark hair and a beard, and a kind face, though it was shrouded in sadness.

Another random thought occurred to Fin as he wondered why a ghost, even a one-legged one, needed crutches. Suzy would probably say something about residual images of the person at the time of death, or a projection of the self-image of the ghost, or something like that.

He wasn't going to ask her, though. She was talking to Caden now.

"I've been in contact with Fiona," she said, her voice expressing a tone of reverence. "She's been so worried about you."

"Ye've been in contact wi' me Fiona?" Caden asked, his face showing a mixture of relief and hope, as his aura glowed a little more intensely. Like Catriona's, his voice was different from the one she heard in Fiona's episodes. Cold, with a bit of an echo, as if it was being transmitted over a long distance. "I've been lookin' everywhere for her. Is she a'right?"

"She's . . . well, you know how much time has passed, don't you?" Caden shook his head. "It's been nearly two hundred years since . . . since you died."

Caden looked shocked. He glanced nervously toward the others with him, then back at Suzy.

"You . . ." Suzy started timidly, "you do know you're dead, right?"

His eyebrows drawn together, Caden seemed as if he couldn't quite understand the concept.

"I'm right 'ere," he said, "standin' in front o' ye, talkin' tae ye."

"Yes, but the year is now 2019. I'm so sorry, Caden. After all that time, though, Fiona's dead now, too. But, like you, she's stayed around. I met her at my home. I'm a direct descendant from her, and I live in the house where she lived, in America."

Caden, leaning on his crutches, stood there mute. He didn't seem to know what to say, but his face expressed anguish, misery at the loss he had been carrying for nearly two centuries.

"I made the trip here for her," Suzy continued, "to honor her, and as a memorial to you, Caden, and her deep love for you."

"So, she went tae America, eh?" he said quietly. "I wondered where she had gone."

"Yes, she did and, as far as I know, she lived a happy life, though she never stopped loving you."

"Ye're verra kind," Caden replied softly, his voice quivering. "What's your name?"

"I'm Suzy. Suzy Quinn. This is Fin MacKinley."

"I'm verra happy tae meet ye both." Fin attempted to nod an acknowledgment to him, but wasn't sure if the command actually made it from his brain to his neck muscles. "So, Fiona spoke o' me, did she?"

"She did," Suzy replied, "but mostly, she showed me her life with you." Caden looked puzzled. "I seem to have this ability to see a story that a dead person transmits to me. I guess that must sound rather bizarre."

Caden shrugged and shook his head.

"Prob'ly no more bizarre than bein' a phantom."

"I suppose," Suzy said with a smile.

"So, I reckon ye're a direct descendant o' mine as well?" Caden asked. Suzy sighed.

"No, I'm afraid not. I'm so sorry, Caden, but your son was stillborn."

"Och, me poor Fiona," he lamented. "That must ha' been so difficult fer her t' bear."

"It was," Suzy agreed. "It was a very difficult episode for me to watch, too. But she was so strong, Caden. She got through it."

"Ye seem tae ha' been a good friend tae her, and fer that, I'm grateful."

327

"It's not like I had much of a say in the matter. I loved her almost from the beginning."

"Aye, I ken that verra well," Caden replied with a sad smile.

"Listen," Suzy said, "I know she desperately wants to know what happened to you."

Caden peered at her for a few moments.

"Ye're able t' read me thoughts?"

"Something like that. What you're willing to share with me, anyway."

Caden nodded, and Suzy felt the episode coming on.

## 69

Caden Loganach, ye'll not be going up there," Fiona said sternly, her fists on her hips, looking at him as if he were a disobedient child.

"I'm feelin' much better, noo," he argued, "And 'tis warmer ootdoors than it is in 'ere."

Fiona responded by raising an eyebrow at him.

"Ye're still weak," she replied. "Ye need to rest. Ye don't want to have a relapse before we set sail."

Caden sighed, knowing she was right.

"Try and get some sleep," Fiona suggested, her voice softening. "That's what ye need more than anything. Maybe in the morning ye can go upstairs."

"Yes, dear," Caden said with a smile and an exaggerated submissive tone. He lay down on the pallet and covered up with the brown wool blanket. "Ye goin' up for your afternoon sun noo?"

Over the last few days, Fiona had made a habit of going outside to enjoy a little sun while Caden napped in the afternoon.

"Aye," she replied. She knelt down and adjusted the blanket for him, tucking it around his neck. Caden looked lovingly up at her and smiled.

"Ah, Fiona, I'm the luckiest jimmy in th' world." Fiona raised her eyebrow again, giving him a skeptical glance, with a meaningful look around their dark, cold cell.

"Of course ye are, love," she said with a smile, and she leaned down and kissed his forehead. "Get some rest."

Caden watched as Fiona disappeared through the doorway, and he listened to her light footsteps as she went up the stairs. There was a moment of bright light as the sunshine bounced off the stone walls and into the flat. Fiona's shadow passed across it, and then the door closed.

He didn't know how long it was after he slipped off to sleep that he heard a loud scraping sound next to him. He turned his head and, in the flickering light of the candle that was still burning on the shelf, he saw two men enter the room.

"What're ye doin' 'ere?" Caden struggled to get out from under the blanket.

"I wanted tae tend t' some unfinished business," the first one said, as he held Caden down.

There was something familiar about him. As he leaned forward, Caden smelled his fetid breath, saw his snarl through the grimy beard and filthy hair hanging down in his face.

Then, the man pulled his shirt away, revealing a scar, two rough white circles below his left collar bone. And suddenly, it all came back to Caden. He saw the dingy little alleyway, with Fiona lying on the ground. He saw the man, this man, who had attacked her and, in that violent act, had been the catalyst that introduced Caden to the love of his life.

"I'd like tae mak yer death as painful as this was," the man said, "but yer body'll fetch a higher price if 'tis nae damaged any more than it already is."

As his friend held him down, the man wadded up the blanket and pressed it against Caden's face. As Caden grappled with them, he knew that this struggle would not have as good an outcome.

## 70

"Oh, Caden!" Suzy said sympathetically as she came out of her trance, bracing herself against the wooden shelves.

"What is it, Suzy?" Fin asked. He was starting to feel a little calmer, but was still tense. He had never witnessed Suzy viewing an episode, and now she had gone into several. The first time it happened, with Catriona, he was afraid that Suzy was going to fall. As she went into the trance, she fell back against the shelves. He was ready to catch her, but she managed to stay on her feet.

Her eyes became vacant, unfocused. Her body was there, but she wasn't, essentially leaving Fin alone with the ghosts. He had to admit that the spirits weren't making any threatening moves against him, but still, being in a dark, underground room alone with a bunch of dead people was definitely not on his bucket list.

"Caden was killed by the man who attacked Fiona," Suzy explained, "the man ultimately responsible for Caden losing his leg."

Fin exhaled and looked at Caden, appreciating the cruel twist that had ended his life. He felt a twinge of sympathy for him, despite the unsettling knowledge that this man standing before him was dead, as were all the other people milling about behind him.

"That were the last thing I remember after me Fiona left," Caden said softly. "The next thing I knew, I were still here. I couldnae figure oot what happened."

"You were killed right there," she pointed at the ground, "where your bed was. In fact, everybody else here was also killed in this room."

"All except meself," said another distant voice to their immediate left, as another man entered the room. His legs moved as if he was walking on the ground, but his body moved more smoothly. He gave the impression of gliding, while his legs just went through the motions. Then, Suzy saw his face.

"Lachlan!" Suzy exclaimed.

Fin looked at Lachlan, shocked. His great-great-great-great-great-grandfather stood there looking no older than Fin himself. Suddenly, Fin felt a little less fearful. He was among family. Like the others, Lachlan appeared diaphanous, with a sort of flickering glow about him.

"Aye," Lachlan replied, "'tis meself. And ye are?"

"I'm Suzy Quinn. I'm . . . a relative of Fiona's." She gestured toward Fin. "And this is Fin MacKinley."

"Nice to meet you," Fin uttered quietly, his voice taking on a tone of awe.

"I'm very pleased tae make your acquaintance," Lachlan replied with a slight bow.

"Wait," Fin said, "I thought you said Lachlan went to America."

"I have traveled tae America on two occasions," Lachlan said, "but Edinburgh is me home."

Suzy was taken by surprise as well, but she turned to Fin as a thought occurred to her.

"I haven't seen all of Fiona's life yet," she said quietly, hoping that Caden, in particular, didn't hear what she was about to say. "In the last episode I saw right before I left for Scotland, she had just married Drummond. Lachlan may have come back to Edinburgh later and died here."

Wondering at the presence of Lachlan's ghost in the vaults, Suzy turned to him and spoke up so he could hear her.

"If you don't mind me asking, sir," she took a breath, "do you know why you're here?"

"If ye mean do I understand that I'm dead," he shot a quick glance at the others, "then aye, I suspected it. Why I'm still doon here in these vaults instead of in heaven, though, I'm afraid I don't know. I don't think I was a bad person."

"How did you die?"

"Me brother lived doon here," Lachlan explained. Suzy nodded. "I paid frequent visits on him, hoping I could inspire him tae turn back from his debauched way o' life and be a respectable person. 'Twas all tae no avail, but I kept trying. Me father gave up on him, but I couldn't.

"The last time I tried, I couldn't find him. That's not an unusual occurrence, as people tended tae move aroond doon here. But I was making me way back and ascending the stairs tae the outside, when I was attacked from behind. I ne'er saw who did it. This was a vile and wretched place, Miss Quinn. There were likely many people living here who would kill a person for whatever money he happened tae carry in his purse."

"But you weren't killed in this room?" Fin asked, the fear gradually lessening. "How is it you're here now?"

"Yes," Suzy said, "and Catriona. I saw her aboveground a few times before I ever saw her here."

"I thought ghosts tended to stay around where they died," Fin said.

"I'm afraid the complete volume of me knowledge of the afterlife is limited tae me oon experience, and that of these few aroond me," Lachlan replied.

"Well, that's more than most of us have," Suzy said. "Yet."

"Aye, right ye are. Well, it seems tae me that some souls, like some living beings, possess a more adventurous spirit than others. They're happy and comfortable wandering the streets above or the vaults below. We tend tae stay close tae where we lost our life, but we feel at ease exploring our surroundings. Catriona is a brave little soul."

Catriona smiled timidly at him.

"Others, lak meself," Caden said, "are creatures o' habit and hold on tight tae what feels familiar. And in me own case, e'en though this room is where I were, apparently, murdered," he didn't seem quite comfortable with the thought yet, "'tis also where I spent the last happy moments o' me life, wi' me dear Fiona."

Suzy felt her heart go out to Caden, and she smiled sadly at him.

"What brought all of you here now?" Fin asked.

"Sometimes we just enjoy being aroond others like ourselves," Lachlan said. "I sometimes see others of ye tramping through here, but ye ne'er e'en notice me. We get lonely, too. I sensed a gathering here and came tae investigate."

Suddenly, Fin and Suzy were shaken by a noise, a distant sound, but one that reverberated through the stone walls and hallways. To Fin, it sounded like a remote roar. Still leaning against the wall, he felt the vibration of it in his whole body. Suzy, though, was reminded of the encounter she had in her carriage house several months ago when she went looking for Fiona. She remembered the phrase, "Leave me alone!" which seemed to resound in her body rather than her ears.

"What was that?" Fin asked, feeling his fear rebound. It didn't help that some of the ghosts also seemed uneasy. A couple of them faded away, leaving their wavering 'heat wave' distortion for a second until it dissipated, too.

"It seems others may be attracted tae our gathering, as well," Lachlan replied grimly.

"There was somethin' of an uprisin' a wee while back," Caden quickly explained. Then, he looked pointedly at Suzy. "Or maybe not so wee a while. A few o' the braver residents o' the vaults decided 'twas up tae them tae protect their loved ones from th' killers makin' money off o' the bodies they killed an' sold."

The noise sounded again, this time a little closer. A couple more ghosts slipped away. Suzy was surprised to see that Catriona was still there among them, though she looked fearful.

"These people banded together," Lachlan hastily picked up the story, "and confronted two o' the men they knew tae be responsible for the killings and chased them tae the north end o' the vaults."

"'*Two* of the men'?" Suzy asked. "Were there more?"

"Reports differ. Some say there was at least one more."

"The man that killed me," Caden said soberly, "was not one o' these men. As far as I ken, he didnae pay for his crime."

"We wish they had taken those men tae the authorities," Lachlan continued. "Instead, they killed them doon here in the vaults and tossed their bodies in a corner of a room under the north end o' the bridge. I can't blame them for their rash actions, considering how little the authorities bothered with the goings on doon here."

The walls shook as the thunderous clamor sounded just up the hall. Trying to quell the panic rising inside him, Fin ran to the door and leaned against it, pushing it closed.

"Ye'll nae stop 'em that way," Caden said.

"What do *you* do when they come around?" Suzy asked, feeling the fear now building in her own chest.

"They dinnae come roond often, but when they do, we jus' go somewhere else. Or jus' wait 'em oot."

"Wait them out? What do they do? They don't hurt you, do they?"

"*They're* already dead, Suzy!" Fin shouted, his eyes wide. "What the fuck are they going to do to them?"

There was a heavy thud against the door, and Fin frantically leaned his back against it, bracing his feet on the floor. The door thumped again, banging hard against the back of Fin's head, but Fin, his body taut and straining, pressed as hard as he could against the door.

Suzy was mesmerized as a glow appeared around the edges of the door and started pouring through like liquid light. It felt as if the room shed ten more degrees as two nebulous arms of bluish-white light reached into the room on each side of the door, then turned toward themselves as if to wrap around Fin.

Seeing the appendages coming toward him, Fin instinctively pressed his head back away from them, but he was obstructed by the door he was leaning against. As the arms stopped inches from his face, the rest of the thing slipped directly through as if the door was completely intangible, totally enveloping Fin in the process.

Suzy watched in horror as Fin was engulfed by the glowing being. She could see him inside the formless translucent body. He appeared to be screaming, but she couldn't hear him. All she could hear was a loud hum, a vibration similar to what she had experienced in her carriage house months before, accompanied by a fluctuation of the pressure in the room.

"Leave 'im be!" Lachlan yelled at the thing. As he did so, the undulating glow surrounding him intensified and turned a reddish color, to match the fury of his command, as if his anger literally blazed.

Suzy didn't expect that Lachlan's command would have any effect, but as she watched, the thing ejected Fin as if spitting him out on the ground. The formless being then settled into a more recognizable hominid shape, albeit a monstrous one.

Suzy knelt beside Fin, shivering on the ground. When she touched him, he felt nearly frozen, and she put her arms around him. When she looked up again, the other killer's ghost had joined the first one.

They had assumed an appearance that more closely resembled the others in the room, including the fluctuating glow or aura. The main difference was their faces. They appeared cadaverous, as if the skin were stretched too tightly over their skulls.

If they had skin. Or skulls.

"Why don' ye go back tae yer hidey-hole," Caden said, "ye cowardly blackguards?"

"Cowardly?" the first one said. His voice, like the others, was otherworldly, with a distant echo and a cold hollow sound. "We came 'ere, didnae we, e'en though we're greatly ootnumbered?"

"Just go 'way!" Caden insisted.

"But we like it 'ere wi' our good friends," the other one replied, "lak li'l Catriona 'ere." He leaned down toward the little girl who, despite cowering away from him, stood her ground. "Yer da wanted t' keep ye," he said. "He liked diddlin' yer li'l cunt. But 'e liked the shillins I gave 'im fer ye more." His aura blazed red as he taunted her, while Catriona's turned a dim bluish color.

"Leave her alone, motherfucker!" Suzy shouted as she stood up to face the ghost. Fin looked up at her, still chilled, but amazed at her bravery.

"Wha's this?" the first cadaverous ghost asked. "The lady has a foul mouth, but qui' a pleasin' form." His companion turned his attention to Suzy and, from the expression on his grotesque face, he seemed to appreciate her appearance, as well.

"You're not welcome here," Suzy said firmly, despite the terror she felt in her chest. She remembered things that Leanne and Lilith had said. "This is *our* realm, *our* domain. You have no place in it. You have to leave."

"Why should we go? This is our 'ome." It was hard to tell if his pallid, emaciated face was smiling mockingly at her, or if it was wearing its usual gruesome expression.

"You must be so proud," Suzy snarked, as she looked around the dark and dusty surroundings, her breath puffing out in white clouds. "Get the hell out of here!"

"I think *ye* should be the one tae get oot o' 'ere," the other ghost said. He stepped threateningly toward Suzy and Fin, and Suzy instinctively stood in front of Fin who was still shivering on the ground.

Both of the ghosts uttered what sounded like demeaning, belittling laughs at Suzy as they both stepped toward her.

"Back away," Lachlan said, gliding between them, "both o' ye. Ye'll nae bother our friends, living or dead."

337

"Ye think ye're enough t' stop us?" one of the ghosts asked. Suzy marveled at the immature, grade school nature of the response. Things haven't changed much.

"If e's not," Caden said, joining Lachlan, "*we* are!"

Lachlan and Caden were blazing red as they faced their foes. The ghosts laughed at them, a cold, hollow cackle.

"Get oot o' our way!" a ghost demanded. Suzy found it difficult to know which one was speaking now, as they were beginning to dematerialize, their bodies wavering and swirling, as if taking on the appearance of flames.

The other spirits remaining in the room, including Catriona, moved smoothly behind Caden and Lachlan, blocking the ghosts' access to Suzy and Fin. Their auras also blazed, casting a red glow on the walls.

The room began to hum, the air pressure increasing uncomfortably, as Suzy was transported back to her carriage house that morning a few months ago. The pressure fluctuated, making it difficult to take a breath, and she felt as if she might vomit.

She pressed her hands to the side of her head, only vaguely aware of the flames blazing from her new, albeit dead, friends, and from the malevolent ghosts in front of them.

Fin, still weak from his moments inside the ghost, felt it too, but his attention was morbidly drawn to the inferno in front of them. He had never imagined such a scene, two lines of opponents facing each other, each individual looking like Johnny Storm, the Human Torch of the Fantastic Four. Their bodies were almost completely lost inside the blazing conflagration that surrounded each of them.

It seemed like a standoff, each side casting fire at the other, as flames licked across the ceiling of the room. Neither side was backing down, until Suzy, to Fin's amazement, straightened up, her hair blowing wildly around her in the commotion.

"Go away!" she screamed. "Leave us alone!"

The two ghosts, blazing red like the others, seemed to hesitate, their individual infernos calming briefly. Then, their flames expanding and turning blue, each of them vanished in a bright flash of white light.

The hum subsided and the pressure in the room diminished to a more normal level. Suzy and Fin immediately felt the effects abate, as the flames died down around their friends. Weak and dizzy, Suzy stepped back and held on to one of the shelves for a moment, hungrily sucking a raspy breath down her throat.

Caden and Lachlan and the others looked at each other in surprise. Their auras gradually returned to the ember heat wave effect that they had displayed in the beginning. Caden turned to Suzy.

"I ne'er knew we could do anythin' like that," he said breathlessly, a little awe-inspired by their own performance.

Catriona was smiling, looking a little awe-inspired herself, and Suzy knelt down in front of her.

"Why did you stay here?" she asked.

"Ye're a crackin' lassie," the little girl replied. "I like ye. Ye didnae deserve tae be treated that way."

Tears sprung to Suzy's eyes, and she put a hand over her mouth as she looked at Catriona's face.

"Oh, you sweet thing," she said, wiping the tears from her face. "Thank you, Catriona. You sure didn't deserve the way you were treated, either." The little girl smiled quietly at her.

Fin struggled to stand up. Suzy turned her attention to him and helped him to his feet. His skin was still cool, but he was warming up.

"Are you alright?" she asked.

"I think so," he replied a little breathlessly. "I'm feeling a little less like ghost guts and a little more like myself again."

"What ye said tae them," Lachlan said, pondering, "that they had no place in your realm, that applies tae us, too, doesn't it?"

Suzy looked at him, hesitant to answer. Caden looked at him as well, then at Suzy, awaiting her response.

"You're not harming anybody else," she said, "so I'd never tell you you have to go." She took a deep breath as she gestured toward the room. "But you're not doing yourself any favors staying down here. If you believe religious dogma, those two may have stayed here out of fear of hell or whatever other final judgment might be awaiting them. But you, all of you," she included the rest of the spirits, "you could move on and hopefully have a happy life, whatever that involves, wherever it may be."

"Can I see me Fiona again?" Caden asked.

"I don't know," Suzy said. "I don't know how the afterlife works. I hope you can. But I do know you'll never see her again if you stay here. And if you go, if you move on, I'll tell Fiona when I get back to America. I'll tell her you're alright, and that you've gone to . . . whatever's next."

Caden gazed at Suzy for several seconds before apparently reaching a decision.

"Aye," he nodded, a bit of a smile interrupting the sadness etched into his face, "ye're a fine friend, Suzy Quinn. Fiona's lucky she foond ye." He pondered a few more moments before nodding. "So am I. Maybe I'll see ye again sometime."

"I hope so," Suzy replied with tears in her eyes.

Caden turned to Lachlan, and to others in the room. Whether complete thoughts were being passed between them in some way, Suzy couldn't tell, but the eyes of several of them did seem to register acceptance. Caden turned back toward Suzy and Fin, and blinked out in a bright flash of white light.

A couple of the others vanished after that as well. Suzy looked at Lachlan.

"What are you thinking?" she asked.

"I'm thinkin' there are too many unanswered questions," he replied wistfully. "Too much I still want tae know."

"That's just a part of life. And death, apparently. Unanswered questions, unfinished business. We never have long enough to get everything done, to learn everything we want to know."

"Nay, I suppose we don't." He looked around for a few moments, then he looked at Suzy and Fin, and he was smiling as he disappeared in a white flash.

Suzy heard Fin sigh heavily beside her, and she looked at him questioningly. His arms folded for warmth, he looked regretful.

"I wish we could have talked more," he said. "I didn't have a chance to tell him I was his great-great-great-great-great-grandson."

Suzy smiled and put her hand on his arm.

"Oh, I know," she said sympathetically. "That all happened rather quickly, didn't it. Well, unfinished business."

"Yeah, I guess so."

Suzy looked at a couple of other spirits, the women who were, earlier, standing on each side of Catriona. Suzy didn't know their names, though she had seen their episodes showing how they died. But she didn't know anything about them or their lives, and she noticed they seemed a little nervous as they looked around the room.

"What's wrong?" Suzy asked. They didn't respond. They just looked sadly at Catriona. The little girl looked back at them and nodded. They looked up at Fiona and faded away, leaving a momentary distortion in the air.

"They looked after me e'er since I came 'ere," Catriona explained. "They been 'ere langer than me, and they cannae leave."

"I see," Suzy said. "What about you?"

"I miss me mum." Suzy saw what looked like a tear in her eye. "If there's a chance I can see 'er again by goin' through that door, I suppose I better go."

"Well, Catriona, like I told Caden, I don't know how it will be in the next place. But I'll bet it's better than this."

Catriona smiled and nodded.

"Goodbye, Suzy Quinn. Mebbe I'll see ye again."

"I sure hope so, honey," Suzy said, wiping away a tear. "I envy the people whose lives you're about to brighten."

The last thing Suzy saw was the little girl's smile, then she vanished in a bright flash of light. Before she realized it, Suzy started sobbing at the sudden and unexpected vacuum she felt.

Her melancholy was lessened a bit, though, when she felt cool hands grip her shoulders. She looked up at Fin, who helped her to her feet. He took her in his arms and, the two of them once again alone in the room, she cried against his chest.

§

"So, any bright ideas on how we're going to get out of here?" Fin asked a few minutes later, as Suzy's weeping subsided and she took a deep breath.

"As a matter of fact," she said, picking up her purse, "I do. I can't say with total certainty that it will be successful, but I'm hopeful." She pulled out her map and studied it by the candle light.

She blew out the candle, plunging them back into pitch black. They quickly turned their flashlights on, Fin especially still creeped out from the ghost episode. Together, they pulled on the door, creaking it back open, and they filed out into the hallway, dark now with the lights turned out for the night.

Suzy went back the way they had come, then took a turn to the right, down a passage which hadn't been on the tour.

"You're not leading us into the lair of Satan this time, are you?" Fin asked quietly.

"Oh hush, you big baby," Suzy replied.

"Says the one who was *not* just swallowed by a ghost."

Eventually, they came to a doorway with a stone staircase, and Suzy began climbing the steps.

"Good," Fin said. "Up is good."

His mood was dashed, though, when the way Suzy led them ended at a locked door.

Suzy started knocking on the door.

"This was your plan?" Fin asked. "Knocking on doors? I'm not sure ghosts can unlock—"

He stopped when he heard the sound of the lock clicking. The door opened and they felt their irises suddenly shrink to pinpoints as they were bathed in bright light. Shading their eyes, they filed into the office, noting the look of shock on the face of the young woman who opened the door.

"Oh my god, I'm so glad someone was here!" Suzy said, her voice sounding much more panicked than it had just a few minutes before.

"How did ye get doon there?" the woman asked in a tone that rivaled Suzy's.

"We got separated from the group," Suzy replied sheepishly. "It's my fault. I wanted to take pictures of the last room without any people in it, and I took too long."

"The—" The woman looked at the clock on the wall. "The last tour ended over an hour ago."

"I know! We were terrified! We've been wandering around down there ever since then."

"I thought we were going to die!" Fin added, getting into the act. Suzy shot him a look that said, 'Don't overdo it,' as she walked toward the front door.

"Well," the woman cast about for something to say, but didn't seem to know what it should be. "I'm afraid I'm the only one here. Do —do you need to talk to the manager? Or the tour guide?"

"Oh, no!" Suzy said. "It's my own fault. I certainly don't want to get anyone in trouble. We just didn't want to spend the night down there!"

"No, I suppose not."

By now, Suzy had gone past the front counter and reached the door. She opened it and, resisting the urge to run screaming out onto the street, she turned to the woman.

"I'm sorry we startled you," she said, "but I'm *so* glad you were here to let us out of there!"

The woman nodded mutely as Suzy and Fin filed out, pulling the door closed behind them. Outside in the late sunshine and the fresh air, they looked at each other for a moment. Then, as if pulled by gravity, they were in each other's arms, their lips locked in a kiss that was a result of their passion and their recent adrenaline rush.

They parted and looked at each other, both of them panting for breath. When each of them saw the need they were feeling in the other's eyes, they took off running for the hotel. As a matter of decorum, they slowed to a fast walk when they reached the lobby, but they ran up the stairs to Suzy's room.

The "Do Not Disturb" sign was hastily hung on the doorknob, spinning around it a couple of times until eventually swinging to rest.

§

The air in Suzy's hotel room was chilly. They had turned the little air conditioner unit up to counteract the friction and kinetic energy they were generating. Now that their lovemaking was done, they were lying under the covers, basking in the warmth of each other's bodies.

"I can't believe we actually go back home tomorrow," Suzy said, her head resting on Fin's shoulder.

"We don't *have* to," Fin said.

Suzy looked at him and thought about what he said for a moment.

"No, I suppose we don't," she said, "but I want to. This has been a fun and informative trip, but I miss home. And I miss Fiona. I'm *really* anxious to tell her what I learned and about what happened in the vaults."

"I still can't believe the power you held over evil spirits!"

"No, that wasn't just me," Suzy said quietly. "I told you about my conversations with Leanne and Lilith. The physical world is *our* domain. Whether you believe we were placed here by God or the universe or whatever, we are the ones given control over it. To an extent.

"And in the end, I couldn't do it alone. It took the intervention of the benevolent spirits in the room to get them to listen."

"Still, when you stood up to that ghost who was taunting Catriona, and then you screamed at them to leave, *and they did*, I felt like such a little baby compared to you."

"Well, it's a good thing we've had this time here so you could prove otherwise." She snuggled closer to him.

Fin smiled at the reminder of the past hour spent in each other's arms, and he kissed her.

"I suppose it *is* time to get back home. I could use a rest!"

"Exactly!" Suzy said, looking at Fin from an inch away. "Besides, you have to get back to work on *A Place Made of Time*."

"Yes, I do," Fin said with an extemporaneous smile.

"You're smiling about that," Suzy said with a smile of her own. "That's a good sign."

"I have some ideas."

"Good! Well, I have an idea of my own. Why don't you postpone going back to Colorado for a day or two? Come to my place. You can meet Fiona."

"Oh great, another ghost."

"No, not just another ghost. Fiona's one of the sweetest, friendliest people I've known."

"A friendly ghost. So this is Casper we're talking about?"

"Oh, she outcaspers Casper."

"Hmm." Fin pondered for a moment. He hadn't been looking forward to leaving Suzy. "Well, I suppose anyone who can inspire such linguistic gymnastics as 'outcaspers' is someone who needs to be met."

## 71

It was eight-thirty when they followed Ocean Avenue across the causeway to Marblehead Neck. The sun had set a few minutes before, and while it wasn't quite dark yet, the harbor was gently bathed in twilight.

Suzy and Fin were exhausted after the long flight. Fin had to admit, though, that it wasn't as bad as his flight *to* Edinburgh, considering that his included the entire breadth of America, and it had been without Suzy.

The flight back included a lot of hand-holding, a lot of quiet talking between themselves, and Suzy's head resting on his shoulder. Even now, it was nice to look to his left and see her at the wheel of her little MINI Cooper, as she veered to the left onto Harbor Avenue, up the west side of the Neck.

Twilight was a bit deeper here, as the road was lined with trees. A few smaller, modest houses quickly gave way to the estates with moss-covered stone walls and tree-lined driveways.

Suzy slowed as she saw, in the shadows of the trees on the left, a parked police car.

"That's my driveway," she said apprehensively. She saw a few bits of yellow crime scene tape fluttering from the trees and hedges in front of her house. As she pulled into the driveway, her headlights illuminated a policeman gathering up the tape and winding it into a big ball in his hands.

She came to an abrupt stop. Beyond him, she saw the carriage house. Its door was open and askew, hanging by one hinge, revealing the blackness of the interior. The front window was also dark, the glass broken out.

"This is not the way I wanted you to see my house for the first time," she said as she opened the door.

"Ms. Quinn?" the police officer asked as he approached. He looked familiar. She recognized him as Officer Miller who had run off the protesters a few weeks before.

"Yes," she replied as Fin came to her side. "What happened?"

"I'm afraid there was a bit of a ruckus here last night."

"I see that."

"Ghost enthusiasts had been camping out around here. They were peaceful, so we didn't run them off. Just reminded them a couple of times to not block traffic, and to stay off your property. Some of the Christians you riled up a couple weeks ago also returned, and they brought reinforcements.

"We determined that you were not home, so we kept your place on our rounds, sent a car around at least every hour to keep an eye on things.

"Around midnight, . . . well, I'll admit I'm not much of a believer in this kind of stuff, but witness testimonies are surprisingly consistent. Sometime around midnight, somebody saw someone in the front window of your carriage house, someone wearing old-fashioned clothing.

"They rushed back to your carriage house," he gestured toward it, even though Suzy knew where it was, "and the Christians followed them. And that's when things got out of hand. Unfortunately, this took place when there wasn't a squad car nearby.

"We're not sure who pulled the door off or broke the window, but several people report being physically thrown back away from the carriage house. The Christians took this as proof that the devil was there, and they wanted him out, and the ghost fanatics thought that the ghost was just defending itself and, well, basically a riot broke out right there in your backyard.

"We ended up arresting four people."

"Oh my god," Suzy said, fascinated, but horrified. "Was anybody injured?"

"Two people ended up being admitted to the hospital, but they're in stable condition and it looks like they're going to be fine. We arrested four people for inciting a riot, assault, vandalism, and destruction of private property. You'll be receiving detailed information about the arrests. We tried to call you, but we got no response."

"We were on a plane," Fin said. "We just got back from Scotland."

"Hmm, well, welcome home," Officer Miller said ironically.

"Thanks," Suzy said, distracted. She walked back toward the carriage house, and Fin followed, while the policeman gathered up the last of the crime scene tape.

Suzy stood at the doorway and looked inside. A waxing gibbous moon, hanging in the western sky, partially illuminated the interior through the side windows, which were also broken.

"People sure suck sometimes," Fin said sympathetically.

"I know," Suzy replied. "But I'm mainly worried about Fiona."

§

Fin did what he could to set the door in place, so it didn't look as if it was standing wide open. There was nothing they could do about the windows, yet. One consolation was that they knew the weather was supposed to be good for the next day or so. And the carriage house wasn't immediately visible from the street.

It was approaching ten o'clock when they dragged their luggage into the house and climbed the stairs, although it felt like early morning to their bodies. Suzy led him to her bedroom, but she stopped just inside the door.

"What is it?" Fin asked. It took a few moments for her to respond.

"I can't do this," she finally said quietly.

"Can't do what, honey?"

Suzy shook her head, looking at the room.

"I shared this bed with Mark for years." She turned to Fin. "You know it took me a little while to be able to begin a romantic relationship with you."

"I was aware of that," he replied lightly.

"I finally got past that hesitation," she continued, looking back into the room, not noticing his tone.

"Yes, I know you did. I remember the Abbey at Loch Ness, and your hotel room last night after the vaults." Suzy turned and looked up at Fin, and her severity briefly gave way to the merest ghost of a smile, before returning.

"But this," she turned back to the room, "this was our room, our bed."

"Sweetheart," Fin said, taking her shoulders and turning her to squarely face him, "it's fine. I understand. I'll sleep downstairs on your sofa."

He noted the look of relief that flashed through her eyes, before changing into a regretful apology. Then, she shook her head.

"No," she said sternly. "No, the least I can do is give you a bed to sleep in. You can sleep in the guest room."

"Sounds perfect."

Tears filled Suzy's eyes as she smiled at him.

"You're the best!"

"I'm just an exceptionally nice guy," Fin shrugged.

"Tell me something I don't know."

Fin pondered for a moment.

"The Church of the Latter-Day Dude, based on the main character in *The Big Lebowsky*, has ordained over 450,000 Dudeist Priests around the world, and includes Jesus Christ in their list of Great Dudes in History."

"Huh?"

"You asked me to tell you something you don't know."

"That's true," Suzy sighed, "I did."

"Then my work here is done."

"Good night, Fin."

"It's okay. I'm way too tired to fool around, anyway."

§

Suzy, despite how tired she was, tossed and turned for nearly an hour before she relaxed enough and was finally

349

able to slip into the beginning stages of sleep. That was when she finally saw Fiona.

"I was so worried about you," Suzy said. "I'm so sorry about what happened last night. I'm sorry I wasn't here to stop it."

"'Twas not your fault," Fiona replied with the sad smile that Suzy had become accustomed to.

"Fiona," Suzy said, quickly changing the subject, "I found him. I found Caden!"

Fiona was clearly taken aback, the sadness in her eyes replaced with surprise.

"Ye found out something about him?" she asked, trying to clarify the thought in her mind.

"No, I found *him*. He was still in the vaults, in your room, your flat. He didn't know he was dead. He stayed there, all this time, wondering where you went."

Fiona put her hand to her mouth in shock and, at least in the image Suzy saw, tears came to her eyes.

"Oh, me poor Caden," she said in a voice barely over a whisper. "Is he there now?"

"No, he moved on." Fiona looked puzzled. Suzy explained. "I told him about you, how you showed me your life with him. I told him you were worried about him and have spent all this time wondering what happened to him. I told him that you were waiting to hear what I found, that I'd tell you when I got back, and that he could go. And it was then that he moved on.

"I . . . I don't really know how it works. I know that people who have come back from a near-death experience speak of seeing a bright light. I don't know if you can see that where you are."

"It's not just a light," Fiona replied. "Not always. It's more like a door, and the light is on the other side. Ye can see it when the door opens, or when ye can get to it."

"There were others there, Fiona," Suzy said, her mood darkening. "There were so many people who were killed in those vaults. Two of the killers were there, too. It was terrifying. But we got rid of them. We got them out of there, with Caden's help. Oh, and Lachlan's."

"Lachlan?" Fiona said, shocked.

"Yes, I assume he went back to Scotland at some point. Apparently he went down to the vaults again to visit his brother and was killed."

"Nay," Fiona said, but she seemed afraid. With a quick look over her shoulder, she disappeared like the swirling dust cloud in which she originally appeared months before.

§

Suzy woke early, while it was still dark, after a fitful night of sleep. Getting out of bed, she got a light robe out of her closet and pulled it around herself. She padded down the spiral staircase in the corner turret and into the kitchen.

She picked up the kettle on the stove and filled it with water. She turned the burner on and set about spooning tea into the infuser basket in her tea pot.

The ritual of making her tea was still comforting to her. But it wasn't comforting enough. She was troubled about her conversation with Fiona, particularly with the puzzling way it ended.

She watched the kettle impatiently, willing it to boil. It wasn't until she left to light a candle on the table of her breakfast nook that she heard the first low note of the whistle. She rushed to the stove and grabbed the kettle off the burner, not wanting to wake Fin so early. After she filled up her tea pot, she slid into the booth.

Gazing at the candle flame, it was only moments before she experienced the tingling sensation and the blurring of her surroundings.

# 72

Fiona smiled as she remembered the night before. Her first anniversary of marriage to Robert had been marked by a dinner with him and his daughter. Martha was getting so big, and they had become best friends.

Robert had given Fiona a lovely pearl necklace. Fiona had given him the news that she was pregnant with their first child. He had been so thrilled, but they both had been particularly happy with the excitement that Martha displayed at expecting a little brother or sister.

Two years and two months had passed since she lost Caden. While her new life with Robert and Martha softened the blow, she still loved Caden dearly, and figured that she probably always would. She thought about him most often in the minutes before falling asleep, and at times like now, when she went out for a walk.

She remembered her father scolding her for her long, aimless walks, and how she would completely lose track of time while wandering. She smiled at the memory, and wondered how he was.

But the wild, rocky Great Neck off the coast of Marblehead was a beautiful place to wander. A few other people had made their homes there in the last couple of years, but for the most part, it still provided Fiona with much untamed, wooded seclusion. And now, in the crisp, cool days of October, she could see the first hints of autumn creeping into the woods.

As she wandered off the trail and toward the house, she knew it was still early. Robert would not be home yet, and Martha would still be with Miss Ewing, her governess. She passed the house and went to the carriage house.

She still came in the carriage house at least once a week. It afforded her time and privacy to sit alone with her thoughts, and with her portrait of Caden. She cherished the privacy, and she was thankful that Robert allowed the carriage house to remain unoccupied.

This afternoon, though, the privacy was shattered by a knock on the door.

"Mr. Mac an Léigh," she said with surprise.

"Good afternoon, Fiona," he replied. Fiona caught the scent of whiskey on his breath. "I just wanted tae call and see if ye were farin' well."

"I'm faring very well, thank ye."

"That's excellent news, lass." He looked at her for a few moments until Fiona started to feel uncomfortable. "Well, aren't ye goin' tae invite your auld friend inside?"

"I don't think it would be proper. I'm married now. Robert and I were married a year ago."

"Ah, even more good news! As a matter of fact, I've been married meself. This calls for a celebration, Fiona!" Ignoring the lack of an invitation, he pushed past her into the carriage house.

"Mr. Mac an Léigh, I'm afraid I must insist that ye leave now."

"Aw, Fiona, dinnae be like that. Your husband wouldnae deny ye time tae see your auld friend, Lachlan."

"As a matter of fact, I believe he would be most interested to see ye, since he still has not been paid for his services to ye."

"Aye," Lachlan said, putting his hand on the side of his head as if he just remembered, "I mean tae pay 'im verra soon. But until then, let's talk aboot auld times, shall we?" He wavered a bit on his feet and leaned against her table, as he made no effort to hide the look he gave her figure. "Ye're still a fine lookin' woman, Fiona."

"Alright, Mr. Mac an Léigh, 'tis time for ye to go," Fiona said firmly.

"Nay," he said, reaching past her and pushing the door closed, "'tis time fer ye to stop bein' such a stuck-up boot."

Fiona silently scolded herself for allowing Lachlan to come between her and the door. There was no way out for her now, unless she broke through one of the windows. But Lachlan had always been so kind and well-mannered back in Edinburgh. She couldn't understand why he was so different here.

She remembered him telling her that his brother had a problem with the drink. Perhaps it was a family weakness, and Lachlan himself had now succumbed. Whatever the case, she needed to get him out.

"Mr. Mac an Léigh, I really must insist that ye leave." She moved toward the door, but Lachlan pushed her away. "Mr. Mac an Léigh!"

"Ye'll stay right 'ere and show me a little hospitality!" He grabbed her arm and Fiona, shocked and surprised by his behavior, struggled to push him away. From this close, the whiskey was strong on his breath. "Ye've ne'er once called me Lachlan. Always Mr. Mac an Léigh. I want ye t' call me Lachlan."

Pressed against the wall between the door and the front window, Fiona twisted her body to try to get out of his grasp.

"Mr. Mac – "

"Lachlan!" he shouted, his face twisted into a grotesque mask, almost unrecognizable from the man she knew. "Call me Lachlan! Ye'll call me by the name I rightly took from me morally superior brother!"

"What?" Fiona looked at him, trying to understand what he was saying.

"Me brother, Lachlan," he sneered. "I know he spoke t' ye aboot his good-for-nothin' brother, Duncan. Always puttin' himself above me."

Fiona had stopped struggling as she looked at him and allowed what he was saying to seep into her mind.

"Two minutes!" he shouted. "Lachlan was born two cursed minutes afore me. And because o' those two minutes, he gets me father's approval and th' family fortune, an' I get nothin' but th' occasional handoot."

"Duncan," Fiona whispered.

"Lachlan!" Fiona cowered under his anger, her ears ringing from the volume of his shout.

"What did ye do?" she asked.

He pushed himself away from the wall and scoffed at her.

"I killed the bastard." He raised his chin as if bragging about the act. "He came t' the vaults as he often did, t' preach at me an' lord it over me. But I had enough o' his morally superior attitude. I decided it was time for me t' have me share, t' get what I deserved.

"So I killed 'im as he left an' I took 'is clothes. I 'ad t' clean meself up and shave, but once I did, I looked just like 'im." He

354

smiled. "Me good and righteous brother was always nippin' at me t' become a better person. So I did. I became him!"

Fiona looked at Duncan in horror as she thought of her old friend, killed in that awful place, like her husband. She stepped to the side, toward the door, but Duncan moved back to hold her against the wall.

"All the lassies loved Lachlan, too," he said, his voice quiet and chilling.

He pressed his lips against Fiona's, but she summoned up all the strength she could and pushed him back. She reached for the door handle and pulled the door open a couple of inches before Duncan slammed it closed again.

The motion of pushing her back against the door caused her to put a foot against it to steady herself. In the moment that she did, she recognized how she might be able to push him farther from her, at least enough to get out the door.

He pressed against her, fumbling with her dress, attempting to open her bodice with one hand as he held her shoulder back with the other. Failing to open it, he yanked hard on it, ripping the fabric apart. He pressed his leg between hers, wishing all that fabric wasn't between his thigh and her groin, but he was encouraged and excited when he managed to rip her chemise, exposing her breasts. Duncan, ignoring Fiona's ineffectual blows, grabbed one of her breasts in his free hand and squeezed.

Fiona, still struggling to push him away, and sickened by his touch, grasped hold of his shirt with both hands. As she tried to push him away from her, buttons popped off and his shirt came open.

"I see ye ha' th' same thing on yer mind," he grinned.

But Fiona didn't hear him. She was looking at his chest, at the scar, the two rough white circles below his left collar bone. She remembered the nippers that Caden held when he rescued her from her attacker, the two narrow ends of the handles that went into her would-be rapist's chest.

As her fear was replaced by anger, she focused all the strength she could muster into the leg she had braced against the door, and she pushed with all her might. She managed to push Duncan back several feet, and he teetered, trying to keep his balance. He staggered back toward her, but being unsteady, when she pushed him away again, he stumbled back.

She watched as he lost his footing and fell backward toward the dining room furniture. As he did, Fiona heard a splintering sound as the loose back rail of the chair that Robert had never fixed broke away. With a soggy cracking sound, the delicate turned stile of the chair entered Duncan's back and protruded from his chest, inches from the first scar, this time impaling him through the heart.

She looked for several moments at the grisly image before her. Duncan's body had come to rest on the seat of the chair, the spindle now coated in blood, as the crimson fluid ran down his body onto the floor.

It took a few moments before Fiona felt the horror of what had transpired. But even then, it was tempered with the knowledge that justice had finally been served.

§

Fiona decided that she had no choice but to tell Robert what had happened. Having closed up the carriage house, she waited until he arrived home from work. She allowed him to greet Martha, but then, she took him aside and related that Duncan, as Lachlan, had shown up at the door of the carriage house.

Then, taking a candelabra, she led him out back and opened the door.

"Oh, dear lord," he whispered. He quickly pulled the door closed. "Fiona," he said, pulling his eyes away from the body and looking at her. "Are you alright?"

"Aye, Robert, I'm fine."

"The baby?"

"He didn't hit me. I didn't fall. As far as I can tell, the bairn was unharmed."

Robert sighed and nodded. Then, he turned back to the dead body.

"I didn't know who to call," Fiona said. Robert glanced at her and back at Duncan. "Should we call –"

"Nobody," Robert interrupted. He looked back at her. Fiona looked questioningly at him, and he nodded. "I know it was self-defense, but think about how this will look." His eyes were drawn once again to Duncan. "I filed a lawsuit against this man, and have been unable to collect what was owed. And now his body is found on my property, having met a violent death."

"But ye didn't do this," Fiona said, "I did."

"It doesn't matter," Robert replied, his voice shaky. "There were no witnesses. Anyone investigating this will find it highly suspicious. All evidence will point to me killing my opponent at law."

That night, Robert dug a deep hole in the brush behind the carriage house and dumped Duncan's body in it, insisting that Fiona not breathe a word of it to anybody. Fiona agreed, though it didn't feel right to her.

She had taken a life and, even though she felt the man deserved what he got, she never felt comfortable hiding it the way they did. Robert was adamant, though. He closed up and locked the carriage house and never mentioned it again.

Their remaining years together felt, to Fiona, more somber than the first. She found deep, abiding happiness with their daughters Finella and Roberta, and their son Patrick. But that dark secret always weighed heavily between her and Robert until the day she died.

## 73

When the episode ended, the familiar surroundings of the breakfast nook rematerialized around Suzy, just as it had been before, with one exception. Fin was sitting there across from her. She looked at him, dazed from the exhaustion of the episode.

"Good morning," he smiled when he saw recognition come back into her eyes. Then, he became alarmed when he saw the expression that her face settled into. "Honey, are you alright? What is it?"

Suzy looked at him silently, in shock. She shook her head as she brooded over what she had just seen. Fin took her hands across the table. "What's wrong?"

"Lachlan died in Edinburgh," she said absently.

"Right," Fin nodded. "I know that. We saw him."

"He died before Fiona came to America."

"Well . . . no, that can't be right. You saw him in your episodes with Fiona, here in Marblehead."

She shook her head and squeezed his hands.

"Duncan killed him. He took Lachlan's clothes, his identity. They were twins." It took a moment for the news to get through to Fin. "Duncan was the man who attacked Fiona in that dark alley. He was the one responsible for Caden losing his leg. He's the one who finally killed Caden in the vaults and sold his body to the university. And he killed Lachlan and came to America with Fiona."

"Oh my god," Fin breathed.

"As Lachlan, he could send back to Scotland for his brother's money and property to be shipped to him. He even got married here as Lachlan. But he always wanted Fiona.

"He got drunk and came back here and tried to rape her again, out there in the carriage house. But when Fiona fought him off, he fell and died."

"So," Fin said, "I'm not descended from a kind, caring philanthropist, but a drunken, murdering rapist."

Suzy wasn't thinking about genealogy. She was thinking that the drunken, murdering rapist was out there in her carriage house now.

"Fiona seemed afraid," she said, thinking aloud, pondering their clasped hands on the table.

"Well, of course. Somebody trying to rape her would be *very* frightening."

"No," Suzy said, "not in the episode. I mean when I spoke to her last night, and I mentioned Lachlan. She looked fearful and she made a motion as if she was looking over her shoulder. Then she disappeared." She looked up at Fin. "Fiona's not the only ghost here. Duncan's here, too. And Fiona still seems to be afraid of him."

Fin looked at her, the wheels turning.

"Do you remember back in the vaults," he said, "how frightened the ghosts in that room seemed to be of the two killers? They outnumbered them, but they still seemed afraid of them."

"Yes. And do you remember how the ghosts of the killers looked?"

"Yeah, their faces were hideous, like something out of a horror movie." Fin shuddered remembering that he had actually been inside one of them. "And they could change form. I mean I don't know if the others could or couldn't do that, but I never saw it."

"Evil is powerful," Suzy reflected. "Even in the physical world, it can take a lot to overcome an evil person, or an evil idea."

"It took all of those ghosts to stand up against them. And one of you." Suzy looked up at Fin again, and she saw the slight smile playing about his lips. "I'm so proud of what you accomplished there."

"I can't do it again, Fin," she said under her breath. "It took too much out of me. I mean, first, before all of this, I lost Mark and Emma. Then, through Fiona and her episodes, I got close to Caden, but he was taken away from me. And the same with Lachlan.

"Facing those ghosts in the vaults was hard. Not just the bad ones, but the good ones, too, seeing their stories, how they died. I feel broken now."

Fin looked at her for a moment.

"Honey, have you ever seen a cracked window?" he finally asked.

"Sure."

"Does that crack keep the light out?"

"No, of course not," Suzy replied. "What the hell does a cracked window have to do with what we were talking about?"

"When the sun shines on that cracked window, it doesn't just bounce off. It still shines through that imperfect glass and lights up the room.

"You can't live your life without getting some cracks. We've all got scars. Some of them are doozies! But those scars don't change who we are or what we can accomplish."

Fin leaned forward, squeezing her hands.

"I can still see your light, sweetheart. It may be shining through a cracked glass, but it's still shining. My god, how it shines! You are the bravest, most amazing woman I've ever known."

With a swelling feeling in her chest, Suzy felt her eyes tear up.

"I never knew you were so deep," she replied.

"I am a many-faceted fellow, Suzy Quinn," Fin said with his eyebrows raised in a mock haughty attitude. "You could do a lot worse than me."

§

"You're sure you want to do this?" Suzy asked.

"I'm game if you are," Fin replied. The look on his face was not quite so confident.

"Try not to get eaten this time."

The sky was clear, the sun shining brightly on this July morning as they walked across the back yard. When they reached the carriage house, Fin carefully pushed the door open and turned it in on its one good hinge. As they walked inside, despite all the windows being broken out, it seemed unusually dark inside.

Still, they were able to see more than they had the night before. One of the three remaining dining chairs had been broken as if a very large person plopped down on it. The wood stove in the kitchen area had been knocked over, the pipe pulled from the wall. The book case was lying forward on the floor, books ripped and scattered about.

The wall above the little table in the sitting area was empty. Suzy rushed over there, slipping on a few of the books. There, on the floor behind the table, she found the portrait of Caden where it had fallen. She sighed with relief as she picked it up.

"Duncan?" Suzy called, her voice lacking the assertiveness she had hoped for. She came back to stand beside Fin. "Duncan!" she tried again. It was quiet. Suzy and Fin glanced at each other.

"Maybe he left when the rioters broke up the place," he suggested. Suzy looked at him skeptically. Fin shrugged.

"Duncan!" Suzy called louder.

They looked at each other again when they thought they heard a distant hum. As it gradually became louder, the hum turned into a stomach-churning vibration that shook their bodies and pounded their heads.

Then came the sensation of fluctuating pressure. Even though the door was open and the windows were broken out, it felt as if the air pressure was increasing, then decreasing, as if the carriage house was breathing. The fluctuating pressure interfered with their own breathing, as the pressure seemed to be greater, pressing against their bodies, when they tried to take a breath, and lesser when they tried to exhale.

Despite the building heat outside, the temperature in the carriage house dropped several degrees and a wave of nausea swept over them. Attempting to fight the pressure of the air around them, they tried to take deep breaths, their exhalations coming out in white puffs of vapor. They fought the urge to vomit, both of them glad they hadn't eaten breakfast yet.

The vibration reached a climax as it finally coalesced into the phrase that Suzy still remembered from nine months before.

"Leave me alone!"

"No!" Suzy yelled, "you need to leave us alone. This is our world. *You* need to leave, Duncan!"

"I'm Lachlan," the 'voice' said.

"No, you're Lachlan's lesser brother, the worthless one, the black sheep, the drunkard, the embarrassment of the family, Duncan!"

"Suzy," Fin whispered, panting beside her, "telling him to get out is one thing. But do you think it's wise to taunt him like that?"

"I want the coward to show himself," Suzy answered, loud enough that she hoped that Duncan would hear her. "I don't want him hiding behind his tricks and special effects. I want to see his ugly face!"

Having seen the faces of the killer ghosts in the vaults, Fin didn't share Suzy's ambition. But he didn't have a say in the matter as dust and book pages and other loose items began swirling around as if caught in a small tornado. The vortex churned in front of them for a few moments. Suddenly, the dust, papers and other detritus were sent flying to all corners of the structure. Suzy and Fin ducked as something began to take shape in front of them.

In the middle of the carriage house, the air turned bright white, the effect Suzy remembered thinking of as liquid light in the vaults. The liquid light swirled in the middle of the room, the white light gradually fading, infusing itself with color, until it finally consolidated into the form of a man, surrounded by the same heat wave aura as the other ghosts they had seen.

Suzy stood up to face the grotesque figure standing in front of them.

"Having just seen your buddies in Edinburgh," she said, "you're even uglier than I expected."

His face bore similar sharp features of skin stretched tightly over a skull, with sunken eyes and acute shadows. Recalling Suzy's enlightenment earlier, Fin thought that Duncan's ghost really did look like the personification of evil.

"Who are ye?" the thing asked, his voice echoing and hollow, as if transmitted over a great distance.

"I'm the owner of this place," Suzy replied, the white clouds of her breath pulled toward the ghost as if toward a vacuum. "I'm evicting you."

Duncan grinned, his thin, tight lips pulling back from his teeth, and he chuckled.

"Ye're a fine-lookin' lassie," he sneered. "Come, tak' hold o' me an' throw me oot."

"This is our realm," Suzy said firmly, "not yours. You need to leave."

"I say again, come, throw me oot."

Suzy's inflexibility faltered a bit when she wasn't able to oust the spirit. Fin saw her hesitation and, fighting his own fear, he stood up beside her.

"Get the fuck out of here!" he shouted, surprised at his own boldness.

"Ah, so the wee laddie has a pair o' balls after all, eh?" Duncan grinned.

Fin took Suzy's hand, and they stood firm, as Duncan's image began to blaze, the heat wave aura turning to flame. He didn't even have to say "flame on," Fin noticed.

"Ye're a couple o' impudent bairns to think ye can stand up against me," Duncan said, the coldness of his voice building. "It's time ye learnt a lesson aboot how t' choose your battles."

Fin couldn't tell what the temperature was in the carriage house. It still felt as if it was freezing in there, particularly at their backs, yet he felt heat emanating from the flames burning from the monstrous image of Duncan's ghost.

The ghost turned into a blazing inferno, blinding bright with blue flames licking at the ceiling of the carriage house. Suzy and Fin both put their arms up to block the heat from their faces. Feeling the fire sucking the breath from their lungs, they were barely aware of something that looked like the trailing tail of a comet fly into the carriage house and place itself between them and Duncan.

Fiona materialized in front of them and began hurling flames at their common enemy. Like a forest backfire or controlled burn, she deflected the blaze from Suzy and Fin, allowing them a moment to catch their breath.

"Duncan," Suzy said, calmly and firmly, "you have to go!"

Duncan's power seemed to falter, and Suzy and Fin looked at each other, as if thinking the same thought. At the same moment, they both shouted at him.

"Get out of here!" Suzy screamed.

Fin thought it would have been much cooler if he had said the same thing instead of, "Go away, asshole!" Still, the solidarity of sentiment seemed to be what did the trick. Duncan gave one last effort to blaze brightly, before blinking out in a flash of white light.

Suzy and Fin felt their clothing and their hair blow forward toward the vacuum where Duncan's ghost had been. Moments later, the atmosphere in the carriage house calmed and the temperature rose a few degrees, though it was still cooler than the summer morning outside.

Fiona turned toward them as her own flames subsided to the ember heat wave aura, and she smiled.

"The two of ye make a good pair," she said.

"Thank you, Fiona," Suzy panted. "We couldn't have done it without you."

Fin, seeing Fiona for the first time, smiled at her.

"Caden's a lucky man," he said.

Fiona smiled back at him, without the sadness in her eyes, Suzy noticed.

"Perhaps I'll be able to see him now," she said.

"I sure hope so, Fiona," Suzy said earnestly.

"I thank ye for all ye've done for me, and for Caden. And for me wee bairn, as well."

"I'm just glad I was able to help." Suzy looked at Fiona, and she could see the goodbye coming. "Are you leaving now?"

"Aye, Suzy. Me Caden awaits."

In that moment, Suzy thought that Fiona's face reflected the eighteen-year-old innocence and beauty that it must have shown in the first episode that she had seen, so many months ago. No wonder everyone had been attracted to her.

"I'll miss you so much, Fiona," she said.

"And I you, child. I'm so proud and thankful. Ye've proven yourself to be a good friend to me, and a worthy granddaughter. I hope I can carry your memory with me into whatever awaits."

"I'll always remember you," Suzy replied, the tears running down her cheeks.

"Goodbye, love," Fiona smiled. "Time for me to go through that door."

After a moment's hesitation, in a flash of white, she was gone.

With her sudden departure, Suzy's body was suddenly racked with sobs, and Fin took her in his arms. He held her for several minutes, rocking her gently back and forth, until her crying subsided. When she finally, weakly, looked up at him, he kissed her.

"Okay," he said, "I guess it's settled. You have a much cooler ancestor than I do."

Suzy smiled and sighed, standing back from Fin to assess the condition of the carriage house. For the first time, she saw the place brightly illuminated, as light was finally allowed into the place.

She realized that she was still holding Fiona's portrait of Caden in her hand, and she held it up in front of them.

"Yup," Fin said, "he's a lucky guy. But not as lucky as me."

## 74

W e've finally approved funding to open up a new position here," said Jay Gilbert, Suzy's friend from the Marblehead Historical Consortium, the local museum. Suzy pressed the phone tighter against her ear. She and Fin were relaxing in chaise lounges on Suzy's rooftop deck, surrounded by a crenelated battlement, overlooking the harbor. "My first choice for the position is you."

"What kind of position are you talking about?"

"I guess you could say it's kind of between an intern and an assistant curator. But it definitely involves more than just fetching coffee, and you might even actually be able to put your history degree to use."

"That . . . well that actually sounds pretty interesting," Suzy replied, intrigued.

"Why don't you come to the museum tomorrow and I can show you what it would involve."

"Yeah, I'll do that. Thank you, Jay. I'll see you tomorrow."

Fin looked over at her as she disconnected.

"I may have a job at the local museum," she said.

"Very cool!" Fin replied encouragingly. "I mean assuming you want a job."

"I think I might. I need to do something more with my life than just sitting around eating bonbons."

"You've got bonbons?" Fin said, looking around. "You didn't tell me there were bonbons."

Suzy smiled and sighed, putting her head back. She closed her eyes, enjoying the sun on her face.

"I am so impressed that you live in a Scottish castle!" Fin said.

"Yeah," Suzy snickered, "a Scottish castle with multiple personality disorder. There's a little Tudor, a little Victorian and even a little mid-century modern tacked on to it."

"I think it's pretty awesome." Fin looked over the battlement at the boats in the harbor. "So what's with all those little white buoys down there? The harbor's full of them!"

"Those are mooring buoys. If you had a boat and you wanted to park it in the harbor, you could go to the harbormaster's office and put your name on a waiting list. In about fifteen years, you might get one." She glanced at Fin who was looking at her skeptically. "That's not an exaggeration. Moorings are often passed down to family members, and they'll stay in a family for years."

"Damn!" Fin said.

"Yeah. That's why it's nice to have a boathouse," Suzy replied. "Although I don't have a boat any longer." That comment brought back memories that she preferred not to remember. "Anyway, you could get a mooring over on the other side of Marblehead, in Salem Harbor, in about a year."

"Really?" Fin asked incredulously. "But Salem's more famous than Marblehead. Everybody and their dog has heard of Salem, Massachusetts." Suzy shrugged. "Obviously, you live on the right side."

"Obviously."

Fin took a sip of his Scotch and put his head back on the lounge.

"I think I could get used to this," he said.

"Yeah?" Suzy replied distractedly.

"I wonder how long it would take to sell my house."

"You're selling your house?" Suzy asked, turning to look at him.

"Well, not yet," Fin said, "but I do kind of have a hankering to live by the sea."

Suzy fidgeted and sat up straighter. Fin thought she seemed a little uncomfortable.

"Fin," she said, "you remember a while back when we were sharing our deepest and darkest, and you said that you've discovered that you tend to jump too quickly into relationships?"

"Yeah," Fin replied apprehensively.

"You're doing it again."

"Too quickly?" Fin asked, his face contorted in confusion.

"Dinnae be such a doltish numpty," Suzy said, lapsing into her Scottish dialect.

"But," Fin said, "I thought we were getting along so well. And you yourself said a few nights ago that you were falling in love with me."

"That's true," Suzy said, "we do get along great." She sighed. "And yes, I do think I'm falling in love with you. But the fact is I also still love Mark. It hasn't even been two years since I lost him, and my daughter. I'm still grieving." Her voice took on a faraway quality as she looked across the harbor. "Being back here in this house has very forcefully impressed that on me." She looked back at Fin who had taken on a crestfallen expression.

"That doesn't mean that you and I will never be together. It just means that I'm not ready yet."

"Okay," he said, feeling somewhat encouraged. "Well, that sounds a little better. I love the ocean. And I can write anywhere. So, what's the problem with getting myself in position?"

"There's nothing wrong with it, if you're doing it for yourself. But don't completely uproot your life to move closer to me before we even know if we have a shot."

"Yeah, that makes sense," Fin said, feeling more disappointed than he was letting on.

"Besides," Suzy said, "I've never been to Colorado. I might want a place to stay if I go to visit."

"You mean *when* you go visit," Fin replied, perking up a little. "Yeah, you definitely have a place to stay. You're into history? We got history, baby. You'll love it." Then, remembering where he was, near the birthplace of America, he looked around at his surroundings. "I mean, it's not as old as the history you have here. Or rather it *is* as old, but it's undocumented. Anything older than about three hundred years in Colorado is basically prehistoric, and is only sur-mised through archaeological findings. But there's a pretty cool museum devoted specifically to the history of Colorado in Denver."

"Okay, okay, ease up, Colorado Kid," Suzy chuckled.

"Sorry," Fin said diffidently. "I just don't want to lose you."

"Honey, nobody's losing anyone." Fin nodded, but not very confidently. "I promise you, though, as soon as I feel like I'm ready to 'take it to the next level,' you'll be the first to know."

Fin smiled. He put his head back and looked up at the clouds sailing across the sea blue sky.

He just had to wait it out. He could do that. For Suzy, he could wait as long as it takes.

# Thanks and Acknowledgments

There's nothing like personal experience in researching a book. Actually visiting the locations can help give a note of authenticity to the story, as Fin was discovering. However, it's inevitable that certain specific and unexpected details may be needed after one has returned home.

For helping me out with some of those details, I want to thank Joanna Stevenson at the National Library of Scotland in Edinburgh.

For similar details about Marblehead, Massachusetts, even though I've visited many times, I thank Anne Thornton at the Abbot Public Library in Marblehead.

I gleaned a great deal of historical information from other books, primarily *Bodysnatchers* by Suzie Lennox, *Lost Edinburgh* by Hamish Coghill, and *The Town Below the Ground* by Jan-Andrew Henderson

I'd like to thank my readers. Even if you didn't read my books, I would still write them, simply because I have to. The fact that others find them interesting is just icing on the cake. ***Please consider leaving a brief review at Amazon or Goodreads.***

Finally, I wish to thank my muse and my biggest fan, my wife Linda, for her tireless enthusiasm, her endless support and encouragement, and all the suggestions she gave, many of which made the story better.

www.ingramcontent.com/pod-product-compliance
Lightning Source LLC
Chambersburg PA
CBHW020324180626
46812CB00001B/41